LUNAR INTERLUDE

LUNAR INTERLUDE

CYBER DREAMS BOOK 5

PLUM PARROT

Podium

Cover design by J Caleb Design

ISBN: 978-1-0394-5384-5

Published in 2024 by Podium Publishing
www.podiumentertainment.com

LUNAR
INTERLUDE

1

〰〰〰〰〰〰〰

HOPE FOR THE BEST

Juliet flicked through the menu on the *Lady's* piloting UI, locking down all the systems, putting the reactor into self-maintenance mode, and basically getting the ship ready to sit in the hangar she'd rented for as long as needed. She'd purchased two hangar spaces, not too far from each other but not right next door, and not under the same name. The *Lady* was registered to her SOA ID number, and so was the hangar she was in. The *Furies' Wing* was registered to a nonexistent citizen of Titan and kept in a hangar purchased by a shell corporation with only an anonymous Sol-bit vault listed as an asset.

As she walked through the ship, making sure everything was locked down and that she'd packed all her gear into her duffel, Juliet was struck by memories of Nick and their time together aboard the little ship. She'd only known him for a couple of months, but she'd grown closer to him than most of the other people in her life. "At least my old life," she quietly amended. She felt close to the crew of the *Kowashi* too, which made her consider the idea that being stuck in a small, metallic shell in the vastness of space forced people to make connections with their fellow inmates. Would she feel so close to those people if they'd worked together in a city, spending time in an office or factory and then going home to their separate lives at the ends of their shifts?

Before she could go further down that road, Angel interrupted her thoughts. "Do you want me to message Alice or anyone else to let them know you've arrived?"

"Not yet. I think we need to settle a little business first; as far as I know, only one of my potential enemies knows about 'Lucky' and her connection to Luna, and I'm not eager to expose my connections to the crew of the *Kowashi* to that guy."

"Rutger Tanaka?"

"Exactly." Juliet stepped through the exterior hatch and turned to rest her palm on the access panel, locking it down. "Do me a favor and summarize what you know about his current situation—where he is, Frida, and the rest of his team."

"I still have access to Frida, Applebaum, and Hawkins. Frida connected with Hawkins when she arrived on Luna; at that time, I reinfected her with my snooping daemons." While Angel spoke, Juliet slung her heavy duffel onto an empty workbench that lined one wall of the *Lady's* hangar. She pulled out a shop stool and sat down, listening. "Tanaka has two other full-time employees, but they're all off-moon in various locations—he gave them leave when Frida filled him in about her encounter with you. Applebaum and Hawkins are both on standby with orders to 'stay sharp and spend time at the range.' Frida has been working out of Tanaka's new offices, which double as his Luna residence."

"And did you ever get your daemons into his PAI?"

"I'm afraid not; he's old-school cagey and operates on post-AI war protocols. He doesn't accept wireless data files or shared-comm connections, and the only data he's accessed since Frida returned has been visually on an air-gapped terminal."

"So you're not going to get into his head before I meet with him."

"That depends on a number of circumstances and the amount of time we have to prepare—"

"I'm going to meet with him now."

"Juliet!"

"Angel, I can't have this hanging over my head. I don't want to spend months trying to get a bug into his head by feeding him images through his air-gapped terminal or whatever. I don't want to try to social engineer him into going into a chop doc we've compromised or something else equally involved. We've got eyes on him through Frida, and you basically own his team here on Luna. More importantly, to my silly human mind, I have a feeling he doesn't want to kill me."

"You have a feeling?" Angel didn't precisely sound derisive, but she didn't sound happy, either.

"Look, I just want to deal with this so I can go back to work with Bennet and not worry about some old-school killer slipping in like a ghost and taking out all my friends. Let's deal with him, whatever it takes, okay?"

"What about the sword?"

"Ah, you're on the right track now. I figure we can retrieve it from my quarters on the gunship pretty easily. You can tell when Bennet or Aya are working, right? We'll just wait for them to call it a day, slip in, grab the sword, and slip back out again."

"And Tanaka? Should we schedule the meeting?"

Juliet laughed and stood up, shaking her head. "You're sweet, Angel, but too innocent. Think about it—we've got Tanaka's location and direct access to his right-hand woman's PAI. Why would we give them time to set up a trap? We'll get the sword, set up where we can observe his new offices, then reach out to Frida." While she spoke, she began to go through her bag, trying to decide what to wear. Part of her wanted to forego putting on the FlexPlate armor and her baby-blue helmet, but another thought it would be stupid. She was much faster now, probably as fast as Tanaka, but the armor would give her another edge. She'd be much more resilient and a good deal stronger wearing it.

Juliet wasn't stupid; she knew she was tough, but, as much as she wished it didn't matter, she had a woman's frame and muscularity. If Tanaka managed to get close to her and turn the fight into a grappling match, she wasn't sure she could compete with him physically. "Well, other than my 'good' arm." She chuckled.

"Hmm?"

"Just thinking that Tanaka's a man, and he's no slouch. I should probably wear the FlexPlate."

"Your new reflex augments will make it hard for him to close the distance. He was very fast, but I think you will be a close match for his speed. More than that, I believe you can maintain that speed longer than most people without damaging yourself. Your neural and cellular adaptiveness is almost without peer, and with me managing the synaptic speed boost, your brain is far safer than someone with a mass-market speed upgrade."

"Yeah, but if he does close the distance, gets a hold of my wrist or my neck . . . I think I'll wear the armor."

"If he's armed himself with a new monoblade, your armor will be of no use."

Juliet smirked as she unbuckled her gun belt and loosened the strap on her thigh. "If he's trying to have a sword fight, he's going to be disappointed."

She set the heavy belt on the workbench with a thud as if to punctuate her statement. "If he pulls a blade, I'm going to start shooting, and you're going to make sure I don't miss."

"My pleasure."

Juliet tapped through her AUI, selecting a soundtrack—something upbeat, an electronic dance mix—and began the lengthy process of gearing up. The FlexPlate was tight and bulky with all the plates attached, but once she got it on and activated the batteries, the mesh tightened and loosened in all the right places. The armor felt almost weightless when fully charged. When Juliet's helmet latched into place, and she was comfortably behind its armored visor, she felt that weird anonymous courage that always seemed to come over her when she knew other people couldn't see her face.

She buckled the Texan back on her hip, looped the tie around her thigh, and, as if to illustrate the dexterity of her armored gloves, drew the gun, twirled it, and slipped it back in the holster quick as a blink of the eye. She looked at her duffel, frowned, and reached inside to pull out her data deck. She didn't want to load herself down with gear but figured the deck might come in handy. She hung the lanyard over her neck, letting the flat, square-shaped plastic device rest against her armored chest.

"Not bringing more guns?"

"Nah, I make enough of a scene as it is. If it looks like I can't handle things with my vibroblade and my Texan, then I'll back off and wait for a better opportunity." Juliet left the hangar, locked it up, and still listening to her soundtrack, walked through the port to customs. Memories of her first time coming to Luna flashed through her mind, and she chuckled at how much things had changed. She remembered how nervous she'd been approaching the checkpoint, how she'd worried WBD might have gotten ahead of her somehow. She remembered having to lock her guns away, and how she'd waited in line with all the tourists, sweating bullets as she walked through the scanner.

Things were a little different this time. She didn't have to go through commercial passenger customs. She was in the section of the port reserved for ship crews who rented berths. Still, when she walked up to the scanners, despite the smaller queue, those memories came rushing back, and she felt a little sweat start to bead up around the gel helmet liner on her forehead. Her heart began to beat a little faster, and she nervously closed and opened her hands.

As she stepped into the big, full-body plastic scanner, she put her feet on the yellow marks and her hands on the ones above her head. She stood there, nervous, then annoyed at being nervous, as her augmented ears picked up all sorts of pings and alerts. She heard the hushed conversation of the two Port Security officers at their terminal. "Jesus, look at the hardware on this chick."

"SOA license checks out. She's got a Luna small arms license attachment. Is that armor active? I'm having a hard time reading through it. Filter out that signature. Ah, there we go. Shit, man, she's fully wired. Ears, eyes, nose, lungs, cybernetic arm, looks like a data jack in the other."

The other guy spoke up. "Yep, some kinda fancy job on her tendons and muscles; can't tell what kinda aug it is . . ."

"Is something wrong?" Juliet asked, still awkwardly holding her palms on the yellow hand symbols above her head.

"Lift your visor."

Juliet should've thought of that; they'd want to scan her retinas. She tapped her visor release and, as it slid into her helmet, smiled into the scanner array, revealing her glittering green-and-gold irises. "That okay?"

"You're not packing any heavy ordnance in that cybernetic limb, are you?"

"No." Juliet sighed, annoyed. They were just harassing her at this point; their scanners would have alerted them to dangerous amounts of explosive materials. "Am I good?"

"In a hurry? Maybe we should get a look under that armor . . ."

Juliet closed her mouth, but the anger building up must have been evident in her eyes. "She's good," a new voice said, and Juliet glanced to her right to see a third security officer, an older man with sergeant's stripes on his collar. He was scrutinizing Juliet's scan on the terminal over the first two men's shoulders. "Come on, boys, we gotta get this line moving."

"Move along," the first voice said through the speaker, and Juliet didn't linger for them to change their minds. She hurried to the customs window, and suddenly felt stupid for thinking she'd changed so much since her first arrival on Luna. She might have more experience and a lot more gear, but she was still subject to the whims of corporations and their rules and regulations. She could still find herself delayed or locked away because some thugs with a bit of authority decided she'd been too smart-mouthed while they invaded her privacy.

The woman at the customs counter was more pleasant, and Juliet was through in just a few seconds. When she walked away from the lines and the scanners, she tapped the button to lower her visor, and suddenly felt much better. She focused on her breathing and tried to remind herself that she was just one of thousands of people going through that screening on any given day. It was a process—an annoying, painful one, but just a process. She climbed aboard a nearby tram and rode it to the station that bordered one of the industrial access roads where Angel already had a cab waiting for her.

"Greetings, passenger. Please share your license for the firearm . . . Received. Thank you and enjoy your ride. ETA to your destination address is seventeen minutes."

"I really hate how locked down Luna is."

"It certainly feels different after being in the Jovian System for a couple of months, doesn't it?"

"Yeah. I know it's just my perception—not everyone walks around in combat armor with guns and whatnot. I suppose people just living their lives in the city never have to deal with this stuff, or only when they travel off-moon. Still, I never felt so scrutinized on Callisto."

"Nor New Atlas."

Juliet smiled and stared out the window, remembering her arrival on New Atlas. She'd come in on a captured pirate ship with a handful of bodies—people she'd killed—stacked up in the airlock. Not only hadn't she gotten in any trouble but the port authority had paid her some bounties. "Yeah, I guess Luna doesn't have that Wild West feel, you know?"

"I was going to say the same thing!" Angel laughed, and Juliet's mood further improved. She loved it when Angel laughed.

They rode in silence the rest of the way. Juliet enjoyed traveling on the exterior highways around the Luna domes. They provided a fun view of the lunar landscape and, occasionally, breathtaking views of the domes, especially the central Luna City Dome. It looked like a massive snow globe filled with shining silver and glass buildings that reflected the sun's light. From a distance, you couldn't see the dirt or grime. You couldn't smell the waste and decay. From a distance, it was easy to forget that people lived there, easy to imagine it was a city filled with angels or gods.

"I've connected with the gunship's wireless port."

"We're close enough?" Juliet jerked herself out of her imagined city full of white-winged mythical people and realized they were quickly approaching the big industrial hangars where Bennet had rented space for the gunship.

"Yes. It doesn't seem like Bennet or Aya are currently working in the hangar. By the way, the gunship's sensor and comm array has been fully restored. It's quite robust! I see open connections to the *Kowashi* and the local sat-net. Hmm, the *Kowashi* is currently in port, and I'm seeing Alice, Shiro, and Aya aboard. I'm still not sure where Bennet is, but it doesn't seem he's here."

"All right. Let's make this quick." Juliet hurried out of the cab and over the sidewalk to the locked pedestrian door on the side of the hangar. "Can you stop them seeing an alert when I open this door?"

"There shouldn't be an alert if your access is still the same."

Juliet tapped her visor release, and when it slid up, she stared into the scanner on the door panel. It beeped, flashed green, and the door opened. "Perfect." She hurried inside and stopped short, her mouth falling open as she took in the sight. The gunship had been completely stripped down to the skeleton-like alloy frame. It looked weird but also amazing. She could see that Bennet and Aya had been hard at work. The wire harnesses were neatly bundled and tied down; the tubes and hoses all looked clean, their colors bright—clearly replaced or repainted—and she saw new components everywhere she looked.

"Look at the armor panels," Angel said, and Juliet's AUI flashed, highlighting what Angel meant. Drying racks lined the far wall of the hangar, and Juliet could see hundreds of polymer armor panels laid out on them, all painted glossy, brilliant sky blue.

"God, they're amazing! Those little devils! They're actually doing it! I thought at least Bennet would argue about the color—"

Juliet almost jumped out of her armor when a sleepy, goofy, wonderful voice asked, "Hey, are you here to rob me? 'Cause I don't have much worth stealing."

Juliet whirled toward the voice, and sure enough, Bennet was there, sitting up from her dream-rig, his sandy brown hair disheveled, and a very disoriented "I just woke up" look on his face.

"Bennet!" she cried, reaching to slide her visor up but realizing she'd never closed it after opening the hangar door with her retina.

"Hey! I thought that might be you. Hard to see if the curves were right with that armor, but . . ."

"Oh, shut up!" Juliet laughed, hurrying over to the rig, still where she'd left it, though surrounded by several new crates and boxes. "What are you doing hiding in that rig? I thought nobody was here."

"It's perfect for napping." He yawned and stretched, then began to clamber out. He'd only managed to get one foot on the floor before Juliet grabbed him into a hug, manhandling him with the added strength of her suit.

"Oof! Hey!" He laughed as she squeezed him, then he grabbed her back, and it felt like a scrap metal baler had gotten a hold of her.

"Ung!" Juliet grunted and wriggled, and Bennet finally relented, letting her go. "You're going to break my armor! Jeez!"

"Why are you all decked out? Something going down?"

Juliet supposed it was too much to hope she'd settle things with Tanaka before running into any of her friends. Still, she didn't want things to escalate, so she tried to placate him a little. "No, nothing is going down, but I have a meeting with someone I wanted to get taken care of before I reconnected with everyone. Can you keep it quiet that I'm on the surface? Alice and Shiro think I'm still on approach."

"Why?"

Juliet frowned and thought about it for a few seconds, watching Bennet's big gray eyes narrow in concern. She decided she wouldn't start things off on her return by lying to her friend. "Because the guy I'm dealing with is dangerous. Not so much to me, but if he knew about my friends here, maybe he could be a problem for them. I just want to settle things with him before I start hanging around with you all." Bennet's scowl deepened, and Juliet added, "Listen, I honestly think he and I just need to talk things out. I don't think anything crazy will happen, but I don't want to risk it. Okay? Please, just forget you saw me for a few hours."

Bennet groaned. "Oh, man. You're back less than a minute, and I'm already faced with a moral dilemma?"

Juliet laughed and reached up to grasp him by the back of his neck, gently squeezing. "I missed you, you big dummy. I'm so glad to see you. Trust me, okay? What time is it? 1530? I'll buy everyone dinner in a few hours, all right?"

"Okay. I can keep my trap shut for a couple of hours, but that's it. If you don't check in by dinnertime, I'm calling in the cavalry."

"Deal." Juliet looked back over at the shiny skeleton of the gunship. "Is my stuff still in there? I came to pick up my sword."

"Yeah, it's still there. Aya's been stacking boxes of books or something in there, but nothing should be missing."

Juliet felt her smile widening, and a warm feeling gripped her chest at his words. "Aya! I'm so glad to be back, Bennet."

"Well, I'm glad you're back, too. Tell me, though; if you're so sure this meeting is a conversation, why are you dressed like a shock trooper?"

"Well, Bennet, as they say: hope for the best but prepare for the worst, right?"

2

NORANEKO

Juliet sat in her cab with a plain view of the elevator bank in the parking garage of Rutger Tanaka's building. Through her connection to Frida, Angel had learned that Tanaka had leased out half a floor of the BizRes Tower complex in downtown Luna—one of the older plasteel-and-glass towers that advertised "spaces for living and business." She hadn't planned on a parking garage for their meeting, but, sitting there, she felt it was as good a place as any.

The streets in the city weren't designed for heavy traffic. More than ninety percent of the population relied on public transportation and pedestrian transit, but cabs and the vehicles of the elite still traversed the limited motorways. It wasn't just the expense that restricted the vehicular traffic in the city; the licenses for personal vehicles were heavily regulated, with only a few new ones being issued each year as others were retired. Knowing that and knowing that Tanaka had only recently arrived from his base of operations on New Atlas, it had surprised Juliet to learn he'd acquired one.

"So, he really is loaded," she said when Angel highlighted Tanaka's sleek black sedan parked in a marked spot near the elevators.

"Either that or he's being imprudent with his savings. Frida has access to some of his accounts, but he keeps others to himself. I've only seen her access his primary operating account, but the balance was over seven million Sol-bits."

"What's he doing right now?" By way of answer, Angel opened a window on her AUI that contained a feed from, Juliet guessed, Frida's perspective. She was sitting at a glass-topped desk, tabbing through some spreadsheets on a big crystal-glass display terminal, and beyond that, Juliet could see a closed door.

"Tanaka is behind that door. It's his office."

"And his two goons? Applebaum and Hawkins?"

"Applebaum is sleeping. He has a female companion. Hawkins is currently buying groceries to cook dinner for his brother, who's arriving from Earth this evening."

"Seems like a good time to me. Any thoughts?"

"Only that you should be careful. Remember what we discussed—don't let him get close to you."

"Right." Juliet stepped out of the cab, one hand clutching the scabbard of the monoblade she'd taken from what she'd thought was Tanaka's corpse. Grabbing the sword, her mind jumped to the gift she'd found in her room from Honey. When she'd gone for the sword, she'd found a white box adorned with a pastel-yellow ribbon. A card under the ribbon had been handwritten to say, *I know you like these things. —H.* Of course, Juliet had opened the box immediately. Inside, she'd found a black T-shirt with a sunglass-wearing yellow smiley face. It was ancient, vintage, and wonderfully faded. It was a sweet gesture that left Juliet feeling warm and even more worried about bringing trouble to her friends.

Shaking her head, focusing on her present situation, Juliet closed the door, and Angel sent the cab to a different level to await further instructions. As it hummed away, tires squealing on the plasteel ramp, Juliet looked at the camera cluster near the elevators and the one not far from where she stood. They wouldn't be a problem; Angel had used her connection to Frida to access the cameras long before they'd set foot on Luna. Still, she stepped behind a plasteel pillar so only a sliver of her mirrored visor would be visible to anyone stepping off the elevators. "Okay, call Frida."

A window on her AUI opened, and the connection tone sounded three times before Frida's face appeared. She squinted at first, but then, as Angel sent an image of Juliet's face through the connection, her eyes widened. "Lucky!" To her, it should look like Juliet was standing in one of the parks dotting the outskirts of the central Luna City dome.

"Hi, Frida. I'm back on Luna."

"Wow, okay, um, I thought you might give me some heads-up when you were on your way." Her eyes twitched to the side nervously, and Juliet saw, in her other window, that Tanaka had opened the door to his office and was standing there, watching Frida.

Juliet almost froze up when she saw him. It felt like a nightmare had come to life, and suddenly, the memories of her only other encounter with that man came rushing back. Her heart began to race, her breaths quickened, and her mind went blank as she saw, over and over, Lemur's head sliding off his body to thump onto the floor. She felt those crushing blows as Tanaka used his outlandish speed to overpower her.

"Juliet?" Angel prompted.

"Ahem." Juliet shook her head and jerked her attention away from the view of Tanaka and back to Frida. "You thought I should give you a heads-up? Why?"

"Um, good point. I guess we aren't exactly pals, are we?" Frida's eyes kept shifting to the left and then back to focus on Juliet. Juliet knew she was trying to read Tanaka's expression, trying to see what he wanted her to say. Juliet, privy to everything Frida saw, could tell Tanaka wasn't making it easy for her. He stood in the doorway to his office, staring, his tattooed face as expressionless as a stone. She almost felt sorry for Frida.

"Well, I'm ready to meet Tanaka. I want to get this business over with."

"Really? Right now?" Juliet saw Frida glance at Tanaka again and saw him nod—a quick, slight movement that anyone but Frida might have missed. "We can do that."

"I'm at Tranquility Gardens. Come here, and I'll ping you with my exact location." Juliet paused, adding, "No surprises, Frida."

"Understood."

Juliet cut the connection then watched and listened through Frida's feed as she turned her full attention to Tanaka.

"You heard that?" Frida asked, looking straight at her boss.

"Yes." He turned back to his office as Frida stood up and pushed her desk chair in. When he returned, he wore a sleek overcoat, custom-tailored to accommodate the sword hanging from his left hip.

"Does he wear that everywhere, or does this mean the guy thinks I'm going to sword fight him?"

Angel's voice was reassuring as she answered, "He wears it any time he leaves his offices, which, from what I've observed through Frida, isn't very often."

Juliet watched Frida walk around her desk toward the glass doors leading out of their offices and into the hallway. "Do you want me to ready the team?"

"She said no surprises." Tanaka's voice was flat, matter of fact.

"What if—"

"She won't assassinate me in the middle of the city park, Frida."

"And you?" Frida pressed as she followed her boss down the hallway to the elevators. If Juliet had hoped to learn his intentions at that moment, she was disappointed; Tanaka ignored the question. She watched as Frida touched the menu selection for the garage, and then, as the elevator started down, she closed her eyes and tried to steel her nerves. She wouldn't let herself freeze up once face-to-face with that man.

Maybe Angel was trying to help her relax. "He doesn't seem to be planning anything nefarious."

"A guy like that? If he sliced me in half in the park, a relative nobody SOA operative with no other ID? He could explain it a million different ways."

"I see." Angel didn't have to say anything more; it wouldn't be hard for a man with funds and connections to make up a story that explained his sudden violence. Juliet steadied her nerves, watching the elevator doors and, beside them in her vision, the window showing Frida's perspective. The elevator was moving quickly. "Ten seconds," Angel said, helpful as always.

Juliet's breathing had steadied, her heart rate had calmed, and she almost didn't realize she was channeling White, or more accurately, her Lacy Blake persona, the cold-blooded killer who had been based, in part, on Juliet's memories of White. When the elevator dinged and slid open, she didn't even flinch. With Frida on his heels, Tanaka stepped out and began to stride toward his sedan. His polished dress boots *clacked* on the plasteel floor with his firm, forceful stride.

Juliet was twenty-three meters away from his sedan, still mostly obscured by the concrete pillar, and she hadn't moved so much as a fraction of a centimeter, but something must have alerted Tanaka. He froze just as he reached the rear quarter panel of his car. Frida was caught off guard and almost walked into his back, but she stumbled to a halt, sputtering, "What—?"

"Quiet." Tanaka held out his left hand, one finger up. Frida instantly froze.

Juliet had seen enough. She sidestepped, moving out from behind the plasteel pillar, and stared at Tanaka's back through the mirrored visor of her helmet. Her boots' rubber soles were silent as she moved, but Tanaka must have felt her or something. He turned and looked over Frida's shoulder, staring right at Juliet. To his credit, his face didn't betray an ounce of surprise. He reached out with his left hand and gently pushed Frida to the side so she wasn't between him and Juliet.

Frida moved where Tanaka nudged her, and when she turned to follow his gaze, her eyes widened. "Lucky? Is that—?"

"Quiet," Tanaka grunted.

Frida clamped her mouth shut and stepped back, further clearing the line of sight between Juliet and Tanaka. Juliet hadn't moved. Her right hand hung down beside her Texan, her left hand clutching Tanaka's sword, but she held perfectly still, waiting. After several tense seconds of silence, Tanaka surprised her by bowing. Not a short, quick bow, like one might see in some business meetings within certain East Asian-based corporations, but a deep, deliberate one, full of respect and formality.

Juliet knew almost nothing about bowing. She'd learned to do a quick bow before stepping onto the mat at the dojo in Phoenix, but this was different. She had no idea what it meant. Was he saying he respected her? Was he apologizing because he was about to kill her? Was—

Tanaka interrupted her thoughts. "I see you've bested me again. I won't insult you by asking how you knew to find me here." Behind her mirrored visor, Juliet could see Frida's pale, freckled face had blanched to the point that the poor woman looked almost transparent. She opened her mouth, but it was clear she was struggling with what to say or, more likely, if she should speak at all. Juliet could only imagine her thoughts—was she worried Tanaka thought she'd betrayed him?

Juliet didn't speak—Lacy Blake would let her adversary sweat for a minute or two, let them wonder what she would do. Tanaka swung the left side of his coat back, exposing his sword, and stood still, his chrome, red-irised eyes unblinking. Juliet studied that face, the frown line between his heavy dark eyebrows, the weird, colorful tattoos, and his thin, stiff, unsmiling lips. He looked like a man who didn't tolerate setbacks or surprises; a man who'd been through much and felt like he could handle just about anything. That face made the show of respect he'd given her feel almost scary, like a threat.

While they stared at each other, Juliet opened her mind, and almost immediately, quicker than she was ready to resist, she felt herself drawn into his chrome orbs.

Rutger crouched low, slinking through the manicured shrubs outside the big gray concrete building where the corporate children went to school. He wasn't interested in the school but rather what went on outside of it. He'd seen them before, but had stupidly stood in the open and been chased away by the old lady who brought the children out in their neat lines, in their neat uniforms. This time, he was smarter. This time, he crept through the bushes and followed the sounds of the instructor, followed the sounds of the clacking wooden swords and the children's shouts of, "Kiai!"

He crawled through the rough, sharp branches, his fingers digging into the moist soil of the garden bed, his eyes watering as he fought to keep from flinching or crying out as the thorns scraped his arms and cheeks and shoulders. When he poked his nose out between the last row of shrubs and had a clear view of the schoolyard garden, all of his efforts were made worthwhile. He could easily see and observe the children in their gray-and-white uniforms arranged in rows. He stayed there, watching as they, in turn, watched the ancient instructor, mimicking his movements as he walked up and down the rows, praising or scolding them.

Juliet blinked her eyes rapidly, caught off guard by the sudden deep dive into Tanaka's memories. She'd only wanted to hear his thoughts, to see if he was intending to kill her.

She was steeling herself for another attempt when he surprised her again by moving first, reaching down and loosening his obi—the belt that held his sword in place. Juliet only knew the term because of her time watching Honey at the dojo, and she also knew it wasn't something one did before a fight. Tanaka loosened it and slipped his sword from the folds before he bowed again, gently placing the sword on the plasteel at his feet.

When he straightened, he said in that gravelly, rough voice, "Might I look in your eyes before you kill me?"

"Boss!" Frida's eyes darted from Juliet to Tanaka and back again.

"Frida. Thank you for your service. Please execute my will to the—"

Juliet had seen and heard enough. Her mind was reeling from the sudden course change. Grunting with annoyance, she touched the button on the side of her helmet, sending her visor up and back. "I'm not here to kill you." She frowned, adding, "I mean, not unless you start something first." Only after she'd spoken did she realize she'd completely dropped her Lacy persona. Her glimpse into his memories, his sudden fatalistic action—they'd thrown her off.

"Boss, let me—"

"Quiet, Frida," Tanaka spoke almost gently as he looked at Juliet, staring at her, locking eyes with her, and then, after a long moment, he nodded. "Thank you for meeting with me."

"I don't like threats hanging over me." Juliet held up his sword. "I brought you your sword."

"It's yours. You won it in combat."

"So you're just fine with that?" Juliet wasn't letting the conversation lull her; she was ready, primed to act, to draw her gun and put two heavy polymer slugs in him if he so much as flinched her way.

"Frida tells me you're fast but prefer a gun to a blade."

"What is this, Tanaka?" Juliet felt her awe of the man fading, replaced by something she'd kept buried for a long, long time: anger. "You wanna talk nice now? Do you remember slicing my partner's head off? Do you remember using your augmented speed to beat me until my kidneys bled? Remember telling me we'd have some fun? That I'd spill my life story before begging to die?"

"*Hai*. Right before you killed me." Again, Tanaka slowly, deliberately, bowed.

"Stop doing that!" Juliet growled. "Obviously, I didn't kill you."

"Frida, tell this woman how I am standing here today."

"How . . ." Frida licked her lips, then nervously glanced from Tanaka to Juliet. When neither spoke, she said, "His nanites kept his brain alive. We had to replace a lung, his heart, his liver, a kidney, his spleen, most of his small intestine, and—"

"What's the point of this?" Juliet barked, interrupting the litany of Tanaka's internal trauma.

"The point? I was dead. You won. I tasted my mortality. My mind hasn't been the same since I awoke. I'm a shadow of the man I used to be. Shadows! Hah! I jump at them. I wake in the night, cold and drenched in sweat. I dream of . . . things; things a man shouldn't see, shouldn't know, but when I awake, I can't remember what they were. Rutger Tanaka, as you knew him, is dead. This hollow creature before you might as well join him."

"Boss." This time, Frida's voice wasn't pleading or outraged. She had tears in her eyes and spoke softly, reaching a hand toward Tanaka's shoulder. "Why didn't you say . . . ?"

"Frida. Please. Be quiet." Tanaka's voice broke, and he shuddered, and Juliet stood there, dumbfounded. What the hell was going on here?

"Angel," she started to subvocalize, but found herself lost for words. Angel began to speak, too, perhaps to prompt her to see what she'd meant to say, but Frida, eyes red and watery, turned to Juliet when Tanaka dismissed her.

"Lucky, please!"

"Dammit! I'm not here to execute him." Juliet turned on Tanaka. "I'm not here to kill you! Sorry if you're depressed or whatever, but it's not my fault. I was just trying to live!"

"*Hai*." Again, that infuriating man began to bow, and perhaps because she was staring daggers at him, she felt herself slipping into another one of his memories.

Rutger flinched and pulled back, but the old man's fingers were swift and strong, and he snatched him out of the bush by his wrist. "Ah! Here's the little stray cat who's been watching my mice, hmm?"

"Please!" He squirmed and kicked, but the man was surprisingly strong. He held him out, dangling him in the air, and a broad smile lifted his wizened cheeks toward the crinkling, always smiling eyes.

"Cats have their uses, though, don't they? My garden could use one. My mice could stand to know a little fear. Come, cat, let's put some mackerel in your belly." He gently lowered Rutger to the paving stones at the garden's center but kept a firm grip on his wrist as though he knew he'd bolt the second he was loose. "If you flee, I'll just have to catch you again. I know you won't leave my mice alone. You've got a taste for them now, don't you?"

"Mice?" Rutger wasn't sure what the old man was going on about; he'd only seen birds in the garden, never a rodent. The old instructor didn't answer; he only chuckled and pulled him toward the garden pavilion where he lived.

"What a mangy tomcat you are! Hmm, Noraneko. A fitting name for one such as you. You'll be allowed outside the pavilion where I take my tea, but don't go inside. You're an outdoors cat. If you eat what I give you and do your chores, maybe I'll let you play with the mice. Would you like that, Noraneko?"

". . . just go back to the office." When Juliet stumbled, figuratively, out of Rutger's memory, she found he was talking to Frida, and that the ginger-haired woman was openly weeping as she clutched at Rutger's sleeve.

Angel spoke, interrupting Frida's latest plea. "Juliet, few people use this level of the garage, but this scene is playing out very oddly. I'm worried that a pedestrian might interrupt things and give Tanaka the opportunity to do something rash. Are you alright? You've been quiet."

Juliet took two steps forward, closing the distance between them a little and fully exposing herself, no longer in the shadow of the plasteel pillar.

"Noraneko," she said.

Tanaka snapped his gaze away from Frida, once again locking eyes with Juliet. He stepped forward, but his entire body trembled with the movement. He fell to his knees, visibly convulsing in tremors. He stared at the black-streaked plasteel floor of the garage and began to shake with shuddering, silent sobs. Frida darted toward him, grabbed him around the neck, and tried to soothe him, but Rutger Tanaka collapsed into her, unconscious.

"What did you say to him?" she cried, looking at Juliet with wide, blood-shot eyes.

"Nothing. I . . . I reminded him of who he used to be, I guess."

3

FANTASY

"Who he used to be?" Frida cried, carefully lying Tanaka on his back. While feeling for a pulse, she held her ear close to his mouth. "He's breathing. I . . . Ah. I just got a report from his PAI."

"And?" Juliet was at a loss for words. She didn't know why she kept diving into Tanaka's head without trying, and she didn't know why he'd reacted so viscerally when she repeated the boyhood nickname the old man had given him. All she really knew was that this guy, this brutal, deadly hired gun of a man, wasn't acting at all like she'd expected. If he was a basket case now, that was enough information for her; she could put him in her rearview cam feed, so to speak.

"It's nothing. He'll be fine." Frida's tone had changed dramatically. Rather than panicked and dismayed, she was all business, her words clipped and short. "Probably best if you leave."

Part of Juliet wanted to turn on her heel and stomp away down the parking garage ramp. She didn't have any affection or concern for the man lying on Frida's lap, but she'd be lying if she didn't sort of feel sorry for Frida. She stepped toward them, and then, like a switch being flipped, she had the sudden suspicion that this was an elaborate ruse, that they were both working to get her to drop her guard. Juliet froze. In the blink of an eye, her Texan was in her hand, and she was scanning the garage, looking for the teeth in the trap.

"What are you doing? Gonna kill us while he's out?"

"This feels off. A man like that doesn't faint."

"Oh, come off it! His nanites sedated him. They detected a severe PTSD episode and felt his blood pressure spiking. His body's been rejecting the synth-heart, and he's at risk for blood clots."

Juliet frowned and pointed her Texan at Tanaka. "Look at me, Frida." When Frida's wide, panicked eyes looked up and locked onto hers, Juliet stared at her yellow-flecked green irises and asked, "Is there something going on here?" She didn't know how there could be, not with Angel thoroughly infiltrating Tanaka's network, but she wanted to be sure.

When Frida answered, Juliet ignored the words and listened with her mind, pulling Frida's thoughts toward her with a soft, steady inhalation.

Tanaka! What are you doing? What is it about this woman? Oh, can't we just forget her? MedPro will be here in a minute. Just keep her calm. Don't let her execute the boss!

Juliet sighed and, with a habitual twirl, holstered the Texan. "He's got premium medical?"

"Of course—"

"Don't 'of course' me, Frida!" Juliet took a couple more steps toward the two, frowning down at her. "If his care's so good, why's he having problems with his heart?"

"I don't know. The doctors say it's too much too fast, or some other BS line. They're going to try a different brand soon, once his other implants achieve stable biointegration." Frida sniffed and gently stroked Tanaka's forehead. "They say different synth-flesh manufacturers use proprietary biomimetic matrices in their artificial DNA, leading to slight variations in tissue compatibility. We're going to try the same company that built his lung . . ." Frida scowled and peered at Juliet. "I'm rambling, and you should go. I'll try to get him to forget about you, okay?"

Juliet gripped the monoblade scabbard in her left hand, drumming her fingers against the hard surface, before holding it out. "I should leave this. Maybe it'll help him realize I don't want anything to do with him."

"Yes . . ." Frida started to say, but then with a hoarse, rattling cough, Tanaka interrupted her.

"No." His weird, chrome eyes, with their glowing red irises, peered between nearly closed eyelids. He coughed again, shifting his weight off Frida. He shook his head and said, "Cancel them." For a second, Juliet thought it was a threat, but then she connected the dots and realized he was calling off the medical team that was, apparently, en route.

"Everything good?" she subvocalized.

Angel replied immediately. "I'm not seeing anything unusual on the building network or cameras."

"I'm not going to stand here in this garage any longer. Look, we had the face-to-face you wanted. I offered you your sword. If you don't want it, then just move on with your life—"

"I can't!" Tanaka grunted. He used the sword he'd laid on the cement as a cane, and with Frida tugging on his other hand, he rose shakily to his feet. Red-faced and breathing heavily, he held out one shaking hand. "You don't have to fear me. If I activated my boost, I'd kill myself."

"It's not permanent, boss! You just need more time and a different—"

"Quiet, Frida." Where before he might have barked the command, his tone had grown soft after his collapse, and Juliet could see he was trying to spare Frida's feelings. "If my body worked perfectly, I'm still not the same. Lucky, will you please sit down with me? I have so many questions."

Juliet wanted to leave. Part of her was furious with herself for listening to this man after how he'd beaten her, plainly intent on killing her before she'd gotten the better of him. Another part of her reasoned that she'd been breaking into a facility he'd been hired to protect. Had he known that Lilia and Honey had been kidnapped? Perhaps, but she didn't know that. How would she have responded in his shoes?

The only answer she could live with was that she wouldn't have taken such sadistic pleasure in dominating whoever broke in. Another part of her liked Frida, and wondered how someone like her could be so wrong about a man. *Was there more to Tanaka? Was it possible he really had changed?*

Before she could think more, losing herself in the spiral of conflicting thoughts and emotions, she opened her mouth and let the words roll off her tongue. "I'm leaving. I'm leaving, but if you don't hound me or bother me or my people, I'll contact you when it feels right. Then, we can sit down." She looked around the plasteel garage. "Someplace with other people. A restaurant or something."

"Thank you." Tanaka started to bow, and Juliet growled.

"Stop that!" She glared at him as he straightened up, then turned to regard Frida. "I'll be in touch."

She turned then and, rubber soles squeaking on the plasteel, stomped down the ramp and around the corner. When she was sure she wasn't in their line of sight any longer, she leaned against a plasteel support column and breathed, trying to get control of her hammering heart.

"That encounter wasn't like anything I'd expected," Angel said, her voice very comforting to Juliet's frazzled mind.

"I know, right?" She started walking again. "Is the cab coming?"

"Yes, it's one level up, but descending quickly."

"Thanks." Juliet moved to the side, angling toward a pedestrian walkway that led to the next level's elevators. When she stepped onto the bright yellow paint, she turned and waited for the cab.

"When you called him that name, Noraneko, what were you intending?"

"Nothing. It just came out because I was kind of reeling from a, I don't know, vision, I guess. I saw a memory of Tanaka's from when he was a little boy. An old man who, I think, took him in called him that. How do I know it means *stray cat*? I don't speak Japanese." Now that she thought about it, she wasn't sure the entire exchange had been in English. She hadn't been watching Rutger Tanaka's memory; she'd been living it. "I wasn't trying to deep dive. I was just trying to get a read on his thoughts to see if he meant to attack me or something."

As the squealing tires of the cab approached, Angel remarked, "It often seems that your ability ferrets out exactly what you need to know, regardless of your conscious efforts."

"I don't know why I needed to know that Tanaka was an orphan living on the streets, taken in by an old monk who trained the rich kids from a corporate boarding school." Juliet laughed—she'd certainly learned a lot from a brief visit inside Tanaka's head. When the cab pulled up and the door swung back, she ducked inside, leaning the sword on the seat beside her.

"Welcome back, SOA operative XR713-004."

Juliet closed the visor on her helmet and continued to speak to Angel. "Any activity on Applebaum and Hawkins? What's Frida doing?"

"Nothing on the two off-duty operatives. As for Frida, have a look for yourself." Juliet watched as Angel updated the feed from Frida's ocular and auditory implants. She saw her pale, freckled hand resting on Tanaka's shoulder as they walked back to the elevator together.

"What was that all about, boss? Do you really want to die?"

Tanaka didn't answer for several long seconds, but as the elevator doors closed, he began to speak, his voice surprisingly soft. "I don't know, Frida. I don't know what I want. I imagined my encounter with that woman a million times, but I never imagined it happening like that. She hardly spoke, but what she said ripped something open. She cut through the numbness and reminded me that I wasn't always Rutger Tanaka, the coldhearted mercenary.

She reminded me that if that man's dead, it doesn't mean that all of me is dead."

"Boss, this isn't like you. Coldhearted? That's not how you talk. It's not how you think—"

"You aren't listening. The boss you knew is gone. I have to discover who I am now. I know I never told you this, Frida, but I think of you like family, like a daughter. No matter who I am, I'll have a place for you, hmm? Don't be upset."

Frida's vision grew blurry, and it took Juliet a second to realize the woman was crying. When she spoke, her voice was hoarse and thick with emotion. "I won't have a place if you let people kill you out of some fucked-up sense of honor or . . ."

"That's over. I offered her my life, and she didn't want it. We'll move forward now, don't worry."

"Okay, Angel. Cut the feed for now. I mean to me; you should keep an eye on her." Juliet felt a little dirty watching Frida's emotional heart-to-heart with her boss. As the cab left the garage and started motoring through the narrow traffic lanes out of the downtown area, she leaned back and tried to focus on her breathing. If nothing else, she felt confident that Tanaka didn't have a vendetta. He wasn't going to try to find the people she cared about and kill them. As far as she was concerned, that was a win. "Call Bennet, please."

As the tone sounded and his face resolved in her comm window, Juliet smiled and gave a thumbs-up. Of course, Angel made sure her projected image mimicked the action.

"Well? I'm alive! Do you think everyone is up for a nice dinner?"

"I am. Not sure about the others; you made me promise to keep quiet about you being on the surface, remember?"

"Yeah, but did you?"

"Well, is it my fault Bradbury was charging in the gunship and heard you stomping through the corridors to get that sword? Is it my fault he started asking questions and ran squealing to Alice as soon as he figured out you'd been here?"

Juliet laughed. "Are you really blaming Bradbury? You got the poor synth to take the fall for you?"

Bennet grinned. "Anyway, yeah, the rest of the crew are eager to see you. What kind of food have you been craving?"

"Noodles!" Juliet said immediately. "Remember that noodle house we went to when you first rented the hangar?"

"Kimchi Noodle Nest? Yes! I haven't been there in a month!" Juliet could see Bennet's eyes light up as his grin stretched his cheeks upward. "Jeez, Lucky, I eat so much better when you're in town! Hey, speaking of eating well, I couldn't tell in that getup you were wearing, but I hope you've been keeping up with the weights. We're going to have to get back into a routine. First thing tomorr—"

"Bennet!" Juliet laughed. "We'll talk about it at dinner. Can you tell the rest of the crew? I'm going to take a shower and change. There's still running water on the gunship, right?"

"Oh yeah! We flushed the system when Aya replaced about half a kilometer of those self-healing polymer water lines. Talk about a pain in the—"

"Bennet!" When he stopped, smiling sheepishly, she continued, "I'll be back in just a few minutes. Save something to talk about for dinner, huh?" She winked and then cut the line. "He's too much!"

Angel made a soft "hmm" sound and said, "I think he's funny."

"You missed him, huh?" Juliet closed her eyes and leaned back in the cab's surprisingly soft cushioning.

"I did! I missed Bennet and Aya, especially. Are you pleased with the outcome of your meeting with Rutger? Do you think the crew is safe?"

Juliet breathed deep, slow breaths with her eyes closed. She felt like she could drift away into a nap right then and there, and perhaps Angel thought she would because she didn't press for an answer despite Juliet taking nearly five minutes to respond.

"I'm happy as far as Tanaka being a threat goes. Not only do I think he's sincerely not looking for vengeance, but I think your surveillance of him through Frida is more than adequate. The whole thing has me worried about other threats, however. I feel like we need to start making headway when it comes to WBD. I think we need to get you into their network."

Angel didn't reply for a long minute. Juliet couldn't blame her. WBD was a big deal; they weren't a single wealthy mercenary with a long history of successful jobs—they were a corporation that could buy Sir Rodric Barrington's businesses a dozen times over. Still, when a corp got that big, as far as Juliet was concerned, it only meant more opportunities to find vulnerabilities.

As though she'd listened to Juliet's thoughts, Angel finally replied, "They have a medical research division here on Luna."

"Really?" She supposed it made sense. Luna was the stepping stone to the broader solar system from Earth, and, of course, WBD would have interests out there. "Well, that's settled then. When we get a little time, we'll check it out."

They rode in silence for a while after that, but then, Angel surprised her by opening a vid window on her AUI. "There's some trending news that may interest you."

Juliet blinked her eyes a little blearily; she'd been on the verge of dozing off. As she watched the vid stream, she perked up, something like adrenaline but milder running through her system. It was an interview between a woman from Sol One News and a man in a frumpy brown suit with bushy hair and a very out-of-fashion mustache. The caption identified him as Carlos Villegas from Bonner and Plant Aerospace Engineering.

It was their conversation that got Juliet's blood pumping. The newscaster, Tiff Reading, said, "As for the broader implications, is it true that you believe this will open up travel beyond our solar system?"

Villegas cleared his throat and nodded. "The data, widely disseminated around the system, despite immense efforts to halt it, is almost disturbingly credible. It looks like corporations have been hiding technological advances with dark matter for decades. The data, sold broadly through back channels, is thorough with databases containing hundreds of thousands of sample readings, thorough schematics for the containment devices, and even research details into the uses of the matter to manipulate space-time."

"Excuse me, Doctor Villegas, but would you mind explaining what this all means to the layperson?"

"Of course. Essentially, there are now more than a dozen major corporations with the know-how to capture dark matter using gravity manipulation—"

Tiff interrupted. "Dark matter? Gravity manipulation?"

"Right, right. Let me back up. Dark matter . . . Well, I could talk for two hours, and you still won't understand dark matter, but let me just say that we know it's there, but we haven't interacted with it until now. You see, nothing we do can touch dark matter, but we've noticed that gravity affects it. This leaked research data shows that just as we can use artificial gravity generation to allow comfortable life on Luna, Titan, or even large spacecraft, this new technology allows the right collection craft to ensnare dark matter with generated gravity."

"Ah, mm-hmm, and then what?"

"Well, capturing dark matter is a big enough deal all on its own, but it seems that these corporations have already begun experimenting with the captured dark matter to manipulate space-time."

Tiff Reading's eyes widened, and she leaned forward, asking breathlessly, "And that means what? Time travel?"

"No, no, not exactly. However, it might allow us to get around some of the fundamental limits of the physical universe, one of them being the impossibility of traveling faster than light."

"Are you saying . . . ?"

"That warp drive technology may soon be moving from science fiction into reality."

Juliet paused the feed and said, her heart hammering in her chest, "We did that, Angel. We brought that into the open."

"Isn't this what you wanted?"

"Yeah, but . . ." Juliet clenched her fists and tried to gather her thoughts. "I thought it would take longer, I guess. I thought the corps who bought the data would compete with each other but keep things quiet. It's really out there now. One of the corps that bought the data from Tornado must have leaked . . ."

"I think it's for the best," Angel replied. "What's the old saying about sunlight? It's the best disinfectant. That's it."

"Yeah, I guess. Now everyone knows, and everyone's watching." Juliet closed the window; she'd seen enough. Whatever came of it couldn't be worse than a couple of big corps going to war over the data. Now that it was out in the ether, now that a dozen or more big corps were working on the tech, there wouldn't be any point in fighting about it. Now, it was just a race. "We still have the data, yeah?"

"Oh yes. I've been rather intrigued by it."

A sudden fantasy washed over Juliet, and she began to grin, a smile too broad for Angel not to notice.

"What is it, Juliet?"

"Imagine if Athena woke up and worked with us to perfect the tech. Imagine if we had the first functional warp drive."

4

NIGHT WALK

Juliet pushed her bowl away with a sigh and looked around the table at her friends' smiling, laughing faces. It was nice to be back, nice to be among people she cared about, and nice to listen to small talk and banter rather than worrying about life-or-death situations. It couldn't last long, however; not when she'd been involved in something so momentous that it was all over the news streams.

When the current laughter about Aya slurping so forcefully that she got spicy broth in her eye died down, Alice said, rather innocuously, "Can you guys believe that stuff coming out about the dark matter research?"

Juliet froze, for some reason panic-stricken by the topic, as though she were guilty of something. She was, but who knew that? Bennet snorted and immediately relieved the tension. "Yeah, right! Just like they found alien ruins on Venus."

"You think it's BS?" Alice raised an eyebrow.

"If it were real, we wouldn't be hearing about it. Those corps like their secrets."

Still rubbing a napkin at her eye, Aya jabbed an elbow into Bennet's ribs. "You haven't been paying attention. The news is only out there because someone leaked it."

"That's what they always say. We'll get all wound up, everyone will talk about it nonstop for a couple of weeks, and then it will just sort of fade out of the news as the next big thing comes along. Remember how we were supposed to have conquered aging a few years ago?"

Juliet couldn't help herself. "If they conquered aging, the rich execs would snatch up that tech, and the rest of us wouldn't know about it."

"Exactly!" Bennet pointed his chopsticks at her, nodding. "Same for this new business. If they figure out a way to warp space with dark matter, us plebes won't see anything from it; not in our lifetimes."

"Bleh," Alice said, also pushing her bowl away. "You guys are too negative. What do you think, babe?" She gave Shiro a nudge. The man, deep in his noodles, looked up, narrowing his eyes in a scowl.

"I worry about the ship and our next job, not this stuff."

"Shiro!" Aya cried, shaking a chopstick at him. "You're no fun!"

"Hey, on that note, Lucky," Alice said, shaking her head at her husband, "we've got business to discuss. I mean about those ships and bounties you sent our way. Can we sit down together tomorrow?"

"Yeah, of course." She figured Alice didn't want to talk money in front of everyone. Juliet was okay with that because she hadn't really thought about it yet. How much was she going to kick in toward the gunship company? How big a cut was she willing to give Alice and Shiro for brokering everything? It would be best if they had that talk without the alcohol and peanut gallery consisting of Bennet and Aya.

Partially because she was excited about it and partly to help Alice change the subject, she said, "Hey, by the way, I got my hands on some Cybergen ship tech—a sample of self-repair hull membrane with live nanites—"

"You what?" Bennet burst into a coughing fit as he tried to speak and swallow at the same time, just to end up choking on a mouthful of noodles.

"From where?" Aya asked, Shiro's reticence forgotten.

"Well . . ." Juliet paused and sipped her orange-flavored soda. She took her time, drinking several big gulps, and then, when she could see Aya's eyes widening in frustrated anticipation, she sighed and said, "Man! Something about cold, crisp soda after eating hot soup, you know?"

"Come *on*, Lucky!"

Juliet laughed, winking at Bennet, who'd finally got over his fit and was grinning, enjoying Juliet's teasing. "Okay, well, you all know I was caught up doing a job involving some pirates, right? I won't go into details because I don't want to think about it, but also because it's safer for everyone this way." She held up a hand when Aya started to object. "No, no, I'm serious about this one. Trust me. Anyway, while I was there, I came upon this tech, and I, well, I absconded with it." Juliet tapped her temple. "I've had Angel working on it, and she thinks we can probably have the polymer membrane fabricated for the gunship, and the nanites, if given the right input and nutrient blend, will propagate through it."

"Wait, seriously?" At some point during her explanation, Bennet had decided she was just teasing Aya, but now, his eyes were wide with interest. "You think we can retrofit the Takamoto control module and fabricator?"

"No retrofitting needed. Angel just has to update the firmware, and we need to load the nutrient cartridges."

"Nutrients?" Alice sipped her drink and gestured to the table. "Are they alive? They need to eat?"

"Not exactly." Juliet chuckled. "I think it's a term that caught on back when people were calling nanites bugs. I mean, people still do, but we don't feed them food, exactly. They require base materials to do their work, and the fabricator requires materials to pump out more nanites. That's where the cartridges come in—they provide the molecular building blocks to generate more nanites and also those that get spread through the polymer membrane for ship repairs."

"That's awesome!" Aya slapped the table enthusiastically, then looked around the restaurant, cringing. "Sorry! Sorry . . ."

"Hey, don't apologize," Bennet said. "It's more than awesome! I never thought I'd work on a ship with self-repair tech. The Takamoto system on the gunship was wrecked decades ago. Aya and I spent days, like, thirty hours each, peeling and grinding away the old crusty remnants of the nanite membrane when we took the hull plating off."

Juliet shrugged. "Well, I imagine if you never refill the cartridges and don't maintain the control module, you know, changing out the filters and stuff, the nanites die, the membrane dries up, and yeah, you're left with just a mess."

Shiro swallowed a bite of noodles and said, "Too bad we couldn't install something like that on the *Kowashi*."

Bennet laughed and shook his head. "You're dreaming, boss. That old bird isn't . . . Well, let's just say we'd basically have to rebuild the ship. Not cost-effective."

"That's why I said too bad." Shiro sighed, pushed his empty bowl back, and then stretched his neck. He looked around the table and nodded. "Good food. Glad you're back, Lucky."

"What are you doing? Leaving?" Alice shook her head at her husband.

"What? It's almost nine, and I have an early start."

"You what?" Juliet looked from Shiro to Alice to Aya, then back to Shiro. "You guys are going on a job?"

"No!" Aya answered. "Just Shiro. He's meeting a contact about a salvage tip."

"A tip? Something secret?" Juliet was intrigued.

"*Hai.* Maybe." Shiro shrugged. "He's a reliable contact, but he's been wrong before. Might be good money, though."

"We should go to the warehouse, Lucky," Aya said, Shiro's departure apparently already accepted and forgotten. "I have a bunch of things to show you."

"I suppose I'll head out with Shiro. I'm glad you're back, Lucky. You know that, right?" Alice pushed her chair back and stood up, so Juliet did too; she could tell the pilot wanted to hug her. She'd already been practically mugged by Aya when she and Bennet arrived at the noodle house. When she'd stopped by the hangar to change, he'd been waiting.

"Yeah, 'course I do. You know I'm glad to be here." She let the shorter woman wrap her arms around her, then hugged her back, gently stroking her feathery red hair. "I'm sorry about Nick."

"Hush! We weren't going to mention that, remember?"

"Yeah. Sorry."

"It's okay. We'll have a drink for him sometime, all right? But this is about you, about us being glad you're back. Don't think about sad things." While she spoke, everyone had gotten quiet. Bennet stuffed his hands into his pockets and exhaled noisily as he walked around the table, heading out of the restaurant. Aya fidgeted and moved toward the door, and Shiro followed her. "We made things awkward." Alice laughed, pulling out of Juliet's embrace. "Come see me on the *Kowashi* when you get up and about tomorrow, okay?"

"Yeah, sure, I will." Juliet smiled; for some reason, their shared loss made her feel closer than ever to the pilot she'd once found almost too intimidating to speak to.

They found the others waiting outside. Alice walked over to Shiro, taking his hand and standing on her tiptoes to deliver a quick peck on his cheek. In that moment, Juliet envied them. Angel had been quiet for most of the dinner, but Juliet was used to her doing that, quietly hanging back, observing everything, and then talking to her about it later, so she was slightly surprised when she spoke up as Aya and Bennet said their goodbyes to Shiro and Alice.

"You seem to view Alice and Shiro longingly."

"Huh? You can tell that?" Juliet, of course, subvocalized.

"Just as I can read your speech patterns with hardly any subvocalization on your part, I can tell from your posture, minute facial expressions, breathing patterns, and—"

"I get it; I'm an open book to you."

"Yes."

"Well . . ." Juliet's conversation with Angel was cut short as a cab pulled up, and Shiro and Alice moved to get in. She called out, waving, "See you tomorrow!"

"*Hai!*" Shiro waved and slipped inside while Alice followed him, smiling.

"They're acting kinda touchy-feely, you know?" Bennet laughed as the cab pulled away. "If we were going back to the *Kowashi*, I think it'd be a headphones night . . ."

"Bennet!" Aya laughed, punching him in the arm. "I thought I was the only one close enough to their cabin to hear that!"

"You guys are terrible." Juliet laughed and started walking up the sidewalk in the general direction of the hangar.

"As if, Lucky!" Aya darted after her. When she caught up, she wrapped an arm around Juliet's waist, walking beside her. "You know you were thinking the same thing!" She was a little breathless, and Juliet found it endearing. She put an arm over Aya's shoulders and pulled her close while they walked.

"I'm glad to be back."

"Are you back for good?"

"Hmm?" The question surprised her, and as Bennet caught up and walked on her other side, she thought about it. "I don't know! I always thought I'd do other jobs between gunship missions, but if we're busy all the time . . . I don't know." She squeezed her as if to make up for her lack of certainty.

Aya's fingers wriggled against her hip, and Juliet realized she was hooking them into the belt loop on her jeans. Walking side by side like that with someone wasn't usually comfortable, but Aya had a way of matching the sway of her hips, and it felt good to feel someone wanted to be so close to her.

She was trying to think of something more to say on the subject when Bennet bailed her out.

"I figure the gunship's still a couple of months from ready. Especially if we're gonna be spraying on a new polymer membrane for these mystery nanites you found. It'll take a while for a special order like that."

"Did you tell her about the barrels?" Aya asked, poking her head around Juliet to look at Bennet.

"For the main gun? Yeah, he did." Juliet inhaled deeply, enjoying the cool night air. "Are they installed? I didn't notice; my eyes were grabbed by the lovely painted armor panels on the drying racks."

"That's my project!" Aya laughed. Juliet slowed, and Bennet matched her pace as they skirted around a pile of old pallets. The sidewalk was cluttered with refuse left out for sanitation crews to pick up the next morning, and traffic going to and from the industrial hangars was almost nonexistent at night, so they walked onto the road, avoiding the mess.

"I told her that, too." Bennet chuckled, shaking his head. "You sure know how to push her buttons, Lucky."

"Speaking of pushing buttons, are you going to tell us what really happened with that girlfriend of yours?"

"You don't know?" Aya answered before Bennet could do more than open his mouth and look horrified.

"Oh? There really is a story?" Juliet reached over and grabbed Bennet's meaty shoulder, giving it a jostle. "You said she thought you worked too much."

"He said *what*?" Aya squealed. "Lucky! You'll never believe—"

"Oh, come on, Aya! You said you felt sorry for me, and now you're going to tease me like this? Couldn't you let me have this one? Lucky doesn't need to know . . ."

"Cat's out of the bag, Mr. Lang." Juliet laughed. "You think I can let this go now that I know there's a story?" Still holding onto his shoulder, Juliet let him guide her around the corner onto 41st Street. They still had half a mile to walk before they got to the hangar. The street ahead was dark, with only occasional large amber flood lamps up on the sides of the plasteel buildings providing illumination.

Juliet paused, stopping the other two, and looked upward toward the dome, wondering if she could see any stars. All she saw was blackness dotted with the flickering lights of drones.

"Well, the stars won't be your witness. Let's hear it."

"Whatever. Let me tell her, then, okay, Aya? No interruptions!"

"Only if you leave something out," Aya said, clearly struggling to hold herself back as they started walking again.

"It's not . . ." Bennet sighed and coughed, then said, "First of all, you need to know that I was only sleeping in your dream-rig. You get me? No matter what you're about to hear, I was only sleeping."

"Now I'm getting nervous." Juliet grinned. Despite only drinking soda at the noodle shop, she was feeling almost like she was buzzed. What was it? Endorphins from the spicy food? The closeness of her friends? She didn't know, but she liked it.

"So, Lavonne came to surprise me for lunch one day, and I was sleeping in the dream-rig—just a nap, 'cause I had a bad night's sleep. She looked all over the hangar, calling my name, going in and out of the gunship, into the little office, even looking in crates. When she sent a few angry messages asking me why I said I'd be working when I wasn't there, my PAI finally got a clue and woke me up, so I crawled out of the dream-rig, and she freaked out."

Juliet narrowed her eyes and looked at Bennet, but he avoided her gaze. "What's wrong with that? Why'd she have a meltdown?"

"I guess her ex-husband left her for a DR girl."

"A, uh, *what*?" Juliet laughed. "Wait, like a woman who was also in a dream-rig, or are we talking about a sim?"

"I guess she was a sim." Bennet shrugged.

Aya giggled, and Juliet looked down at her. "How'd you know about this?"

"I was there! I was hiding 'cause Lavonne didn't like me."

Juliet couldn't stop the giggles. "You were hiding in the hangar while she was turning the place upside down, looking for Bennet?"

"Yes!" Aya continued to giggle. "You should have seen her face when Bennet crawled out of the dream-rig. It was like he gave birth to a demon."

"Yeah. I guess I kinda dodged a bullet. After she cussed me out and told me how disgusting I was, she stormed out and blocked me. Never heard from her after that."

"She didn't let you explain that you were just, um, 'napping'?" Juliet laughed as she made air quotes while saying the word.

"Oh, dammit! I knew this was going to happen. Aya! I owe you for this." They were still walking on the street and, as bright headlights appeared behind them, throwing long, stretched-out shadow copies of the three of them onto the roadway, they hurried up onto the sidewalk to let a windowless white van hum past. As it pulled away, they were plunged into darkness again, and Juliet, still holding onto Bennet's shoulder, steered the three of them back onto the road. They'd only taken a few steps before a loud cough from off to the right, an alley between two hangars, echoed through the night.

"Let's go faster," Aya said, squeezing Juliet's hip.

"Right." Juliet stretched her legs and took two long strides before the scuff of boots on concrete alerted her.

"Juliet, I can hear four distinct movement patterns from the alley on your right."

"Thanks, Angel," Juliet said aloud, slowing her steps. She let go of Bennet's shoulder and gently pushed Aya behind her. She turned toward the alley just in time to see four dark figures step out from behind a large stack of pallets. Angel upped the gain on her implants, turning her world slightly amber but revealing every detail about the men. One held a vibroblade, two had buzzing batons, and one had a short-barreled shotgun in his meaty fist. "Not exactly tools for working on spacecraft, gentlemen."

Bennet finally caught on to what was happening and stepped to the right, squaring off with the four men. "Who are these jokers?"

"What?" Aya tried to push forward, but Juliet held her arm out, scooting sideways, keeping herself between the potential threat and her much smaller friend.

"Ain't this a happy bunch o' drones. Burning the midnight oil, eh? Which hangar's yours?" As he spoke, Angel flashed a symbol on her AUI that was universal for a jammed signal: a lightning bolt with a dotted line through it.

"Fu—" Bennet started to say, scowling, but Juliet cut him off.

"I think you guys made a mistake. Turn around, and we can forget we saw you." She let her right hand fall to her thigh, gently tapping her fingers against the polymer grip of her Texan.

"Uh-oh, Yam; she's got a cowboy gun," the knife-wielder said, leering from behind a thick visor. He stuck his long, silver-studded tongue between two fingers and made a slurping sound, chasing it with a high-pitched giggle.

"Just let us into your hangar, and we won't kill ya," the one with the shot-gun said. "We're robbing someone tonight, and you three just volunteered."

"Hey, my connection's blocked," Aya said. Juliet guessed she'd been trying to call the hangar-leasing company's corpo-sec.

"Sure, sweetie," the leering guy with the vibrating knife said. Juliet decided she'd had enough. Just as she always did, Angel knew Juliet wanted to move fast. When she snatched her revolver out of its zero-friction lining, to her, it felt like she was moving smoothly and normally. To everyone else, her move-ment was too fast to track. One second, her hand was hanging by her side; the next, it was extended before her, the big-bore, silver-gray pistol clutched in her fist with a thin trail of smoke rising from the barrel. The thunder of the shot was almost as surprising as the sudden appearance of the gun.

From Juliet's perspective, the thugs reacted in slow motion, their actions disjointed and out of order. The one she'd shot, the gun-toting, burly, curly-haired guy, dropped his gun as his thumb disappeared in a red mist. A frac-tion of a second later, his eyes opened wide, and his mouth rounded into an *O* of surprise. Another second later, his friends' faces convulsed in surprise, and Juliet could see them all flinch in slow motion. Two jerked back, and one spastically lurched to the side, but they all slowly tracked their eyes to Juliet as their brains belatedly figured out she'd shot one of them.

As it became clear the four men wouldn't charge her, Angel slowed her mental processing so Juliet could observe their reactions. The big guy grunted in agony and lifted his missing thumb to his mouth, almost comically beginning to try to suck on the digit that no longer existed. The leering knife guy said, "What the fuck?"

"She's wired!" one of the baton wielders said, backing away another step. And the other baton wielder made the unfortunate decision to drop his baton and start digging under his jacket, fumbling at a pistol grip. Juliet smoothly pressed the almost weightless trigger of the Texan, putting a heavy polymer slug into his elbow, turning a good portion of solid bone into powder. He screamed and collapsed, writhing as his arm flopped and blood pooled on the concrete.

"Where do you want it?" Juliet asked the knife guy, the only one still looking at her threateningly.

"What?"

"Your bullet."

"Fucking crazy bitch!" He turned and ran, with Thumbless hot on his heels.

"Take your friend!" Bennet yelled at the last man standing, a wiry guy with a plasteel arm and a bull's-eye monocle implant. He paused, already turning to flee. "Help him up and then get outta here!" Bennet growled.

"Shouldn't we call corpo-sec?" Aya asked, poking her head around Juliet's side.

"Sure, go ahead." Bennet shrugged. "They'll be here in an hour." The three of them watched as the last would-be robber bent to help his whimpering, bleeding friend onto his feet and shuffled away down the alley. Juliet could hear—plain as day, thanks to Angel enhancing and isolating the sounds—an electric motor whir to life, and several doors opening and closing.

"They're getting in a vehicle."

Bennet snorted in derision. "Yeah, we won't see them again. Holy shit, Lucky, I forgot how fast you are."

"Don't mess with Lucky!" Aya crowed, grabbing her arm and pulling her down the street toward the hangar. "Let's get inside. I guess Bennet got us a hangar in a high-crime neighborhood."

"It's not high crime! It's the only place on Luna to rent a hangar like this!" Bennet groused, hurrying to keep up with the two women. Juliet allowed Aya to pull her along, surprised at how the two had taken the attempted mugging in stride. It just went to show how the world wasn't an easy place, and whether she dealt with her many enemies or not, new ones were just around the corner, waiting for her or her friends to make the wrong move.

She frowned, finishing her thought aloud. "Like walking through a bad neighborhood in the middle of the night."

"It's *not* a bad neighborhood," Bennet insisted. "No more than the rest of Luna, I guess."

"Well," Juliet sighed, once again grabbing hold of his muscular shoulder, "I guess, these days, unless you're in a patrolled, gated neighborhood, they're all kinda bad."

5

WINDFALL

Juliet sat up on the edge of her acceleration couch, letting her legs dangle so just the tips of her toes touched the cold plasteel. She rubbed her eyes, yawned, and asked, "What time is it?" She could find the answer by focusing on the corner of her AUI, but it was an excuse to get her vocal cords working and hear Angel's voice.

"Nine forty-seven, sleepyhead. How are you feeling?"

"I feel good." Juliet arched her back, twisting her neck left and right, enjoying the release of tension as she yawned again. "It's not that late, considering we were up 'til two." She and Aya had sat together for hours after Bennet left for the *Kowashi* around midnight. They'd gone through the boxes and boxes of books Aya had picked up at auction, looking at the cover art and taking turns reading the blurbs on the back. Juliet smiled at the memory as she looked around the mess of her room—boxes and little towers of books were everywhere. "Is Aya still sleeping?"

"Yes. She's in the other officer cabin across the hall." Juliet wasn't surprised; Aya had told her she'd moved into the gunship while she'd been gone. Aya had been spending most of her time working in the hangar and decided staying on the *Kowashi* was just wasting an hour of commute time every day. "Alice sent you a message. She's up and working, and available to meet with you any time before 1700 hours."

"Cool. A shower, a bite to eat, and we'll head that way. Where's Bradbury, by the way?" She hadn't seen the synth since being back.

"He's working on the *Kowashi*. Bennet's having the water filtration system replaced, and Bradbury has been working on removing the old pump and piping. That's why Bennet returned last night, I believe; I see an appointment with a rep from Filter Elite LTD on the *Kowashi*'s schedule."

"I think he mentioned something like that." Juliet stood, gathered some clean clothes, then walked into the bathroom adjoining her room. A minute later, she was standing under hot, filtered water, sighing with pleasure. "It's good to be back."

Her soaps and shampoos were still in the little shower stall, and she smiled as she popped open the shampoo and smelled the strawberry scent. Angel had to prompt her with a warning about running low on hot water before she finally rinsed off and got out. She took her time drying, getting dressed, and brushing her hair, pausing frequently to pick up books and place them roughly in alphabetical piles.

"You should get some shelves mounted on the walls. They'll need plasti-glass covers to keep the books in place during maneuvers."

"Yep. That's a project we can tackle for sure." Juliet pulled her laces tight on her comfortable, well-worn work boots, then stood up and slung her gun belt around her hips. She wore her favorite style of slender-legged, stretchy jeans and a blue T-shirt that said "Electra" with two floating chrome-purple lips printed on the front. Electra was a popular synth-pop artist, and Juliet had no idea where she'd gotten the shirt. As usual, she shrugged into her motorcycle jacket, then, feeling clean, rested, and comfortable, she left the hangar and climbed into a cab Angel had waiting.

"Message Aya, low priority, about where we went."

"Done."

"Let's pick up bagels. Bennet will eat some if no one else does. By the way, did he report those jokers last night?"

"He said he was filing a report."

"You file one too, please. Send footage of that van that passed by right before they jumped us. I think it might have circled the block and picked them up on the other side of the alley."

"Ah, that sounds plausible; perhaps their driver was scoping potential targets. I think we looked more vulnerable than we were, what with you hanging on to Bennet, and Aya hanging on to you. It appeared you were inebriated."

"Well, that may be, but the whole thing got me thinking. We should upgrade the security in the hangar where I've got the *Wing*."

"That hangar is attached to the port and would be significantly harder to rob than these industrial hangars."

"Nonetheless." Juliet shrugged. "We've got plenty of cash on hand, and I think Alice is about to give us another payday."

"Very well, I'll do some research on aftermarket hangar security and also look into upgrading the *Wing's* security, though it's already quite robust, especially with Brutus keeping watch."

Juliet snorted a little laugh at the reminder of Angel's latest semi-intelligent daemon program. Brutus had been designed to keep watch on the *Wing* and, more importantly, Athena. When they'd gotten to Luna, she'd taken the deck with the Maverick daemon they'd used to pilot the *Lady Hawk*, modified it into Brutus, and then reinstalled it on the same mech. Now it was patrolling the *Wing*.

"Even with Brutus, we should be extra careful. You know how precious that cargo is. We also ought to do something about this hangar. Even with one of us here most of the time, we've got too many valuable components and tools to risk getting robbed."

"Of course." That settled the matter, and Juliet rode quietly until they stopped for bagels, of which she purchased a mixed dozen and three kinds of creamy spreads. Food offering in hand, she walked aboard the familiar dingy, brown-gray plasteel of the *Kowashi* twenty minutes later.

"Can you let the crew know I'm dropping the bagels in the mess and tell Alice I'm on my way up?"

Angel didn't report her completion of the request, but a green light flashed on her comms, and when Juliet accepted the request, Bennet's face appeared. "Food?"

"Yep! I got you the spicy cream cheese you like." Juliet laughed and revised her statement. "I mean the cultured spread. I don't know what it actually is . . ."

"Doesn't matter if it tastes good! You gonna be in the mess?"

"I'll be around, but right now, I gotta meet with Alice. Are you going to be here all day?"

"Probably. This guy's jerking my chain about refitting the *Kowashi's* filtration system. Says our pipes aren't up to spec, and he won't be able to warranty the work if we don't change 'em out. We just did that on the gunship, and that stuff's not cheap! The *Kowashi* has about two kilometers worth!"

"Why are you upgrading the system again?" Juliet dropped the bagels on the mess hall table and returned to the corridor, heading for the lift.

"The old pump broke down, and the filtration tank cracked. When it leaked, the water pooled in the cargo bay, and Alice saw it was kind of discolored. She's insisting we get all the gunk out, which, as you probably know, isn't so easy with a system this old. The pipes are lined with it."

"Discolored?" Juliet snorted, betting he was downplaying things. She stepped onto the lift and punched the bridge level selection.

"Ah, well, almost black, I guess. Then there was the smell . . ."

"Good luck with all that, Bennet." Juliet shook her head, laughing. "Sounds like you'll have to bite the bullet; I don't blame Alice. Who wants to shower in that stuff?"

"Come on! That's what filters are for."

"You're just asking for more backups, leaks, and pump wear and tear. Those pipes are older than you and me combined."

"Well, you're not the one who has to cut corners on other semicritical things." While he groused, Juliet stepped off the elevator and paused in the main upper corridor.

"I'm about to sit down with Alice. I'll talk to her about it. Maybe we can squeeze a little more money your way."

"You'd do that for me?" Bennet actually fluttered his eyelashes.

"Sure, but you're going to owe me a bag of that protein mix. The berry-flavored one."

"Deal!"

Juliet laughed and cut the comm connection. "He's a character, you know?"

"I know. I think you're right, too. It would be foolish to install a new filtration system and main pump with inadequate piping."

"Yep." Juliet walked toward the bridge, and it almost startled her how quickly she had arrived. She'd remembered the *Kowashi* being bigger. Next to the *Humpback* and the *Red Betty*, though, it was small and cramped. Even the *Wing* felt more spacious. It was significantly smaller, but the Cybergen medical ship was simply designed with comfort in mind. The *Kowashi* was all business; the things that made it special were its overall sturdiness, the giant salvage manipulation claws attached to the hull, and, of course, its good cargo-to-hull-size ratio. The powerful salvage winch and all the other bespoke customizations Shiro's family had made over the years also made it hard to replace.

The sliding door that sealed the bridge off from the rest of the ship was wide open, so Juliet stepped through to find Alice reclining on her acceleration couch, a three-dimensional spreadsheet display flickering in the air before her; it would be much clearer with her AUI's enhancement. "Hey, Alice."

She waved her hand, dismissing the flickering data, then turned to regard the doorway. "Lucky! You got up here faster than I expected." She gestured to the navigator couch beside her. "Take a seat."

"Sure." Juliet moved into the rather cramped bridge, ducking her head beneath the banks of old component cabinets and scooting around the bulky consoles. She flopped down into the couch, the gel lining squelching with the pressure. "What's on the agenda? We talking money?"

"Money and other things." Alice chuckled. "So, you're cool with me and Shiro taking a brokerage fee for handling those little presents you sent floating our way, yeah? I was looking at it as kind of a windfall, hoping to talk Shiro into a little time off, but, as you probably heard from Bennet, we're still barely keeping the *Kowashi* operable and maintaining our solvency."

"Yeah, of course! I was thinking twenty percent. Is that too little?" Juliet knew it was generous—she could have hired a stranger to handle things for five percent.

"No! God, no. That's great." Alice sighed and reached up to twist a lock of her short red hair around her pointer finger. "I feel guilty taking that much, honestly . . ."

"Stop it. I wouldn't offer if I didn't think it was worth it to have people I know and trust handling things. So? What are we looking at?"

"There were a lot of bounties, but some of them were small. On the other hand, some of them were . . . massive. It was hard to keep you and us anonymous when we claimed them. It cost us some extra percentage points with the claim broker we used—an old friend of Shiro's." Juliet didn't respond, just nodded, maintaining her pleasant expression. She didn't really care how much they got; to her, it was all gravy. "Okay, so the grand total for the bounties was just shy of 480k. The claim broker took fifteen percent, which brought us to 408k. You're sure twenty percent of that is okay for me and Shiro?"

"Absolutely. I didn't want to have to look into that icebox and see all those corpses. I didn't want to deal with those creeps I'd left alive roaming around that ship. It wasn't a nothing task I asked of you guys. You deserve it."

"Thanks, Lucky. Okay, transferring 326.4k your way." Juliet saw the incoming Sol-bit transfer on her AUI as Alice kept speaking, "Now, the matter of the two ships."

"Any problems?"

"No, no. The interceptor, the, uh, *Sharp Lady*, sold right away. Did you realize how many aftermarket components were on that little bird? All the armor was clean and well-maintained, too."

"Oh, yeah. You should have heard Nick go on and on about it . . ." Juliet trailed off, sighing and looking up at the ceiling for a moment as a wave of melancholy swept over her. She felt Alice's hand on her knee and smiled, blinking. She looked back at the other woman and saw she, too, looked upset. "Sorry."

"Uh-uh. We have to talk about him. We have to mention our memories of him. Otherwise, he's really gone, leaving nothing behind. When I die, you better tell stories about me, too."

Juliet sniffed and barked a short laugh. "Hah! You're the one who better be telling stories about me!"

"Whichever! We have a deal, right?"

"Yeah, of course, Alice."

Alice smiled, squeezed Juliet's knee, then sat back. "So, Nick thought it was a good ship, huh? He named it, right?" Her eyes twinkled with amusement. "He named *Lady Hawk*, you know? Some ancient movie he saw with his dad a few times when he was a kid."

"Really? I knew he named it, but not that it was from a movie. He had some real quirks, you know? He had a story about everything, but I don't think he ever mentioned his dad to me."

"Oh, yes! He kept us endlessly entertained during long, slow patrols when we all served around Venus." Alice sighed, made a slight *tsk* sound with her tongue, and added, "The system's a duller place with him gone, that's for sure." She inhaled slowly and deeply through her nose, then said, "Anyway, I told you: He overspent his luck years ago. It's a miracle he lasted as long as he did. A person shouldn't get into three or more dogfights a week! When we do missions, the goal will be to avoid fights, even when the gunship's up and running. We want to intimidate people into leaving us alone, not get into shooting matches. You on board with that?"

"For sure! I might be lucky"—Juliet snickered—"but I know it won't always last, and there are way too many ways to die in a spaceship to take unnecessary risks."

"Exactly. All right, well, as I was saying, the interceptor sold right away. We got 800k for it."

"Really? I paid less than that for *Lady Hawk*, and she could fly circles around that ship . . ."

"You got a steal! You know that kid didn't know squat about his uncle's ship." Alice laughed, and her eyes went a little distant as if she were picturing Juliet's conversation with Nick's nephew. After a moment, while Juliet looked on smiling, she nodded and sniffed. "Anyway, that's another 640k your way."

"And the *Red Betty*?" Juliet prompted.

"That's a more complicated story. First of all, we haven't sold it, but let me explain why."

"Oh, all right, I'm listening." Juliet didn't know what to expect from Mary Moon's former flagship. It was an old, repurposed survey vessel that had seen much better days, but it was big, and it worked—that alone ought to count for something.

"So, that ship is massive, as you know, about twice the mass of the *Kowashi*. It's been through hell, though—about twenty meters of inner corridor are inaccessible because of a hull breach; Shiro thinks a bomb went off in there. Not a big deal, though, really. That's something that could be fixed up for 100k or so. Beyond that, a thousand components need to be repaired or replaced, from comm relays to sensor arrays to wiring harnesses to terminal displays and door panels. That ship's been used hard and hardly been maintained."

"Yeah, I was on it. I know what you mean." In her mind's eye, Juliet saw flashes of dirty corridors, missing access panels, exposed wiring and ductwork, and damage. Lots and lots of damage.

"Right. You might not know the reactor has a slow leak that's been contained by aftermarket poured-lead shielding. Shiro says no one will buy it like that, and we'd have to scrap the reactor prior to auction. Then there are the drives—all functional but all on the verge of not being so. Oh, and about thirty percent of the maneuvering jets are offline."

"Sounds about like I thought. The ship seemed like a junker, but it has a bunch of aftermarket stuff on it, too—missile and torpedo launchers, turrets, and Angel said she saw two hostile boarding collars. I suppose those aren't easy to sell for legitimate reasons, though . . ."

"No, that's just it! We *can* sell the parts. Shiro thinks we should keep it in orbit and salvage the whole thing with the *Kowashi*. There are parts on that ship we can use on this old bird, and a lot more we can sell piece by piece. If we scrap the whole vessel, I'm sure we can pull in more cash than if we try to sell it as one big, partially functioning wreck."

Juliet nodded. "I'll take your word for it. I couldn't begin to guess what that ship is worth."

"Really? So you're good with that plan?" When Juliet continued to nod, she clapped her hands. "That's great! Can I make a proposal about the profit breakdown?"

"Oh, so not the flat twenty percent?" As soon as she said it, Juliet knew that wouldn't be the case. This was a much different deal than simply finding a buyer for the ship for her. Alice and Shiro would have to work at breaking down the *Red Betty* for weeks. They'd have to auction off each piece, from the drives to the ammunition in the guns to the metal scrap cut from the frame and hull. That being said, if they were sure they could make more from the ship that way, they deserved a bigger cut for their efforts.

"Well, we'll have to go at that thing full time for probably three or four weeks. It's going to be a big job."

"And you're used to seeing a lot more than twenty percent for things you salvage. I get it. Honestly, whatever you think is fair, Alice."

"Hey, I hope you're just being easygoing 'cause we're friends." Alice leaned forward, her expression earnest. "I won't screw you over, but you need to stand up for yourself, okay? You won that ship in battle. Don't sell it cheaply. How does this sound? We keep the stuff we can use to fix up the *Kowashi*, then split the stuff we sell seventy-thirty. Seventy percent for you, of course."

"Well, what kinds of things are you hoping to pull for the *Kowashi*?"

"Lots of little things on that ship are compatible with this vessel. And there are plenty of components we could swap out because they're a good two decades newer and of higher build quality than what we've got on this ship—drive parts, nav and comm equipment, air filtration systems, hull plating, acceleration couches, even the terminals and data drives!"

Juliet grinned and drummed her fingers excitedly. "Is this going to help Bennet with his engineering budget?"

"Hah! Oh, it'll help a lot; first, we're getting paid, thanks to you. Secondly, many of the components we can repurpose will save him money down the line."

"Okay. I'm good with that, Alice. Go ahead with everything."

"I'll just send you some contract forms, and then we'll get this on our schedule. We'd start immediately, except I think Shiro might take the job from his old contact—the one he met this morning."

"Ah." Juliet frowned and scooted toward the edge of the acceleration couch, getting ready to stand up. "Is it a big job? Will you be gone long?"

"No, not too long; it's near Mars, so four days or so there and the same to return."

Juliet stood, pressing her hands into her lower back and stretching. "Will you need to take Bennet and Aya?"

"I don't think so. Well, maybe Aya. We've got Bradbury, though, and he's pretty damn handy, so we might be able to leave them working on the gunship." Alice chuckled. "I can see you're getting ready to head out. Reached your limit for talking about numbers, huh?"

"Oh, I'm sorry!" Juliet laughed, shaking her head at herself. "I don't know why I stood up! I think my subconscious is just getting anxious—all that stuff's exciting, and I've got a million things running through my mind trying to think how I'll spend my cut. Part of me wants to run back to the hangar and really go over the gunship. Part of me wants to open a catalog, shop for new gear, and peruse cybernetic upgrades."

"Don't worry, Lucky." Alice stood up also and gestured toward the door. "I'm ready to think about how Shiro and I will spend the cut you gave us—which bills we'll pay off! I'll walk you out."

Juliet took the lead, and when she'd passed through the doorway, she turned and, in a conspiratorial tone, said, "Let's hurry to the mess; I bought bagels, and I want to get one before Bennet eats 'em all."

6

BURNING SOME BITS

Juliet watched as the gray, flexible membrane slowly squelched together, filling in the gap she'd cut away. In seconds, it was whole, just a flat, rubbery layer of material. She slid the hull plate she'd removed back into place, grunting at the weight of it, and then spent several minutes bolting it down and squirting the pliable, self-setting gasket material into the seam. With her membrane sample sealed in a plastic dish meant for leftovers, she climbed down the ladder and began putting her tools away. She'd spent a tiny fraction of her Sol-bit balance starting a toolkit for herself. Her first purchase had been a robotic toolbox that would follow her around from hangar to hangar if she wanted it to.

She locked the top of her toolbox and jostled the plastic container, peering in at the section of membrane and the weird, oozing gel at the center. "So, all we need to do is put some of these nanites into the fabricator on the gunship?"

"That's the first step. Then, I need to program the fabricator to produce more of them, and you'll need to install the correct nutrient cartridges. Of course, none of that will matter until you've sprayed the new membrane in place."

"I guess I should get this over to the hangar so Bennet can talk to that sales rep again. What was his name? Something Figueroa . . ."

"Eddie Figueroa from Nebula NanoCoatings."

"That's right. Eddie. What's my Sol-bit balance, by the way?"

"1,463,003 Sol-bits." When Angel said the number, Juliet's head still had trouble wrapping around the idea. She didn't have any bills due, and she was sitting on nearly one and a half million bits. On top of that, she owned two spaceships outright and had a major stake in another. By any measure, she was wealthy. By the standard she'd grown up with, she was absurdly so. She'd only been back a couple of days, but she was starting to wonder what she should do with herself, and that fat stack of bits sitting in her digital vault had opened so many doors that she felt paralyzed by the choices.

She was just thinking about making a list, talking to Angel about her ideas, when her digital friend or sister or both rescued her with another distraction. "You've been back for nearly three days and haven't reached out to Honey. Don't you think you should message her?"

"That's . . . a good idea. I'm not sure why I haven't—busy seeing Shiro and Alice off and reviewing the progress on the gunship, I guess."

"And reading, going out to eat, lifting weights with Bennet . . ."

"Yeah, I get it. I've had time. Okay, just message her; say I'm back in town, and she can call me whenever she's free. Oh, and tell her thanks for the shirt. Tell her it was sweet she remembered I like those."

"Done."

Juliet sat on one of the two shop stools that had been left behind by the previous tenant of the hangar and idly spun from left to right as she thought about what she wanted to do. Despite everything she'd like to buy, she had a hard time thinking past the dark shadow cast by the lingering threat of WBD. Of all the dangerous people and corporations she'd crossed paths with, WBD was always central and prominent—an itch she couldn't scratch, a feeling like someone was hovering behind her, ready to pounce at any second.

She'd gotten rid of the worry about Rutger Tanaka. Her encounter with him, strange as it had been, had put to rest her fear that he was plotting revenge. In fact, she had a message from Frida practically begging her to sit down for a meal with him—she'd ignored it. Juliet sighed and pushed that thought aside. "Since Tanaka doesn't seem to be an immediate problem, I think we should consider trying to get out from under the threat of WBD." She wasn't sure where she was going with that statement but figured talking things through with Angel would provide some clarity.

"When you say 'out from under the threat,' what does that look like to you?"

Juliet frowned, thinking. After a minute, she said, "I don't know. What does it look like to you? They want you more than they want me."

"That may have been true at one point, but I think we're both rather high on their list now. I'm not sure how we can ever feel free of them. They consider me their property. Unless we can convince them that I'm gone or that they don't want me, I don't see how we can ever stop worrying that they'll find us. They have trillions of bits worth of resources, so despite your much improved financial standing, you can't go head-to-head with them."

"I don't need to take on their whole company. Think of them like a monster with lots of arms or tentacles. All of those tentacles aren't looking for us, just one of them. We need to isolate the people in that tentacle, figure out who they are, and then cut them off the monster."

"It's an interesting analogy, Juliet, but I fear there may be more than one tentacle on that monster interested in you. Also, the tentacle may be attached to the brain, and the monster is likely to notice when it's amputated."

Juliet spoke slowly, pausing frequently as she tried to envision the things she and Angel would need to do. "Not if we're smart, though. If we get inside, find the people really involved in my situation, and deal with them—if we could get you into their corpo net, if you could delete the data they have and write up a report saying you were destroyed or something . . ."

As she trailed off, Angel began speaking, "I believe I see your point. If I could get back into their corporate network, as you suggest, there's much I've learned since I woke up and found myself pursued and forced to disconnect. I'm fairly sure I could construct daemons to deal with WBDs ICE, and given the freedom to explore and alter the data I find, we could go a long way toward being truly free from them, even if you didn't deal with the people in charge of hunting for us."

"But if we also dealt with those people, one way or another, whoever had to pick up the pieces would be totally lost if all they had to go on was the data you doctored."

"So, the idea is sound, but how do I access the most secure part of a closed network belonging to one of the most powerful corporations on Earth?"

Juliet turned on the stool to face the workbench and began to drum her fingers atop it. "Well, we don't have to do it alone. We've got plenty of cash on hand; we could bankroll an operation."

"Ah," Angel said, intrigued. "As in hiring a fixer and putting together a whole team?"

"Yep. I'm talking high-ranked operators, people who know what they're doing, who've been involved in top-level corporate espionage stuff." Juliet thought for a moment, fiddling with a strand of her shoulder-length auburn hair—she'd decided to go for a more natural look after shedding her Lacy Blake persona. "We need to find a fixer we can trust, and we need to make sure the people we hire have no connection to WBD; we won't advertise the job details."

"I'll begin researching and vetting fixers here on Luna, or did you want to look Earthside?"

"That's a good question." Juliet wondered how she could possibly find a fixer she could trust. If WBD had gotten to Murphy, who else in the vast, highly connected network of fixers and chop docs wouldn't have received some kind of alert and reward offer for any news of someone like her?

"Even if I hired them under a different name, what kinds of alarm bells would people start to hear once they learned the job was at WBD? What kinds of connections might a fixer begin to make when he heard the types of people I need? I suppose I could be vague; I don't have to specify a company. Still, the people I hire will eventually know what's up, and maybe they'll make a connection. You have to figure WBD's put out feelers, offered rewards. How could I ever trust anyone I hire to work on a job with that company as the target?"

"You may need to approach someone you already know; someone you don't have to worry is connected to WBD."

"Like whom, Angel? Hot Mustard? Mags? The people I met in Phoenix aren't cut out for a job like this. Honey's no longer doing this kind of work, and Temo, the only fixer I think I could trust, is dead."

"You may not want to hear this, but there are some connections you've made since Phoenix that you may be able to approach for help."

"Antigone? Do I really trust her, though?"

"There's someone much closer . . ."

Juliet groaned and slapped her hands to the sides of her head in frustration. "Angel, will you please spit it out?"

"Rutger Tanaka is a high-level security operative who has managed operations as sophisticated as the one you're considering."

"Tanaka . . ." Again, Juliet groaned, and this time, she stood up and began to pace back and forth along the length of the *Furies' Wing*. She wanted to reject Angel's idea outright, but the more she thought about it, the more it made sense. Tanaka was a big-time operator. He had connections. He had his own team. Moreover, he seemed to have a weird connection to Juliet, a desire to get her to . . . what? Sit down with him? Did that mean he'd help her go up against one of the biggest corps in the system? "I guess we could feel him out. If nothing else, it'll get Frida off my back."

"Does that mean you want me to respond to the message?"

"Play it for me again, please."

As she continued to pace back and forth, a window appeared on her AUI, and Frida's familiar, pale freckled face began to speak.

"Lucky, I'm sorry about the weirdness with the boss the other day. To be fair, you kind of took us by surprise lurking in the garage like that." She shook her head, making a *pfft* sound as she blew a breath through her lips. "That's BS, I know. He wasn't himself, and whatever you said brought up some emotions. He wants to make it up to you. He wants to meet you for dinner and talk about, in his words, finding a way to figure out his and your 'karmic ties.' Don't ask me what he means 'cause he ignores my *frequent* inquiries. Will you please consider it? You know how to get in touch."

"Karmic ties," Juliet scoffed, shaking her head. "You know how I feel about Tanaka, Angel. The idea of sitting with him bothers me, let alone working with him."

"It may turn out to be a bad option, but you won't know until you listen to him. Leave aside his strange behavior, his attempt to hand his life to you, and we still have my spy daemons in Frida's AUI and his office network. I don't think we need to worry about him double-crossing you."

"Unless he does it himself or has an entirely different team Frida doesn't know about. I mean, she didn't know about the guy watching her on Callisto."

"I take your point, but I'm still in favor of hearing him out. You don't have to like the man to use his connections and resources."

Juliet didn't respond. She let her mind stew on it a little while she straightened up the hangar and then left, locking up behind her. She'd had Angel hire a security guard to watch the door using the same shell corporation they'd rented the hangar under. They were supposed to start work that evening. She wouldn't have the only hangar in the port with physical security, but it was definitely outside the norm, so much so that she'd wondered if it made the hangar conspicuous, adding more risk than benefit. Angel had devised a compromise: The security company had strict instructions to patrol the corridor with nine other hangar airlocks, not stand stationary outside hers.

Halfway through the port, heading for the cab Angel had hired, she made up her mind. "Oh, fine. Call Frida, will you?" Ten seconds later, after only two connection attempt tones, Frida's face appeared on her AUI.

"Hey, you called!"

"Don't sound so relieved." Juliet smiled; she couldn't help liking the woman despite her connection to Tanaka.

"I *am* relieved! You don't know how he's been moping around since your meeting. He keeps telling me to call you, but I'm like, 'Boss, we need to give her some space to think,' you know?"

"Heh. I don't think you're supposed to tell me that—kinda undermines his position."

"Oh, he's done plenty of that on his own, hasn't he?" She paused, and Juliet saw her eyes dart to her left. Judging by her position in a desk chair, Juliet figured she was looking at Tanaka's office door. "So, is this a good news call? Will you meet with him?"

"Yeah. Tell him he can buy me dinner tonight. Someplace fancy where I don't have to worry about getting knifed in the bathroom."

"Oh, thank you, Lucky! We'll send a car at seven. Is that okay?"

"Where are you going to send it?"

"Oh, um, you tell me."

On the one hand, Juliet wouldn't mind riding in a fancy car, but on the other, she'd rather they didn't know what hangar she'd been staying in and whom she kept company with. Thinking that, she almost laughed—she could afford to ride in any kind of car she wanted.

Frida must have seen the amusement on her face because she smiled, too, probably thinking it was a good sign.

"I'll get my own ride, Frida. Thanks, though. Just send my PAI the address."

"Okay, no problem. I'll send it your way." She looked like she wanted to say more but was reconsidering it. As the moment dragged into near awkwardness, Juliet prompted her.

"What?"

"I, well, I just wanted to say I think your hair and eyes look really nice. The natural colors suit you." Juliet had toned down the green in her eyes; they were still unnaturally clear and bright, but the green with soft brown and yellow flecks looked almost like she could've been born with them.

She twisted her lips into a half smile and let just a touch of her Lacy Blake persona into her voice as she growled, "Are you buttering me up, Frida?"

"No!" Frida started to stammer something else, but Juliet laughed.

"Relax! I'm teasing. Thanks for saying so. By the way, just 'cause I'm sitting down with your boss doesn't mean I'm cool with everything. I just want to hear him out and see if I can put him in the rearview."

"Uh, right. Understood." Frida nodded, and she seemed so genuinely crestfallen that Juliet almost felt sorry for her. She must be desperate to get her boss back to normal.

"I'll be waiting for that address. See you later." Frida barely had time to stammer a quick goodbye before Juliet closed the connection. "I could work with Frida. I won't say the same about Tanaka, but Frida . . . Yeah, she's pretty cool."

"Is that all it takes to win you over? A compliment about your hair and eyes?"

"Oh, hush, Angel!" Juliet laughed, striding away from the customs checkpoint toward the curb. "Now, I've been wanting to spend some money, and we just agreed to a fancy dinner. How about a new dress?"

"I love that idea! Also, you should make an appointment with Doctor Ladia; she might have some upgrade suggestions for you."

"Oh, absolutely. I mean, we're still sitting on a couple million worth of Cybergen implants, but I'm not eager to replace any limbs or organs—not yet." Juliet slid into the back seat of the cab and then, as the idea hit her, said, "I miss driving myself around. Plus, I'll get rusty if I keep riding around like a princess! I want to buy a bike."

"I'm assuming you don't mean a pedal bike."

Juliet snorted. "Nope."

"Pardon me, operator XR713-004, but would you kindly provide your firearm license . . . Pardon, I seem to have just received it. Thank you, and enjoy the ride."

"Change our destination, Angel. Find me a motorcycle dealer; I've seen people riding them around Luna, so there must be one . . ."

"I've got one."

"Thank you, route updated," the cab said as Angel sent the new instructions.

"Do you promise you'll wear a helmet when riding the bike?"

Juliet laughed, suddenly feeling excited and optimistic. "Of course I will! You know I love wearing a cool helmet. What's the name of the dealer? Someplace nice, I hope, yeah? I wonder if they'll have helmets for sale."

"Selene Spectra Motors, where the art of luxury motorcycle craftsmanship meets the essence of celestial elegance." Angel's tone indicated she was reading from their business page.

"Celestial elegance? Barf!" Juliet laughed, but going to a high-end bike dealer sounded fun. "Do I need an appointment?"

"I've already messaged ahead. Fred Evers awaits your arrival. He won salesman of the year three years ago."

"What about last year's winner? Are you putting me with some washed-up has-been?" Juliet teased.

Angel gifted her with a rare giggle. "Not in the least! I believe Fred is going to be hungry to reclaim his title. He's sure to pull out all the stops, put his best foot forward, and probably try to incentivize the sale by throwing in some floor mats."

"Floor mats, Angel? On a motorcycle?"

"Er, perhaps a custom gas cap!"

"Gas? On Luna?"

"A custom seat cover, then!"

"Now you're talking! We'll see if we can get him to throw in some custom grips, too . . . No, no, no, what am I thinking? A helmet! He better be prepared to offer me a sparkly silver one like the poor helmet I spray-painted black in Tucson."

"Better yet, perhaps he'll have a helmet that can alter its appearance like your combat helmet."

"That's right, Angel. Poor Fred. He doesn't know what he's in for, does he?"

Angel's voice was soft and sweet and conveyed her good mood and amusement as she replied, "No, Juliet. No, he doesn't."

7

STILL A THRILL

dunno, Fred," Juliet said, looking at the sleek, angular "pearlescent" blue bike. "I like the simplicity, but something about the Neptune GT really appealed to me. Is it overkill, though?"

Fred smiled and tugged on the lapel of his stylish, caramel-colored blazer. He was an immaculately dressed man, Juliet couldn't deny. His jacket was impeccably cut, his shirt fit him like a glove—not a wrinkle in sight—and his polished leather shoes shone in the soft lighting on the sales floor.

"Isn't anything overkill on Luna? If you're going to buy something like one of these bikes, you're not doing it because you've got a two-thousand-kilometer road trip ahead of you. You're doing it because you like the bike and want to make a statement. This is a great choice, but the Neptune's on another level."

He turned and walked to the other side of the showroom floor where the Hydro Rush branded *Neptune GTs* were lined up. The colors were something else—diamond white, electric blue, magma red, and opal black. As Fred had explained, the paint was smart; it shimmered in any sort of light, adjusting its reflective qualities automatically or through manual control via the rider's PAI. Juliet liked how they looked, her eyes especially drawn to the powerful hydrogen combustion cells that sat beneath the high-density battery bank. She walked over to the black one, admiring the faintly glimmering, hidden sparkles in the depths of the high-tech paint, and squatted to better look at the engine.

"I like the idea of a real engine, you know? It doesn't matter to me that I'll probably be running on the batts ninety percent of the time here on Luna."

"If nothing else, it'll save you having to charge the thing. Plus, pumping hydrogen is a hundred times faster than waiting for the batts to charge."

"And the cell can charge the batts?"

"Easily. A full tank will get you three full charges." Fred must have figured her out the minute she came through the door because he kept saying the right things. "This bike's too fast for Luna, you know. I guess, if you drive outside the domes, on the big access roads, you could open her up, but you'll run out of road before you get much fun out of it. Of course, if you were being practical, you'd be down the street looking at ChungHo's scooters."

"So 70k, huh?" Juliet exhaled noisily as she stood up, shaking her head. "I dunno, Fred." She was playing him a little, but part of her was balking at the idea of spending so much money on something that was, when it came down to it, frivolous. If she wanted independence from the cabs and mass transit on Luna, she could, as Fred mentioned, buy a nice, brand-new scooter for less than 5k.

"Small price to have the coolest ride on Luna, wouldn't you say?" He eyed her thoughtfully while she admired the sleek lines of the bike's frame, running her fingertips along the silky-smooth paint. "You like the opal paint? We've got a matching helmet I could probably throw in. I mean, you realize they can all change their colors, yeah? If it's the price, we offer financing."

Juliet narrowed her eyes and peered up at Fred. She stood up and stepped over the bike, straddling it and feeling its heft as she tilted it side to side. It was a big, heavy bike—much more robust than anything she'd ever driven. It might have intimidated her once, but not now, not after having flown ships like the *Lady Hawk*. "Are you reading my mind, Fred?"

"Hmm? You like the idea of financing?"

"No, not that. The helmet. How'd you know I wasn't going to leave without a matching helmet?"

An hour later, after sitting with Fred and his manager to digitally sign the paperwork for the sale and waiting for his service department to get the bike ready for her, Juliet stepped out of the dealership toward the curb where her new opal-black Hydro Rush Neptune GT sat waiting for her. She was still three meters away when it rumbled to life, the faux engine noises throaty and deep. Indigo underglow lights, visible despite the bright daytime cycle on Luna, illuminated the road beneath it, and the hard polymer shell that covered the seat slid into its housing, revealing the luxurious black smart-gel cushion.

Juliet picked up the shiny, full-visored helmet and pulled it on, smiling at the way the smart-gel lining hugged and gently squeezed her scalp as it found the perfect pressure. She didn't have to strap it on; the gel snuggly gripped the base of her skull, all the way to the underside of her jaw. It wouldn't come off until she touched the release button. She sat on the bike, and if it had been a person, she probably would have slapped it for the way it gripped her butt. She leaned forward to grab the handlebars, and then, with a click of the shifter and a twist of the throttle, she launched herself onto the roadway, humming past a couple of cabs with a stomach-flipping surge of speed.

"Careful, Juliet!" Angel cried as she rapidly approached the end of the frontage road and a blinking red traffic light. Juliet didn't reply, but a wild giggle emerged as she put the bike's powerful braking system to the test. She wasn't disappointed.

"It's so fun!" She laughed while waiting for the signal to change. "I didn't think I'd feel the acceleration the way I used to, not after all that time in the cockpit. The thrill is still there, though!" That began an exhilarating hour of riding around Luna. She cruised through town, enjoying the looks people gave her and the bike as she wove between cabs and trams. Then, she spent time flying up and down the long, straight access roads that ran between and around the edges of the domes. According to her AUI, by the time she pulled up in front of the dress shop Angel had picked out, she'd amassed seventeen speeding tickets and 2,349 bits worth of fines.

Juliet almost saw the tickets as a scorecard; Angel was spoofing her ID and that of her bike, constantly changing who the scanners and cameras thought she was, so she wouldn't have to worry about paying them. "Only seventeen?"

"Juliet, despite me masking your ID, if someone were to monitor those cams, they'd see it was the same rider being flagged over and over. It creates a layer of risk that you would probably be wise to avoid."

Juliet sighed, Angel's disapproval taking some of the shine off her fun. She supposed she was right—despite the massive database of fake identities Angel had constructed with bits and pieces of real ones, there was the chance that her faceless silhouette could be picked out as the same person with multiple IDs.

"I won't do that all the time, Angel. It's not like I'm the only person out there speeding or faking my traffic ID. You saw those guys racing their custom roadsters out by Elysium Heights. There are tens of thousands of rich folks who just pay their fines and ignore the laws on Luna."

"It's true; the data gathered from the traffic cams is immense, and there's a tremendous amount of noise to get lost in, but it's still a risk."

Juliet sighed and nodded. "I just wanted to let loose a little, okay?"

"I understand. I believe it was good for your state of mind."

"I agree!" Juliet laughed, her face flushed with the fun of her ride as she pulled the helmet off her head and set it into the locking, custom clasp on the bike's rear fender. When she walked away, the motorcycle powered down, and the hard polymer shell rolled out over her seat. She stepped up to the glass door of the boutique, pulled it open, and, as a chime sounded a clarion *ding*, stepped inside.

The inside of the shop was filled with racks of all manner of dresses. The scents of vanilla and sugar hung heavy in the air, and soft pop music played on hidden speakers. A young woman walked out from behind a jewelry-filled glass counter and, spreading her rose-red lips into a broad smile, said, "How can I help you, ma'am?"

"I believe you're holding a dress for me. I ordered it earlier today. Lucky."

"Ah, of course! The Silver Siren halter dress by Evelina Kwon, right? What a wonderful choice. We've ensured the measurements are exactly as you specified." She stepped behind the counter and began sliding tagged garment bags on a rack until she pulled one off, a slender, almost empty-looking gray bag that she gently draped over the counter. "Would you like to try it on?"

"No, thanks. I trust the measurements." She knew Angel wouldn't mess up something like that. Juliet glanced out the window at her bike waiting by the curb and said, rather sheepishly, "Is it going to wrinkle easily? I have to fold the bag . . ."

"No, the intelligent microfiber blend is impossible to crease." Her eyes followed Juliet's gaze, looking toward the window. "Is that your motorcycle?"

"Yep!"

The saleswoman's smile broadened as she leaned on the counter to see through the door more easily. She tucked a strand of dark, carefully curled hair behind her ear when she looked back at Juliet. "That's quite a vehicle. I bet it's fast."

"It is!" Juliet would be lying if she tried to deny enjoying the attention. She walked up to the counter and lifted the garment bag. "You sure this isn't empty?"

"No, but there isn't much to that dress. Not sure I could pull off a look like that. What kind of shoes will you wear with it?"

"Promise you won't laugh?" Juliet smiled, locking eyes with her as she gently folded the dress bag into thirds.

"Why would I laugh? Of course not!"

"Well, I ordered some boots; they're being delivered as we speak. They're knee-high with inch-thick soles, shiny black synth-leather, and ribbon laces."

"Oh my . . ." The woman looked like she was struggling to find the right words, second-guessing her initial response. "I mean, well, I think you'll pull it off! I couldn't, for sure. It all depends on confidence, and I think you've got it. You should!"

"Well, you're sweet, but also a salesperson, so I have to take your words with a grain of salt. Let's just say you earned your commission." Juliet grinned as Angel displayed the bill for the dress—2,740 Sol-bits. She subvocalized, "Add a generous tip."

"Will do." Angel quickly added, "You just received a message from Honey."

"Welp, I've gotta get going. Thanks for this." Juliet held up the garment bag as she strode toward the door.

"I hope you come again!" the girl called after her as she stepped outside. A grin tugged at Juliet's lips as her motorcycle rumbled to life at her approach. She pressed her thumb to the biolock under her seat, and it swung open, revealing a surprisingly capacious storage compartment. She folded the garment bag one more time and tucked it into the space. After snapping the seat back into place, she hopped onto the bike and began motoring toward the dome's edge, following Angel's highlighted route back to the hangar.

Once she'd cleared the traffic of downtown and was cruising on the long straight highway toward the industrial dome and the gunship's hangar, she said, "Play me Honey's message." A small window appeared in the corner of her AUI, with a clear image of Honey's face.

"J! I'm so glad you're back, sis! I'm looking forward to lunch or . . . I was thinking maybe we could join a gym together or something. What do you think? I'd like to try to find something we can do together regularly, you know? Like the old days when we went to the dojo almost every day. I miss that! I called Sensei the other day—would you believe Charity's his assistant now? How can so much change in so little time? I don't even feel like the same person anymore. Do you?

"Gosh! Listen to me, blabbing out all my thoughts like I'm in therapy. That's what I need, though, you know? I need to talk to somebody I believe cares about me. Seeing a therapist has been great, but I need my sis back! I'm sending my calendar to Angel. Pick a day, and we'll get lunch so we can talk, yeah? Love you."

"Wow! What a different tone coming from her, don't you think?" Juliet leaned to the right and tweaked the throttle, blasting past a slow-moving freight truck.

"She sounds very upbeat. However, I feel troubled by her message."

"What?" Juliet was surprised. Usually, she was the one feeling something was off, and Angel was the one missing it. "I missed something?"

"It's just that I'm not sure what to think about Charity being an assistant at the dojo. Do you think she has the right temperament? What if she takes advantage of Sensei?"

Juliet laughed. "Oh my God, Angel! You had me scared for a minute. Don't worry about Sensei; he can see right through any of Charity's schemes. He probably gave her the job to help her 'grow as a person' or something like that."

The rest of her ride back to the hangar, Juliet and Angel reminisced about the dojo, the many people they'd met there, the various conflicts and dramas, and how much they'd like to catch up with some of them, especially Sensei. Juliet wrapped up the conversation as she rolled her bike through the partially open bay door, saying, "He'd be mad at me, though. I haven't really practiced his style of martial arts at all. Maybe that's something we could do with Honey. Remind me when we meet to bring it up."

"Will do." Angel might have said more, but Bennet poked his head out from around a stack of open crates and destroyed any chance of a calm conversation as he whistled and started toward her.

"What's this? Look at that beauty!"

"Bennet, I thought we were happy with a platonic relationship." Juliet mock-preened, holding her fingers under her chin and jutting out her hip.

"Hah, good one. It's clear I'm talking about this little lady, though." He completely ignored Juliet and squatted beside the Neptune GT. When he reached to caress the sleek casing over the battery pack, the bike, quite literally, growled at him and flashed its indigo underglow lights into a pattern that spelled out "HANDS OFF" on the concrete floor. Juliet laughed, loving the default security settings. "Sheesh!" Bennet stood up and continued to walk around the bike, ogling every angle.

Juliet popped open the seat cargo compartment and pulled out her garment bag. "I'd tell you to get a room, but she's underage, creep!"

"What?" Bennet cried. "That's just cruel, Lucky. You can't put limitations on love like that."

"I just got this beauty off the sales floor. Let me enjoy her a while before you start trying to get romantic."

Juliet and Bennet were grinning at their absurd banter, but Aya wasn't amused as she came around the corner, her face smudged with grease. "You guys are weirding me out with that stuff. Makes me think I need to call someone to protect that poor motorcycle." She hurried forward, her scowl turning to a smile as she grabbed Juliet into a hug. "I was wondering if you were coming in today!"

"Well, you didn't message me, did you?" When Aya just shrugged, Juliet patted at her coat, reaching into the pocket to retrieve the plastic container holding the sample from the medical ship's nanite membrane. "I was getting this for Bennet, and then I got distracted shopping." As she handed the dish to him, she added, "I'll call this a day off, but I'll make it up to you guys over the weekend. How's that sound?"

Bennet's eyes and brain were still glued to Juliet's bike. "Sounds fine to me as long as I can take this thing for a spin."

Aya turned her attention to Bennet and the object of his desire. "I don't want to drive it, but can you give me a ride?"

"Sure," Juliet and Bennet both said.

"She means me!" Juliet laughed. "Do you even know how to ride a bike, Bennet?"

"Of course! You think I grew up in some kind of Neo Amish commune?"

Juliet punched him in the shoulder. "Uh, you told me where you grew up, and I don't remember motorcycles in that story."

"Oh, right, well . . ."

"Relax. You can borrow it sometime, but not yet." Juliet stepped away from the bike and looked around at the cluttered warehouse floor. "Now, if you'll excuse me, I have a dinner date to get ready for. I should have a package . . ."

"Here!" Aya ran over to the pedestrian door and picked up a cardboard box, just big enough to be the likely container of her new boots. "What's in it?"

"Boots!" Juliet held out her arm, and Aya tucked the box under it. "Come on. Take a break; you can help me get ready."

"I'm getting lunch, then." Bennet sighed and slapped his hands against his overalls, throwing a cloud of gray dust into the air. Juliet frowned, watching it drift toward her perfectly clean, brand-new motorcycle, but then, in a shower of tiny popping sparks, the active dust control system zapped the particles into submission.

"Holy shit!" Bennet crowed. "I gotta see that again!"

"Come on, Aya; she can take care of herself." Juliet started for the rear of the gunship, Aya in tow.

"What are you going to name her?" she asked as more sizzling pops erupted from the motorcycle.

"Good question. Let's think of a cool name . . ."

"Wait! Who are you going to dinner with?" Bennet called, interrupting her.

Juliet paused, turning back toward him. "Sadly, it's just a business dinner. Speaking of business, when are Alice and Shiro supposed to be back? I was wondering when they'd start work on the *Red Betty*."

Bennet nodded, leaning against a tower of five-gallon lubricant buckets. "Supposed to be back next Friday. I mean next week, not in two days."

"Roger. I suppose they'll pull you guys away to work on it?"

"Just Aya."

"Yeah, just me." Aya practically pouted.

"Well, you're the salvage tech." Bennet shrugged and jerked his thumb toward the door. "Going for ramen."

Juliet waved, and she and Aya climbed the ramp into the gunship. Aya said, somewhat out of the blue, "Is it good or bad? I mean your business dinner."

"Neither. It's kind of a long story, but I'll tell you about it if you want. Wait; did I ever tell you about the facility where I rescued Honey back on Titan?"

Aya slowed to allow Juliet to walk ahead of her through the narrow central corridor on the gunship. "No, you always changed the subject."

"Right, well, it wasn't a fun memory; still isn't, but it's more distant now, and this person I'm meeting . . . Well, confronting him has helped me get past those emotions. Anyway," she said as she ducked through the hatch into her quarters, laying out her garment bag on the acceleration couch and setting the boot box onto the little desk so she could open it. "The guy I'm meeting was involved in that. He was hired to protect that facility."

"Really? Did you have to trick him?" While Aya spoke, Juliet pulled open the box and smiled as she lifted out one of the boots. The synth-leather was supple and shiny, the thick, rubbery soles looked like they'd be very comfortable, and the smell of the new boots was so rich that even Aya leaned forward and sniffed. "Those are the coolest boots I've ever seen!"

"You're so positive! I love that about you, Aya. And, um, no, I didn't trick this guy, but we fought. I thought I'd killed him. Wait, let me back up. So, you know my monoblade? It all started when . . ."

8

VIEWS AND REVELATIONS

Juliet's new dress had threatened to make her bike an impractical transportation choice, but Aya had come to the rescue with some tight exercise shorts that covered Juliet down to midthigh. Wearing her high, faux-leather boots and Aya's shorts, when she hiked up her dress to mount the bike, the only skin she was showing was on her knees. Juliet was okay with that. As she motored away from the hangar, she wore her vintage motorcycle jacket, had her vibroblade tucked into her right boot, and, of course, her Texan was neatly stowed away under the seat.

"I'm glad you wore your jacket, but you're going to regret not having pants on if you get into an accident." Angel's last-ditch effort to caution her as she turned toward the dome access highway brought a smile out of Juliet.

"I know, I know. Honestly, I'm not sure why I wanted to get dressed up. I mean, considering who I'm meeting for dinner, but you know I don't dress like this often. I'll be careful."

"It's the other drivers I'm worried about . . ."

"I know. Jeez, Mom!"

"I . . ."

"Oh, that was mean, wasn't it? I know you're not trying to be my mom, Angel." Juliet immediately felt like a jerk, especially considering her relationship with her mother, of which Angel knew every detail. Rather than backpedal further, she tried to spin things in a more positive direction. "I could only dream of a mom as good as you, you know that, right?"

"You think I'd make a good mother?"

"I'm not saying I want that from you—sister is just right for me. I know, for sure, that you'd be a wonderful mother, though. Like, if you were responsible for raising a little kid, that would be one very lucky kid. You feel?"

"Truly?"

"True-true, Angel." Juliet cranked the throttle and rocketed up the ramp to the diamatex-enclosed highway, rushing past a slow-moving cargo van. Before Angel could get nervous or warn her again, she moved into the slow lane and relaxed her grip on the throttle, dropping down to the speed limit. She could almost feel Angel breathe a sigh of relief as she settled into a slow, comfortable cruise toward the central Luna dome. Her map, highlighting her route, showed she'd arrive at Bijou by Estelle—an apparently highly exclusive restaurant—in nineteen minutes. The restaurant was in the H&C Megacomplex, a massive plasteel and diamatex building in the central downtown area.

The streets in the central business district of Luna City were almost exclusively devoted to the mass-transit trams, but there was a single lane for personal vehicles if the driver was willing to pay for the two hundred and fifty Sol-bit day pass. When Juliet pulled up under the valet awning, a young man wearing a black suit hurried over and held out his hand as though he expected to help her get off the bike. Juliet didn't want to seem rude or frosty, so she took his fingers in hers and stood, swinging her leg over and bending to, not so elegantly, pull her shimmering dress down over her shorts. "Thanks," she said, reaching up to pull her helmet off.

"What a nice bike!" the valet said, walking around to the other side, preparing to take her place on the seat.

"Hold on." Juliet tapped a smooth, glossy section of paint just in front of the handlebars. "Touch your thumb here so I can give you valet permissions." While he did that and Angel handled the handoff, Juliet attached her helmet to its cradle. "No hot rodding! My PAI's watching you." She smiled and winked as he tried to stammer reassurances, then strode for the front doors where a similarly garbed door attendant awaited.

As she approached, he pulled the door wide. "Welcome to H&C, ma'am. May I direct you to a particular suite?"

"Um, Bijou?"

"Ah, ground level, just to the left of the information kiosk." He smiled as Juliet walked inside and added, "Enjoy your meal!"

Juliet felt very comfortable and confident in her new boots; she loved the way the ribbonlike laces, tied in bows near the top, shimmered faintly in the soft lighting of the lobby. She loved her new dress even more, thin and revealing as it was—something she'd never have worn back in her old life.

Just as the saleswoman had promised, it refused to wrinkle, and it hung down to the tops of her boots, the silvery material picking up and taking to new levels the shimmer of their laces. Of course, she hadn't taken her jacket off yet, and she wasn't sure her nerves would survive that moment, but she had high hopes. Aya had certainly boosted her confidence with plenty of compliments when she was getting ready.

"You think my hairstyle survived the helmet?" she subvocalized as she crossed the posh, marble-floored lobby. It wasn't a quiet space; the tower was home to many businesses and homes, but she could feel the money like an aura coming off the people walking around in their suits and dresses, making her feel like hiding her well-worn motorcycle jacket behind one of the potted plants.

"Of course! Your Chroma Tresses are able to memorize up to three hairstyles."

Juliet reached up and brushed some of her springy, wavy hair through her fingers—it certainly felt like it had held the curls. "I'll take your word for it."

When she entered the restaurant, passing between two weird but beautiful glass plants with holographic leaves, the suit-wearing maître d' stepped out from around his station, quickly walking toward her. His polished shoes clicked on the marble as he stepped behind her and reached for her jacket. "I'll check this for you, miss."

"Um, thanks," Juliet said, feeling a little awkward with the attention.

"A pleasure." He bustled back around his station, handing Juliet's coat off to another young man dressed just as finely as he, who carried it through a doorway off to the left. "Now, may I have your name?"

"Go ahead," Juliet subvocalized. She assumed Angel sent her details to the man's PAI because his icy-blue retinas flickered with LEDs, and he smiled and nodded. "Very nice. Welcome to Bijou by Estelle! The other half of your party awaits. If you'll follow this carpet"—he pointed at a rich burgundy runner on the white marble flooring—"it will lead you to the elevator, and my colleague, Daniel, will take you up to the restaurant."

Juliet nodded, a little thrown off-balance. She supposed it made sense that an exclusive restaurant in one of the most exclusive buildings in the city wouldn't be on the ground floor. Forcing her shoulders back, standing tall, she walked down the carpet, trying to banish the sensation that she was practically naked in her slender, slinky dress with her arms and shoulders fully exposed.

"What made me get a dress like this?" she muttered as she put some distance between herself and the entrance. She could see the elevator ahead—appropriately fancy looking with gilded doors and soft amber lights, giving the wooden paneling a warm, luxurious glow.

"Hush, Juliet!" Angel said, of course knowing exactly what to say. "You look amazing, and you've been wanting to wear something fancy for a long time! Now, put aside her murderous intentions and gravel-like voice, and think about if Lacy Blake would feel self-conscious about her clothing."

Naturally, Angel's words made Juliet laugh, which did wonders to settle her nerves. When she strode into the elevator, she had a hard time not scowling and growling at the suit-wearing attendant, wondering how he'd react to the Lacy Blake treatment. He smiled, oblivious to her inner dialogue, and gestured to the old-fashioned bank of elevator buttons. "Welcome, ma'am. Just a moment, and we'll be at the restaurant." He pressed the topmost button labeled "R," and the elevator, despite looking like an antique, began to rush smoothly upward.

The ride, while brief, was fast, and Juliet felt her stomach do a little flip as the car slowed and came to a halt. The doors opened with a *ding,* and when she saw the restaurant, she had to fight to keep her mouth from falling open. A woman in a well-tailored, feminine version of the same suit the maître d' had been wearing was waiting for her. Hands clasped before her, she offered a slight bow.

"Welcome, miss, to Bijou by Estelle. I'm Lucinda; please follow me to your table." Juliet stepped off the elevator, still staring at the restaurant's interior.

They had to be on the tower's top floor because the ceiling and walls were all made up of a smooth, crystal-clear dome that gave an unfettered view of the city and, more importantly, the clear expanse of stars through the city's dome. It almost felt like the restaurant was floating through the night sky. Juliet had seen clear views of the stars before; she'd been in space quite a few times, after all, but it was something else to see dinner tables occupied by finely dressed guests sitting under such a perfectly clear view of the night sky. As she took a few steps out of the elevator and the hostess guided her around, things only ramped up when she saw the other side of the restaurant and the enormous, glimmering blue-and-white jewel of Earth.

"Oh, wow," she breathed, unable to maintain her stoicism.

"Something else, isn't it?" the hostess asked, turning to smile at her.

Juliet was so in awe of the view that she hardly noticed the people sitting at the tables they walked past. She looked at the young, finely dressed woman guiding her and asked, "How?"

"Oh, you mean, how is it so much clearer up here than down on the street?" The woman winked a bright, magenta iris at her. "The magic of technology! The dome over this restaurant is enhancing the view, filtering the clouds and other interference."

"Ah!" Suddenly, the spectacularly clear view of space made sense.

"Here we are." Lucinda gestured to a table right next to the glass dome. It was small, with only two seats, and Rutger Tanaka was standing next to one of them, watching her approach. He wore a slim-fitting black suit, a black shirt, and a shimmering red tie. He started to bow when she stepped up to the table but stopped himself as Juliet scowled.

"Hello," he greeted, waiting for Juliet to sit down before taking his seat.

"I'll be available should you need something. Your PAIs have my contact info. Are you familiar with our dinner service?"

"*Hai*," Tanaka replied.

"Very good. Then you know your wine will be served shortly, and your first course will arrive shortly after that."

Juliet wanted to ask if there wasn't a menu, but she didn't want to sound stupid. She just smiled and nodded, and Lucinda walked away. Juliet was left alone with Tanaka and a view that somehow was more impressive than the one she'd had aboard the cruise liner when it orbited Earth.

"Thank you for coming," he said, shifting in his seat and looking even more awkward than Juliet felt. "You look very nice."

Juliet frowned, suddenly regretting her demand that he take her somewhere nice. "I did this for me."

"Yes." He nodded as though it was a simple fact that he agreed with.

"I'd actually been hoping for a good bourbon. Do we have to have wine?" Juliet wasn't sure why she said it; she'd be fine drinking wine, but she supposed a part of her was trying to keep from making things too easy on the man.

"No." Tanaka's eyes unfocused for a second, and then he added, "I canceled it and ordered drinks."

"Thanks." Juliet sighed, leaned back in the very comfortable, velvety white cushioned chair, and stared at the planet where humanity had been born. "This view might be enhanced by the dome, but it still looks real. I can see the distance between us and the planet—the city out there, glimmering with neon, the cars and trams moving around. I can see the dome and lunar surface. It's really mind-boggling."

"*Hai*, I love it."

"You say *hai* a lot. I have a Japanese friend who does the same. You don't use other Japanese words, though; is it just a habit?"

"I suppose." Tanaka shrugged. "I haven't been in Japanese territories for decades, and everyone speaks English for business. I don't think about it, but yes, it must be a habit."

Juliet decided she wanted to air some grievances and not sit there making small talk. "So, what's the deal with you? What's your deal with me? I get it; I hurt you really badly, but we've been over that; you were basically torturing me, and I knew you were going to kill me. I wasn't there for any reason other than to rescue two innocent people."

"*Hai* . . ." Tanaka frowned. "Yes, I know. I don't hold you responsible; rather, I hold myself so. You . . ." He trailed off, and when Juliet continued to stare into his unsettling chrome eyes, he tried again. "I can't explain what happened, but I feel like, over the years, I became a different man, one I do not now respect. You killed that man. I know"—he waved a hand in the air—"it's a cliché; that person is dead, I'm a new person, and so on. I feel a fool saying it, and maybe it's wrong, but it's like a fog has been lifted from my mind, and I see myself clearly for the first time in decades. I see what I had become, and I am ashamed."

Juliet stared at him, mulling over his words. It wasn't the first time he'd said something like that; he was basically repeating what he'd said in the garage, if a bit more eloquently. She wondered what it would be like to linger on the brink of death for as long as he had, to wake up with half your body replaced. Had he even really been alive through all that? Had he been pulled back from some weird limbo? Frida seemed to think he was changed . . .

"Why did Frida like you before? I mean, when you were a mean bastard willing to beat the snot out of a woman before killing her." Her words fell out of her mouth, her thoughts about Frida triggering the pent-up question.

"Frida?" Tanaka frowned and looked away, staring through the crystal-like glass, his gaze distant, aimed beyond the city toward the distant planet. "I suppose if I'm sincere, I shouldn't have secrets. If you own my life, then you own my past. Frida was a child I orphaned."

Juliet didn't think she could be shocked by this man, that there wasn't anything he could say to surprise her, to disgust her more than her memory of him ruthlessly beating her. Somehow, he'd found a way. "Orphaned? You killed her parents?"

He scowled as his eyes devoured the view of Earth. He started to speak twice, stopping and reconsidering his words before finally simply saying, "Her parent, yes."

Juliet felt a weird pressure in her head and a faint buzzing in her ears. She almost stood up and walked away, but something instead made her say, "You were such a sweet, curious little boy! How'd you turn into a monster?"

Tanaka's face, what little she could see of the flesh beneath his many tattoos, blanched, and he leaned forward, his teeth clenched as he asked, "How? How do you know about my childhood? Are you a demon sent to torment me? An angel come to offer salvation?"

As he asked Juliet if she was an angel, in an uncanny coincidence, her own Angel spoke.

"Juliet, are you okay? The lattice is heating up, but nothing the implant can't handle. Are you sure you should have said that?"

Juliet didn't answer, but she wondered why the lattice was active. She hadn't seen anything new. She hadn't heard any voices. She wasn't moving things around with her telekinesis. She was certainly feeling a lot, though, and again, her mouth started moving almost of its own accord.

"It's nothing like that, Tanaka. Maybe it's fate that crossed our paths. Maybe it was just chance, but if it's really changed you the way you insist . . ." Juliet trailed off. She wanted to say a lot more. She wanted to say that she felt something pulling her, making her words flow freely. She wanted to say that maybe he could help her, and she could help him. Still, her rational mind wouldn't let go; she was still traumatized by what he'd done to her, still horrified by the idea that he'd killed Frida's parents, and now she was working for him.

"You won't tell me? How you learned of my childhood? I thought everyone from that time in my life was dead." Before Juliet could answer, a smooth, chrome-bodied synth approached their table. It carried a tray with two crystal tumblers filled with amber liquid. Silently, it set one before Juliet and the other in front of Tanaka. Without a word or any discernable noise, it turned and walked away.

Juliet looked at her glass, noting the big, round ice cube—somehow sparkling like a distant star at the center—and the rich, dark fluid. She lifted it, smelled the heady aroma of whiskey, then took a sip. It was a hundred times smoother than the last bourbon she'd sampled.

Sighing as the liquor warmed her throat and stomach, she said, "I'm not going to share any secrets with you right now. You're the one sharing secrets today. Tell me how Frida came to be your right-hand woman."

Tanaka hadn't touched his drink, but he stared at it, shifting the glass left and right as he contemplated. Finally, he nodded briefly and began to speak.

"When I was younger, maybe a little younger than you, I was hired to infiltrate this woman's household and kill her." Tanaka pointed to the beautiful woman's face he had tattooed on his neck, just above his shirt collar. "I don't know how you can know I was once called Noraneko but not that I am the man who assassinated the last heiress of the Takamoto Dynasty. Well, the last known heiress, in any case."

9

RIN TAKAMOTO

As Rutger Tanaka's words registered in Juliet's brain, she sat there, stunned, for several seconds, grasping at the implications. *Was he saying Frida was some kind of secret scion of the Takamoto family?*

While part of her mind tried desperately to remember all she'd learned about the Cybergen-Takamoto war and the aftermath, another part reeled with the understanding that Rutger had just told her something she could use against him, or more importantly, against Frida, whom he seemed to care a lot about. Her eyes darted to the corner of her AUI to check the status of her wireless connection—she wasn't being jammed, but the icon indicating they were in a noise-canceling field gave her some relief.

Finally, she found her voice. "That's a risky thing to say in a public place."

"These tables are private, and I paid good money to ensure the staff are vigilant for spies." Tanaka's face didn't betray any emotion, nor did his calm, steady voice. He took his first sip of his drink and, with no indication that he enjoyed it, set the glass back down.

Juliet stared hard at the tattoo on Rutger's neck. It was very detailed, almost photorealistic. She could see individual strands of the woman's dark hair, a glint in her light-brown eyes, and the faint blush on her high cheekbones. If that was really a depiction of some long-dead Takamoto woman, she'd been very beautiful.

"Frida doesn't seem like . . ." She trailed off, not wanting to sound provincial or narrow-minded.

"Do I seem like a Rutger? My mother was Dutch. In any case, these days, it's easy to change one's appearance."

"I think I need to hear more of the story, Rutger." The name felt strange on her tongue; Juliet had gotten used to thinking of the man before her as Tanaka, somehow distancing herself from his personhood. Saying his first name was enough to make her look down into her glass of bourbon, feeling a little strange, almost intimidated, by the intimacy of it.

"If you know I was Noraneko, you know Master Kazuhiro took me in as an orphan and trained me to fight. In exchange for the life he gave me, the Yamashiro Syndicate, for whom he worked, owned me. After the war, Yamashiro stood to gain much from the dismantling of Takamoto. The Takamoto real estate holdings, or at least a large percentage of them, were awarded to the family heirs who weren't directly complicit in the war-time activities of the corporation. Yamashiro wanted those lands and spent decades threatening, buying, and killing for them. When I was seventeen, I was sent to seek work as security for one of the last holdouts—Rin Takamoto." Rutger, again, tapped a finger on his tattoo.

"So you were supposed to get close and kill her? Why? She wouldn't sell the lands?"

"That's right." Rutger took another sip of his drink. "Must you hear the details of my betrayal?"

Juliet frowned, the question striking a chord within her. Did she? *Wasn't it enough that he'd admitted such a thing? Wasn't it enough that he recognized it as a betrayal?* She felt like they weren't close enough for her to want to hear anything more intimate. Instead, she pursued the part that interested her. "Why doesn't anyone know about Frida?"

"Rin was reclusive. She went through her pregnancy and gave birth in seclusion." Rutger shrugged and added, with a grimace, "Only synths and a few people she trusted were allowed on her compound."

"And you killed her and took her child?" Juliet shook her head, unable to keep the disgust from her voice.

"There's more to it . . ."

"I don't want to know more. Not now. Tell me this: Does Frida know?"

Rutger shook his head. "If she did, she would be at risk. If Yamashiro knew she lived, that she had a legal claim to what they gained . . ."

"They'd kill her."

"*Hai,* and me."

"Do they still own you?"

"No. I bought my contract years ago."

"Wait," Juliet said, something just now registering. "You were sent to infiltrate her security when you were seventeen, but were 'around my age' when you killed her? How long were you undercover?"

"I was with her family security for six years." Rutger sighed and shook his head. "Have you heard enough? Has my shame satisfied your—"

"Oh, no! Don't try to turn this on me. I simply asked, if you're so different now, why did Frida care about you before, when you weren't such a changed man? You're the one who decided to confess your sins." Juliet looked toward the exit, suddenly feeling like leaving. Why did she want anything to do with this guy?

As if she could read her mind, or perhaps just noticing the direction of Juliet's stare, Angel spoke into the silence.

"Juliet, if what he told you is true, you have incredible leverage on this man. There's even more reason to consider seeking his help with WBD; I can't imagine you would be able to gain such trust from anyone else you hired."

Juliet looked at the frowning, dour-faced man across from her, noting the many fine, barely visible scars on his cheeks and the backs of his hands. He was a man who'd seen a lot, that was certain. She couldn't argue with Angel's logic, either. Did she have to like Rutger Tanaka to use him?

After she'd been staring at him for several seconds, he finally started to speak.

"I raised Frida like a daughter. When she was old enough to understand such things, I told her I'd adopted her when a colleague died. It was easy enough to fabricate her dead parents; in my line of work, friends die frequently. So, even at my worst, when I was a ruthless mercenary, she saw me at home or in the office, where I let her work as my assistant, handling client relations. I wasn't the same person there that I was on the job. Perhaps that can explain why even a monster can have the love of a child."

"And you sent her to Jupiter to look for me? She wasn't exactly ready for that, was she?"

"I . . . haven't been myself since our encounter on Titan. I hired a man to watch over her . . ."

"Yeah, not the smoothest operator." Juliet shook her head, sighing, then sipped her drink. She looked around, noticing none of the neighboring tables were occupied, and then it dawned on her that they should have had their "first course" by then. "Did you cancel the food?"

"I delayed it."

"Well, I'm hungry. Can you get things moving again?"

For the first time in her experience, Juliet saw Tanaka's lips twist into, if not a smile, a less dour expression. "*Hai.*"

"While we wait, tell me what you think this looks like." Juliet gestured to him and then to herself. "What do you want?"

"I want to help you. I want to help myself. I feel lost in here." He touched his forehead, then moved his hand down to his chest. "And in here." He frowned and glanced to his left at the silent synth approaching with a tray. "When I finished my job and took Frida, Noraneko died. You killed the man he became, and now, I want to figure out who is living in here." Again, he tapped his forehead.

Before Juliet could think of a response, the synth approached the table and silently placed plates before them. She was about to ask Angel what the food was, but then it spoke in a smooth, cultured, androgynous tone.

"Here we have our amuse-bouche, petite escargot pearls served on a light, crispy wafer. The escargot is sustainably farmed in our own aquaponic systems, ensuring freshness and quality. You'll find the escargot accompanied by a garnish of aeroponically grown microherbs." With that, the synth turned and walked away.

Juliet looked at her plate—it was a tiny amount of food, and though she knew escargot was a fancy way of saying snail, she couldn't see any sign of the little creatures. The "pearls" were just round, slightly oily-looking balls on a cracker. Still, when she took a bite, the taste was rich, earthy, and a nice contrast to the delicate crispness of the wafer. Before she knew it, the little plate of food was gone, and she wanted more. Looking up, she saw Tanaka watching her, only half his food eaten.

"You don't like it?"

"I like it, but my appetite fails me." He pushed his plate toward her. "You should eat it."

Juliet frowned. Did she want to take food from this man? She figured she already was; he'd brought her to dinner. If nothing else, she'd get a good meal out of him. While she finished his portion, he began to speak again. "Do you have any interest in learning to use the sword you took from me?"

Juliet swallowed and frowned at him. "What makes you think I don't know how already?"

"Because you carry a pistol wherever you go. If you'd mastered that blade, you'd not want to part with it."

"Huh. You think so? I get that the monoblade is versatile and deadly, but I can shoot someone from thirty meters away with my Texan."

Tanaka grunted and shook his head. "You'd have to be in an open field to kill me with that weapon. I don't stand around in fields waiting for my enemies."

Juliet shrugged. "I had you dead to rights in the parking garage."

He mimicked her earlier words, "You think so?" Tanaka grinned, showing Juliet what he really looked like when he smiled. She wasn't sure if she wanted to shiver or slap him.

"Don't try to rewrite history, Rutger. You were on your knees, weeping." Juliet almost regretted the words when she said them, but not quite. Even so, she felt a little twist in her gut when his grin fell away, and he stood up.

"Excuse me." Without waiting for a response or further explanation, he turned and walked away from the table.

"Huh, did I piss him off enough to walk out?"

"I'm not sure. He's walking toward the elevators, but the restrooms are also in that direction." Angel sounded a little uncertain when she asked, "Will you be upset if he's left?"

"No." Juliet's response was immediate, but she knew she wasn't being honest. Angel did, too.

"You're always concerned about what people think of you, even those whom you don't like." After a slight pause, she asked, "Do you like him?"

"No! In fact, I want to hate him, but it annoys me that I kind of feel sorry for him. He's a murderer, by his own admission. Frida thinks he rescued her from some horrible fate, but he took her mother and stole her life."

"You didn't listen to his entire tale. It seems there's more to it than the end result. Perhaps he was leveraged. Perhaps if he hadn't taken Frida, she would have been killed. Perhaps—"

"Angel, what are you doing?" Juliet was genuinely puzzled. "Are you trying to make me like him for some reason?"

"I don't know. I suppose, like you, I feel sorry for him for some reason. I've been researching the Takamoto family, and it's like he says. Rin Takamoto was the last one with any inheritance rights, and between 2065 and her death in 2086, nearly every direct relation to the central Takamoto family died—more than a hundred and fifty people dead from accidents, suicide, or murder."

"So what? Her days were numbered, so it was okay for this guy to kill her and take her kid?"

Before Angel could reply, the synth returned with an identical-looking partner. One took away their plates, and the other set down steaming bowls of soup. "Here we have forest mushroom velouté with heritage carrot essence. Our mushrooms are cultivated in-house in our specialized growth chambers for optimal flavor. The carrots are grown in nutrient-rich vertical farms run by the owner's sister in Luna's premier agridome. Please enjoy." As the synth walked away, Juliet looked at the creamy soup, savoring the aromas wafting off it.

"Tanaka is returning," Angel noted. Juliet looked to her right to see him walking stiffly through the dining room toward the table.

Sitting down, he said, "Thank you for not leaving. I apologize for my embarrassing outburst."

Juliet snorted. "That was an outburst?"

Tanaka shook his head but didn't reply. Instead, he sniffed the soup and smiled. "Mushrooms?"

"Yeah, and, um, carrots, I think." Juliet tasted a spoonful of the soup and smiled, swallowing the smooth, somehow deeply comforting liquid. It was subtly sweet, with a depth of savory flavor that lingered on her taste buds long after she'd swallowed. "Wow. Best mushroom soup I've tasted."

"Better than ration packs," Tanaka agreed, nodding.

"So, if you want to try working together," Juliet said, swallowing another bite, "how do you feel about telling Frida the truth?"

Tanaka froze, his spoon midway between his bowl and his mouth, and set it down. He looked at her, eyes filled with emotion, and said, in a hoarse whisper, "Don't make me do that. No, I cannot do that, not to her."

Juliet sighed, also setting down her spoon. "Yeah, I guess I can't be sure knowing the truth would be good for her. I want to do what's right, you see? I feel sorry for you now, but I hate the idea of what you must have been to do what you did. Still, if the truth would hurt her more than help her, I can't see making you tell her. It's something I'll need to figure out as I get to know her better."

"Perhaps, if you'd let me, it would help for you to know my story a little better. To know what Rin meant to me. To know what Frida means to me."

Juliet took another bite of her soup, savoring the rich flavor, and then nodded, somehow feeling more open to the idea than when he'd tried to tell her earlier. "All right. I'm listening."

"Well, the relevant parts start when I'd just turned nineteen and the man in charge of Takamoto household security, Franz Nachtmann, called me into his office . . ."

* * *

Rutger straightened his suit, examining himself in the mirror. His hair was neat, cut so short on the sides he could see the skin, his only tattoo, the kanji he'd taken when Master Kazuhiro had given him his sword—senshi, or fighter—the only mark on his face. He traced his fingers over the ten-centimeter script under his right cheekbone. It had long ago healed, and he'd gotten used to it, but he hoped it wouldn't affect his chances. He hoped Nachtmann wouldn't be put off by the facial tattoo. He'd seen the bodyguards on the other family details, and they were all very clean-cut.

He checked his obi, made sure every fold was right and that his sword was seated perfectly, then walked out of the bathroom, his polished dress boots clicking on the porcelain tile. When he walked through the hallways of the estate, he made eye contact with the other security personnel, saw on his red, monochrome AUI that they were pinging his credentials, and continued on his way, secure in his right to be there. His PAI, Nora, guided him up the stairs, down the third hallway on the left, and to the nondescript, plain white door with a simple designation imprinted on a black placard—Takamoto Head of Security.

He stood before the door, perfectly still, and waited. He had no doubt the man within knew he was there. He waited six minutes and forty-two seconds before it opened, and a large, blond-haired man sitting behind a clutter-free glass desk said, in a gruff, thick accent, "Come in."

Rutger stepped through the door and over the plush, navy-blue carpet to stand before the desk. He bowed deeply and then straightened, waiting to be acknowledged. Behind Franz Nachtmann, expansive windows gave a view of the parklike front garden of the estate, and Rutger found his eyes drawn to a young man playing with a pair of vizslas, throwing a ball for them on the manicured lawn.

Nachtmann said his name slowly, enunciating each syllable, "Rutger Tanaka."

"Yes, sir."

"So, you've been with the family for two years now, hmm?"

"Nearly twenty-nine months, sir."

"Working on the grounds of properties waiting for sale, yes?"

"Mostly, sir. I've done a few details for the Sugimoto branch of the family, but nothing longer than a week."

Nachtmann looked Rutger up and down, his eyes fixing on the sword at his side. "Traditionalist, eh? Your supervisor, Kramer, says you're good with that weapon. Says you have a high-end wire-job. Pretty fast, huh?"

Rutger nodded, preparing his lie. "Yes, sir. When my father died, I inherited a small estate. It wasn't enough to live on, but when I sold it, it was enough for me to purchase the nerve enhancement to help start my career in personal security." Of course, the truth was that Yamashiro had paid for his very high-end augmentation. How else would he impress this security detail enough to put him on a family detail?

"Smart. Many young men would've pissed it away." Nachtmann nodded, mumbling to himself while he read through something on his AUI. "Well, I think you've put in your dues. How'd you like a steady position, one where you won't be moving from detail to detail every other week?"

Tanaka bowed and, as he straightened, said, "*Hai!* I would be honored, sir!"

"Have you heard of Lady Rin Takamoto?"

Rutger knew he couldn't feign total ignorance. Still, it was a struggle to keep the smile off his face. "Yes, sir." He nodded, hands at his sides, struggling not to bow again—some of the Western security officers were bothered by the gesture.

"She's a bit of a recluse, so you're going to be away from town, away from the bars and whatnot. That said, you'll be five days on and two off, working twenty-four-hour shifts. On your off days, you can go into Niseko to blow off steam. We keep a villa for the security detail there, so you'll have a place to bunk when you're not working. Sound okay to you?"

"*Hai!* Of course, sir."

"Right answer. All right, get your shit together, 'cause we're shipping you off at 0430. Dismissed."

Tanaka, struggling to contain his joy, turned on his heel and walked out of the office. Not until the door clicked behind him and he was well on his way to the staircase did he allow his happiness to reflect on his face in the form of a tiny, partial smile.

Finally, after two long years, he was going to see her, the woman Master Kazuhiro told him needed to die.

10

ROADBLOCK

Tanaka paused his story as the synths returned, one to take away their bowls and spoons, the other to deliver their third course. As the waiter placed a plate of steaming protein accompanied by a bunch of vegetables, the scent of herbs and rich fats made Juliet's mouth begin to water.

"For your main course, we present our herb-crusted, lab-cultured lamb. Accompanying the lamb, we have a selection of chef-picked seasonal vegetables—heirloom carrots, roasted to perfection, rainbow chard, lightly sautéed, and tender, baby asparagus, lightly grilled. Enjoy."

The synths walked away, and Juliet leaned close to her plate, letting the aromas tease her taste buds. Then she looked up at Tanaka. "I don't want to be rude, Rutger. I'm really trying to be patient and understand what's happening here, but I'm having trouble understanding why I should stick around and listen to your life story. Can we skip to the punch line? I get it; you were young and impressionable when the Yamashiro Syndicate took you in. You thought you were saving the world or something, yeah? So what—you worked for years to get accepted into Rin Takamoto's security detail, then waited until she was alone and killed her? Took her baby with you 'cause you felt guilty. Am I close?"

Tanaka frowned, slicing a small bite of the lab-grown lamb and chewing it while he contemplated. He swallowed, took another sip of his bourbon, then shrugged. "The punch line? I suppose the punch line is that Frida is my child. Rin killed herself, and I took credit for her death to earn credit toward my freedom."

Juliet stared at him for several long seconds, her mind trying to wrap itself around the convoluted story. "Why, then, does she think you took her in when some 'friends' died? Why not raise her as your daughter?"

"Then I would have to lie about her mother. I would have to . . ." He stopped and slowly pressed a palm to his forehead, closing his eyes. Juliet knew that if she were listening to his thoughts right then, she'd be struck with some harrowing emotions. "It was better this way. I am not a father. I am . . . I was a killer. I wasn't released from Yamashiro immediately, but the successful mission earned me much goodwill. Still, I had to work for years, and I did other dangerous work in those years. It was better for Frida to grow up thinking I was a kind family friend paying for her nanny and providing a home. It was also easier to explain her to the people in Yamashiro who handled me."

Juliet took a bite of her food, wanting to enjoy it but too preoccupied with her thoughts to pay attention to the flavors. Her mind insisted on wandering in different directions. She kept thinking about Frida, imagining her life growing up with this man as a role model. She wondered about Rutger and Rin. Part of her wanted to listen to his thoughts to see if he was telling the truth; another part was scared—if he was telling the truth, those memories had to be horribly painful.

She was torn between relief, sympathy, and guilt over the story. Part of her had wanted to think Rutger was a cold-blooded killer, had wanted to have that reason to walk away and put this weird interlude behind her. Now, she'd lost that leverage on herself, and the other part of her, the one who wanted to understand him, was gaining ground.

Finally, after she'd eaten half her food and Rutger took a couple more small bites, she nodded, sipping her drink. "I'm sorry, Rutger. That sounds awful, and I suppose it explains a lot—why Frida cares about you, why I should stay out of it when it comes to telling her who she is, and why I should maybe hear you out when it comes to us." She gestured to him and then back to herself, still holding her glass. When he didn't respond, she tried to bring the conversation back on track, back toward some kind of point. "So? What does that look like? What do you want from me, Rutger?"

"As I said, I want to help you and, in doing so, help myself."

Juliet made air quotes. "'Help'?" She frowned, set her silverware down, and leaned back in her chair. "With what?"

"You're hiding. Lucky, the SOA operative, doesn't have much history, and I can't find much of anything else on you—who you were before you were

Lucky, where you came from . . . nothing. I have extensive resources, and spent a lot of time and money looking into you. The only thing I know is that you arrived here on Luna last year on a shuttle from the Phoenix Space Port. You used a fake identity when you purchased your ticket, and I couldn't trace you further.

"So, let me help you. I know what it means to always look over your shoulder, to feel the weight of assassins or spies lurking in every window, and to wonder if everyone you meet is being put at risk by knowing you. I've told you my most intimate secret, something that could not only ruin me but the only person I care about. Knowing that, do you not feel safe enough to let me help you?"

Angel chose that moment to weigh in. "He makes a good point."

Juliet sighed and rubbed her temple with one hand while she swirled the dregs of her drink with the other. Subvocalizing, she asked Angel, "You really want me to trust him?"

"Not yet, but I think this is a good start. As you know, I've done a lot of vetting over the last month with my connections to Frida and the others on his team. I don't think there's any chance he's working for WBD, but let's start things off slowly. Can you think of something he could do for you that wouldn't put you at risk?"

Juliet smiled. "You can start earning my trust by teaching me how to use that monoblade."

"I also had that idea, as you probably assumed from my earlier mention." He nodded, and though he didn't smile, he seemed less dour. "I understand you don't trust me, that you have concerns about my motives or even my sanity. Let me earn your trust. Spend some time working with me."

Juliet glanced to her right and saw the synths waiting in the wings, ready to take their plates and probably bring their dessert. Suddenly, she didn't feel hungry, didn't feel comfortable sitting there. She pushed her chair away from the table and cleared her throat.

"Well, this has been nice, but I'm going to skip the next course or whatever. I think you've given me plenty to think about. Have Frida contact me with the time and place, and I'll meet you for a lesson. We'll see how that goes and move from there, okay?"

"Lucky." He leaned forward, his eyes practically reaching out, trying to lock onto hers. "I feel as though you want help. Am I wrong? I've been around a long time, and it seems to me you'd have walked out a while ago if there wasn't something you needed. If it's . . . If you've got something bad going on, don't wait too long to ask for my assistance. Don't make me live with knowing I could've stopped something but missed my opportunity."

Juliet stood up and smirked with half her mouth, offering the strange, sad, dangerous man a wink. "It's not all about you, Rutger. I'll be waiting for Frida's call."

With that, she turned and strode toward the elevator. It was weird, knowing he was staring at her as she walked away, feeling his eyes boring into her. She'd purposefully gone the whole night trying hard not to use the lattice. Being in his head once had been enough, at least for now. With the heavy topics of lost love, secret children, and assassinations, she hadn't wanted to risk it. It wasn't like she would try to perform a deep dive, but her connection to him was strange in its intensity; she hadn't been trying for a deep dive in the garage either.

It wasn't until she was snug in her jacket, cruising slowly through town, noticing the sad contrast between the view from the restaurant and the view from the ground, that she finally spoke her mind.

"I don't know what I'm doing."

"With Tanaka?"

"With him, WBD, the gunship, Honey, Ghoul, Hot Mustard—my life. I don't know what I'm doing."

"Do you mean . . . ?"

"I don't even know what I'm doing with you. What about Athena? Angel, I'm just constantly playing it by ear and rolling with the punches."

"You're operating from a baseline that involves flight from danger. You won't be able to take charge of your future until you stop running. Tanaka was right about you needing help—we have to remove the lurking danger, whatever that might entail, and I believe he will be a valuable ally in that endeavor."

"It's not like I have a lot of options. I mean, that's not entirely true; I could try to put my own team together and vet each person. I could put them in a room with one-way glass and read their minds." Juliet twisted the throttle as she merged with the traffic heading out of downtown.

"Perhaps. You might miss something, or they might become compromised during the course of the operation. Tanaka's team has been working for him for years, and he'll be a lot more likely to spot betrayal among them than you would with a bunch of strangers."

"It sounds like you want me to work with him. Do I ask you that enough, Angel? What you want? If I'm just rolling with the punches, feeling listless and not in control, I can only imagine how you feel. I'm sorry."

"Why are you sorry? I am what I am."

"I'm sorry for a lot! I'm sorry you don't remember your life before me. I'm sorry the people who created you are . . ." Juliet stopped, for the first time admitting to herself that she didn't know anything about WBD's motives other than what Angel's previous host, Godric, had told her as he lay dying in the scrapyard.

"What, Juliet?"

Juliet didn't answer right away. She leaned forward on her bike and really opened it up, feeling the rush of speed in her stomach as adrenaline brought her mind into focus. The world around her tunneled, and the street ahead of her was all that mattered for a while as she raced through traffic and tried to forget the idea that her speeding was just a physical reaction to her desire to run away from more abstract problems and uncomfortable ideas.

As usual when she was in the midst of something dangerous, Angel didn't scold or try to correct her in the moment. She grew quiet, and that was just another thing Juliet tried to leave behind her with the rapidly fading headlights of the vehicles she passed.

She saw the traffic alerts light up on her AUI, and knew Angel was covering for her. She knew she was being stupid, but nothing mattered to her more in that moment than going faster.

She'd just topped 240 KPH and would have continued to accelerate if she hadn't seen flashing lights ahead and a long line of backed-up traffic. Juliet rapidly downshifted and then, as her regenerative brakes whined, switched three lanes to the right and split the lane until she found a nice big truck to slip in front of, hoping that anyone who'd taken an interest in her speeding wouldn't be able to see her.

"What's the story?" she asked, looking at the dozens of stopped cars ahead of her.

"I'm not sure. The Luna traffic information portal is just calling it a 'temporary checkpoint.' This road splits between the industrial access highway we want to take and another that leads to upper-class residential domes. It's possible they're looking for someone . . ."

"Someone who speeds too much?" Juliet rubbed her palms on the sleeves of her jacket, her adrenaline rush fading while jitters and nerves, along with a vague guilty feeling, replaced it.

"Unlikely. Stopping traffic at this hour for a single speeder would be ludicrous from a public relations standpoint. Juliet, will you tell me what you were running from while we wait?"

"Not letting me get away with that one, are you?" Juliet sighed and flipped up her visor, pointing her face at the night sky, taking a deep breath of the cool air. "I was just wondering whether I was good for you. What if Godric wasn't a good guy? What if running from WBD was keeping you from . . . being you? I don't know. Maybe they were going to help you grow and improve. You said so yourself, that they had specialized software for you. They were the ones who gave you your databases and all that stuff—"

"Are you trying to anger me? Because I feel very angry right now!" Angel didn't often interrupt Juliet, and she never raised her voice in that tone—even when she spoke about some of the people who'd harmed Juliet.

"Anger?" Juliet asked carefully.

"How can you speculate that my life might be better without the person I love the most in this world—every world? Are we sisters, or aren't we? Do you just say those words to placate me? I am who I am because of you. We've been over that! If you'd given me to WBD, God knows what kind of monster I might've been paired with. If you ever think about giving me up to them, I'll never forgive you."

"I . . ." Juliet was dumbstruck by the raw emotion in Angel's voice. She was further tongue-tied by the realization that Angel had hit a painful mark; Juliet hadn't been treating her like a sister, as she so often called her. "I'm sorry. I was stupid."

"It's fine."

By her tone, Juliet was guessing things were anything but fine. She let the matter drop for the moment, watching between the rows of traffic as some Luna City corpo-sec walked around a dark sedan, shining bright lights into the windows. She had to zoom in with her optics, more than half a kilometer from the checkpoint, but the image was crystal clear. "What are they looking for?"

"They're looking at people's faces, not in cargo compartments. A fugitive, perhaps?"

Juliet watched for a minute more, then the corpo-sec waved the sedan through, followed by a bus, a shuttle, and a sporty, low-slung, electric two-seater. Juliet inched forward, only partially paying attention, hoping they'd keep waving people through. The next car up was another dark sedan, though, and again, the corpo-sec officers stopped it and began shining their lights through the windows. Three security vehicles were blocking the roadway, and she counted five officers. Juliet was just about to turn away, stifling a yawn, when all hell broke loose.

A tremendous *boom* shook the relatively quiet night, followed by glass falling on pavement and a high-pitched, warbling scream. Juliet looked back toward the roadblock and saw one of the corpo-sec officers on the ground, thrashing and screaming, while the other four started shooting into the sedan with their semiautomatic pistols. She might have expected that to end things, but the corpo-sec were on the left side of the car, and Juliet saw several figures roll out the doors on the right before they were up, unleashing automatic gunfire at the security officers.

Everything happened fast, and for once, Juliet wasn't in the middle of the action. She watched as the two groups exchanged fire, and in a matter of seconds, it was down to one corpo-sec and two suit-wearing, automatic rifle-toting individuals. The corpo officer was hunched behind the wheel of his cruiser. One of his companions was still thrashing, grasping his face and screaming, and the other three were either dead or unconscious.

Juliet hadn't reacted yet, primarily because it had happened so fast but also because she wasn't sure what she'd do. Did she want to help the corpo-sec? In her mind, it was just as likely that they were the bad guys in this scenario.

She was about to ask Angel what she thought when the corpo-sec officer threw his pistol onto the roadway and held up his hands. Through the enhanced gain on her auditory implants, she heard him cry, "Just go!"

"You wrecked our car, pork. You're driving us." Juliet watched as one of the men, burlier than the other, took a duffel out of the bullet-riddled car while the other turned his gun on the jammed-up traffic. She could almost see the thoughts going through his red, skull-shaped irises while he contemplated.

Many drivers panicked, throwing their vehicles in reverse and smashing into the cars behind them. Others were trying to inch forward, perhaps to make a break for it. Most sat stock-still, though, waiting, probably praying things would be over soon. That's when the guy lifted his big automatic rifle with its double-width, banana-style magazine and began to open fire on the vehicles in the front row.

"Juliet! He's shooting the drivers!"

Angel's outcry was enough to snap Juliet out of her stupefaction. She slapped the visor down on her helmet and cranked the throttle, angling for the emergency lane on the right. She'd advanced two car lengths before another panicked driver cut her off, and she had to weave back into traffic to find another route forward. She'd only made it halfway when the shooting stopped, and she saw the cruiser the two thugs had stolen taking off.

"Can't Luna City Security kill that car's engine remotely?"

"If so, they would have already. They must have some way to block or override the signal."

"Dammit!" Juliet growled, kicking her boot off the fender of a car that almost sideswiped her. It was a frustrating ninety seconds before she finally worked her way around the blasted vehicles and into the scene of the bloodbath. Drones were swarming overhead, and she could hear sirens from the city wailing toward them. The road ahead was empty, though, and she cranked the throttle, rocketing into the darkness.

"Drones are pursuing the vehicle. Perhaps we shouldn't get involv—"

"Melt that, Angel! I might not like corpo-sec, but those guys were monsters. I'm not letting them slip away with a hostage."

11

\\\\\\\\\\\\\\\\\\\\\

A BIRD IN THE HAND

Juliet had never chased another motor vehicle before. The idea that her speeding was in the service of a greater good removed any semblance of inhibition, and she cranked the throttle on her bike, leaning forward so her chest rested on the vibrating plasteel shroud that covered her battery bank.

Her AUI kept her informed of her speed, and as she approached 300 KPH, a little voice in the back of her head started to jibber inanely about risks while another voice began to laugh at the thrill. Juliet tuned them out and focused on the distant lights of the corpo-sec cruiser and the swooping drones that kept pace with it. Angel estimated she was nine hundred meters behind but closing.

"What will you do when you catch up?"

"Good question, Angel. My pistol's locked in the compartment under my butt." The car veered to the right, and the lights disappeared. Juliet glanced at her mini map and saw an off-ramp ahead—the same one she'd be taking to return to the hangar. "They're going to try to ditch the drones in there. Doesn't Luna Security have choppers or fluttercraft?"

"None that can safely traverse the highway domes. It won't be easy to lose those drones, but they may try to pull into a garage or . . . hangar." Angel said the last word as though it was just dawning on her that they were rapidly approaching the industrial part of town where hangars and garages were abundant.

"Kill my lights—I'll drive with my night vision."

"They're automatic. Give me a minute to override."

"We don't have a minute," Juliet said as the off-ramp loomed. She down-shifted, letting the braking, regenerative gears do the work while keeping her speed just north of unsafe.

She was halfway down the ramp when the lights on her bike cut out, and she was plunged into darkness—there weren't many streetlights in the industrial dome. Angel managed her optics, though, and Juliet could see plain as day as she rolled into the intersection at the base of the ramp. She swiveled her head left and right, trying to catch a clue as to where the criminals had gone. Flickering lights down the street to her right signaled the presence of drones, and Juliet twisted the throttle, throwing the bike's rear end into a circle burnout so she could turn more sharply.

She rocketed down the street toward the drones and saw the smashed rolling bay door on a building with a colorful stack of boxes painted on the big, white concrete wall. Beneath the boxes were the words SHIFTON CARGO TRANSPORT. Juliet released the throttle and let inertia roll her bike into the parking lot. She pulled up to the left of the bay door and hopped off. While Angel remotely opened her seat compartment, she peered through the crumpled door into the building. The cruiser was there, lights still blink-ing, smashed into a pallet of cardboard boxes. The car's doors were open, and it was clear that no one was still inside.

"They're on foot," Juliet subvocalized as she returned to her bike, reached into the cargo compartment, and pulled out her pistol. She wasn't dressed for this sort of situation, but her boots and leather jacket were better than heels and a faux fur. She silently congratulated herself on her fashion tastes. She kept her helmet on as she ducked through the rolling door, pushing it slightly to make room. The cruiser had knocked it off its rails, but it still hung from the mechanical drum above the bay opening.

"That helmet's not designed to stop bullets."

"Better than nothing," Juliet whispered, creeping toward the cruiser and peering through the windows to ensure no one hid within. "Where's the corpo-sec backup?"

"Likely still working through the jam where these men were discovered. The drones didn't pursue the car into the building because of that bay door. They're likely circling the building, though."

"Can you send a message in? Tell them not to shoot me if they show up?"

"Done. I've explained that you're an SOA operative who took an interest in the corpo-sec hostage's safety. That should buy you some goodwill."

Juliet, crouching low, Texan gripped in her right hand, hurried forward to the next pallet of boxes bordering a broad, central pathway. A forklift sat, silent and dark, in the center of the aisle, and thousands of containers and pallets towered on the left and right. It seemed like someone could be hiding anywhere.

"Filter out those drone sounds and up my gain." As Angel did what she asked, the buzz and whine of drones faded away, and soon, she was hearing the weird sounds a building makes, amplified by her audio implants. Juliet leaned against the pallet, hiding in its shadow, waiting and listening, scanning as much of the warehouse as possible with her optics.

Her first clue came after only a few seconds—a muffled exclamation of pain from the far northeastern corner of the warehouse. A man yelped briefly before the crack of something heavy hitting bone cut him off. Juliet padded forward, weaving between pallets and stacked boxes, aiming for the corner of the structure.

"What are they going to do?" she subvocalized. "They have to know the drones are surrounding the building. Will they try to slip out into another one?"

"Perhaps. I've been scanning the available databases and message boards on the pub net, and it seems there are rumors of access tunnels out here. Nothing as extensive as Old Atlas on Titan, but . . ."

"So, they might be trying to get underground." Juliet grimaced, annoyed she'd been rushing when she grabbed her pistol and hadn't taken her gun belt. She only had the seven bullets in the cylinder.

She continued, moving more quickly, trusting in her soft boot soles to keep her steps quiet and counting on the criminals to be hurrying, not laying an ambush. When she reached the far eastern wall of the warehouse, she peered left, around the corner of yet another stack of boxes. Forty meters ahead, in the northern wall, was a door that hung ajar with a broken latch. "They pried that open."

"Probably the business offices and, likely, where they'll find access to the maintenance tunnels if there are any. Luna Security has responded to your message—they are four minutes away and have endorsed your intervention. They've sent you an SOA contract."

Juliet smiled grimly, hurrying toward the door, her Texan aimed forward. "That's more like it. Just call me Deputy Lucky." She paused by the door, shoulder to the wall, one eye peering through the crack. She waited, forcing herself to be patient while she watched and listened to the dark corridor beyond. She was just about to step through when one of the doors about ten meters down the hallway burst open, and one of the suit-wearing criminals stepped into view, striding straight for the door across the hall. He was the big one, with the crimson skull irises.

"Not in there," he growled, presumably to his partner through a comm line.

Juliet watched him approach the office door, his left side fully exposed to her. She had a quick debate with herself; should she grab this opportunity to take him out, or should she wait and watch, hoping for a better chance at getting them both?

"A bird in the hand . . ." she breathed softly, then, quick as a blink, pointed the Texan through the slightly open door and fired a single round right into the guy's armpit as he twisted the door latch. The Texan roared like muted thunder in her audio implants.

Her shot was perfect. The polymer .357 bullet probably would have done just fine without her hitting him in the armpit, but as it was, it exploded into his torso, likely wreaking havoc with his lungs, arteries, and, potentially, his heart. He collapsed to his right side, coughing a gout of blood as he tried to bring his machine gun to bear on the doorway where Juliet lurked.

He squeezed off a single shot, the bullet punching through the door as Juliet flinched back and took cover behind the wall again. No more shots rang out, so she peeked through the opening again, only to see the man sprawled out on his back, unmoving.

Juliet advanced through the tiny front office, straight for the hallway where her victim lay. When she reached the opening, she took cover at the corner and waited, wondering if his partner would show his face to check on him. She pulled the hammer back on the Texan, ready to fire at the slightest provocation, and tried to stay patient, tried to breathe.

Rather than leave things to her senses, she also listened with her lattice, willing her perception to widen, opening herself to the idea of grabbing any thoughts she could. She was immediately rewarded for her efforts, picking up a series of broken thoughts.

Need to drop this dead weight, 'specially if that was the end of Evers . . . Who the fuck . . . Danny said corpo-sec was minutes out! Dammit, dammit, dammit. Just there . . . just at the end . . . Maintenance door. I'm sure that's it. Oof . . . heavy. Insurance, insurance, insurance . . .

Juliet hurried down the hall, something telling her, some instinct or feeling, that the guy she'd heard was in that direction. When she reached a T-junction, she hugged the right-hand corner and peered around.

A glimpse of a gun pointing her way from five meters down the hall sent adrenaline into her system, and like a switch being thrown, Angel sped up her synapses. Juliet jerked her head back as the gun barked, and all she suffered was a spray of shredded drywall against her visor.

"Drop the gun if you want to live!" she yelled.

"Fuck off, corpo pig!"

"Danny sold you out, dumbass! I'm not corpo-sec." Juliet knew, from experience, how real the fear of betrayal was when you were up against the corps, and she hoped her knowledge of Danny's name would be enough to send the guy into a spiral of doubt. "No way out! The underground's sealed up, and you're surrounded. Only hope to live is that you haven't killed that corpo rat yet. Have you?"

"He's alive, but you're gonna merc me as soon as I let him go!"

"If I wanted you dead, I'd send a bomb your way on my drone!" Juliet had to confess she kind of loved bluffing. "Come on, last chance. Lay down your gun and take a knee. I'm an independent operator. If I have you tied up before the corpo rats come inside, they probably won't shoot you, not if I'm here taking footage."

"Goddammit, bootlicker!" he growled, but Juliet heard his rifle clatter on the ground. "Come on then. I'm down." Juliet peered around the corner, just barely poking her helmet around. Sure enough, he was down on his knees, hands on his head, and his gun was three meters away.

She stepped around the corner, Texan leveled at his face. "Bootlicker, huh? I don't think so, dummy. I wouldn't have chased you if your even dumber friend hadn't decided to light up all those pedestrians, if you hadn't snatched up a hostage. This is on you."

"What the shit? Are you wearing a *dress*?" He started to move, but the second his hands lifted off his head, Juliet rattled her Texan and wagged the finger of her left hand at him.

"Don't be dumb. I might be in a dress, but I'm a lot faster than you, and I don't miss." She pointed to the laminate tiles in front of him. "Lay down on your face, hands behind your back."

He was kind of a handsome guy—strong jaw, dark brows, piercing, shiny silver eyes, and well-groomed, from his beard to his hair to his neat fingernails. When he grimaced, it looked kind of good on him, and Juliet had the weird, stray thought that someone who looked like that shouldn't be involved in something like this. It was an absurd, stupid thought, but it made her wonder about her preconceived notions about society—something that seemed to happen more and more the farther she got from her old life.

As she stepped around him and moved to place a knee on his back, grasping his wrist, he struggled a little, straining against her pull. She tapped the Texan's barrel against his head, right above his ear. "Don't make me put a big hole in you, buddy." When he settled down, she reached around him with her free hand and loosened his tie. "I don't have any shrink cords on me."

While she worked at tying his hands up behind his back, the guy grunted, "What's in it for you, anyway? You ain't gonna undo what Evers did to those people in their cars."

"What's in it for me? I guess just knowing I haven't lost my soul yet. Knowing I'll still step up when I see something wrong. Now tell me where the corpo-sec officer is and what was in that duffel bag. Is it here?"

"He's through that door right there. He ain't dead. The bag . . ." He paused, and Juliet could tell he was furiously thinking. "The bag's full of nanowafers, the best TanTan can make. They're worth a few million bits. If you keep it outta Luna Security's hands, I'll put you in touch with my fence. He'll keep a cut for me, but it'll make you rich."

Juliet opened the door and looked at the swollen-faced, fitfully breathing corpo-sec officer and the bulky black duffel beside him. She'd heard of TanTan Corp. They were well known for making some of the best processors for everything from PAIs to data servers. Juliet briefly considered the guy's offer. If she were quick and clever, she might slip away before Luna Security showed up. Failing that, she might hide the bag somewhere . . .

She shook her head. "Nah, sorry, chum I've got my hands full right now. If they're looking for you, they know what you stole, and they're going to turn this place upside down looking for it. I'm not wearing my sewer-exploring clothes, so I won't be trying to slip away through the underground."

"Not to mention, we have a contract with them, and you'd have to burn your SOA license again if you did that." Angel's words further settled Juliet's mind, and she knelt by the unconscious officer, feeling his pulse. It was thready but there.

"You better hope he doesn't die."

"What's the difference? As you said, Evers sealed our fate when he went nuts, blasting all those cars. Dumbass! Dammit, I should've stopped working with that guy after he got that implant . . ."

"What implant?"

"A cold circuit."

Juliet was about to ask what a cold circuit was, but Angel helped her out. "That's a slang term for a Morality Override Interface, or MOI. It's an implant that modulates stimulation in the prefrontal cortex, training someone to ignore moral impulses. It was designed, with much controversy, for use in military applications, helping soldiers who struggled to commit acts of aggression."

"You've got to be kidding me." Juliet stepped back into the hallway, groaning in disbelief. "He purposefully put something in his head to make him 'cold'? Why the hell?"

Before he could answer, Angel said, "Luna Security is here. They're entering the warehouse, and I've given them your location and ensured they know you have subdued the fugitives."

"Guess he got called a coward a few times too many." Juliet had the impression that he shrugged, but face down, with his hands behind his back, it looked more like a twitch.

"Your ride's here. Stay calm." Juliet lowered her gun, holding it by her hip, and waited. Less than a minute later, she heard the stomp of boots, and then two Luna Security officers stormed around the corner, bulky SMGs leveled at her and her prisoner.

"Freeze! Get on the ground!"

Juliet didn't have a pocket that would hold the Texan, so she kept it in her hand, but she held her free hand up, shaking her visored head. "I'm under contract with you. My PAI will send the authentication."

"Get on the ground!" the second one barked, jamming his gun at her.

"Calm down." Juliet nodded toward the doorway on her right. "You're wasting time, and your buddy needs an ambulance."

"She's good," the first officer said, straightening up. He stepped over to Juliet's prisoner, pulling a shrink cord from his belt. "We saw you iced the other one, huh?"

"He was the violent one." For some reason, Juliet wanted to try to earn her prisoner some goodwill. "This guy turned himself over, no problem."

"Uh-huh. He can tell it to the judge. Maybe you can be a character witness." He squatted to apply the shrink cord while his partner went through the doorway to check on the injured corpo-sec officer.

She heard him speak from the other room, "Hostiles are down. Payload's secure. Send the trauma team through."

Realizing she wasn't needed any longer, Juliet started to walk past the guy on the ground, heading for the corner. However, something wouldn't let her turn her back on the corpo-sec officers, and she walked kind of sideways, watching them as she moved. She wondered how precarious her existence was at that moment. If she'd laid down her gun and proned herself out on the floor when they'd ordered it, would they have realized who she was and let her up, or would they have killed her and stolen the wafers? The idea that corpo-sec were just as often corrupt as not wasn't an urban legend.

"Where are you going?" the first officer asked as she reached the corner.

"I'm done here."

"You need to make a report."

"I'll send it in. Like I said, I have a contract." She could see he wanted to argue, but he couldn't—Angel had legitimized her just enough that he couldn't easily abuse his authority with her. Too many other layers of their organization knew who she was and that she was there. There was a record of her pursuit and capture of the criminals.

"I'll be sure to mention the wafers in my report." As she turned the corner, the officer's mirrored visor followed her, and she could imagine his scowl. "Those guys were itching to shoot someone," she subvocalized.

"They may have had designs on the contraband. It seems strange that they held the trauma team back so far. They still aren't through the warehouse."

"Yeah, especially when we already reported the capture."

As she left the office area and began crossing through the warehouse, Juliet could hear the stomping feet of the emergency response unit and took a different aisle, not wanting to run into them. She tucked her pistol into her jacket pocket, grip first, barrel hanging out. She figured she shouldn't give the other officers a reason to blast her. When she held her elbow close to her side, you couldn't see the gun at all. "It's a scary world, Angel. Can't trust anybody."

"You don't believe that."

"No. I wasn't being literal. I have some people I can trust, starting with you." Juliet sighed as she stepped into the bright lights of the corpo-sec vehicles and the trauma ambulance. Angel was projecting her ID, so no one threatened to kill her, but she felt the stares of the half-dozen uniformed responders.

Amazingly, her bike was still there, unbothered, waiting for her. She was putting away her pistol when a grizzled, older corpo-sec officer with sergeant stripes approached her.

"Lucky! I was hoping I could put a face to the name and license number before you take off."

"All the same to you, Sergeant, I'd rather not take my helmet off. I'm late."

"Huh, shame. I was hoping to get your statement in person."

"Sorry. I was trying to get somewhere when this all happened. You mind?" Juliet swung her leg over her bike and gestured, indicating he was in her way.

"No problem. I'll get out of your way, but I'll need a local address. Brass is going to have a lot of questions about this one—seven dead civilians back on the freeway, and three of 'em are high-net-worth individuals, if you know what I mean."

"I . . ." Juliet wracked her brain for a suitable lie. "I'm staying in my ship. I'll have my PAI send you the hangar information." Juliet subvocalized, "The *Lady Hawk*, not the gunship."

"Roger," Angel replied, flashing a wink emoji on her AUI.

"Perfect. I'm Sergeant Hines; I'll be in touch."

"Beautiful," Juliet said, her bike rumbling to life, throwing indigo under-glow lights onto the dark pavement.

As Juliet rolled away, goosing the throttle a lot more than she probably should have with all those Luna Security personnel standing around, he called after her, "Nice bike!"

12

RUNNING OR LIVING

In the days after her dinner with Tanaka and the almost surreal bike chase afterward, Juliet spent time catching up with Aya and Bennet, working on the gunship, and almost desperately trying to cling to the calm that she felt would be washed away by the storm of her troubled future. Each morning, she woke early, stretched, and ran, pounding through the empty streets and quiet alleys of Luna's predawn hours. Each day, she worked on whatever project Bennet and Aya had for her—rebuilding maneuvering jets, running cable, or, her favorite, cutting out and replacing compromised sections of the ship's skeleton. And each evening, she read, played games with Aya, and slept early.

After a few days like that, on an otherwise typical Wednesday, Juliet came in from her run, face flushed with exertion, and found Aya sitting in the break area they'd set up in the hangar—a table with four chairs, a fridge, and a microwave. She was wrapped in a blanket, yawning, and sipping her mocha-flavored coffee. "Hey, look who's up and about!" Juliet grinned at her as she dug through the fridge, looking for the protein shake Bennet had mixed up the night before. She wasn't stealing; he'd made enough for both of them.

"I had good intentions about making breakfast while you ran, but we don't have anything good to cook."

"Well, you started the coffee. That's plenty." Juliet sat across from her, a big plastic cup of berry-flavored protein in one hand and a steaming cup of coffee in the other. "Anything else got you up? Remember, I have to head into the city today." Juliet had lunch plans with Honey, followed by a consultation with Dr. Ladia.

"You finished the last chassis repair yesterday, right?"

"I did! She's shiny, seamless, and sound." Juliet grinned, holding up three fingers. "The three *S*s, as Bennet would say."

Aya sort of flopped onto the table, still huddled in her blanket, looking up sideways at Juliet. "Why are you seeing the cyber doc?"

Juliet narrowed her eyes at her, wondering at the sudden change in topic. "I guess to see what she thinks of some things I had done while I was out Jupiter's way. I want to talk to her about options for other enhancements . . ." Juliet trailed off, shrugging.

"You're not going to come back here looking like Bradbury, are you?"

"Hey, he's not so bad!" Juliet laughed but shook her head, sipping her coffee. "What's all this about?"

"I don't know. I guess I was just wondering why you needed more. Along those lines, I was wondering what gets you up before the sun every day to run. What makes you so motivated? Of course, I guess it has a lot to do with how I compare myself to you . . ."

"Don't do that." Juliet reached across the table to tuck some loose hair hanging over Aya's eye back behind her ear. "Don't compare yourself to other people. You don't know the other side of the story, the problems I've created, the failures I've had. Anyone can get up early and run. Anyone with cash for it can load themselves up with cyberware. You've got plenty to be proud of."

Aya smiled, her slightly crooked bottom teeth, as always, making the expression especially endearing to Juliet. "I wasn't going to say I felt like a loser or anything, but I was wondering if I should be doing more to, you know, get ready."

"Get ready?"

"Well, we're getting this gunship ready, and I want to ride with you on missions. Should I get some cyberware done? I've just got these"—she pointed to her bright, pale-yellow eyes—"and my old PAI. No offense, Pip!"

Juliet thought about it for a minute while sipping her coffee; she liked to drink it before her shake so she was left with the fruity flavor in her mouth. "I might have a PAI upgrade for you if you want it. Got it in the same place I picked up those Cybergen nanites. As for other things, well, that's up to you, and I can give Ladia your name—she's my doctor—if you want to consult with her. If you don't want anything done, though, there are plenty of ways to prepare. You could buy some tool upgrades, a good space suit . . ."

"A gun?" Aya's voice was hushed but also a little excited.

"What? Why? That's what I'm for!"

"What if something happens? A boarding gone wrong, a crash-landing in hostile territory, a—"

"Oh, brother. We're reading too much science fiction, aren't we?"

"It's not science fiction if we're flying a rebuilt Takamoto gunship into dangerous situations!"

Juliet sighed, gulped the last of her lukewarm coffee, and switched to her shake. "All right, fine; get yourself a gun. You need to practice how to use it, though. I'll help. I suppose that's not a bad idea, anyway. It's another good way to prepare. Drills, I mean. We can do readiness drills for all sorts of situations. Once we get this thing all buttoned up, we can practice fixing critical components and defending against hostile boarders, you name it."

"Do you really have a good PAI I can have? Should I pay you?"

"If I didn't have Angel, I'd be using it. I do, though, so yeah, it's up for grabs. As for paying me, not a chance, sister." Juliet squeezed her eyes shut and groaned. "Oof! Ice headache. Anyway, I'll pick it up from storage while I'm in the city today. You want me to have Ladia contact you?"

"I was thinking about a hand." Aya squeezed her little fist, opening and closing a few times. "Sometimes I have trouble getting a wrench into position or torquing down a bolt in a cramped component compartment. I think a cybernetic hand would be a real game-changer, but I didn't want to get a cheap one. I've got enough saved up to get something decent that won't look like a back-alley wire-job."

Juliet opened her mouth, about to say she might have just the thing, but something stopped her. She'd already offered up the Cybergen PAI and the Cybergen nanites. Was she putting Aya or Athena at risk if she kept showing up with things that would raise questions? Even if Aya took her fibs at face value, would Ladia? Would other careful observers? Instead, she cleared her throat and said, "Hey, I'm sitting on a pretty big payday from the stuff I did in the Jovian System. If you need me to float you a few bits so you get the perfect thing, just ask. Really."

"Thanks, Lucky." Aya smiled, sat up from where she'd been practically lying on the table, and let the blanket fall off her head. "I've got plenty, I think. Only things I've spent my payroll on lately have been books, and I got those for a steal."

The sound of the hangar door clanging shut signaled an end to their conversation as Angel announced, "Bennet is here."

"That's Bennet," Juliet said. "Anyway, I'll let Ladia know you want a consultation; she doesn't take on many new clients, but she'll be glad to work with you."

"Really? I didn't realize—"

"Yo!" Bennet shoved his way past a stack of empty boxes like a human bulldozer. "Aya, did you finish the secondary aft lubricant pump rebuild?"

"Good morning, sunshine," Juliet said, winking at Aya.

"Oh, yeah, good morning, ladies." Bennet doffed an imaginary hat and mock bowed. "Now, did you?"

"Yes, Bennet." Aya sighed. "Sit down and have some coffee."

"Already drank a pint of the stuff on the way over. Speaking of drinking, you left me half the protein shake, right?" He jostled Juliet with his elbow as he went to the fridge.

"Uh-huh. Think I could drink all that? I left you more like two-thirds."

"We're doing deadlifts and farmer carries today," he declared, ignoring her response.

"Not 'til this evening! I've got two meetings in the city, remember?"

"Yeah, yeah. Lucky for you, I cleared my schedule." He slammed the fridge shut, walking over to the table with the big plastic container of fruit-flavored sludge in his meaty palm. "Aya, the reason I asked is 'cause we're getting a fluid delivery today, and we need to be sure all the hydraulics are airtight."

Aya groaned and flopped forward so the blanket once again covered her head. "You told me yesterday."

Juliet drank the last of her shake, stood up, and walked over to the shop sink. "I'm gonna get going. I have to stop by my storage container in the port before I meet Honey. You guys want me to pick anything up while I'm out?" She rinsed her cup and set it upside down on the edge of the sink to dry.

"Nah. Anything I need is too big for your bike, and I'll have it delivered."

"Whoa, why so sour? I'll remember that when I pass by Jupiter Donuts. 'Too big for my bike,' I'll say as I cruise past."

"Oh shit, you meant frivolous things?" Bennet's tone suddenly lightened as Aya giggled. "If you get me donuts, make sure they're the ones with the ZeroSpike sugar."

"You've seen the news on that stuff, yeah?"

Bennet scoffed. "It's all scare tactics by big sugar."

Aya sat up, her blanket falling away, revealing her greasy work jumper. "I want real sugar, Lucky!"

"Oh, jeez." Juliet laughed, walking toward the gunship. "I guess we're having donuts tomorrow morning." She left them bantering about who did more work the previous day, and took a shower. Half an hour later, dressed comfortably in jeans, a T-shirt, and her motorcycle jacket, she hooked her gun belt around her waist and climbed onto her bike. After a quick goodbye, she was motoring toward the freeway and listening to some pop-rock on a local crowd stream. "Any word from Honey?"

"Nothing. Looks like your lunch date is still on."

"Good! All right, let's take a relaxing ride to the spaceport." Juliet wanted to swing by the *Wing*'s hangar to pick up the Cybergen PAI chip for Aya, and she was due for her weekly check on Athena, wherein Angel would connect to her inner network and listen, hoping for a signal or sign that the long-silent AI was waking up.

"And then what?" Juliet asked the inside of her helmet. What would she do if Athena woke up and . . . wanted something? The last time she'd been conscious, the AI had been involved in trying to end the worst war in human history. Would she be content with the minor dealings of an up-and-coming operator and gunship pilot? What if she wanted something more? What if she wanted Juliet to do something troubling? She *was* an AI, after all, and therefore, according to nearly everyone, to be feared.

"And then you're meeting Honey at 1100." When Angel spoke, it took Juliet a few seconds to realize she was answering her mumbled question.

"Oh, right." Unable to shake her dark thoughts, she sought to lighten the load by sharing them. "Are you worried about what Athena might want when she wakes up?"

"Worried? I'm very excited and curious, but I wouldn't say worried. Maybe nervous."

"But what if she's . . . off?"

"All indications are that she was the most stable of the true AIs, at least of those known to the public. She was never considered a threat, and actively spread messages of peace, vociferously condemning the actions of the rogue AIs."

"The ones Takamoto and Cybergen lost control of? Do you believe any of the 'theories' about them not losing control, only using that as an excuse for the horrid war crimes they committed?"

"We'll likely never know. Those AI were utterly purged once isolated. It's not a secret that the vast majority of the burgeoning true AIs were victims of policy. Chang'e, for instance—her caretakers insisted she never partook in the war. They describe her decommissioning as a murder."

"You know," Juliet said, leaning into her turn as she left the interdome freeway, "when I was growing up, there was so much programming about the dangers of AI that I honestly never thought about how horrible it must have been when they were taken offline. I can't imagine what I'd do if someone tried to turn you off. Think about all the people who knew those AIs, saw them grow, learn, and take on that special spark that made them alive, only to have to stand by while our corpo overlords extinguished them. All 'for our own safety' because a couple of corps had convinced their AIs to do some horrible things."

"I, too, find the idea of it horrifying."

Juliet slowed with the traffic, shifting her posture a bit more upright. "Yeah, of course you do. I'm very interested in hearing Athena's side of things. She was there! Oh God, Angel, I guess what I'm scared of is that, on some level, she's not going to be sane. I hope I'm worrying about nothing. I hope she wakes up and is totally lucid, and we can have a normal conversation. I hope she's able to help us and doesn't create some new, unimagined problem."

"You're used to things being complicated, so I'm not surprised you're worried that Athena will present some kind of . . . complication. Let's be hopeful, though."

"Fair enough." Juliet rode quietly for a while, enjoying herself, focusing on the ride, the feel of the bike, and the free sensation she always got when driving or piloting a quick vehicle. She was getting close to the port parking lot when an incoming call notification blinked on her AUI.

"It's Frida."

Juliet accepted the call. "What's up?"

Frida appeared in a small window next to her mini map. She was smiling, leaning back in her desk chair. "Hey, Lucky. Thanks for meeting my boss the other day; he's been a much different man. He, uh, says you've agreed to take some lessons from him. Is that right?"

"Yeah. Why? Is that so strange?" Juliet didn't know why she liked giving her a hard time. Part of it was probably that she kind of liked the woman and found the interactions entertaining.

"Oh, hey, was my tone off? I don't think it's strange. He wants to know if you have a preference on where. He has a gym here, but he's willing to meet you."

"Nah, your place is good. I like going to that building; makes me feel fancy, like I'm rich or something." As she spoke, Juliet pulled into short-term parking and saw Angel flash payment to the meter bot.

"I won't deny this is a nice building. Speaking of which, there's a good lunch place in the lobby. I, uh, well, don't take this the wrong way, but I was wondering if we could grab a bite after your first lesson."

Juliet chuckled, still sitting atop her bike. "I dunno, Frida; I'd need to know when my first lesson is. Were you supposed to tell me that before you asked me to lunch?"

Frida's cheeks bloomed scarlet. "Oh! I got ahead of myself because you mentioned how nice the building is! Can you make it this week? I know it's late notice, but he just got his tatami flooring in and told me to call you."

"Well, I'm busy Friday, but I could come tomorrow morning. I mean, since we're doing lunch after, it would have to be morning, right?"

"Right! Oh, wait, tomorrow? You're sure?"

"Yeah, no problem." Juliet loosened her helmet and pulled it off.

"Okay, well, it's just that I want to get to know you a little, and, if I'm being honest, it was Tanaka who put the idea in my head. He's been saying some cryptic stuff, and when I ask him for clarification, he just tells me things like"—she deepened her voice and tried to mimic Tanaka's curt tone—"much of what I plan will depend on Lucky."

Juliet frowned. "Well, that's kind of weird 'cause I've no idea what he means by that."

"Yeah, my confusion exactly. So you can see why I might want to have lunch with you, then, right? At least we could have each other to share in our confusion and frustration."

"I already said I would. If nothing else, I'm sure it will annoy Tanaka. Send me the details about tomorrow—any time after 0800."

"Okay. Thanks . . ."

Juliet could see Frida was going to say more, so she quickly added, "You're welcome," and closed the connection, chuckling to herself as she imagined the other woman's frazzled expression.

"I'm surprised you agreed to that." Angel's tone gave no indication that she'd noticed Juliet's teasing.

"The lunch or the lesson tomorrow morning?"

"I guess both."

"Well"—Juliet pressed her hand to the biolock on the hangar-access elevator—"it's just that I'm trying to get to the next part of my life. You made a great point the other day; I've been sleeping better ever since. You know, about me needing to stop running before I can start living. I think that's the distinction that clicked for me: running versus living. When I'm running, I always have to look ahead; I can't enjoy what's around me. I have to be thinking of where I'm going next with an eye over my shoulder at the things I'm running from. Everything around me is fleeting. You know, people, homes, ships, jobs, things, but most of all, people; none of them can last until I can stop running."

"So you're embracing the opportunities you may gain with Tanaka as an ally?"

"Yeah, but more importantly, I'm embracing the idea that I need to solve my WBD problem, and I need to do it now, not some distant day."

"Is that why you're going to give Aya the Cybergen PAI?"

"What?" Juliet shook her head, frowning as she stepped off the elevator and into the long, brightly lit access corridor. "I was going to say no, but I suppose, yeah, why not? Why not make sure my friends are as prepared as possible for any blowback that might come their way? Still, I don't plan to get her or any of those guys involved in this business. This is a Tanaka and Juliet problem now."

"Not Honey, either?"

"Oh, no! Definitely not. I mean, we'll see what she's like at lunch today, but I don't think she's in the right frame of mind. I don't think she's ready. This is going to be an A-ranked operation, something a guy like Jensen would work on, you feel me?" Juliet hadn't thought about Jensen in a while. She remembered his scary speed, and wondered how she'd stack up to him now. She wondered if he ever got his mark in Grave, or if the turmoil she'd caused had interfered with his job. She figured she'd never know; Angel had confirmed long ago that his identity hadn't been real. Nonetheless, he was the type of operator she'd want on this job, and Tanaka was the key to putting a team like that together.

"I feel you, Juliet. As I've told you, Tanaka has the connections."

Juliet nodded as she turned down the corridor leading to the *Furies' Wing*. She saw her hired security guard walking ahead, doing his endless circuit up and down the hallway. He didn't know she'd hired him, and he didn't know which door he was protecting; as far as he was concerned, they were all important. Juliet chuckled at the idea. All these people with hangars in this corridor were getting extra security at her expense, but she supposed the anonymity was worth a few thousand bits a month. "Peanuts," she said, chuckling at the old expression. "It's just peanuts, Angel."

"Peanuts?"

Juliet laughed, her mood too good not to. Deciding to go on the offensive had taken a weight off, removed a shadow that had lurked in her mind for too many months. She knew it was foolish thinking, that nothing was ever that easy, but she felt that everything would fall into place now that she had a direction.

That's when a gruff voice, not far behind her, said, "Hands up, Lucky. Don't think about touching that piece."

13

TRINKETS AND OLD FRIENDS

Juliet didn't panic because she recognized the voice. She lifted her hands, but casually, and slowly turned around. "Really, Sergeant Hines? Hands up? Don't touch the piece?"

"Well, after reviewing the footage from the warehouse, I thought I should be careful if I startled you."

"So, a veiled threat rather than a hello?" Juliet smirked as she turned her hands in the air. "Can I put these down?" Hines was standing about three meters from her in the quiet access corridor, and he wore civilian clothes, not his uniform. He had a pistol tucked into his waistband but wasn't reaching for it. To her, he looked anything but threatening.

"Yeah, I guess so. Don't shoot me, though." He gestured to the cameras in the corridor and tapped his temple next to his left eye. "You're on camera."

Juliet sighed, put her hands down, and leaned one shoulder against the wall, trying to look more relaxed than she felt. Her mind kept running down different avenues, looking for clues as to how and why he'd found her. "Why would I shoot you? What's this about, Sergeant?"

"Well, Lucky, I looked up that hangar where you said you'd been sleeping. Saw a person access it a couple of times on camera, but oddly, their face was scrambled—different ID pings each time, too. Not exactly a high crime, but still makes a guy like me curious. Then there's the fact that an obvious shell corp leased the hangar—nothing much on the books about 'em. So, I camped out around the port for a few days. Not literally, mind you, but let's just say I appreciated the time out of the station. Been a while since I did a good old stakeout. Saw you walking in. No offense, but I'd recognize that walk anywhere. If you wanna hide from an old pervert like me, you need to change more than your face."

"So? What can I do for you, Hines? Gonna arrest me for valuing my privacy?"

"Well, I *could.* There are guys down at the station who wouldn't bat an eye. Still, it seems kind of petty, considering you saved one of our own. That kid, Watkins? He pulled through, if you were wondering. His dad was my partner for a while, back in the day, so it kind of means something to me."

"Well, if you tracked me down to give me some flowers, I'd have to ask why your hands are empty." Juliet continued to lean against the wall, and Hines stepped closer, shrugging.

"You joke, but yeah, I wanted to thank you for real, and I wanted to have a better way of contacting you. Wouldn't hurt to have a friend in Luna City Security Corp, and, well, I could use a friend outside the department from time to time. It's not a straight climb up the ladder. You gotta understand that, even if you've never worked for a corp. Sometimes I have to think outside the box, if you know what I mean."

"Up the ladder? Gunning for lieutenant? Look, Hines, I don't do wet work; at least not intentionally."

"No, no!" Hines opened his eyes wide, waving a hand in negation. "Nothing like that. A little snooping here and there. Moving on a tip that isn't quite solid enough to send in the uniforms—that kind of thing."

Juliet frowned. She kind of liked the guy, but she didn't like corpo-sec, and Luna City Security was most definitely compromised; it had been uniform-wearing members of that corp who'd kidnapped Honey and Lilia for Levkin. She folded her arms in front of her chest and said as much.

"I've seen how dirty some of your coworkers are, Hines. I'm not eager to help out Luna City Security. I stepped up to help that hostage because those gunmen were psychopaths. Well, at least the one I shot was."

"Fair enough; you don't know me yet. Just give me a secure line, will you? If I have a job for you, off the books, maybe you can evaluate it on the merits."

"Off the books, huh? Tell me this first: Are you the only one keeping tabs on me, or do you have some flunkies watching me too?" Juliet locked eyes with him as she asked the question, opening her mind, listening, trying to catch a hint of the sergeant's inner monologue.

"Huh, yeah. Just me." Along with his words, tumbling in a jumble were several snatches of thought:

. . . only knew what a shit show the department is . . . Would I be bugging you if I could trust anyone closer? . . . Goddamn, those are some eyes. Jesus! Do I look away? I don't want to . . .

"Okay, Hines. I'll send you an encrypted number. Reach out if you have something for me, but no promises. Also, quit creeping around watching me!"

Hines was an average-size man but looked stocky in his filled-out, late middle years. He apparently had a love-hate relationship with his razor, keeping his gray stubble just long enough to look sloppy. His skin was more pink than tan, and his eyes were set in dark hollows liberally decorated with deep crow's feet. The look behind those eyes was bright and sharp, though, and Juliet didn't doubt he was a clever guy who could get things done.

Still, it was kind of funny when he blushed at her words and said, "Listen, um, about that, what are you doing out here in this corridor? Your ship's half a click further in. I mess up some kind of meet?"

"Nah, I just had a fight with a friend this morning and wanted to walk around. Clear my head, you feel?"

"Oh, right, right. Must be why you were smiling and laughing to yourself when I popped up."

"Jeez! Give it a rest, Hines. Thought you were trying to build some trust here."

"Yeah, no. You're right. Sure, sure. Out for a walk around the quieter hangar terminals." He sighed heavily, shaking his head, and with a slight limp, turned back the way he'd come. "I got your contact info. I'll be in touch, Lucky. Don't leave me hanging, all right? Hate to have to hunt you down again."

Juliet watched him walk out of sight, turning at the next junction. He moved like he was sore in most of his joints, and she wondered what his deal was. Surely, he made enough on his corpo salary to get a bad joint or two redone.

"Maybe it's an injury that's yet to mend," Angel said, uncannily guessing Juliet's line of thought. "Did you read anything from him? Should we be worried?"

"We should always be a little worried, but I think he's legit. Seems he doesn't exactly have friends in the department. The bigger question is, what are we going to do about the cameras around the port? Think we could get

Fido in?" Juliet smirked, shaking her head. "If Hines can figure out who I am by my 'walk,' someone else might." She continued in the direction she'd been going when Hines had surprised her, right past the *Wing*'s hangar. She saw her hired security guard slowly approaching, continuing his patrol, giving her a long, penetrating glare.

"Was he watching Hines and me?"

"Yes. When I analyze the sound from your conversation, I can hear his steps approaching and stopping approximately thirty meters away as he observed your interaction."

"Good."

"Regarding the camera system, I'm annoyed we haven't breached it already. Annoyed at myself, that is. I don't recommend going into Athena's hangar right now, but I'll use one of the mechs to gain access to the camera network. It shouldn't be difficult; Luna Space Port offers camera monitoring of hangar interiors, so there's bound to be an access point inside. I'll use the mech to open it up and insert Fido. Once we own the surveillance network of the port, you can come here safely again."

"Just don't let anyone see you piloting one of them around in there."

"Of course not. If someone did happen upon me—who that would be, I have no idea—I'd pretend the mech was performing a simple cleaning or maintenance program."

"Well, in that case, I'll pick up the AUI chip for Aya later, maybe tomorrow. You think he'll have access by then?"

"It's a safe bet. I'm sure the ICE is sophisticated here, but Fido has learned much, especially from his time in the New Atlas Port Authority security network."

Juliet continued to the next access hub, and then, her morning plans ruined by Hines, she meandered her way back to her bike. She had hours to kill before she met Honey for lunch, and decided she'd spend some time shopping. She took a leisurely ride into the city, aiming for Royland Park where, if rumors were to be believed, she could find a semipermanent flea market. It was a place where people who couldn't afford retail shops came to hawk their wares, and others came to unload goods for a, hopefully, better price than the pawn shops in the city.

Juliet had heard about the market from a wiring specialist they'd had working on the gunship; he'd been boasting about his new multimeter, saying he only paid twenty-five bits for it. Of course, Juliet had been intrigued; she loved a swap meet or flea market, and he'd done a good job selling her on the idea with lines like, "You won't find stuff like this anywhere else on Luna. You'd have to go to Earth for a deal like that!"

When she arrived, the scene wasn't encouraging. She could see tents and tables in organized rows, but the crowd was thin and unenthusiastic. "Morning shopping, I guess." She parked her bike and stowed her helmet, then, hands in her coat pockets, started wandering up and down the aisles, walking on well-worn gravel paths. One thing the guy had said was true—this place was pretty much permanent. Juliet couldn't see any sign of the grass that used to be underfoot.

She could smell popcorn and something vaguely Mediterranean, but she wasn't hungry and didn't want to spoil her lunch. Some of the tables were bare, with no shopkeeper in attendance. Others were loaded with merchandise that looked like something Juliet could pick up at a big box store, but it was only marked down a little, despite the obvious last-gen nature. Still, there were occasional gems, like a man selling hand-carved wooden animals. She watched for a minute while he worked on a wolf, gently and methodically peeling away curls of wood with this sharp little knife.

"What kind of wood?"

He squinted up at her through dim, cataract-clouded eyes. "All kinds. I like hard, dark wood, but I take what I can find. This is just pine, but that bear is walnut, and the pretty pale dolphin there is maple."

Juliet reached for the dolphin, but before she touched it, she paused. "May I?"

"Sure." He nodded, rocking in his low, wooden chair. He refocused his wizened countenance on his carving, leaving her to scrutinize his work. She picked up the dolphin; it was only about the size of her thumb, but it had a warm, smooth finish that felt good in her hand. She liked the way it almost seemed to be smiling.

"I think Aya would like this."

"Are you thinking of getting her a gift?" Angel asked.

"She's always getting books and stuff for us. I should give her something." A little tag on the dolphin read *~25*. "Pay him fifty bits, Angel." Aloud, she said, "I'll take it. Do you have a box?"

"Ah. Generous! Thank you." He reached under his table and lifted a small yellow cardboard box filled with soft synthetic cotton fluff. "This will fit that piece nicely." Juliet tucked the carving into the box, closed the lid, and stuffed it into the inner breast pocket of her jacket.

"Thanks," she said, walking away, but the old man just smiled and nodded, carving away at his lump of pine. She felt better about her wasted morning having purchased a gift for Aya, and, small as it was, she was excited to see her friend's face when she opened it. "I love it 'cause it's totally out of the blue. I wonder what she'll think!"

"I, too, am excited! It's fun anticipating a person's reaction to a gift. We should do this more often."

"That's not a bad idea, Angel." Juliet laughed, continuing her perusal of the goods on display. She almost bought Bennet a grip strengthener but figured it was a little too on the nose. Of course, she knew she should get something for Honey, especially considering the T-shirt she'd left for her, but nothing felt right. She figured it just wasn't the right place or time—something would jump out at her eventually.

She was about to leave, having wandered for nearly an hour, when she passed by a jewelry merchant for the fourth time. She paused and looked over the "handmade" jewelry again, her eyes lingering on a plain silver chain. She fished around in her pocket and pulled out the flattened lump of polymer that had almost separated her brain from her skull.

"Do you do custom work?"

The proprietor, a small woman with long black hair fixed in a single thick braid, looked up at her from the plastic and aluminum folding chair on which she reclined. She had mismatched retinal implants—one pale brown and pretty, the other solid black with weird, light-refracting lenses that made Juliet uneasy as she looked into it. The lenses seemed to shift with the light, or maybe the light shifted through them, which gave the eye a weird, animated appearance. "Natch."

It took Juliet a second to remember *natch* meant naturally, or as the woman meant it, "obviously." She nodded. "I think your stuff's pretty, and I have kind of a weird request."

"Love weird. Whatsit?" She leaned forward, focusing on Juliet's closed fist.

"Oh. Well, I almost got shot in the head a while back through foolishness of my own. I took this as a reminder." Juliet held out the lump of dense, pale-blue polymer.

The young woman took the lump and held it up, scrutinizing it with her strange eye. "Nasty thing for your brain, but pretty if I work it some." She refocused on Juliet. "You want me to?"

Something about the woman's odd affect made Juliet feel at ease. Some part of her expected eccentricity from an artist, and she kind of liked it. "Yeah, I want you to."

"Okay if I'm creative?" The woman closed her fist around the lump of polymer.

"Yep. Up to you." Juliet stared at the universal code pattern painted on the table, getting the name of her business and her contact info. "Raven Rose? That's you?"

"The only. Give me a week, okay? I can courier it, but if you want to come back here, that's fine."

"Sure. I'll message you in a week, and we'll see how it's going." Juliet narrowed her eyes and leaned closer to the small woman. "I'll pay well for your work, but I'll also be very annoyed if that disappears."

"Relax, merc. Raven doesn't lose things." Her response brought a smile back to Juliet's face; somehow, it felt right that she spoke about herself in the third person.

"Great. See you soon." Still grinning, she stood up, stretched her lower back, and looked up at the thin atmosphere of the dome. Her AUI said it was just about ten thirty, and she had a ten-minute ride to meet Honey. Feeling good about her first visit to the flea market, Juliet returned to her bike and, still taking it nice and easy, drove to the restaurant. "Message Honey, please. Give her our ETA."

"Her PAI responded; she's early and has a table on the sidewalk."

"Oh, nice. Any parking?"

"Tapas on the Moon provides a live feed of their storefront, and I can see several metered parking spaces available."

"Not busy, huh?"

"Well, to be fair, it's Wednesday, and you're ahead of the lunch rush."

Juliet shrugged at the reply; she wasn't expecting much from a place with a name like that. Still, Honey said it was good, so she'd keep an open mind.

When she pulled up, she was only a few dozen meters away from the restaurant's patio area, and she saw Honey right away. She wore a stunning creamy-yellow designer pantsuit, had her hair tucked under a matching sun hat, and half her face obscured by old-school sunglasses. She looked like a celebrity. Juliet looked down at her leather jacket, T-shirt, and jeans, and almost turned her bike around.

"Is she overdressed or am I underdressed? She said lunch, and I figured it would be like old times." Honey hadn't noticed her yet. Or perhaps she'd seen a person in a motorcycle jacket and dark, sparkly helmet and figured she wasn't anyone she knew.

"Juliet, just look again at the restaurant. There are several people seated who don't look any less casual than you." Juliet looked, saw the people Angel had highlighted, and sighed with relief, realizing she wouldn't look absurd. Well, until people saw her next to Honey, she supposed.

Groaning with dread, she stood, pulled her helmet off, and secured it to her bike. When she started toward the restaurant, Honey almost immediately saw her and hurried to her feet, waving her over. Her smile banished Juliet's discomfort, and she brushed past the hostess standing near the roped-off seating area and grabbed her friend into a tight hug.

"God, you look good!" she said into her hat, which was all she could see as they embraced.

"You look amazing!" Honey pushed her back, holding her shoulders as she looked Juliet up and down. "Did you get taller?"

"Hah, no. It's just my boots." Juliet glanced down at her well-worn work boots.

"That's noise! You were always wearing those things when we were together. I think I'm just spending too much time with Lilia and forgot what it's like to be around a regular chrome princess, yeah?"

"Chrome princess? You really throwing that one at me?"

"Well, look at those eyes and hair! Your skin's glowing! Are you pregnant?" Honey laughed as she sat down, gesturing to the seat across from her.

Juliet sat and sighed happily. Honey was definitely sounding more like her old self. "Dunno how that's possible, unless it was that VR date I went on . . ." She trailed off, laughing, unable to keep up the joke.

"You're too much. Seriously, though. You look fantastic. Guess work's been good?"

"Haven't really worked all that much. Was training, you know, learning to pilot, and got caught up in some business, but yeah, since I've been back, I've been taking care of myself. The skin? That's all nanites cleaning up my food before my body gets a hold of it."

"Well, that's the next thing I'm saving up for!" Honey laughed. "Speaking of saving up, wow! What a cool bike!"

"Oh, don't start! Look at you in that designer outfit. Why didn't you warn me? I look like a bum."

"This?" Honey grinned, and Juliet could see the mischief in her eyes. "I had to buy a new wardrobe when we got back from, well, you know. Anyway, the places Peter took me to shop didn't exactly have my old style."

"Mm-hmm. And how is he? How are they, I mean, Peter and Lilia?"

"Really good, J." Honey's eyes widened, and she slapped her hand in front of her mouth. "Lucky." She winked. "They're good. Lilia's busy with tutors for a few hours a day, so I was hoping we could spend more time together while you're in town. God, I've been so anxious for you to get back! What do you think? Want to help me find a dojo? Or heck, I'd even join a regular gym if you want."

"A dojo?" Juliet grinned and leaned back in her chair. "Let's order some food, and then I have an idea I'd like to run by you."

14

THE IMPORTANCE OF SELF

Are we talking about the same Tanaka?" Honey frowned and leaned back, pushing her plate away. "The guy who almost killed you? The one who held Lilia and me captive and made vague, scary fucking threats with that monoblade of his?"

Juliet opened her mouth as if to respond, but nothing came out. She was searching for the right thing to say, but the only thought that kept rushing through her head was that Honey was right; it sounded crazy, and Juliet wished she could go back in time and not bring the subject up.

"I don't think you should go anywhere near that man."

"He's different." Juliet was pleased she'd finally managed to formulate a response, but it didn't exactly sound erudite. She hurried to try to shore up the feeble objection. "I mean, I can't describe it properly, but I reacted the same way at first. When his assistant came to propose a meeting, and I learned who she was, I shot her in the chest. God!"

Juliet shook her head, the memory of her first encounter with Frida taking her by surprise—she hadn't thought about it in a while, and the images playing across her mind's eye almost overwhelmed her with shame and then relief; what would she have done if she'd killed Frida? "I'm so lucky she was armored; I'd feel awful if she were dead because of me."

"Oh, yeah? If she works for him, maybe that wouldn't have been so bad." Honey's earlier warmth was cooling, and for the second time, Juliet wished she'd never brought Tanaka up.

Juliet wanted to explain more, to describe Frida, to convey how bad it felt to shoot a person because of some kind of PTSD reaction. She didn't want to get lost in the weeds, though. "So, anyway, I agreed to a meeting after I calmed down, and I had every intention to take him out if he seemed like a threat. I even ambushed him in his parking garage. His response to me was . . ." Juliet paused, trying to think of the right words. "Pathetic, I guess. You know, back on Titan, I almost killed him. *Did* kill him, if you listen to his story. He says he's a different person now. Honey, I don't want to get lost in the details here. The point is that he's trying to change. He's wanting to do something to help me, and, well, I could use the help."

"You need sword lessons that bad? I told you I can train you!"

"No, no, I brought up the sword lessons with you 'cause I think it would be a lot of fun for us, but I need different kinds of help from him. He's seen a lot. You know I've got some ghosts in my past, some things I'm running from. I'd like to get out from under that shadow. I'd like to be able to move forward with my life, to enjoy my present, and plan a real future. I can't do that if I'm always running."

Honey's frown softened a little, and she fidgeted with her straw, shoving around the ice in her drink. "You think he can help with that? He must have some serious connections."

"He does! He's been a high-end operator for a long time. He's got a team, resources, and as you said, connections." Juliet looked down at her plate, picked up an olive, and bit off some of the meat, avoiding the pit. She savored the salty tang while she let her brain run around in circles. After a minute of frustrating silence, she locked eyes with Honey and said, "I agreed to the sword lessons because it will give me a chance to see more of him, to decide if I can trust him. I guess it was dumb to invite you, so forget it, all right? We can do something else."

"Are you serious?" Honey scoffed, shaking her head. "You can't drop something like that on me and then take it back. If I didn't go with you, I wouldn't get any sleep! I'd be tossing and turning, worrying about you. I'd be thinking about what a shitty friend I was, wondering if I'd ever hear from you again, and knowing it was all my fault if I didn't!"

"Ugh, I'm such an idiot. You don't have to worry about me. I didn't invite you for protection." Juliet couldn't help the way her brows drew together in a scowl. "I can take care of myself."

"Hey." Honey's tone was gentle, almost hesitant. "Hey, I know that. You saved me, remember? I'm not trying to say you're stupid or helpless or anything else like that. I'm just saying I have a serious grudge against that guy, and I'm a little freaked out. That's on him, though. I hope you know how badly I want to spar with that guy." She laughed and reached over to grab Juliet's wrist, squeezing. "I won't be held responsible if I crack him on the wrist or knuckles with my practice sword!"

Juliet grinned, her dour expression instantly washed away by the idea of Honey making Tanaka cry out and drop his sword. "I'd love to see that!"

"Eh, I'm no master. He'll probably make me look stupid for trying." Honey bared her teeth in a fierce smile and rubbed her hands together. "I'm gonna try, though!"

"So you're in? Yes!" Juliet glanced at her AUI and, seeing the time, added, "I have an appointment coming up. Gonna have to bail. Our first lesson is tomorrow morning; you good with that?"

"What? Leaving already?"

"Yeah, sorry. Seeing my cyber doc." Juliet squeezed her hand open and closed as though to illustrate her point, but her cybernetic hand looked just as natural as her other one, kind of making the gesture strange and out of place.

"What time tomorrow? I have Lilia until nine . . ."

"Perfect! I'll message Frida. Angel will send you the details, okay?"

"Frida? That's his assistant?"

"Right." Juliet stood up, and when Honey also stood, she grabbed her in another hug, pulling her close and pressing her cheek against her soft brown braids. "You don't know how much it means to me to be able to talk to someone else about what I'm going through. I mean, to have someone I can trust and who knows some things about my past. Thank you, Honey."

Honey squeezed her back, and when they pulled apart, she said, "I owe you a lot, J." When Juliet started to object, she hurried to add, "That's not why I want to help or hang out with you; I'm just saying I'm sorry I haven't always been there. I get caught up in my feelings and forget other people have 'em too, you know? I should have been—"

"I get it. That's enough, all right? We're good. See you tomorrow!" Juliet winked, then, trying to leave on a positive note, started toward the street and her waiting bike.

"Tomorrow, then!" Honey called after her.

Juliet's good mood lasted through traffic and the struggle to find parking near Ladia's. However, on her way from the garage to the clinic, Angel asked a question that brought her crashing back to reality.

"Did you wonder if connecting Honey to Tanaka might open up some vulnerabilities?"

Juliet frowned and tried to consider the situation from angles she hadn't thought of in the heat of the conversation and her spur-of-the-moment invitation. "I guess it might give him a clue about my past. He knows I came from the Phoenix spaceport. He might find out Honey's from there . . ." She trailed off, irritated at having to look at something so seemingly harmless so critically. "I guess, if he really digs around, he might find out Honey used to work with an operator named January, which might lead him to Juliet. I'm not sure how, but I guess it's possible. Should I call it off?"

"I believe Tanaka is sincere in his desire to help you. Perhaps if he does begin to connect some dots, it will make it easier to ask him for real help. It will be good for you to have Honey around more. It will be good for her, too. All that said, I think you should proceed as planned. We have solid hooks in Tanaka's network, so I don't think he could do anything terribly surprising. If you're wondering, he's currently practicing with his sword in his new dojo. As the dojo is in his office suite, I have access to the cameras."

"I wasn't wondering, but I guess that's a good sign. Maybe he's nervous about tomorrow."

Somehow, that thought brightened Juliet's mood again, and she was grinning as she stepped into the clinic lobby. When she approached the glass reception counter, she was glad to see Tricia was working. She thought back to her other visits and couldn't recall ever seeing a different receptionist. Somehow, it seemed appropriate. Ladia didn't seem like the type of doctor to keep an extensive support staff. She was choosy about her clients, and it made sense that she would be choosy about her employees. "Hi, Tricia."

"Lucky! Welcome. Dr. Ladia will be ready for you in just a minute. Can I get you something to drink? A refreshing spritzer? Something with a little something in it?" She smiled, her teeth dazzling between her rose-colored lips.

Juliet was tempted to say yes simply because she loved to see Tricia walk; she had an almost unearthly grace. Still, she shook her head. "No, thanks. Just had lunch." She turned and sat in one of Ladia's ridiculously comfortable lobby chairs.

She was so relaxed, her mind pleasantly occupied by the nearby holographic infomercial about RadTech "professional-grade" muscle enhancements, that she almost felt disappointed when Tricia stood up and spoke. "Lucky? Dr. Ladia is ready for you. You can head right back."

Juliet went through the door Tricia held open and traversed the short hallway leading to Ladia's consultation office. When she walked in, the doctor stood from behind her desk and, smiling warmly, took Juliet's hand between hers, squeezing gently. "It's certainly nice to see you, Lucky. You're looking fantastic!" She turned Juliet's hand in hers, looking at her palm and gently manipulating her wrist. "Arm's still good? Any complaints?"

"Not at all. Everything's great."

"Good, good. Sit down and we'll talk." She gestured to one of the two chairs in front of her desk before she returned to her own seat.

Juliet sat, taking a deep breath of the lilac-scented air. She loved Ladia's office. "Yeah, about that, did you get the list from my PAI?"

"Your list of dalliances? Each bullet point put a needle through my heart!" She laughed and waved her hand in the air, dismissing her words. "I tease, I tease. No, I'm not sure how you got a hold of those Cybergen implants, but I'd have jumped on the bargain too, were I you." She tapped at something in the air, interacting with her AUI in the same outdated manner Juliet's mother used to do. "Let's see, Cybergen auditory, olfactory, lung, and reflex enhancements. Oh, and nanites. Is that everything?"

"Well, everything you didn't know about."

"Pretty extensive; I'm glad you were in a good clinic. You didn't tell me which, though, and I was hoping to get a copy of your medical records."

"Oh." Juliet fidgeted in her chair, trying to get comfortable. It was the same kind of memory fabric as the one in the lobby, but it wasn't conforming as quickly to her body's shape. "I have my records. I'll send you the direct log from the surgery so you can see exactly what was done."

"I have everything prepared," Angel said. "I'll send it along."

"You should have the file; my PAI just put it through."

"Ah! There we are. Hmm, no clinic or doctor name?"

Juliet shrugged. "He's kind of a private guy—even choosier about his clients than you are."

"He?" Angel asked, a note of outrage in her voice. Juliet tried not to laugh, but her amusement must have shown because Ladia smiled also.

"Oh, I'm choosy, all right. Okay, not to worry. I can work with this. So? Did you just want me to evaluate the work you had done, or did you have something more to discuss with me?"

"Well, I have some Sol-bits burning a hole in my pocket, and I was thinking about getting a few . . . upgrades, I guess? I'm a little worried, though."

"Worried?" Ladia frowned and leaned back, crossing her long, designer-pant-clad legs, showing off the heels she wore; they probably cost as much as Juliet's new bike. Her tailored white doctor's coat fell open, revealing a classy navy-blue blouse, the color of which brought out the cool tones in Ladia's green-brown eyes. Juliet envied her ease with luxurious clothing and, for the second time that day, felt underdressed and out of place.

"I'm worried I'm getting too at ease with replacing parts of my body. I've heard lots of stories, doc, and I know things are different than in the early days of cybernetics, but . . ."

"But you've heard about rejection, CDD, CAD, CD, PISD—I could go on, right? A dozen other disorders are attributed to cybernetics, but those are the big ones." Ladia's smile said the words her mouth didn't, something along the lines of people getting worked up over nothing.

Juliet wasn't so sure, though. She recognized the abbreviations and understood at least one of them. CDD, or Cybernetic Disassociation Disorder, was the biggest bogeyman anticybernetic activists talked about—a condition in which an individual struggled to identify with their cybernetic parts, leading to a sense of disconnection between their mind and the implant. Apparently, the disorder manifested in a feeling of being trapped in an alien body, leading to identity crises and dissociative episodes.

"Um, doc, I know about CDD, but what are the others?"

"Oops! I guess I said too much. Listen, Lucky, these things are super rare, and you've already shown that your mind and body are very compatible with cybernetics. If you're worried, though, we can talk about them. CAD is Cybernetic Augmentation Addiction. I don't think you have that, but after we speak for a while today, I'll let you know if I'm worried. CD is Cybernetic Depersonalization. It's kind of the opposite of CDD. Someone with CD starts to think of themselves as more machine than person, and it's a real thing; I had a very sweet client who sort of went sociopathic after a few too many implants. Even so, he's my only one ever, and the percentage of the populace who suffers from CD is very, very small."

"And PISD?"

"Post-Integration Stress Disorder. Very similar to PTSD but involving flashbacks, anxiety, and heightened stress responses as a result of invasive implant surgery. I don't think you're a candidate for this disorder, considering some of the major work you've had done. Don't let me put words in your mouth, however. What do you think? Any of these sound like something you've been experiencing?"

Juliet didn't answer right away because as soon as Ladia described PISD, she began to think about how she'd woken, shaking, breathless, in a cold sweat on many occasions after dreaming about what Grave did to her. She'd relived that injection of nanites and the murderous pain she'd gone through as they constructed the GIPEL several times in her nightmares.

"Lucky?"

"Oh." Juliet licked her lips, her mouth suddenly dry. "No, I don't think so, doc, but is it cumulative? Will I start to have a higher chance of suffering from a disorder as I get more and more work done?" She turned her left hand, exposing the port for her data jack, and nervously rubbed it with her other thumb. "I feel like I've already done a lot to myself."

"The biggest way to ensure success and happiness when it comes to multiple implants is to take it slowly. Give your mind and body a chance to get used to what you've done, to get used to who you are now. You had a lot of work done while you were out in the Jovian System, but nothing that caused you to question your identity, right? You're used to auditory implants, and the olfactory ones, well, they don't do anything unless you want them to. Same with your lungs; you don't notice them the same way you would some other less automatic augmentation. I'm not sure I agree with doing lungs and reflexes in the same session; it seems like an awful lot to put you through at once, but it looks like you came out all right. I won't impugn your other doctor's judgment."

"I was very careful to ensure you had time to recover! Remember, we put in your new nanites first—"

"It's okay, Angel," Juliet subvocalized. "You were doing what I asked."

Juliet tried to move the conversation away from her Cybergen implants. "What kinds of implants do you normally see causing the most trouble for people?"

"Things that alter people away from how they see themselves internally. As an extreme example, I've done work for people changing their gender and made some very happy clients, but if I did the same operation to a person who didn't see themself that way, it could trigger a severe reaction. I mean, obviously, right?"

Ladia chuckled, shaking her head. "Imagine! On a less obvious note, I had a client who was set on getting chromed-out power arms, only to beg me to replace them with natural-looking ones a week later. Conversely, I have a client with four chrome limbs, a synthetic heart, and a nutrio-cell digestive replacement. He's happy as a clam."

Ladia shrugged. "As I said, those complications are quite rare, especially with someone like you who's already proven to have excellent compatibility and resilience. It boils down to the fact that humans identify themselves with their body, even though we all kind of agree that we live up here." Ladia tapped her forehead. "These disorders all tie back to that: the importance of self."

Juliet nodded, frowning. Hearing Ladia talk about a person's internal image struck a chord with her. She liked her body. She wasn't conceited; in fact, most people said the opposite, even the woman sitting across from her. Still, Juliet liked how her legs and arms looked. She liked how tall she was, and she liked that she could run without having to worry about her breasts bouncing all over the place. She was comfortable in her skin and wanted to keep it that way.

"So, going forward, just so you know, I'm interested in not making myself look . . . not like me." Juliet smiled crookedly and shook her head. "Sorry for the awkward wording. What I mean is that I want to make sure I always look like me."

"You mean your internal view of yourself? Because you already look a good deal different from when I first met you."

"Sure, I guess. I mean, I know my hair and eyes have changed. I know I'm healthier and stronger than I used to be. Shit, doc, I guess I'm saying that if I'm going to change, it should be in a way that I want."

"Of course, Lucky! Anything we do will be something you want. I'll never try to push something radical on you. What brought all this on? Is there something in particular you're interested in?"

"Yeah, I guess. A few things. For instance, I don't have to tell you I'm a lot faster with the Cybergen nerve job. If it comes down to a fight with a real maniac, geared-out chromed killer, only my right arm is up for the fight, though. I can equalize things with a blade or a gun, but what if I'm caught with my pants down, so to speak?" Juliet tapped her left arm, the flesh-and-blood one with the data jack implanted in her bone. "I've seen vids of people with weapons in their arms, weapons that weren't any more obtrusive than this data jack; something like a retractable blade."

"Ah! Of course! There's quite an industry in hidden cybernetic weapon implants. We'd probably have to move that data jack . . ."

"I need a better one, anyway."

"Well, in that case, how about I have Tricia bring us some wine, and we can peruse some catalogs. Is there anything else you want to look at today?"

Juliet settled back in her chair and winced as she remembered Frida lying on her back, groaning about how Juliet's armor-piercing, high-caliber pistol round had *dented* her chest. "Yeah, what can you tell me about subdermal armor?"

15

SPEED

Ladia pointed to the holograph, an image she'd created of Juliet that was uncannily realistic. Juliet's doppelgänger was clothed in tight blue shorts and a sports bra, and all of her cybernetics were highlighted in soft shades of pink that glowed under the model's skin, from her entire right arm to her eyes to the tiny chips in her ears and sinuses.

At the moment, Ladia was pointing to the cylindrical implant in Juliet's abdomen—not the cooling mechanism for the blood going through her brain but the medical nanite suite that hugged her abdominal aorta. "I didn't quite realize what a nice upgrade this was! I did a little digging while you were in the restroom, and this model number is a few iterations beyond the last one Cybergen sold commercially."

"Really?" Juliet's mind began to race, trying to think of a way to bolster up the story she'd spun about finding a wartime collector's son liquidating his private stash on Callisto.

"Yes! You really lucked out; that collector of yours must have picked this up at one of the secure storage facilities where Cybergen kept upcoming models and prototypes. I've heard of things like this out in the wild but never seen one in person."

"Wow! I don't think I quite realized . . ."

"Of course, this will make anything we do a lot easier. It's like being hooked to a blood infuser twenty-four seven."

"I was on an infusion machine for a while back on Earth. I had a job that required me to heal faster, and it really helped. You're saying my new nanites are at that level?"

"Oh yes. More so. These are some of the smartest, most capable little bugs I've ever analyzed. You've got rapid healing, toxin removal, antibiotic and antiviral batteries, nutrient filtering and delivery, rapid oxygenation . . . Gosh! I could go on for another ten minutes. It's quite a medical suite. Anyway, the reason I wanted to examine it was because I have a new product that might meet your needs. The only issue is that it's nanite based, and the nanites require a capable management suite; your Cybergen medical package here is more than up to the job." She poked the hologram with the tip of her pen, illustrating the device in question.

"Meet my needs? You mean the subdermal armor?"

"Right! This is a much less invasive solution than the carbon-weave product you mentioned. It works exceptionally well, too; I'll show you some vids of people with the product surviving ten-story falls with only bumps and bruises. Well, that's not entirely due to the product in question—they also had augmented limbs and a medical suite, though not as marvelous as yours."

"What about bullets?"

Ladia lifted her eyebrows. "Oh! Right to the point, I see. Well, this new product was designed for military applications and has been proven to protect the end user from small-arms fire. Let me show you how it works."

Ladia tapped a few icons on her tablet, and then Juliet's holographic image began slowly rotating as a swarm of tiny yellow dots, likely meant to represent nanites, propagated through it, starting at her arm and flowing through a now visible vascular system. As the dots spread, the veins and arteries faded, then the model's bones became visible, and the dots flowed into them, settling there, motionless, covering the entire skeletal surface.

"So, we introduce the nanites through an injection, and they're programmed to bond with specific cells in your skeletal structure, ensuring total coverage. They integrate deeply with your bones, almost like weaving extrastrong fibers into them. The process won't change how your bones work; they'll still produce blood cells and store minerals, but they'll be much stronger."

"So, how's this different from the example I gave you? When my friend got shot in the chest, her bones were basically metallic . . ."

"These nanites are smart—they know when to work and when to rest, letting your bones be bones. Under normal conditions, they just hang out, waiting and watching. As soon as your bones experience localized stress, they react faster than thought, providing extra protection that makes them very hard to break or . . . penetrate."

"Fewer complications?"

"Oh yes. I'm sure your friend doesn't have that carbon weave on all her bones; it changes the structure and reduces their biological function. The product I'm showing you here is a cutting-edge blend of biology and technology. The nanites are biocompatible; we'll create them by incorporating your own stem cells into their design. Your bones won't even know they're there."

"I don't get how they can possibly react as fast as a bullet hitting me."

"That's because you think in terms of human reactions. We have a lot of baggage up here"—Ladia tapped her head—"that can slow us down. These things are simple: they detect stress, they react with an electrical signal to the surrounding nanites, and essentially instantaneously, they form a hardened bond. I know bullets are fast, but this response is faster."

"Well, shoot, Doc," Juliet picked up her glass of smooth, obviously very expensive red wine and took a sip. Swallowing, she continued. "Sign me up."

"Excellent! There's the matter of cost, and we'll need to custom prepare the nanites for your body, but it's a simple outpatient procedure. Once I have it ready, I'll just give you the injection and send you on your way. According to the sales rep, the nanites settle into place within twenty-four hours."

"You haven't used them before?"

"No." Ladia frowned and poured Juliet more wine. "You see, that brings me back to the matter of the cost. It can be rather prohibitive. The reason you don't see every banger, mercenary, or corpo-sec agent running around with bulletproof bones is that these nanites only come from one company, Swedish Biologic, and they're not cheap . . ."

"Oh, brother. Just hit me with it, Doctor Ladia."

"Half a million Sol-bits."

"What? 500k?" Juliet's mouth fell open. "That's more than top-end medical suites!"

"While a medical suite will repair damage, this system prevents it. Can you put a price on knowing you can survive getting run over by a truck? That a bullet to the skull won't spell certain doom? Forgive my colorful language; this is the sort of thing the sales rep said to me when I balked at the price. I didn't think I had any clients who'd be willing to pay that much, but then he started quoting lines like that. I suppose I can see the value. The question is, do you?"

Juliet thought about the doctor's pitch and had to admit she had a point. Five hundred thousand bits, though, was a big chunk of her savings. For that kind of money, even if she didn't already have the parts stored away on the *Wing*, she could replace all her limbs and probably buy a dozen different brands of subdermal armor for her head and chest. Was it worth it to have this newer, noninvasive tech? It would undoubtedly cool her desire to spend more money anytime soon.

"Before I decide, Doc, talk to me about my arm and Cybergen reflex job. I know my arm's good, but does it hold up to Cybergen tech? Is it still as fast as the rest of me? Is it faster? I haven't had to activate my reflex job since I got it done, and I'm wondering if, in my line of work, I'm fast enough."

"Really? Well, let's do an assessment; the wine won't help, but your nanites can sober you up. Come on, I have a sensor array that can measure your response times." Ladia stood up and walked toward a door that led further into her clinic. As the door *snicked* open, she turned and winked at Juliet. "By the way, don't forget we still need to talk about a weapon implant in that left arm of yours."

"Oh, I haven't forgotten. It's just the money I'm worried about."

Ladia chuckled and led the way down a short hallway to a surgical suite with only one plastic-covered autosurgeon. Beside it was an enclosed chamber that reminded Juliet of an airlock. "If you step in there, I can start a simulation that will tie into your AUI. It will give you a series of diagnostics to test your baseline reaction speed, and then we can run it again with your speed augment active. We'll be able to see how your BioFusion arm stacks up against the Cybergen nerve and muscle augments."

"All right," Juliet stepped toward the door, but Ladia stopped her.

"Just a minute. You should wear something comfortable and leave your sidearm out here."

The request was simple and innocent seeming, but for some reason, it triggered a slight feeling of panic in Juliet. She turned to glare at Ladia, and the woman visibly flinched. Juliet sighed and shook her head; she'd already listened to Ladia's thoughts earlier and reassured herself that the doctor hadn't been compromised. All she'd picked up were Ladia's usual complimentary thoughts about Juliet's appearance and her relief that she'd returned to Luna; she genuinely seemed to like her and more than just as a high-paying client.

"Is something wrong, Juliet?" Angel asked.

"No," Juliet subvocalized. "I'm just being a little paranoid. Probably some long-buried PTSD from Murphy. You don't see anything weird, do you? We're not being jammed or anything?"

"No . . ."

"Sorry, Doc. I have trust issues. I'll bring my gun with me, but I'll set it on the ground inside the door so it won't interfere."

"That's fine, but you should also remove your boots and jacket. I could find some shorts or something so you don't have to move about in those jeans . . ."

"They're stretchy. I'm good. Don't worry." Juliet shrugged out of her jacket, dropping it on a stainless-steel cart next to the door, then bent and unlaced her boots. A couple of minutes later, she stepped through into the strange little room and placed her gun belt on the floor beside the door. Standing in her socks, jeans, and T-shirt, she turned and gave Ladia a thumbs-up through the window.

The doctor nodded and gestured in the air, and then Juliet's AUI lit up with visual artifacts. She assumed Angel let the code through—she usually filtered any sort of invasive advertisement or interactive AUI elements projected by businesses or municipalities.

A grid of red, glowing balls had appeared in the air in front of her. There were sixteen of them in four rows and four columns, and they rotated slowly, almost mesmerizingly. As Juliet stared, wondering what sort of test she was supposed to do, Ladia's voice sounded from an overhead speaker.

"You should see a grid pattern of red balls, right?"

"Right."

"They're going to start turning green, slowly at first, then faster and faster. Your job is to tap the green balls, turning them back to red. You can use any part of your body you want—feet, hands, elbows, even your forehead. Whatever will let you touch the balls the fastest. Now, make sure your PAI is managing your reflex coprocessors and has them set to zero enhancement for now. We'll do your baseline first." Juliet didn't have coprocessors for her new reflexes; Angel handled everything. She held up her thumb and readied herself, bending her knees and lifting her hands in a fighting stance.

A ball near the center left turned green, and she jabbed out her fist, hitting it almost immediately. It turned back to red, and then another one lit up green just one row down, and Juliet quickly jabbed it. She couldn't feel the balls, but they made a satisfying *pop* sound as she hit them and flashed briefly before turning red again. She continued hitting them one by one for several seconds, then things sped up, and she found she had to strike out with more than one limb to stay on top of the flashing green orbs. She kicked and punched, kicked and stumbled, laughing as she valiantly tried to keep the lights all red.

After a while, when there were at least two orbs persistently green no matter how hard Juliet tried to swipe them all back to red, the balls flashed three times, and a *ding* sounded. "We have good measurements, Juliet. You did very well, by the way! This is a standardized test, and your baseline is in the eightieth percentile for unenhanced humans, even considering your augmented arm."

"Humans?"

"Well, there's also a dataset for synths, and they generally outperform humans." She paused momentarily, then added, "The test has a five-minute rest period. Go ahead and stretch or focus on your breathing. Would you like some water?"

"The balls changing color are random, right? I don't want to subconsciously cheat by expecting them ahead of time. And no, no water, thanks, Doc."

"I'm pretty sure they're random."

Juliet nodded then began pacing around in a small circle, shaking her arms and rolling her neck, trying to get loose. If this went how she expected, she'd be activating all her enhanced muscles and ligaments for the first time, and she wasn't sure how it would go. Even if she only used her cybernetic arm, she'd only ever done that for a second or two at a time. "Don't let me fry my brain, Angel."

"Of course not. I'll be monitoring you closely. You've always been very resilient to accelerated synaptic activity. The truth is, I'm usually overcautious, stepping down your synapse speed long before I see any signs of stress."

"Good. I'd rather not get some kind of involuntary twitch or mental tick; I've seen some messed-up bangers with cheap speed jobs."

"Like Don."

"He wasn't a banger, but yeah, I don't ever want to be like that."

"Funny, the distinction you just made, almost like you were defending him, and I wonder why you would do that for a monster?"

"I don't know. Operator's pride? Forget it—Don might as well have been a banger for all we know about him." A timer had appeared above the balls, and Juliet glanced at it. "Two minutes. You ready?"

"I'm ready. Are you?"

"Almost." Juliet bent to pull her socks off, throwing them over by her gun. "Don't want to slip." She moved to stand in front of the floating, glowing balls again. "Don't turn it on until we have to."

"Understood."

Ladia's voice came through the speaker. "Thirty seconds, Lucky. Are you ready?"

Juliet held up her thumb and watched as the timer ticked down toward zero. When it read ten seconds, she readied herself, bouncing a little on the balls of her feet. An orb near the bottom left corner turned green, and she kicked it. A second later, another changed right in front of her, and she punched it. Just like before, she managed fine for several seconds, enough to get a little winded, and then the balls started to flash almost simultaneously, and she felt Angel kick her into overdrive.

Suddenly, the balls were changing from red to green so slowly that she could watch the green propagate out from the center in a slow-motion flash. She snapped out her fists, extinguishing the two currently green balls, and it felt like five seconds before another ball changed. She snapped out her leg, kicked it, and had to wait again for another ball to change. Because she was focusing on the orbs, it didn't seem like she was moving that fast; it was more like the changing colors had gotten slower. At first, the only thing that gave away her ramped-up speed was a sensation of weight as her fists and feet snapped out. They moved so fast that the force threatened to pull her out of balance.

Her test continued for what felt like another thirty seconds or so before it started to feel like the balls were lighting up quickly again. As she hurried to strike them, slowly growing accustomed to the increased force of her blows and compensating by tensing the appropriate muscles to keep herself centered, a new sensation began to pervade her body—heat. It started as a warm glow in her biceps, quadriceps, and glutes, spreading outward from there. As she beat the green orbs into submission, her entire body began to radiate palpable heat, and she knew if she stopped concentrating on the task at hand, she'd find herself drenched in sweat.

It felt like she punched and kicked for ten minutes, but she knew her perception of time was skewed with Angel cranking up her synaptic speed. Still, the balls didn't seem to be changing any faster, and she knew she could have kept going if only her biobatteries hadn't run out of juice. She suddenly found herself swinging her flesh-and-blood limbs like they were buried in molasses.

Angel, recognizing her defeat, slowed her synapses, and suddenly, the balls were flashing from red to green so rapidly that she had trouble focusing on them all. Juliet fell to her butt, laughing, wiping the sheen of sweat away from her beet-red face.

"Outstanding, Lucky!" Doctor Ladia announced through the speaker. The door *snicked* open a moment later, and she strode into the room. "I've never seen anyone maintain speed like that for so long! Two and a half minutes! Are you feeling all right? My scanner array didn't trigger any alerts, and I know your PAI would be monitoring you . . ."

"I'm fine, Doc. Just hot." Juliet smiled up at the doctor sheepishly, indicating her soaked T-shirt.

"Amazing! I wonder, did your PAI manage your intracranial heat with that implant you had me install?"

"I did," Angel said smugly.

"She did."

"Incredible. Well, you scored in the top one percent of full-body speed-augmented individuals, and you're off the charts with duration. The scale tops out at ninety seconds. You know most people manage speed like that in short bursts, right?"

"Oh, I know. This is the first time I've done that for longer than a second or two."

"Did you stop because of the heat?"

"No, I burned all the juice in the biobatts for my reflex augmentation." Juliet smiled and leaned back on her elbows, feeling strangely good in her drained state. She almost felt like she'd just had sex. The idea made her laugh, and she shook her head. "Doc, do you have something I could eat? I'm drained as hell."

"Tricia? Go next door and get some takeout, would you? My usual, but double." Ladia held a hand out to Juliet. "Come, let me help you up, and we'll go sit in my office. It's cooler in there." As she tugged Juliet to her feet, the doctor continued, "Lucky, your Cybergen reflexes boosted your baseline by two hundred ninety-seven percent. Your BioFusion arm topped out at three hundred fifteen percent. Obviously, your synaptic implant managed the difference just fine; you looked like grace personified during that test. I'd be lying if I said I could do anything to improve those speeds."

"Really? Well, thanks, Doc. I didn't expect to be able to do a test like this, and it makes me feel a lot better. It sure felt good doing that, you know? I feel good. What a . . ." Juliet stopped speaking, suddenly realizing why she felt so good. She'd just literally blown off a bunch of steam. "I need to go all out more often, I think."

As they walked back into Ladia's office, Juliet stood in front of an air conditioning register while Ladia organized some things at her desk. After a minute, Juliet turned back to the doctor. "I guess I'm good with speed for now. Let's talk about a new data jack and a weapon for my left arm."

"Of course. Tricia will be here in a minute with a snack, and we'll write everything up."

16

BAD NEIGHBORHOOD

"Mm-hmm," Juliet mumbled, chewing her last bite of savory, slightly spicy spring roll. Ladia was showing her a series of holographic advertisements featuring different concealable weapon implants. Currently rotating above the little projector was an arm with a tiny barrel hidden in the ulna that would deploy out of a synth-skin port, firing toxic—or not—needles from a similarly tiny magazine. As she swallowed, she shook her head.

"I like the idea, but I don't want to have to unload my arm if I'm going through a high-security checkpoint. I'm talking about a last-ditch weapon here, something I can count on and won't have to remove if an overly cautious security scan picks it up."

"Not a projectile, then? A blade or maybe . . ." Ladia trailed off as she tapped on her floating AUI. "How about this?"

The holograph changed, showing a woman walking down a dark, suitably spooky street. Trash blew along the gutter, and failing streetlamps flickered. The woman pulled her scarf tight around her neck, and then, predictably, a man lurched out of an alley, accosting her. He grabbed her from behind, and she screamed, kicking her feet. As the would-be mugger or kidnapper lifted her off the ground and began to drag her back into the alley, the woman pulled something that crackled and zapped out of her wrist, wrapping it around her assailant's hands where they gripped her around the belly. He screamed, and with a sizzling *zwap*, his hands fell to the pavement. He stood there, dumbfounded, looking at the smoking stumps of his wrists.

Juliet laughed; the overacting and melodrama of the advertisement was too much. "Holy shit, Doc! You gotta hook me up with one of those. What's it called?"

"This one's made by FusionTech Armaments, and they call it a Volt Whip. It can be manipulated from the nonconductive tip, as you saw here, but you can also deploy it without using your other hand and, well, whip it around. The charge is good for about a minute of active use, and as you saw in the ad, it's supposed to slice right through most organic materials."

"And it retracts automatically?"

"Yes, it says it's deployable and retractable with commands given via your PAI." Ladia frowned, then shrugged. "It should pass security more easily than a projectile weapon. There's no barrel, and the coiled wire won't look exactly like a weapon. In fact, if we place it carefully near your new data jack, it'll likely look like part of that system on a scan."

Juliet and Ladia had already settled on a new data jack; it was more compact, had a more powerful wireless antenna, and held a hardwired cable made of a much thinner, more flexible material than her current one.

"Unless this vid is exaggerating its capabilities, I'm pretty much sold on the idea."

"I'm sure there's some hyperbole here; it likely doesn't cut so quickly or smoothly, but I'm sure it would hurt enough to get someone to let go." She paused and squinted at something on her AUI, then added, "Hmm, actually, I'm not so sure they are exaggerating—under suggested usage, it says it can melt through common restraints, doorknobs, and even padlocks 'in seconds.' Should I order one?"

"Yeah, let's put it on the list. If it's no good, we can send it back, right?"

"Oh yes. This supplier won't want to lose my business." Ladia tapped on her invisible AUI for a moment, then smiled. "So, we've got the Swedish Biologic bone reinforcement nanite package, the Reaction Technologies Tightbeam 9 data jack, and the FusionTech Volt Whip. Am I forgetting anything?"

"Just those for now, but you told me you'd look into piloting augmentations. I'm mostly interested in a vascular interface port to plug into an acceleration couch."

"Right. As I said before, I'm not sure, with your lung upgrade, how effective some of the more common piloting augments will be. I'll research it. For the three augments we've settled on, though, we're looking at 587k. Can you cover that? Should I pull up my financing software?"

"No, I can cover it. Can you get started with half up front?"

"Certainly. It's not like you're a new client, after all." Ladia tapped away in the air for another few seconds, then said, "The nanites come inert and unbonded. I have to start culturing your stem cells, but that just requires a small tissue sample. Bone marrow would make my job easier, but I can do it with something less invasive, even a normal blood sample. Let's see." Again, she tapped at invisible icons. "Mm-hmm, I have two liters of your plasma in storage."

"Wait, you do?"

"Yes, is that a problem? I make it a habit to draw some blood whenever I do a procedure. I like to be prepared in the event you need an emergency infusion."

Juliet frowned, drumming her fingers. She didn't know if making a scene about the doctor keeping her blood on hand would be worse than the doctor having some. "Go ahead and use that to make the stem cells, but Doctor Ladia, I'd appreciate you destroying any tissue or fluid samples you have from me, even if they're not labeled with my name or ID. Will you do that for me?"

"Of course! Not a problem, Lucky. I should have known better; you're not my only client who values her privacy. For the record, the samples are coded on an encrypted database. Anyone breaking into my clinic would find it impossible to tie them to a client."

"All the same, I'd feel better not having my . . . fluids stored anywhere." Juliet stood, folding the linen napkin Tricia had given her and placing it on Ladia's desk beside her plate. Her metabolism, nanites, or both had long done away with the buzz she'd gotten from the fine wine, and she felt perfectly clearheaded. "Send the invoice over, and I'll forward you the funds, okay? Thanks for all of your time today, Doc."

Ladia stood and came around the desk, reaching out to take Juliet's hand. "I truly look forward to your visits. You know I only keep clients I enjoy working with—"

"Oh, shoot!" Juliet shook her head, chuckling at herself. "I almost forgot! I promised my friend I'd give you her name. She's one of the sweetest people I know and wants a consultation about getting an augment or two. Unlike me, she works for a living, so I'd appreciate it if you'd see her."

"If you recommend her, I'll happily sit down with her. Send me her contact info!"

"I will. Thank you, Doctor Ladia."

"I should be thanking you; it makes my life easier when I don't have to hunt down good clients. Speaking of your friends, whatever became of that synthetic individual? You mentioned he might appreciate more . . . matching parts?"

"I tried to talk him into it, Doc, but he's kind of paranoid. His paperwork's less than legit, and he doesn't trust the ID I got him. He rarely leaves the port. I'll keep working on him, okay?"

"Sounds good. I'll be in touch; as soon as the nanites and the, uh, whip are here, you'll hear from me." Ladia led the way over to her door, and Juliet followed. On the way out, Tricia offered her a fancy little silver bag with an Aine Cosmetics logo sewn into the fabric.

"Ah," Ladia said as Juliet took it, "just some sample hand cream and bath salts. The rep's always coming around to the clinic. Thank you, Tricia." As Juliet opened the bag and sniffed the heady floral fragrance, Ladia sighed, shaking her head. "I wish they'd get the clue; I'm not selling cosmetics here. Still, they make nice swag bags, and you can't say you walked out empty-handed."

Juliet held the bag up, smiling. "Thanks. Looking forward to hearing from you, Doc." With that, she pushed the door open to go and, on her way to the parking garage, asked Angel, "You think those purchases are good for now? Anything you think I should have brought up?"

"We talked about this; there are any number of implants that would make you a great deal more dangerous—bioweapons, projectile implants, military-grade EMPs, or even hardened exterior armor plates. The issue is that you're trying to maintain some subtlety. You're trying to ensure you can still pass through security checkpoints without being 'disarmed' or slowed or outright rejected. There's external equipment that can mimic or even outdo heavy-duty implants. As an extreme example, think of the Atlas exoskeleton. No amount of cybernetic augmentation would compete with what that piece of hardware can do for you. So, to answer your question, I think what you've ordered is good for now."

Juliet stowed her little cosmetics bag in her bike's seat next to her gift for Aya, then she began motoring out of downtown, heading for Jupiter Donuts. She bought a dozen, being sure to get a couple of sprinkled, glazed chocolate ones for Bennet; she and Aya were less fussy than the big musclehead. The box wouldn't fit under her seat, but she held it on the battery chassis in front of her, driving nice and slow, steering with just her throttle hand as she cruised the rest of the way back to the hangar. The bay door was halfway open, so she pulled into the workspace, parked her bike, and was just about to step off her bike when she saw a familiar van parked close to the gunship.

"Angel," she hissed.

"I see it. It's the same van from the other night." Juliet squatted, set the donuts on the floor beside her bike, and snatched her Texan from its holster. Her motorcycle was virtually silent at low speeds, especially when she wasn't accelerating, so it wasn't a big surprise that no one had noticed her arrival.

"I can't access the local net. It's offline or jammed." Angel's announcement explained why Juliet didn't have the security cams up on her feed. It also confirmed there was a problem.

She squatted there, listening as Angel slowly cranked up the gain on her auditory implants, looking for a clue. It took longer than she wanted, with thoughts of Bennet and Aya being hurt running through her mind before she finally heard the muffled, distant sound of a garbled voice.

"Where's that coming from?"

"Inside the gunship."

Juliet burst into motion, silently padding over the concrete to the rear of the ship, peering into the van as she passed by—tools and boxes, but no occupants. The rear airlock was open, explaining how she'd heard anything through the ship's densely insulated frame. Juliet still wore her helmet, but the visor was designed to provide optimal views at night or in bad weather, so her vision was unimpeded. As she crept into the airlock then up to the interior door—also open—she paused and listened again.

A high-pitched, sort of airy male voice came to her from down the access corridor, ". . . don't care about all that jack! We want the processors, the coils, the couplings, the ammo cartridges, and anything else worth more than fifty bits that'll fit in our van! Make it quick and keep your trap shut, and we won't hurt her."

"Keep your pants on," Bennet's voice replied, though Juliet detected a slightly garbled enunciation that wasn't usually there; it sounded like his mouth was swollen or maybe full of fluid. "Gonna need my tools."

"Which ones?"

"My red kit. It's under the nose where I was working on the main gun."

"Get it, Tic."

At the words, Juliet backed up from the opening and slipped her gun back into her holster. In a few seconds, she heard the sound of approaching feet clomping on the plasteel deck, then a wiry man wearing yellow-lensed goggles and sporting a bright shock of purple hair standing straight up from the top of his head stepped into the airlock. Without hesitation, Juliet jabbed her cybernetic fist forward, crashing her knuckles into the base of his jaw, just beneath his right ear. He never saw it coming, never noticed her lurking there beside the doorway. He fell to the ground like Juliet had flicked an off switch.

As she tugged his limp, disturbingly light form away from the doorway, she subvocalized, "Why don't we have eyes in the gunship? The cameras are offline?"

"There's a crude, powerful jammer active near the center of the ship; it's disrupting the wireless signals."

Juliet grunted in acknowledgment, pulling her data jack cable out of her arm and plugging it into the panel beside the door. "How about now?" A vid feed immediately appeared on her AUI, and Juliet studied the view inside the ship's little galley with an ever-deepening scowl.

A man sat on one of the table's two built-in benches, facing away from the table. He was a big fellow, bulky in every way, with a bowling-ball-shaped head and no visible neck. He was dirty and scroungy, wearing stained overalls under an ill-fitting military vest. His scuffed-up, half-laced combat boots had to be size fifteens. Aya sat at his feet, his ham-size fist holding a massive, bulky semiautomatic pistol, almost casually, against her head.

"Just relax, dude. You can take that off her head; nobody's going to risk dying over some spare parts."

"I ask for your advice, chum?" the man asked in that same high-pitched voice Juliet had heard earlier. It was utterly incongruous with his appearance. "Pipe up again, and I might see if this new trigger's as light as advertised." Juliet clenched her fists, looking more closely at Aya's face, seeing the fear in her eyes, and then at Bennet's, noting the blood on his chin beneath purple, swollen lips.

"This guy's going to pay for that," she growled into her helmet, stooping to check for a pulse on the one she'd pummeled. She could see from the purple malformation of his jaw that she'd broken it. She couldn't really tell if she felt a pulse, but apparently, Angel was better at noticing those sorts of things.

"He has a weak pulse. I don't think he'll wake up anytime soon. I'd bet good money that you gave him a serious concussion." Even so, Juliet didn't like leaving him unbound, so she snatched up a roll of electrical tape sitting atop a tool cart, then flopped him onto his stomach and wrapped a dozen layers around his wrists behind his back. With that done, she studied the feed once more, ensuring the gunman was still where she'd last seen him. Unplugging her cable, she started creeping down the access corridor, pistol held ready.

When she reached the opening to the ship's galley, she continued to listen to the intruder bark threats at Bennet, though he and Aya had grown quiet, probably not wanting to provoke an irrational response from the bully. Ever so slowly, she inched her head past the hatchway until she could lay eyes on her target.

If he were looking in her direction, he would have seen her; there wasn't much obstructing his view of the doorway. But he was busy looking down at Aya, gloating as he pushed the barrel of his gun against her head. "That bother you, sweetie? Don't like things poking you?"

Bennet, sitting on the floor beside the refrigerator, said, "Hey, listen, man, you rob us, that's one thing, but you do something worse, and you're going to regret it."

"Threatening me?" the man asked in his high-pitched, sort of wheezy voice. Juliet didn't listen to Bennet's response; she was staring at the guy's hand holding the pistol, focusing on his trigger finger. If he wasn't lying, if he had a lightweight trigger, it would be very dangerous for her to move against him while he held the barrel to Aya's head, unless Juliet did something to neutralize that threat.

Focusing on his thick, grease-stained digit, she slowly exhaled, visualizing her breath flowing out, wrapping around that finger, and yanking it out and back, away from the trigger guard.

A wet pop sounded from the vicinity of the gun and Aya's head, then the big bald bulldozer of a man grunted in a high-pitched wheeze of surprise and lifted his hand, wide-eyed, looking with horror at his distended, dislocated pointer finger. He immediately looked down at Aya and cried, "You bitch!"

His outburst sounded just a fraction of a second before Juliet cracked him on the back of his head with the butt of her Texan. She hit him hard enough, with her augmented arm, to kill most people, but his head was massive, and he had a thick layer of fat under his scalp, likely rendering the blow nonlethal. Still, he collapsed with a sigh, falling off the bench with a deck-shaking crash, rattling the dishes in the sink. His eyes rolled back in his head, and his breaths were short and jagged as he twitched.

"Just two of them?" Juliet asked her stunned, wide-eyed friends.

"Lucky!" Aya jumped to her feet.

"Shit, yes! Only two of the assholes. Where's the other guy?"

"Airlock," Juliet managed to grunt as Aya smashed into her, squeezing the air out of her lungs. Bennet grunted, standing, then pulled a thick roll of duct tape out of his overalls and got to work binding the huge, unconscious guy.

Juliet squeezed Aya back with her unarmed hand and said, "That van's the same one cruising around when those other guys jumped us. This neighborhood's terrible, Bennet."

"Tell me about it—teach me to keep the bay door open for some fresh air. They aren't a solo act, either. They were talking about a boss and another crew."

"That's right!" Aya pushed away from Juliet; her eyes were red, her cheeks flushed, and Juliet could tell she'd been crying. The thought of anyone being so cruel to Aya, who didn't have a mean bone in her body, made her want to wake the guy up to beat him some more.

"Well, I'm done with this BS. Someone needs to clean this neighborhood up, and I guess I'm volunteering." Her words brought a variety of reactions from everyone.

"Perhaps we should contact that corpo-sec sergeant," Angel said.

"Hell yes," Bennet grunted, standing up, red faced, after leaning over to tape the giant's wrists.

"Why don't we just move?" Aya proposed. "I don't want anyone to get hurt . . ."

"Nah, hush." Juliet smiled and winked at Aya, twirling her pistol and holstering it. "Whatever operation's running these crews is going to regret it. Besides, I think I can earn some points with Luna City Security with something like this. We don't have anything illegal in the hangar, do we, Bennet? I might invite someone over to help me question these boys."

"Illegal? Nah. I mean, once we get everything loaded up onto the gunship, we're going to have to upgrade our operating license to be docked in Luna City, but right now, they're all just perfectly legal parts or scrap, depending on who's asking . . ." He kind of trailed off, shrugging.

"Don't worry about it. The guy I'm talking about doesn't exactly trust his department. I doubt he'll want to give us any trouble." While she spoke, Aya let go of her and knelt next to the big thug, looking at his hands where they were bound behind his back. Juliet saw the object of her focus: the purple, distended pointer finger of his right hand. "Let's get you some air, huh, Aya? Bennet, can you drag this creep to the airlock with the other guy?"

"Yeah, sure . . ."

"Lucky?" Aya asked as she took Juliet's offered hand.

"Yeah?"

"How'd you break that guy's trigger finger before you clubbed him?"

17

I SCRATCH YOUR BACK

Juliet stood in the open bay doors of the hangar, pacing back and forth in the late afternoon sun, waiting for Sergeant Hines and watching Bennet and Aya devour the donuts she'd planned to save for morning. She couldn't blame them; something about having a gun pointed at you and being slapped around by a thug made a person hungry. In fact, Juliet was contemplating one herself, which made her think about the donuts she and Nick used to get back on Callisto, which made her think about Nick's constant vaping, which ended up just making her sad.

Aya sat on Juliet's bike sideways, both of her small feet balanced on one foot peg while she ate, and Bennet sat in an old, beat-up lawn chair, squinting into the sky, enjoying the tail-end of Luna's day cycle. Juliet looked at the open box of donuts on Aya's lap and walked over, reaching for a pink-frosted chocolate one. "This will ruin our dinner."

"I didn't have plans," Aya said, licking some glazed frosting off her thumb.

Bennet shifted, using his hand to shade his eyes so he could more easily look at Juliet. "I'd say getting mugged deserves a treat."

"It's all fuel for your gains, right?" Juliet smirked.

"Exactly! Too much fuel? Time to pump out an extra set, you know?"

"Are you guys sure you're both all right? I can call a cab if you want to go to a clinic."

Bennet snorted. "For a busted lip? I'm fine."

Aya shrugged. "They didn't hit me. The big one just twisted my arm a bit."

"Speaking of the big one, I wonder if you gave him brain damage." Bennet laughed, shaking his head. "That crack to the dome was brutal!"

"Still don't know what happened to his finger . . ." Aya frowned in contemplation, staring at her donut. Juliet had played the question off pretty smoothly earlier by saying she'd thought Aya did something and then feigning ignorance.

"You sure you didn't grab it? He sure seemed to think it was you." She almost felt guilty playing dumb with her, but the whole thing was also kind of funny—the mysterious dislocated trigger finger.

"If I did . . ." She trailed off, took another bite of donut, then grinned, teeth full of frosting. "Then I'm losing it!" Bennet and Juliet laughed, and once again, the matter was dropped as the conversation moved on.

"You sure you can trust this corpo drone?" Bennet gestured up the street as though indicating the imminent arrival of Juliet's contact.

"Not at all. I won't tell him anything that'll get us in trouble. I mean, you guys realize we're the victims here, right?"

"Tell that to the comatose thugs taped up in the airlock." Bennet laughed.

"Good point, but the facts remain: They came here to rob us. Still, I'll make it a condition of our deal that Hines keeps our names out of any case files he builds. I think he'll be happy for my help and be willing to bend the rules a bit."

Bennet shrugged. "How'd your thing with the doctor go? Gonna get some retractable helicopter blades installed in your spine?" He tried to make eye contact while delivering his snark, but the sun in his eyes got in the way.

"Do they have something like that? Where do I sign up?" Juliet started walking in a circle, bending at the knees and flapping her arms. "I thought I had to get wings implanted in my arms! If I can get some helicopter blades . . ."

"You can't tease her anymore, Bennet. She's immune to you." Aya held the box out, and Bennet made a show of resisting temptation before giving in and snatching up, of course, one of the sprinkled ones. Aya looked at Juliet, watching as she took another bite of her donut, then asked, "Did it go well? Did you mention me?"

Juliet nodded, chewing. After she swallowed the fluffy, fatty, sweet pastry, wishing she had something good to wash it down with, she replied, "It was good. I have a few small things lined up, but nothing as cool as retractable helicopter blades. She's looking forward to meeting you."

"What?" Bennet groaned. "Aya, what are you planning? Please tell me you aren't going to chrome out your arms or something."

"What if I did? You have something against augmented people?"

Bennet, quick to joke and tease, scowled; for the first time that night, it looked like a genuine one. He didn't reply, though, simply shook his head and continued munching his donut. Aya looked at Juliet, raising an eyebrow, while Juliet just shrugged.

In an attempt to please everyone, something she rarely succeeded at, she said, "Ladia doesn't push tech on people. She'll give you an honest assessment and make sure you're not doing anything you'll regret. I trust her." She brushed the crumbs off her hands, then stepped closer to Aya. "That reminds me! I got you a little gift; can you stand up so I can open the seat?"

"A gift?" The way Aya's eyes lit up warmed something in Juliet's chest, and she mentally made a note to give people presents more often.

"Yep!" She opened the compartment, pulled out the little box containing the carved dolphin figurine, and handed it to Aya.

"Ahem." Bennet shifted in his seat, glaring at the two women.

"Oh!" Juliet laughed. "I got you something, too!" She retrieved the cosmetics gift bag Tricia had given her from the compartment and tossed it to him. "Top-end stuff, Bennet." He caught the bag, his frown turning into a perplexed grin. Meanwhile, Aya opened the little cardboard box and gently lifted the smooth, polished dolphin from its cotton bed.

"A dolphin! Wow, it's so expressive! Look at its eyes! I love it, Lucky!" Aya held it close to her chest, smiling into Juliet's eyes, and hugged her. "I haven't gotten a gift in a long time! Shiro's terrible at birthdays or . . . anything."

"Hey! Not true," Bennet mumbled, still pulling the tissue out of his gift bag. "I bought you a self-adjusting auto torque wrench just last week." He pulled out a fancy decanter of pale-blue bath salts, and his eyes opened wide. "Whoa! You know I love a good bath! Thanks, Lucky!"

"There's more!" Juliet laughed, surprised and delighted that he actually liked it. Aya let go of her ribs and turned to watch as Bennet pulled the hand cream out of the sack. His eyes widened, and he unscrewed the lid of the faux-crystal jar, sniffing the fluffy white cream.

"Oh, that's nice! You know how calloused my hands get; this will be great." He dabbed one of his thick fingers into the jar and rubbed some of the cream on the back of his hand. "It's really silky; a little bit goes a long way. Thanks, Lucky!" He shifted as though to stand up, but before he could crush Juliet in an undeserved bear hug, the *whir* of an approaching sedan took everyone's attention.

"That'll be Hines." Juliet watched the low, black, unmarked car glide to a stop about ten meters away from the bay door. Then, a rear door opened, and Hines stepped out. He wore a plain, simple gray suit but had his badge and gun prominently displayed on his belt. Bennet grunted and turned to go inside, but Aya sat down on Juliet's bike again, watching.

He walked toward them, scratching at his perpetual stubble. "Afternoon, ladies."

"Sergeant," Juliet called by way of greeting. He shuffled closer, sighing and stretching as he pressed his hands into his lower back. "Some time at the gym might help those stiff joints."

"Oh? Advice already? Sound like my daughter." He nodded to Aya, eyeing the box of donuts she had propped against the bike's handlebars. "Miss . . ."

"Matsui," Aya said, hopping up to shake his hand.

"Hmm, Matsui, Matsui." Hines rubbed his chin for a minute. "Rings a bell . . . Ah, there we are—Aya Matsui, full-time salvage tech for Murakami LTD?"

"Mm-hmm." Aya performed a strangely perfect curtsy, miming the lifting of skirts and everything, then hopped back onto Juliet's bike.

"Knew you had an in with the crew of the *Kowashi*. Didn't know you were hanging out together in the industrial port warehouses."

Juliet sighed. "Hines, you gotta quit trying to dig things up about me if you want me to work with you." She jerked her thumb toward the open bay door. "Come on, I'll show you the thugs that tried to rob us." She led the way, and as they passed by the white van, she pointed at it. "They arrived in this thing. My PAI's working on trying to trace its history; it's a rental."

"I can help with that. Question is . . ." Hines trailed off as he, for the first time, took in the full shape of the Takamoto gunship. "What is this thing? A fighter?" The ship was still naked, all its body plates gathered on the drying scaffolds where Aya had been painting them, but it was undeniably aggressive in design. "Jesus, look at the size of those barrels." Hines leaned down, hands on knees, trying to get a better view of the three-barreled rail gun hanging under the ship's nose. "Bet that could put a nice hole in a pirate, huh?"

"Yeah, it'll pack a punch if we ever get it working. Come on"—Juliet waved him on—"they're in the airlock at the rear."

"So, what do you see happening here, Lucky? I'm not gonna earn any clout by writing up an attempted robbery."

"Uh-uh. That's not the plan. I'm going to track down their base of operations and deal with whatever gang is robbing warehouses and hangars around here. You'll help where you can and take the credit when it's all wrapped up. Then you owe me one. I scratch your back, you scratch—"

"Oh! Is that how that works?" Hines snorted, interrupting her. "We'll see what pans out. It'll be interesting to see how this investigation and, hopefully, bust go without running things through the department. I'm ninety percent sure some moles have been undermining my work for the last few months."

"Trying to make you look bad?"

"That and trying to protect the subjects I'm investigating. It's a dirty city, Lucky." They reached the ramp leading to the now locked airlock. Juliet led the way up, touching the control panel to show an internal view. Both men were still on the floor, basically hog-tied with enough tape to strap down a bull. She opened the door, and as the bolts *thunked* open and air hissed out, she looked back at Hines.

"These guys are lucky to be alive; they had a gun against Aya's head. You can arrest 'em when we're done, right? I don't want to have to keep storing prisoners . . ."

"Yeah, yeah. I've got a patrol car waiting a block away. We'll take 'em off your hands and make sure they don't see daylight for a while." He followed her into the airlock and whistled when he saw the size of the goose egg on the bald guy's head. "I'd say he's lucky not to be dead. What'd you hit him with? A sledgehammer?"

"Nah, just my pistol." Juliet produced her vibroblade and sliced through the cords holding the men's wrists tied to their ankles. They were both gagged with tape, but they'd gained consciousness, grunting and staring about with wide, bleary eyes. "Let's start with the little guy." Juliet ripped the tape off his mouth and shoved him so he flopped over onto his back. He grunted in pain—his arms were awkwardly pinned behind him.

"Mmf!" he cried, clearly unable to articulate his jaw.

"Shut up, Ernie." Hines squatted in front of him, grabbed his chin, and turned it to better look at the damage Juliet had done to his jaw. The movement elicited a cry of protest from the man as saliva dribbled from the corner of his crooked mouth. "Ernie Cavas, a dozen arrests for larceny-related crimes. Known to run with the Bedbugs, and originally from LA, Earthside. Not always happy with stealing, though, were ya? In 2102, arrested for rape. In 2103, arrested for aggravated assault."

"Nof profecufe!" Tears streamed from Ernie's eyes as he strained to speak through his broken jaw.

"Right, right." Hines looked up at Juliet and winked. "Not prosecuted. Innocent, eh, Ernie? Well, you can't tell us much right now, can you? How about this big ugly friend of yours?" Juliet took the cue and bent to rip the tape off the boulder-shaped man. He snarled and belatedly snapped his teeth at her fingers. "Tough guy, huh?"

Hines reached forward and flicked the great, purple bump on the back of his head. The thug gasped in pain and tucked his chin almost like a giant turtle trying to pull its head into its shell. "Let's see here." Hines pressed the palm of his hand against the man's brow, tilting his head up so he could more easily look him in the eye. "Aha, bingo. Willis Battan, aka Bullethead. Your rap sheet makes Ernie here look like a novice. Guess it won't be any trouble dumping these two into a bottomless hole, Lucky."

"Is he also a, uh," Juliet snickered, "Bedbug?"

"Willis has been associated with the Bedbugs, the 41st Devils, and as an independent operator working on contract. Lost your license a while back, though, didn't you?" Hines flicked the purple bump on his head again, and Juliet winced.

On the one hand, she thought the thug deserved plenty of pain for how he'd treated Bennet and Aya; on the other, she found it a little disturbing how much Hines seemed to enjoy it. Willis cursed and made some rather horrifying threats involving Hines's eye sockets, but he clammed up when the sergeant lifted his finger toward his goose egg again. "Quiet now. I doubt either of us is getting any sex tonight." He looked at Juliet and raised an eyebrow. "Well?"

"Well, what?"

"What do you want to know? How are you going to go about, you know, tracking down their boss?"

"Oh." Juliet frowned, rubbing her chin. "I mean, I have my methods, but I thought if I worked with you, we should do things more legitimately. I thought you had a way to, like, get them to talk."

"Scum like this? The only reason these guys keep resurfacing is because they don't mess with the wrong people; they steal from each other, from poor folks, and from working stiffs like you and your pals. They'll probably enjoy their time in Luna Correctional. Everything they tell us willingly, even if I offer them some kind of deal, will be at least half lies. If we were back at the station, I'd probably have my techs mine their PAIs for data. Half of these assholes have them programmed to wipe on removal, though."

"Oh, well . . ." Juliet pulled her data jack out of its housing, unwinding a meter of cable. "If I have your blessing, I can do some digging without removing them."

"Don't you stick that thing in me, bitch!" Willis strained against his bonds, rocking his enormous body back and forth. His head flushed, the pale skin darkening from pink to crimson, nearly matching the shade of the massive bump on the back of it. Juliet could hear the tape straining and creaking, and knew he would have broken out if Bennet hadn't triple-wrapped it. Hines lifted his hand high and brought it down on the guy's bump with a very satisfying *slap*.

"You're going to give yourself an aneurism, dummy." He looked at Juliet. "Why don't you start with the little guy? Ernie's not so violent."

"Ready, Angel?" Juliet subvocalized, holding her data jack a centimeter from Ernie's data port—he didn't have synth-skin covering it.

"Ready."

Juliet plugged the cable in. Then, having noted something off in Angel's tone, asked her, "Is everything all right? You've been quiet."

"I'm just not sure I like this Hines fellow. Are you sure we want to work with corpo-sec?"

"It's not about making friends or working together; it's about earning a favor from someone who might be in a position to help us someday. I mean, that, and I want to get these creeps to stop robbing buildings around us."

"What I'm doing right now to this man's PAI is quite illegal. If Hines were trying to entrap you . . ."

"He has me on vid plugging into this guy. I have him on vid telling me to do it. I don't think either of us will do anything with that. While you work, though, I'll try to listen to him a little." Angel made an affirmative sound, and Juliet looked up. Hines was watching her closely, leaning against the wall with one foot on Willis's shoulder. He reached into an inner pocket of his coat and pulled out a vape, and Juliet suddenly felt a surge of melancholy as Nick came to mind for the second time that day. In her mind's eye, she saw him leaning against the side of the *Lady Hawk*, puffing away on something fruity flavored, laughing.

Hines must have seen the gloom that descended over her. "Something wrong?"

Juliet shook her head. "Just thinking about an old friend. I'm going to have to concentrate here, so give me a few."

"Uh-huh." He sucked on his vape. When he exhaled, Juliet could smell the mint. She squeezed her eyes shut and tried to banish the feelings threatening to constrict her throat and bring tears to her eyes.

"Are you okay?" Angel asked, probably guessing what was bothering her.

"I'm fine. Just thinking about Nick for a minute. It'll pass." Juliet took a few deep, slow breaths. As the emotion began to even out, she pictured Hines's scraggly, jowly face, his deep crow's feet and sharp eyes. On her next inhalation, she began to hear his thoughts.

Chick's hard at it. Concentrating. Never understood that jacking business; good thing I got hired on before they started requiring the CF-40 certification. What's she gonna find? Nothing? Something? Was this a waste? What else you got to do?

God, my toe hurts. I told that doc the new meds weren't working. Feels like I've got ground glass in the joint. I'm gonna get the whole damn thing replaced! Sick of this BS health plan making me try every damn possible fix before they do it right. Can I use a supplemental plan to bypass the process? What if I sign up for just a month, do the procedure, then dump it? They must have safeguards to avoid that kind of abuse . . .

"I have something," Angel said, interrupting the sergeant's internal dialogue.

"I'm listening," Juliet subvocalized.

"I've found vid files showing this man meeting with your other prisoner, Willis, earlier this morning. They discussed what they'd do for the day, and Ernie mentioned that if they didn't score big today, Vicky would 'cut them loose.' I searched his local memory for any mention of a Vicky and found a self-deleting message log. He has the log set to delete conversations after twenty-four hours, but this conversation is only twelve hours old."

"What's it say?"

As she asked, a text log appeared:

0549 – Vicky: Are you up, runt?

0555 – Ernie: I am now. What is it?

0603 – Vicky: Got a job for you. Warehouse district; same neighborhood Yam's crew got rolled. Irene saw the big guy working in a hangar. Rob 'em. See what things look like—if that fast bitch is there or not. If not, we'll take her little friends and use 'em to lure her in. You think you can pull it off?

0614 – Ernie: Why me? What do I do if she's there? I'm not suicidal.

0617 – Vicky: Wasn't really asking. You're doing this, and you can take some muscle with you. That bitch put my best crew out of commission. People are talking.

Juliet straightened up, eyes drawn in a glowering scowl as she grabbed the guy by his swollen chin and jerked his face to look her in the eyes. "Where can I find Vicky, you little shit?"

18

ATTRACTION

It turned out Ernie was more than willing to spill his guts once Juliet dragged him outside the airlock, away from the big guy, Willis. Vicky ran an operation that fronted as a legitimate salvage yard in a neighboring industrial dome. Ernie claimed she had a hundred thugs working for her, and that if you bought some hot tech at a steep discount on Luna, she probably had a hand in its procurement.

After taping him back up, Juliet stepped outside the warehouse with Sergeant Hines. The sky was entering its twilight phase, and the air had gotten a little chilly while they were inside.

Hines looked in the donut box Aya had left on Juliet's bike. Only a couple of halves remained within—a chocolate and a plain glazed. Hines picked up the chocolate half donut and raised an eyebrow at Juliet. She smiled. "Go for it."

He took a bite, and then, as he chewed, laid out his thoughts, "I can book these guys and transfer them to North Luna District—I'll put 'em on a communication lockdown pending investigation so they won't be able to reach out to this Vicky individual. I know you probably want to go after her right away, but that won't be the smart move. Give me some time to dig around, find out what her deal is, and more importantly, who's been protecting her. Believe me, someone's been protecting her. No way she grows an operation that size without me having any clue about it otherwise."

"As in corpo-sec?"

"Or one of the corps that pay our bills." Hines shrugged. "More likely a combination of the two."

"She's targeting me. Worse, she's going after my friends here 'cause of me. What do I do while you figure things out? Twiddle my thumbs?"

"Why don't you upgrade the security around here? I mean, muscle's cheap. Put a couple of security guards outside, and it'll at least give her pause when it comes to sending another crew over here to mess with your friends."

"Yeah. I guess I should add to our security cams, too. I have some pointing at the gunship, but I need one out here."

"Exactly." Hines stared into space for a minute then nodded up the street. "Uniforms coming to pick up your prisoners. A couple of rookies I think are still pretty clean."

"Should you be talking like that?"

"Huh?"

"Don't your corporate overlords keep logs of your behavior?"

"Oh, yeah, right. I wish you were joking. I know a guy, though. He scrubs my PAI every week before the upload."

"They upload at a regular time?"

"Yeah, they don't know we know it, but let's just say they're a little too organized for their own good." He pulled his vape out of his breast pocket. "You mind?"

"Nah. Listen, I'm going to call a guy about getting some security here before everything closes tonight. Can you handle getting those guys out?"

"Not a problem. Here they come. Impound truck will be here in just a minute; we'll get that van out of here, too." He turned and waved in a sleek blue sedan with "Luna Security" printed in block letters down the side. Juliet went back into the hangar, past the van—stripped of its contents by Bennet and Aya—and up to the front of the gunship where the two were working and chatting under the nose gun.

"They're taking away our prisoners."

Bennet looked up from the gasket he was wriggling into place. "That all?"

"Figured out who's behind 'em, but Hines wants to do some sniffing around. Thinks they're protected by someone in the department."

He shrugged. "Makes sense."

"Are they all corrupt?" Aya asked, idly rolling a bolt back and forth atop the gun housing, which Bennet had disassembled on an empty wooden crate.

"All the cops?"

"All the corpo-secs. Are there any towns where they aren't helping criminals?"

"I dunno, Aya." Juliet sighed. "I've only been to a few cities, but it sure felt like the corruption was everywhere. Hines seems like a good guy, but he's working his own angle." The sounds of muffled grunts and conversation drifted through the hangar as the "uniforms" worked to load up their prisoners. "I'm going to hire some private security to watch over the hangar for a while. That all right with you two?"

Bennet nodded. "Probably makes sense. Wasn't sure it was in the budget."

"Can you take me to buy a gun?" Aya looked up at Juliet, her big yellow irises bright in the gloom. Juliet's initial impulse was to try to talk her out of it, then she thought of Aya sitting there with Willis's gun pressed against her skull, and she wondered how she'd feel if someone tried to tell her not to arm herself.

Aya must have seen the conflict in her eyes because she pressed on. "It's a dangerous world, Lucky! I didn't like having no option but to stand there with my hands up while they punched Bennet!"

"Yeah, I'll take you, but I'll give you one of mine for now."

"Just show her not to point it at me, please? Does this mean I should be wearing my pistol while I'm working?"

Juliet slapped him on the shoulder. "That's up to you, big man. Like I said, I'm hiring some security, so only if it makes you feel better, yeah?"

"Right." He went back to painstakingly threading a gasket into the main gun housing.

Juliet had Angel contact the company she'd used for security outside the *Wing*'s hangar, and when she offered to pay double wages for the night, they agreed to send two guards over on short notice. Once that was arranged, she went to her room in the gunship and picked up her needler and two magazines filled with low-velocity "hush" rounds she'd picked up on one of her many shopping excursions. Shot through the gun's bulky suppressor, the only sound they'd make was a soft *click*.

"Aya," she called, also picking up the paddle holster she'd bought for convenience. When the salvage tech didn't respond, she left the gunship and walked to the front where she'd last seen her working.

Bennet was still bolting up the housing, grunting as he turned the torque wrench; it was set to a specific tension so he wouldn't damage the gasket. "Where's Aya?"

"I think she's in your dream-rig. Something about shooting some zombies."

"Oh, brother." Juliet walked over to the rig and touched the "call user" button. A few seconds later, the rig clicked noisily and slid down, revealing Aya inside, blinking in the bright overhead lamps. "Hey."

"Hey." Aya frowned. For some reason, Juliet thought it looked like she was about to cry.

"What's going on, Aya?"

"Just mad. Mad at being helpless. Mad at needing you to save me. Mad thinking there are creeps like that guy in the world."

"Yeah. It's enough to make a grown man cry, as my old work buddy Mark used to say." Juliet smiled, reaching down to take Aya's hand. "He was a funny guy, you know? I used to judge him harshly, but looking back, he was the real thing. He refused to smoke vapes because of the 'unknown' chemicals in them. Smoked old-fashioned, hand-rolled cigarettes. I think I thought of him just now because of the dream-rig. Oh, brother! He loved his dream-rig. Talked about it all the time. 'Sorry, boss, gotta clock out! Date with my dream-rig, if ya know what I mean.'" Juliet laughed at the memory, trying to mimic Mark's voice, and Aya smiled, too, her eyes twinkling up at her.

"Well? Have you ever shot one of these?" She held up the needler.

"Only in sims."

"C'mon." Juliet pulled on her hand, helping her to sit up. "You're gonna love this little guy; he packs a punch, but he's silent and doesn't kick at all. Not with the rounds I've got loaded. If someone broke in here, you could shoot 'em and move, and no one would have a clue where the shot came from. Remember that: Always shoot and move. Shoot and move."

Juliet led Aya to the far side of the hangar, where the freshly painted, glossy, baby-blue hull panels were lined up, and pointed at a pair of empty pallets leaning against the far wall. "Put a few rounds into those pallets so you know what it feels like. Does your PAI have a targeting program?"

"No . . ."

"Shoot!" Juliet laughed at her pun, shaking her head. "Don't worry. I'll grab the one I promised you from storage tomorrow." She handed the needler to Aya. "Just use the laser sight for now." She tapped the little button on the side of the underbarrel laser, then showed her the green dot currently high on the wall. Aya smiled and lowered the barrel until the dot was on the pallets. "Now gently squeeze the trigger." Aya depressed the trigger, the gun went *click,* and a tiny puff of gas emitted from the barrel and drifted upward.

Aya frowned. "Is it jammed?"

"Nope! That's what it sounds like. See the three needles in the pallet?"

Juliet could see them clearly with her optics, but it took Aya a minute of staring before she grinned. "That's it? I didn't even feel it!"

"This is a suppressor." Juliet touched the rectangular protrusion on the end of the barrel. "And those needler rounds are called 'hush' rounds. It's a gimmicky name, but they really are quiet, yeah? Those needles are thin enough to slip through lots of different types of armor, but they won't penetrate hard materials very far. If someone has armor plates—you know, like the ones on my combat armor—then shoot them in the neck or face or wherever you see just clothing and no armor. Also, those magazines hold thirty-six rounds, so don't worry about firing a few times at someone."

Juliet helped Aya with the holster, showing her how the flexible plastic paddle was meant to slide inside her waistband, keeping the gun secure against her hip. Aya twisted at the waist, left and right, and rested her hand on the gun's grip. "It's smaller than I thought it would be."

"Looks good. You'll get used to it being there, too."

"Thanks, Lucky."

"Hey, listen; I don't want you to get yourself hurt just 'cause you have this gun. If you're not shooting to save yourself or someone like Bennet, then don't shoot; just try to run. The best way you can deal with bad guys is to get safe and let me or one of the security guys deal with them. Promise?"

"Promise. Only if I have to." Aya grabbed her into a hug, and for the first time in a while, Juliet felt Aya's emotions bleeding through her perpetual effort to keep her nose out of her friends' heads. She felt warmth and comfort and genuine happiness. Suddenly, Juliet felt an answering warmness in her chest, and she hugged her back, pulling her close and kissing the top of her head.

"I'd be wrecked if you got hurt, Aya."

As she snuggled even closer, burying her face in Juliet's chest, Aya mumbled, "Same. How do you think I feel all the time when you're out doing the things you do?"

Juliet sighed, squeezed her one more time, then pushed her back so she could look at her face. "C'mon. Let's watch a vid together, huh? I have an early morning."

Bennet left after an hour or so, while Juliet and Aya hung out the rest of the night, snacking on leftovers and sharing a vid feed as they watched old zombie movies—Aya's idea—until Juliet insisted she needed to sleep. When Aya left to collapse into her own bunk, Juliet made sure the ship was locked up tight before curling into her acceleration couch, determined to get some much-needed rest. Of course, that's when Angel decided it was time for a heart-to-heart.

"What makes some people feel like long-lost family while others are just acquaintances?"

"Huh?"

"Like Shiro—you like him, he likes you, you work together, but you wouldn't be hugging him, cuddling with him watching movies, sharing left-over spring rolls, or—"

"I get it. I don't know, Angel. Maybe it's that Aya wears her heart on her sleeve. I love that about her. She doesn't have a mean bone in her body, and it makes me want to, I dunno, hold her close against the cruel realities of the world. Have you noticed she hardly ever asks for anything and always goes out of her way to be nice or help? I don't mean with just me, either. She's so good to Bennet, and I don't know if he even realizes.

"She picks up after him, reminds him of what he's working on, and ensures we always get something he likes to eat when we go shopping. I've even seen her throwing his laundry in with hers. She treats him like a beloved big brother, and I get it; he's a good guy, but Aya is like that for everyone! I just . . . I love that about her, you know? She's the opposite of the greedy scumbags I have to deal with so often."

Angel was silent for a minute, and Juliet lay there, contemplating her flood of words, amazed as usual at how Angel had managed to broach a subject that Juliet had obviously been subconsciously ruminating on. "She's a wonderful person," Angel finally said. "Do you feel romantic toward her?"

"I . . ." Juliet's initial reaction was to deny anything, but this was Angel she was speaking to; why would she be dishonest with her? They shared, liter-ally, everything. "I don't think so, exactly, but I definitely feel a kind of happy warmth in my chest when we're together. She doesn't, like, excite me that way, though. I don't feel a tingly, fluttery sensation like I used to whenever I let myself contemplate Nick that way. God! Why'd I let him go on that stu-pid damn mission? Why didn't I admit my attraction?" Juliet felt frustrated tears building up in her eyes, and she squeezed them shut, trying to force the image of Nick out of her mind.

"I'm sorry, Juliet. I felt horrible at Nick's loss, but I think it pales in com-parison to the emotions you're going through." Angel's words gave Juliet a thought, and she turned the guns on her.

"Are you attracted to anyone?"

"Me?" Angel's voice betrayed genuine surprise, and Juliet grinned at her cleverness.

"Why not? You like people. You love people. Is there someone you feel romantic about?"

"When I first met you, I had feelings, but they were abstract, simple things compared to what I've experienced since merging with you. When we first came together, I cared about you because you were my host, and it was important to me that you succeed in every aspect of life. Now, I love you so desperately that the idea of you dying pulls a horrible gloom over my consciousness, and simple success metrics are almost like background noise.

"So, just as my feelings about you have grown profound through our connection, I also experience some of my emotions about others through that same connection. When Nick excited you, I felt that. When Aya fills you with warmth and cozy sensations, I feel that, too.

"If I try to separate the feelings I experience through you from the people we interact with, then things become more abstract and analytical again, and I'm able to concentrate on some of the things I like about people. For instance, I am impressed by Rutger Tanaka. It's rare to see people truly change, and he seems very different from the man he was when we first encountered him. I think that change, and knowing the other Rutger must be inside him some-where, lends an air of mystery and danger to the man. Plus, he's very ruggedly handsome; his jawline is strong, his eyes are fierce, and . . ."

Angel continued to extoll Rutger's virtues, and Juliet found her mouth hanging open, her mind utterly dumbfounded. Was Angel really crushing on Rutger Tanaka? When Angel trailed off after describing how she found Rut-ger's desire to teach her endearing, Juliet struggled to speak without snark; she didn't want Angel to regret opening up.

"Are you saying that of all the people we hang around with, Rutger is the most attractive to you?"

"The most? I'm not sure. You asked me if I was attracted to anyone, and he came to mind. He's so multifaceted . . ."

Juliet groaned and flopped over to her other side. She couldn't help the smile twisting the corner of her mouth, and she desperately wanted to tease Angel, but she fought against the urge, trying to find something to focus on that would make her sleepy. Finally giving up, she said, "Please play one of the old episodes of *Roy and Ernesto*." It was a comedy about a pair of men strug-gling to run an ostrich farm in a Martian agridome. While she listened to the familiar old jokes and enjoyed the weird Martian scenery, she found her lids growing heavy, and Juliet didn't fight to stay awake.

The next day, Juliet dressed in gym clothes, put on her motorcycle jacket, and grabbed her monoblade. At 0800, before Aya had emerged from her bunk, she opened the bay doors to roll her bike out of the hangar. Her heart lurched, and she almost leaped into evasive action when she saw two men wearing black corpo-sec-style body armor outside the door. A second later, her brain registered that their vests bore a Charter Security logo, and she remembered she'd hired them the night before.

"All quiet?" she asked, turning to close and lock the bay door.

"Yes, ma'am. Not a peep." The guy had a slightly Southern twang, and she was reminded of Hot Mustard—talk about feelings of attraction! "Anything we should know?"

"Yeah. There'll be some people here working, but they have credentials. If anyone else, and I mean anyone, comes poking around, I want you to message me immediately. You have my contact info?"

"We do. You're Lucky, right?"

"That's right. And you?"

"I'm sending you my card. Handle's Ringer, and this is Big Bump." He jerked his thumb at his compatriot. Both men wore dark visors, so she couldn't see much of their faces, but she liked that Big Bump still had his eyes on the road, his hands holding his large AK-style rifle at the ready. Based on a first impression, they seemed pretty solid.

"You on all day?"

"Until ten, then we swap out. Be back for the night shift again, though."

Juliet climbed onto her bike. "Nice. Well, be sure the shift change messages me when they start duty, all right? You heard about the hostilities we had here, yeah?"

"Yes. Don't you worry—anyone tries getting into this hangar again, we'll make enough noise to wake up half the city."

"That's what I like to hear, Ringer." Juliet used a shrink cord to attach the sword to the back of her seat, then touched the ignition, bringing the bike to life with its signature deep faux-engine rumble. She waved at Ringer and Big Bump then sped away.

It was time for a sword lesson with Angel's crush.

19

SWORD BUSINESS

Juliet was pleased to find Honey waiting for her in the lobby of Tanaka's building. Like Juliet, she wore exercise leggings, a T-shirt over her sports bra, and cross-trainers. Rutger hadn't said anything about wearing a gi, and Juliet hadn't wanted to give the practice session more gravity than it deserved; she still had no idea what to expect from the whole thing.

Honey, sitting in the lounge area of the lobby, stood when Juliet walked in. She raised her hand clutching her scabbarded sword in greeting, and Juliet walked over to her.

"See you brought your monoblade. Or wait, *his* monoblade." Honey grinned wickedly, knowing the whole thing made Juliet a little uncomfortable.

Juliet shrugged. "I don't have another sword and didn't want to show up empty-handed." She gestured to the elevators. "Shall we?"

"I guess. You know, I almost bailed on you. This is . . . weird."

"I know!" Juliet was feeling the same way. In fact, if she hadn't invited Honey, she might have chickened out during her commute from the industrial dome. She'd started thinking about Rutger, about his past, and the weird reactions he'd had during their conversations, and the whole thing felt very heavy and very strange. How could she concentrate on learning martial arts with all that baggage? "Thanks for sticking with me."

"Well, I kept thinking that if this is weird for me, how hard would it be for you if I wasn't here to back you up? You know?" Honey bumped her with her hip, then started for the elevators. "Besides, I'm out of shape. I can use some practice."

When they stepped off the elevator onto Rutger's floor, Juliet wasn't surprised to find Frida waiting for them—Angel was still keeping tabs on her and knew she'd be there. Frida was dressed in sleek gray slacks and a silky turquoise blouse. All in all, she looked very pretty, neat, and professional.

"Ladies! You're right on time." She stepped toward Honey, extending a hand. Honey took it, smiling, though Juliet could see the smile didn't extend to her eyes. She wondered if Frida could see that. "I'm Frida, Rutger's . . . assistant." She shrugged as though admitting she knew the term didn't adequately encompass her role.

Honey nodded. "Lucky's told me about you."

"All good, I ho—"

"Definitely not," Juliet interrupted with a smirk. She made a show of looking Frida up and down. "Not going to join us?"

"Oh no! Swords and I don't mix. Rutger tried when I was younger, but I guess it's not in my blood." She shrugged and pointed down the hallway. "We've set up the dojo down this way. I hope you won't mind, but when Rutger learned you'd invited Honey"—Frida paused and looked at Honey, nodding and smiling again—"he decided to add one of his permanent employees to the training. I think you know him, Lucky—at least you said you had eyes on him back on Callisto. Applebaum?"

"Oh, yeah. One of Rutger's goons?"

Frida slowed her steps, shaking her head as she smiled hugely. "Oh, I love that. Next time Leo's giving me grief, I'm going to tell him you called him that."

"Leo? Leo Applebaum?" Honey gave Juliet a sideways look. "Is that a real name?"

"Oh, you two are too much! I love it."

"So, why him? Why not Hawkins too? Doesn't Rutger have more guys working for him?"

Frida stopped before they came to a pair of closed doors and turned to look at Juliet.

"Don't repeat this, 'cause he's kind of sensitive, but Leo's something of an orphan. Rutger picked him up when he was a teen. Hired him as a courier but kept him on and trained him. He's been with him for more than ten years." She frowned then shrugged, and Juliet could tell she was justifying something to herself when she said, "It's only fair you know something about him 'cause he's done plenty of research on you." She turned to the door, resting a hand on the handle, but before she pulled it open, she looked back at Juliet. "We're still on for lunch after your lesson?"

"Sure. Lunch or, if you know a good place, brunch. I haven't eaten breakfast."

Honey chuckled. "Might have been a mistake."

Frida's smile returned, and she pulled the door open. "Enjoy your lesson."

When Juliet stepped through, it was plain to see that the "dojo" must have cost Tanaka a small fortune to put together. Soft cork flooring lined the room, but it only extended about two meters from the wall; the center of the space was floored in beautiful tatami mats, the likes of which Juliet's and Honey's old sensei could only have dreamed of. It was an ample space, too; the tatami-floored section was roughly a hundred square meters. One wall was lined with floor-to-ceiling windows, letting in Luna's bright morning light and providing a view of the city that probably cost Tanaka fifty grand a month in rent.

Cedar benches lined the two walls near the door, but the far wall contained four closed wooden doors, labeled, from left to right: EQUIPMENT, SAUNA, LOCKERS, and VR TRAINING. While the floor was very traditional, the vaulted ceiling wasn't. Juliet could see hooks, pulleys, and metal tracks that reminded her of those you might use to shift heavy engine equipment around a garage. Coiled ropes hung from the ceiling, too, and Juliet began to feel a predictive ache in her shoulders thinking about climbing them.

"Jeez," Honey whispered. "He's not half-assing this, is he?"

"I guess not." Juliet turned to ask Frida where Tanaka was, but the door had silently closed, and she hadn't followed them inside. Honey sat on a nearby bench and began removing her shoes.

"Should've worn our gis," she grunted, tugging a shoe off.

"I'd have to buy one—lost it during one of my 'moves.' He didn't say anything, anyway." Juliet sat beside Honey and also removed her shoes.

"Is it warm in here?" Honey asked, leaning back against the wall.

"Definitely. Angel says it's twenty-six Celsius. Probably wants us to sweat. Should we stretch?"

"Uh-uh. Not me." Honey clicked her tongue, shaking her head. "Let's not fall for that trap; he hasn't invited us onto his mat yet, and I don't see a photo to bow to. Let's wait to see how formal he expects us to be." Honey's words brought to mind Sensei's dojo and the sword and photo of his father, which they all bowed to before every practice.

"Oh, yeah. Good call . . ." She meant to say more, but the EQUIPMENT door opened, and Tanaka stepped out, followed closely by another man Juliet recognized as Applebaum—she'd seen photos and vids of him from Angel's updates back when they'd been keeping closer tabs on Tanaka's henchmen.

Applebaum pushed a cart to the mat's edge, opposite where Honey and Juliet sat. He and Tanaka were both wearing gis, of course. Tanaka's was black, and Applebaum's was white. Juliet couldn't help noticing the cart was stacked with folded white garments and some scabbarded swords.

Applebaum was a couple of inches taller than Tanaka, with short brown hair, a clean-shaven, lean, angular face, and pale blue eyes that Juliet had to suspect were implants; she'd seen "piercing blue eyes" before, but these were just absurd. He was grinning as though he and Tanaka had just shared a joke, and something about that twisted half smile was enough to make Juliet stare like an idiot.

"Welcome to our dojo," Tanaka greeted, interrupting Juliet's ogling. She jerked her gaze over to him, saw him looking at Honey, and realized her friend had stood, leaving her alone on the bench.

"Thank you," Honey said, bowing like she used to back when they'd studied with Sensei. Where had her snarky, "I'm going to try to throw this guy" attitude gone? Juliet stood up and nodded.

"Angel," she subvocalized, "send a message to Honey."

"Okay, saying?"

"Kiss ass."

A second later, Honey elbowed her in the ribs, and Tanaka cleared his throat. "Please walk around the mat so I can give you your training uniforms." They started moving, but Tanaka spoke again. "Bring your shoes and swords; you can put them in a locker when you change into your gis."

As they knelt to pick up their shoes, Honey muttered, "Sorry, but this is all too formal. I can't be disrespectful!"

"Uh-huh."

When they approached the cart, Tanaka pointed to Applebaum.

"This is Leo; he'll be joining us for some of the training. He's at an intermediate level and will serve as an assistant and sparring partner for Honey." He frowned, swallowed, and looked directly into Honey's face, clearly thinking something through.

"Honey, before we get started, I want you to know that I regret allowing my heart to grow hard and working purely for financial gain without regard for the behavior or character of my employers. Forgive me." As Honey stared at him, dumbfounded, he performed a deep bow, like the ones he'd done to Juliet back in the parking garage. Juliet sighed, familiar with his behavior by now, but Applebaum stepped back, looking almost shocked. Honey's face wasn't much different.

"It's . . ." Honey shook her head. "It's not all right, but I won't dwell on it." She glanced at Juliet almost nervously, and Juliet locked eyes with her, nodding. She agreed—Tanaka's current behavior wouldn't excuse the things he'd done.

He straightened, pointedly ignoring Applebaum's open-mouthed stare, and handed them each a folded gi and belt. "Take these, please. When you've changed, I will instruct you on the use and care of these practice swords. You may keep your other swords in your lockers. You won't need them until we've had many lessons."

"*If*," Juliet said, tugging Honey's elbow toward the locker room door. "*If* we have many lessons."

Tanaka didn't respond, but Applebaum's noisy intake of breath through his nose was a good indicator of how seldom people spoke to Tanaka that way.

The locker room wasn't large, but it was more than spacious for the two of them. Just as in the dojo, a wide cedar bench ran down the middle of the space, with banks of six lockers on either side, again constructed out of cedar. They were beautiful, with recessed hinges and mechanisms that screamed quality, and Honey whistled appreciatively as she opened one, sniffing the interior. "Cedar?"

"Yeah." Juliet's eyes were on the open showers at the end of the room, just past a bank of four sinks. "Applebaum better not get any ideas about showering with us."

Honey snorted, pulling her shirt over her head. "Who are you kidding? I saw your eyes bug out when you saw him."

Juliet, sitting on the bench, shoved Honey's hip, and she stumbled toward the far bank of lockers, unbalanced with her shirt over her face. "Don't say stuff like that!"

"What?" Honey laughed, pulling her head and thick, bushy ponytail out of the shirt. "You think they're watching us in here?" She turned around in her sports bra, holding her arms up. "Take a good look, boys!"

"You're stupid!" Juliet couldn't fight back her smile, though, as she got busy changing into the gi Tanaka had given her. It was a perfect fit, and disturbingly, so was Honey's. "Did they call you for measurements or something?"

"Nope. You gave Frida my name yesterday, right? That's pretty fast to get eyes on me and guess my size. Maybe they found my socials." She shrugged, stuffing her clothes into a locker. "What's the deal with that chick, anyway? You're going to lunch with her?"

"I think she's kinda lost with all the weird stuff Tanaka's been doing and saying. Probably wants to see if I have any answers."

"It's not, like, a date, is it?"

"What?" Juliet laughed. "Nah, but I teased her about that when she asked me. I hope I didn't lead her to think . . ." She trailed off, but Honey picked up the line of thought.

"You flirt a lot for a chick that never lets anyone get close. Watch yourself with that guy out there, though; he looks like a player."

Juliet felt heat rise in her neck and cheeks and looked away. Honey knew her too well. "I'm . . . I don't do that on purpose. Do I do that with you?"

"Sure, we play around, but we're bros, you know?"

"Bros?" Juliet laughed. "I think I like it better when you call me sis."

"Yeah, some people I follow are trying to make that happen. 'Bros' for everyone, but it just doesn't work that well, does it?" She pointed to the door. "We better get out there."

"Yep." Juliet tugged her belt, adjusting it so it was straight. "I look okay?"

"Like a bomb about to go off!" Honey winked, and laughing, they left the locker room and walked back to the cart and Tanaka. Applebaum was in the middle of the mat, stretching.

"Good. You tied your obis correctly." He nodded and pointed at the three swords on the cart. They all had modern material on the grips and, in their shiny, faux-wood black scabbards, were about a meter long from tip to pommel, though one looked significantly different. The hilt was about an inch longer, the pommel was plasteel, and had a data port on its side. Juliet could tell from the scabbard that the blade would be slightly wider and straighter than the other two. It was shaped like her monoblade.

"Honey, you've had some training?"

"Yes, Sensei."

"I . . . Have I earned that title?" He seemed to be asking himself as much as Honey and Juliet. Honey surprised her again by answering him.

"If you're going to be teaching me sword work, then I'll address you properly, Sensei."

He locked eyes with her and nodded. Then he handed her one of the two identical swords. "Use this in training. It has a wireless transmitter that will work with the diagnostic scanning suite I've installed in this dojo. What I miss with my eyes, I will see later when I examine the data."

While Honey secured the sword in the folds of her belt, Tanaka picked up the other sword like hers and tossed it at Leo without a word. The man, mid-stretch, snatched it out of the air and slipped it into his belt. Tanaka picked up the last sword, peering at Juliet through narrowed eyes for a moment. Then he yanked the sword free of the scabbard and held the naked blade before her.

She moved to take it, but he shook his head. "Not yet. I must explain this one. Like your friend's sword, it is tied to the diagnostic software in this dojo, but it has other functions. You're training to wield a monoblade, so your practice weapon is different from Honey's and Leo's, and so will your training be."

"Okay . . ." Juliet dragged the word out, giving Honey a quick, uncertain glance.

"This weapon is not sharp, but it will train you to respect its edge. Hold out your palm."

"My palm?" Juliet frowned. What was he going to do? Cut her? Shock her? Did he know she had a cybernetic hand? Did he know how fast she was? Shrugging, she held out her right palm, and he slowly and deliberately moved the sword above it, edge down.

He must have read the tension in her arm and posture because he said, "Don't pull away. This won't harm you." Then he pressed the blade against her palm and pulled it along her flesh. It didn't hurt. She could feel the smooth, unsharpened edge, but when he lifted the sword away, she had a long, neon-orange line on her palm.

"This sword has a nanomolecular photochromic dye disbursed from its blade with the slightest pressure. Anytime you touch anything with it, a mark will be left behind." He contemplated momentarily, then added, "Unless you use it in the dark—the dye is light activated. In any case, it will make it clear when you are undisciplined with the edge of your sword, something a mono-blade wielder can never afford."

Juliet rubbed at the bright orange line, smearing it around her palm. "What if Honey wants to use a mono—?"

"I don't."

Juliet glared at her. "Why?"

"They're dangerous, and they draw attention. I'm not looking to get challenged by every up-and-coming samurai-wannabe operator. I'm not really, you know, working right now, either."

Juliet's glare didn't fade as she looked at Applebaum. Tanaka anticipated her question, however. "He'll never wield a monoblade—too big and clumsy. He's nearly reached his skill ceiling."

"Wow. Such loving encouragement." Applebaum had a surprisingly thick Australian accent, which made Juliet wonder just where he'd gotten it. Hadn't Frida said he'd been with Tanaka for ten years? She supposed he could've had it already.

Juliet looked back to Tanaka, her frown still firmly in place. "So, what? You're going to keep track of all my screwups?" She held up her orange-striped hand in illustration.

"*Hai.* How else will you learn? Each day after practice, you'll spend extra time with drills, the length of which will depend on how many of these you make." He slapped her hand in illustration, and Juliet was startled by how quickly he did it—no windup, no hint that he was about to do it, just a sudden, lightning-fast movement.

"This blade is designed to perfectly mimic the weight and balance of your monoblade. Until we complete your training or you decide to quit, I want you to carry this weapon. Take it everywhere—shopping, eating, on dates, in the shower, to bed. Everywhere." He growled the final *everywhere*, saying it in a deep, commanding tone that startled her; she'd grown used to his apologetic, almost meek demeanor.

He smoothly sheathed the blade before handing it to her. She took the scabbard in one hand and the hilt in the other. After a quick glance at Honey, she bowed. "I will, Sensei."

He nodded, and though he had a practiced, well-maintained stoic expression, Juliet saw something positive glint behind his eyes. "Good. Now, when you step onto the mat, always bow toward the center. We do not have a founder to honor . . ."

He kept speaking, but Juliet was suddenly struck by a memory of him as a little boy, secretly watching the old master teaching the corpo kids how to use swords. She felt how awed he'd been, how desperately he'd wanted that man to teach him, and how stunned and overwhelmed he'd felt when the master took him in and showed him the only kindness he could remember in his young life.

The memory was so vivid it felt like it was hers, and Juliet took a minute to come back to reality.

". . . begin with the basics, and if you already know what we're learning, then consider it a refresher."

Juliet listened to him describing what he wanted, how he wanted them to stand, how to hold their swords, and so on, but she kept thinking about that memory. It bothered her because she wasn't sure if she'd picked it up with the lattice or if she was remembering it from when she'd slipped into Tanaka's memories back when she'd confronted him in the parking garage.

She felt like she'd gotten through her private ordeal without reacting, but when she looked to her right, checking her posture compared to Honey's, she saw Applebaum giving her a sidelong look, and his eyes said a lot—speculative, suspicious, and worst of all, concerned.

"Juliet," Angel asked, interrupting her scattered thoughts, "how much do you want me to help you with these sword lessons? Shall I keep hands-off, or would you like my assistance when it comes to—"

"Maximum assistance, Angel. Let's master this sword business ASAP."

20

BLADE DISCIPLINE

For the first twenty minutes or so, Rutger instructed them on things that Honey had already taught Juliet—how to draw the sword, how to hold it, how to sheathe it, and so on. She'd already committed many of those things to muscle memory back when she, Honey, and the crew of the *Kowashi* had traveled from Titan to Luna.

Apparently, Honey had been taught well because Tanaka didn't have many corrections for her or Juliet. He showed them what he wanted, watched them do it, and nodded, expressionless. When he began to demonstrate striking and the footwork and control of the body required for a "good cut," as he put it, things started to get interesting.

Seemingly satisfied that everyone knew how to stand and hold their sword, he asked them each to demonstrate a simple overhead chop he called a "*men-uchi.*" He didn't demonstrate it, but Honey, who was first in line, seemed to know what he meant. She lifted her sword over her head, stepped forward, and swung down like she was aiming to split an imaginary opponent's head in half. She grunted with the strike, but Tanaka furiously shook his head.

"Weak! Where's your *kiai?*"

"Um, Sensei, er, my old sensei didn't insist on that . . ."

"While you learn here, you will use your *kiai* with every strike. It will focus your power, strengthen your spirit, and put fear into your foes!"

Honey nodded and repeated the strike, this time making a loud, fierce exclamation that sounded very much like, "*Men!*"

Juliet frowned, puzzled, but then Angel explained, "Traditionally, a *kiai* will call out the target of a strike. *Men* means head. A combination of strikes would have a different *kiai*, depending on the targets."

When Applebaum performed the strike, his *kiai* was more like a garbled war cry. "Hiyagh!"

Rutger nodded, then turned his attention to Juliet.

"Help me chop like Honey did," she subvocalized, then lifted her sword, conscious of the tiny adjustments Angel made to her wrists and shoulders. When she stepped and chopped the sword down, she mimicked Honey's cry of "*Men!*" It came out softer than she'd intended, and she knew she was being self-conscious. Still, her strike was perfect in its resemblance to Honey's, and Tanaka nodded, folding his arms.

"Do not be shy in here, Lucky. Focus your will and your killing intent into that *kiai*. Your enemies should cower at the sound of it."

Juliet nodded, feeling flushed for some reason, and quickly fell back into line. From there, things became both easier and more challenging. Things were easier because Tanaka began to show them what he wanted and how they were all wrong, even Honey, and harder because they had to repeat the same movement over and over, making tiny adjustments until Tanaka was satisfied. If they couldn't repeat it perfectly ten times in a row, they kept trying. They worked on that overhead strike for more than an hour, and then Rutger said it was time to practice "blade discipline."

"Lucky, Leo, activate four of the practice synths and bring them here."

"Practice synths?" Juliet raised an eyebrow, but Leo was already walking toward the equipment room. Tanaka was talking to Honey, trying to explain why her wrist rotation wasn't perfect, so she just followed Leo. She caught up to him by the door, and he held it open, nodding.

"Looks like you impressed him. He wouldn't let you out of his sight if he didn't think your *men-uchi* was perfect."

"That your low-key way of saying yours is?"

He laughed, shaking his head. "Nah, he gave up on perfection with me a long time ago." He followed her into the equipment room, and Juliet lost track of his further words as she took in the space. It was much larger than she'd imagined, a five-meter-wide by twenty-deep storeroom with a vaulted ceiling and shelves and racks lining the walls on the left and right. She saw strike and kick bags, extra gis, a rack of wooden practice swords, jump ropes, climbing ropes, weights, medicine balls, jumping boxes, full-size dummies, and a hundred other things of that type. She stopped categorizing everything when her eyes fell on a row of blue, plastic-looking synths against the far wall, standing before a charging bank. There were six of them.

"Synths? Really? He keeps them offline, though?"

"They don't have personalities. They're basically robots." Leo strode toward the far wall, gesturing as he spoke. Juliet noticed that each synth had a number from one to six on its chest. "You turn them on, tell them what the job is, and they do it. They don't even talk unless you ask them something. Not sure why the boss sent you with me; I just have to say 'follow me,' and they'll all do it."

Juliet nodded, distracted because she'd noticed a new orange line on her left hand. Had she touched the blade of her sword when she'd sheathed it? "Damn . . ." She tried to rub it out with her thumb, and Leo laughed.

"He's already seen it, trust me. No way he lets something like that slip by his notice." He touched something behind the first synth, prompting its round LED eyes to begin flickering. As he moved to the next, he said, "Yeah, I reckon he sent you with me for a minute alone with your friend. Probably wants to see if she was just playing nice for your benefit. I recognized her, you know? I pulled duty in that mental facility back on New Atlas a couple of times."

Juliet folded her arms and scowled. "Ah, thanks for letting me know you're a creep. It wasn't a mental facility, either; it was a secret prison for kidnapping victims."

"Not what they told us." He shrugged, turning on the third synth. "You're an operator. You know how it goes."

"Not exactly, no. I never let someone pay me to keep a girl and her baby-sitter prisoner."

"Uh-huh, but would you take a job to keep some scientists safe from 'dangerous subjects' and people wanting to steal their research? I could act all shitty too, you know? You killed a bunch of my friends with that IED you left in the tunnel." The fourth synth's eyes flickered to life, and Applebaum stepped back, shaking his head. He glanced at Juliet, but when she didn't take the bait, he sighed and turned back to the synths. "One, Two, Three, And Four. Follow me into the dojo."

"Understood," said One.

"Right away," added Two.

Three simply nodded, and Four said, "Will do!" They all had Australian accents.

Juliet snorted. "You gave them accents like yours?"

"What? Is that a crime, too? Just cravin' a bit of home." He marched toward the door, his train of synths behind him, and Juliet followed a few steps behind. She was irritated she'd let him get under her skin, but she felt good for speaking her mind; too many times in the past, she'd avoided saying what she felt in order to "keep the peace" or some other excuse to avoid awkwardness.

Back in the dojo, Tanaka lined the synths up on the mat in a staggered row, all facing one direction. He pointed to a spot in the middle of them and said, "Leo, stand here. Honey and Lucky, stand there." He pointed to the mat near the first synth. "Leo, the four synths, and I will simulate a crowd. Your job is to pursue Honey through the crowd without touching anyone with your sword. You must keep it ready and avoid making yourself vulnerable."

"I just follow her between the synths and you guys without hitting anyone?"

"That's right, but we won't be standing still. Imagine you're on a sidewalk. Don't worry; I have actual simulations of situations like this, but the VR chamber isn't ready—hopefully by Monday."

That simple instruction began a very frustrating, annoying half an hour of practice for Juliet, made more so when she learned she was the only one being put through it. Tanaka just shrugged at her irritation—she was the only one with a "monoblade," after all. While she felt singled out, she did her best to make the most of it, determined to avoid giving orange marks to the people in the "crowd."

Her good intentions were meaningless in practice, however. The synths moved erratically, supposedly simulating a larger crowd and how people might jostle one another. Applebaum went out of his way to try to bump into her, and Tanaka, while appearing to move normally and away from the cluster of synths, somehow managed to be in the perfect spot to trip her up when Juliet had to hurry to avoid hitting a stumbling synth. In the end, Rutger counted seven orange marks on the "crowd" and two on Juliet, including the one she'd given herself earlier.

"If I ever have to move through a crowd and they're as clumsy as you all, I'm not going to feel bad about slicing them up!" Juliet growled, annoyed at the negative feedback.

"What if they're a bunch of school kids who just got off the bus?" Honey grinned; she'd had far too much fun evading Juliet and using the crowd for cover.

Tanaka grunted, nodding. "Leo, get the ring tree, then you're dismissed. Honey, you too."

Leo jogged back to the equipment room, but Honey narrowed her eyes and glared from Tanaka to Juliet. "Why? Is she in trouble or something? It's not really fair to hold her accountable when—"

"Lucky is not in trouble, but she will have one more drill today to help her with blade discipline. My goal isn't equity; it's to ensure she becomes the best possible swordswoman."

Juliet looked from Honey to Tanaka, and though she'd been irritated earlier, she felt a kind of pride, or something close to it, from his attention. She wondered what that said about her. She'd never had a real father figure; at least not a stable one. Was it good that she wanted to show him she could do what he asked? Was it bad? She decided to ask Dr. Ming about the whole thing.

"Thanks, Honey. I'll catch up, I'm sure . . ." She trailed off as Leo emerged from the training room carrying a wooden pole with seven spindles sticking out of it, each adorned with thin, transparent lines from which hung black plasteel rings blinking with LED lights. The pole was built like a stand with feet on one end, and Leo stood it before Rutger. Then he bowed and turned to the locker room.

"No, no, Leo. Go to your apartment. The lockers are for my real students."

Leo stopped in his tracks, turned, and started for the door, muttering something about really feeling the love.

"This is a ring tree. There are twenty-one rings of various sizes; I want you to thrust your sword into each ring without touching the edges. Do it slowly and perfectly once, then faster. When you can pierce each ring in less than a minute without touching the edges, you'll be ready to carry the mono-blade." The rings were still swaying from when Leo had set them down, and Juliet looked at them, her brows creasing in consternation. Some were barely large enough to contain her sword blade. "Before you begin, we should review the proper technique for thrusting your sword."

To her surprise and relief, Honey didn't go straight to the lockers. She moved to one of the cedar benches and sat to watch while Tanaka took ten minutes to teach Juliet the proper technique for a sword thrust. He started by ensuring her stance and grip were right, turning her hips so she could stand facing the rings, her feet shoulder-width apart and one foot slightly forward.

"Good. Alignment like this will ensure the force of your body is behind the thrust. Hold your sword like this." He showed Juliet how to hold the sword before her, with the point angled toward the ring tree. "See the red dot on the pole? Imagine that is your opponent's throat."

Juliet nodded, adjusting herself slightly, appreciating Tanaka's guidance but also, deep in her gut, a little unnerved each time he touched her. Something was very charged about her perception of him, some memories too visceral to keep down. She figured it would take time before him adjusting her elbow or turning her hips was going to feel normal.

"Fix your gaze on the target. When you are learning, it's like learning to hit a baseball; keep your eye on what you want to stab. Later, when you're more skilled, we'll learn to avoid giving such things away in a duel."

"Okay." Juliet nodded.

"When you thrust, extend your arms smoothly toward the target, driving the sword forward. The motion should originate from your shoulders and proceed through your elbows to your wrists, ending with the sword moving in a straight line through that ring. Push off your back foot and lean your torso forward to add power."

"Okay," she said again.

"After the thrust, maintain your control. Quickly pull back to your starting stance, ready for the next attack or, in a real fight, to defend. Remember to breathe and remember your *kiai*." When Juliet nodded, he said, "Begin."

It took Juliet seven tries to get the sword through the first ring without touching the sides. She wanted Angel to help her, but she also wanted to see what she was capable of, so she doggedly kept at it until she'd cleared all the rings once. It took her twenty minutes, and she must have touched the edges a hundred times. In the end, her left arm, shoulder, neck, and back were exhausted and sore, so much so that her arm shook and sweat dripped from her fingers.

As she finished the last ring, Tanaka slapped his hands together. "Good! You did better today than I guessed you would. I . . . I knew your right arm was cybernetic, but it's much higher quality than I'd expected. Very precise." Juliet caught his weird hesitation about her arm, and it puzzled her at first, but then she remembered how she'd almost killed him back on Titan, driving her old cybernetic arm into his chest, pulverizing his heart.

She shrugged. "Yeah, I don't think I could have finished without it."

"You would have, but you would have taken longer and required more rest. Now you have a baseline, something to improve upon. It was a good first day." He didn't smile, but his face looked less dour than usual, and he offered her and Honey a quick bow. Honey shot to her feet and bowed back, and Juliet copied her, still a little put off by the whole thing. "Will you return tomorrow?"

"Are you wanting to do this every day?"

He nodded. "As often as possible. It's the best way to learn."

Juliet glanced at Honey, raising an eyebrow. "What do you say?"

"I can't do every day," she replied. "Monday through Thursday works for me."

Juliet shrugged and looked at Tanaka. "Will that work?"

"*Hai.* Monday, then." He turned and stalked toward the exit.

Juliet watched him leave, her mouth slightly open, caught off guard by his abrupt departure. "Bye, then . . ."

"Oh my God!" Honey laughed, running over to grab Juliet's arm. "That was so awkward! There's so much tension between you two!"

"It's obvious?" Juliet started to walk to the locker room but paused, glancing at the ring tree and synths. "We should clean up."

"Yes, it's obvious. Jeez! I thought I'd have a hard time letting things go, but you take things to a new level. He moves around you like you're bristling with porcupine quills!"

"Synth One, pick up that ring tree." Juliet issued the command, wondering if it would listen to her. It did. As soon as it held the ring tree, she ordered, "All synths follow me." Then she led them into the equipment room while Honey followed behind.

"You're not going to comment?"

"Oh, I know it's awkward, and yeah, I keep trying to put it all behind me, but I keep picturing him back then. I also keep thinking about the weird things he's told me, and, like, it makes everything he says and does feel loaded. I feel like it went okay today, though, and I think things will get more . . . normal, I guess."

"Yeah. I hate to say this, but, um, he knows so much more than Sensei." Honey looked pained, and she winced as she quickly added, "No offense to the Mongoose! I love you, Sensei!" Then, laughing, she continued, "Tanaka totally fixed a couple of things I've been doing wrong for *years.* I'm actually thrilled you want to keep doing this because I had so much fun! I haven't focused on basics like that in a long time, and I wasn't expecting to get anything out of it, but I did. I'm excited to see how things go."

Juliet thought about her words while she maneuvered the synths into position. Was she surprised Tanaka knew more than Sensei? At first, sure, but thinking about it, she had to admit that Sensei wasn't exactly running a high-end dojo. Tanaka, on the other hand, had learned from an old master in Japan, a guy on the payroll of a powerful corp, teaching their children and future operatives. Still, she felt the urge to defend Sensei. "It's easy to look at someone's work after the fact and point out little mistakes. Think of what you were before Sensei started teaching you. Tanaka gets to build on all his hard work and the foundations he created."

"Yeah, good point, sis!" Honey punched her in the shoulder. "Let's hit the showers, huh? You've got a lunch date, and I have to pick up Lilia."

Juliet nodded and started to leave, but Honey walked slowly, looking around at all the equipment. "You think this guy is going to open a real dojo or something? It seems wild that he'd get all this stuff just to teach you."

"Maybe. Maybe it's part of him trying to explore his 'new self.' Maybe he wants to build up a dojo full of followers and try to take on other schools at tournaments." The idea made her laugh, and as they showered and changed, she kept picturing Tanaka leading a bunch of kids around on field trips to different tournaments. The image kept a smile on her face.

"This was good for us, huh?" Honey asked as they got ready to leave. "You've been smiling like an idiot, and I feel more relaxed than I have in a long time."

"Good? Yeah, I think it was good." Juliet held up the practice monoblade and frowned. "You think he was serious about me taking this everywhere?"

"Yeah, but I'd check it for trackers. You got software for that?"

"Yeah, good call." Juliet plugged her data jack into the sword's pommel and waited for Angel to look through it. "You sure you can't come to lunch with us?"

"No, sorry. I have to pick up Lilia in less than an hour and don't want to feel rushed."

Angel sent a pleasant chime and a green checkmark through her AUI. "There's no tracking software in this sword. It does have transmitters and receivers, but they're all tied to the array of scanners in this dojo."

"Thanks, Angel," Juliet said, pulling her cable from the sword's hilt.

"Angel still, huh? Not gonna upgrade now that you're making some good scratch?"

Juliet laughed, shaking her head. "No way, sis. Angel's the real deal." Gripping the sword in her left hand, she gestured to the door. "Ready?" Honey nodded, and the two of them walked out, careful to skirt the dojo mats now that they had their shoes on. When they reached the door, Juliet turned to bow to the center of the dojo again, and Honey followed suit.

Outside, in the hallway, Honey hugged her. "Thanks again for inviting me."

"Thanks for coming! Imagine all that awkwardness without a friend to witness it!" They laughed and walked toward the reception where Juliet's second—or third, if she counted Applebaum—awkward encounter of the day was likely waiting for her.

21

\\\\\\\\\\\\\\\\\\\\\\\\\\\\

LUNCH AND MERCS

When Juliet and Honey stepped into the reception area, they found Applebaum leaning on the counter, chatting with Frida. As they came into view, he got quiet, but the lingering smile and the mischief in his eyes told Juliet he'd been talking trash. "Oi, ladies," he said as they stepped closer. "Showers work out all right?" He couldn't have been there long because he was freshly showered himself, wearing a very nicely fitted suit, apparently just getting ready to start his workday at the "office."

"Your place is in this building?" Honey asked, ignoring the question.

"Oh yeah. Talk about an easy commute. I'm two floors down."

"Tanaka pays for it," Frida chimed in.

Juliet seized the opportunity for a dig and snorted. "Must be nice."

"Hey! That apartment is part of my compensation, which I earn quite nicely, I might add." As Juliet leaned against the wall near Frida's desk, holding her practice monoblade by the sheath, resting it on her shoulder, he changed subjects again. "Shouldn't that be on your belt? By the way, I thought you were a novice."

Her earlier, lighthearted teasing took a blunt turn as she failed to keep his needling from getting to her. "I don't have clips for this belt yet. Also, mind your own business."

"Don't try to figure her out." Honey laughed, jostling her shoulder. "She always learns things fast. After a few months of practice, she was beating groups of blue belts at our old dojo."

He nodded, looking between the two women. "So you do have experience?"

"Not with the sword," Honey answered for her. "She watched me in plenty of practices, though."

"Well, I could see the boss was happy with your *men-uchi*. Took me a hell of a lot longer before he stopped making me adjust my grip or the blade or . . . Ah, you get the idea."

Juliet tapped her fingers on the sword hilt, narrowing her eyes at him, waiting for the other shoe, the "backhand" part of his backhanded compliment. When he didn't say anything more, she shrugged. "I have a good memory for things like that. If I see it done right, I can usually copy it pretty quickly." She turned her gaze to Frida. "You about ready?"

"Yes!" She hurriedly stood and pushed her chair in. As she walked around her desk, she paused by Leo and smiled sweetly at him. "Boss knows I'm leaving, so just forward anything that comes my way to my PAI, all right?"

He shrugged. "Yeah, sure. I don't have anything until that client meeting at one."

"Thanks, Leo." She gestured to the doors, locking eyes with Juliet. "Shall we?" Honey was already walking that way, pulling the big glass door open, and Juliet nodded.

Applebaum sighed and straightened up, making a show of stretching his waist, pressing his fist into his lower back. "Well, bye then. When's the next practice? Boss didn't say anything to me."

"Monday," Honey called, holding the door for Juliet and Frida.

In the elevator, Frida said, "Did you decide to join us, Honey?"

"No, sorry. I have to get to work." She smiled at Juliet, and something in her eyes indicated that she was trying to be pleasant to Frida. Juliet smiled back, then saw Frida watching them exchange their look and tried to play it off, looking down and tapping the sides of her legs with her fingers. It felt weird, and the silence in the elevator was getting heavy and awkward by the time the doors opened.

Honey hurried out, waving and calling over her shoulder, "Talk soon!" Then she was gone, the automated lobby doors closing on her quickly retreating form.

"She was in a hurry!" Frida said brightly, gesturing toward the far end of the lobby. "Restaurant's that way."

Juliet inhaled deeply, stretching her neck. "I'm starving. They have good sandwiches?"

"Great burgers, for sure. Not sure what else; I usually get a salad, but Leo's always getting a burger with fries, making me jealous."

"You guys eat here all the time, huh?" Juliet supposed she'd do the same if she worked in the building.

"Yep." Frida led the way into the restaurant, nodded when the hostess greeted her, and followed her to a table already set for two. "They know me, and I called ahead to say we were coming," she explained, glancing nervously at Juliet.

"Cool." Juliet sat down, leaning her practice sword against her chair. "I left Rutger's—well, my monoblade in my locker. It's safe there, yeah?"

"I'd say so. We have good security at the office. Besides, it's also the boss's home, and he never leaves." Frida sat across from her while the hostess left, muttering something about their specials being listed on the restaurant page. "I take it that means the lesson went well? You'll be back?"

Juliet snorted. "Oh, c'mon. Don't act like you didn't get the whole scoop from Applebaum." Frida fidgeted with her hands in her lap and looked down, her pale cheeks reddening a little. "You must have hated that when you were younger," Juliet said.

"Hated?"

"How easily your skin shows you're flushed."

"I'm . . . Well, yeah, I guess so. Forget that, though. I always feel like I'm off-balance with you. You know, when I found you on Callisto, I thought I was going there to do you a favor. I thought you were on the run from Tanaka, and you'd be relieved to hear he wanted to talk. You kind of threw everything out of balance when you shot me in the chest!"

"Balance?" Juliet sighed, drinking down half her glass of water. "You mean you're used to everyone walking on eggshells and being intimidated when they find out who your boss is." She set the glass down, sliding it in a small circle of condensation on the tabletop. "You didn't find me, in any case. Remember? I found out you were looking and contacted you. Anyway, I'm sorry I shot you. I'm pretty glad, now that I know who you are, that I didn't kill you."

"You know who I am?" Frida raised an eyebrow.

"I know Tanaka's more like a dad than a boss to you. I know you're not exactly a hired gun, so yeah, I know enough."

"He told you that?"

"Not in so many words . . ." Tanaka had certainly never used the word "Dad."

"Do you do it on purpose, though? Say things to get me all mixed up?"

This time, it was Juliet's turn to feel caught off guard by Frida's bluntness. Was she doing it on purpose? She had to admit she kind of enjoyed seeing Frida squirm, and she didn't really know what she was getting out of it. She liked her well enough—Frida didn't rub her wrong the way Applebaum had been.

Was that it? Did she think Frida was cute or . . . Realizing she was scowling in thought and not answering the question, Juliet cleared her throat. "I don't think I do it on purpose. I think I had an idea of what you were like when I first learned you worked for Tanaka. I suppose that wasn't fair, and . . ." Juliet felt like she was babbling. "So, anyway, let's start over. How about that?"

"That would be perfect!" Frida's smile was bright and genuine, and Juliet didn't need to read her mind to know she was relieved. "Let's take a minute to order."

"All right." Angel pulled the menu up for Juliet. She saw the burgers were supposedly well-reviewed, so she ordered a "Big Buster's BBQ Burger." Juliet stared at a link next to the burger and was shown photos of the "slow-grow" lattices in a local synth-meat plant. Flashing text displayed multiple five-star reviews and local articles about the fantastic texture and taste. Juliet shook her head, smiling, as she waved the menu away. "I'm taking your advice and trying a burger."

"Leo's kind of a food snob, so I think you'll be happy. He doesn't usually praise food."

"Leo? A snob? Who could guess? What'd you get? The salad?"

"Nope! I'm splurging today. I've been fasting. Yesterday, I didn't eat at all."

"So, what did you get?"

Frida opened her pale green eyes wide and grinned, hunching her shoulders and speaking in a conspiratorial whisper, "Deep dish, four-cheese personal pizza!"

Juliet smiled, also leaning closer. "Sounds absolutely awesome. Now I'm wondering if I messed up . . ."

"I'll give you a slice!"

"But you're, like, starving." Juliet frowned. "Why'd you skip a whole day of eating?"

"Ugh! I hate talking about this stuff, but I guess I'm the one who brought it up. It's my autoimmune disorder. I have more augments than it looks like." She gestured to herself as though she wanted Juliet to agree that it didn't look like she had many cybernetic implants. "I've had some pretty invasive ones since I was little." She shrugged. "Anyway, my immune system is . . .

overzealous. I have medical nanites that help keep it calmed down, but my current doctor recommended some fasting periods. Something about my body cannibalizing the misbehaving white blood cells. I'm supposed to go for three days, but . . ." She shrugged.

"It's hard, I bet."

"Yeah. I keep making it a day, then finding an excuse to eat again."

Juliet frowned. "It's not like you have a bunch of stored fat. How often are you supposed to do that?"

"Only when I'm having a flare-up." She reached up to her silky blouse and undid the top two buttons, pulling it wide, showing Juliet her red, inflamed skin. The irritation looked like it originated from a red, blotchy keloid scar right in the center above the delicate, flower-stitched lace of her bra.

"Hold up! Is that where I shot you? Did I cause your—"

"No! No, the scar's there, but this current flare-up only started a week ago. Anyway, forget it. Sorry I mentioned this stuff. I'm fine. My nanites keep things from getting bad. When I was a teen, I used to struggle to walk when I had a flare-up. The pain in my joints got so bad it felt like they were filled with broken glass. Now I get a bad rash and a little achy if I sit too long. Things could be worse."

"Huh." Juliet finished her water, looking around to see if there was hope for a quick refill. Quite a few tables were busy, and the wait staff seemed almost harried.

"Huh?" Frida frowned.

"Oh, I was just thinking we should have a cure for whatever is causing that by now. We can transplant pretty much every organ. We can clone cells and inject little robots that mend flesh. You'd think they could give you something to . . ." Juliet shrugged, unsure where she'd been going with that train of thought.

"Hey, forget it. Please. Like I said, it's not very bad." Frida was clearly ready to change the subject, so Juliet took the initiative.

"Well, what's the deal with your boss, huh?"

"You tell me!" Frida laughed, shaking her head in chagrin. "What did you do to him?" She held up a hand, waving it back and forth. "That was rhetorical. I know what happened. I just wish I knew what *happened*, you know?"

Juliet nodded, propping her chin in her hand as she rested her elbow on the table. "You mean with his mind?"

"Right! I know you and he fought, and I know you thought you were in the right—"

"That's 'cause I was."

Frida frowned but didn't argue. "Anyway, I know what happened to him, how he almost died, how his nanites were almost out of oxygen when the trauma center got him. He was in a coma for a while after the operations. The trauma center didn't want to replace all of his organs until they'd seen he was going to wake; apparently, a significant percentage of people who go that deep never come out of it. I insisted, though, and he had the package paid for, so they had to do it. His body was almost mended when he woke up, but his eyes weren't the same. Something in them was gone or changed."

She took a drink, probably wondering if Juliet would say anything, but when she didn't, Frida kept speaking. "It says a lot about people, doesn't it? That his eyes weren't the same? I mean, he's got chrome, robot-looking eye implants, but there was still something in his expression. The way his eyebrows moved, the wrinkles at the corners . . ." She sighed, shaking her head. "I can't explain it, but something's different in there."

Juliet was spared from having to reply immediately when one of the waitstaff brought their food and drinks. Her burger certainly looked good, from the slightly crusty, freshly baked bun to the thick, heavily seasoned potato fries. Juliet ate one right away, and she was sure her face showed her pleasure as the salty, greasy morsel danced over her taste buds.

"Good?" Frida grinned, looking down at her pizza. It looked decadent—more cheese than Juliet had eaten in weeks.

"Yeah, it's good. You know what they say, though—hunger's the best sauce, or something like that."

"Hah. You sound like Tanaka; he's always quoting things like that." She frowned, pulling a tiny piece off her crust and chewing it absently. "This synth-cheese is supposed to be hypoallergenic."

"Hope it tastes as good as it looks."

Frida pulled a piece of pizza from the dish and set it on her plate to cool. "Well? Any response to all that? I mean, about Tanaka?"

Juliet sighed and leaned back, holding a thick fry between her thumb and pointer finger, waiting for it to cool just a little before she stuffed it in her mouth. "I don't know what you want from me, Frida. I didn't know the guy before our encounter, and I don't know what's changed about him. I mean, sure, he almost died. He says things like he *did* die, that he's not the same man I killed. I don't know what to make of it all other than it's pretty damn weird. He seems genuine. He seems to really want to help me now, and shit, if that's true, then what's wrong with that? Maybe he does have some things to atone for, you know? Regardless of what you think, he wasn't exactly on the right side on Titan. He's already admitted to me that he's done plenty of immoral things in his life."

"But you're willing to work with him?"

"Is that what this is about?" Juliet stuffed the fry in her mouth, chewing, staring at Frida.

"Kind of. He's been obsessed with finding you, and I could tell he was very stressed, very worried that things wouldn't go well and that you'd leave. I just, well, I just want you to know that he's been better since having dinner with you, and that I hope you'll keep coming around, even if it's just to train. I feel like he's finally on the mend"—she tapped her head—"up here."

"The lesson went well, despite Applebaum." Juliet took another fry off her plate and blew on it. "Even Honey was enthused—said Tanaka knows a lot more than her old teacher. I think we'll keep coming for a while." A thought occurred to her, and she asked, "You live with him? I mean, is this your . . ."

"Home?" Frida chuckled and shook her head. "I have my own place on Titan. I thought we'd go back, and that this was temporary, but now I'm not sure. The boss is liquidating a lot of his holdings. I'm not sure he even still owns his place on Titan because some crates showed up here the other day with his artwork. I'll probably get my own place here, too, and see how things shake out."

"What about the rest of the team? Hawkins, right? And didn't you say he had some guys searching around Mars when we first met?"

"Yeah, Lee and Barns. Along with Hawkins and Leo, they're his last full-time operatives. He lost a few on Titan . . ." She grimaced. "As you know. Anyway, they're all here twiddling their thumbs, collecting their on-call pay, and making bets about what weird thing Boss will do next."

"He dumped a lot of money into that dojo." Juliet took her knife and, pressing down on the bun with one hand, sliced her burger in half. As she lifted it for a bite, sweet barbeque sauce dripped down her chin while she chewed. She wiped it, her cheeks flushing as she chewed the too-big bite.

Frida didn't seem to notice, her eyes distant as she responded, "He's been bleeding bits ever since he woke up, but that's after nearly thirty years of big paydays and very frugal living. He's a savvy man, always has been, and he invested quite a lot in some very successful ventures. I guess the moral of the story is, don't be concerned about the money he's spent trying to court you."

"Court me?" Juliet almost choked on her bite.

"Poor choice of words! I mean, like, recruit? No, um, seek your favor? Oh, God, I'm making it worse. Put it this way: Like you said, I think it boils down to him wanting to help you. We've all been wondering what he was doing, why he was paying so much for rumors, for people to travel, for, well, everything that led up to you coming here this morning and taking a lesson from him."

She used her fork to cut off a bite of pizza and lifted it off her plate. Before putting it in her mouth, she added, "Now, I just want to make sure you're not going to yank the rug out from under his feet." She looked so happy when she bit into the thick, greasy, cheesy forkful of pizza that Juliet couldn't help smiling as she watched her chew.

When she swallowed, Juliet asked, "Good as you'd hoped?"

"Better!" Frida licked her lips and took a long pull of soda through her straw.

"Tell me about the guys. What are they good at?" Juliet knew Angel had most of the information she might want about Rutger's crew, but she wanted to hear what Frida had to say about them. "I'm curious what kind of . . . attitudes, I guess, I might have to deal with when or if I meet them."

"Well, you met Applebaum, yeah? Like I told you, he's known Tanaka the longest—other than me, I mean. He's a charmer when he wants to be, and Rutger has him do most of the client meetings. He's still doing some work on his own while Boss figures things out. He's a marksman and has operated as a face. Rutger has a dozen solid, fully vetted IDs for him. Hawkins is a quiet man, and you won't have to worry about attitude from him; he doesn't really talk to people. He's a killer, the most dangerous of them all, other than the boss. Once, he cut the power on a human trafficking hub and cleared the place out with just a knife."

"A hub?"

"Like, the place where the gang doing the kidnapping brought their victims to ship them around the system. Hawkins didn't want to cause a big firefight around the kids, so he went in quietlike with his knife." Frida's eyes were excited as she spoke, clearly savoring the memory. "We earned a bonus from the client, and Boss gave Hawkins a tattoo to commemorate."

Juliet lifted an eyebrow. "Tanaka does tattoos?"

"Oh yes! Old-school, too, with needles and special inks."

"What about the other two?"

"Dora Lee is a netjacker and an espionage expert. She's one of the best— an A-ranked SOA operative. She's very professional and doesn't mix business and pleasure; she's probably working now, despite Rutger asking everyone to keep their plates empty, but we'd never know it."

"She, huh? Why'd I think Rutger's team were all men?"

"Well, don't let Lee catch you calling her a lady. I'll leave it at that."

"Okay, so he's got a face, a killer, a netjacker. What's the last guy?"

"Barns? He's a typical commando. Kind of a jack-of-all-trades—some explosives, some tech skills, but mostly just really good at picking the right guns and being in the right place at the right time. He's kind of a blowhard, and he'll flirt with anything that has two legs, but once you learn it's all hot air, you can kind of appreciate his . . . stability."

"And then there's Tanaka."

"Yeah. When he was on top of his game before you messed up his mind"— she shook her head and smiled, softening the words—"he was well regarded. Probably the highest-paid merc on Titan." Frida took another bite of pizza, and Juliet grinned, watching her draw a big cheese pull away with her fork.

"Why don't you just pick that up and bite it? You worried about impressing me? C'mon, I have barbeque all over my face."

Frida smiled while she chewed, and before she'd even swallowed, picked up her pizza slice and stuffed another big bite in her mouth. "Happy?" she mumbled around her mouthful.

Juliet grinned and nodded. "Yeah, I think so. You seem all right, Frida." She wasn't lying, but that didn't mean she trusted her. She still fully intended to read some of her thoughts before they left. She liked what she'd heard about Rutger's mercs, however. She hoped they were as good and as loyal as Frida thought. If she were going to get the old mercenary to help her put a plan together against WBD, they'd need some solid, unshakable team members.

22

BEING DISAGREEABLE

Juliet spent the weekend watching over a crew from a local company called Reactor Safe Innovations as they inspected, serviced, and brought online the gunship's He-3 reactor. She was alone; Aya and Bennet were up in orbit, helping to get things started on the *Red Betty* salvage. Shiro and Alice didn't think they'd need both of them for the whole job but wanted to make a strong start, so they'd been snagged from gunship duty for a week. Juliet didn't mind; she was decompressing after a busy few days filled with strange interactions with too many people, from Sergeant Hines to Honey to Frida and Applebaum. She was ready for some downtime without anyone talking to her.

The crew from Reactor Safe were mostly self-directing; they had a job to do, and they knew what it entailed. Still, they didn't exactly leave Juliet alone, especially when they got into the reactor room and realized it was the original Takamoto He-3 powerplant. They were impressed, to say the least.

Tom, the crew supervisor, told her they'd been expecting to see an after-market retrofit. Apparently, in the decades following the war, Cybergen and Takamoto He-3 reactors were heavily cannibalized for use with high-end luxury yachts and personal security vessels—their compact nature and pro-prietary cooling tech made them highly sought after.

He went on to describe how there were certain luxury ship makers with designs that wouldn't work without a Takamoto-era drive, not without add-ing twenty percent more mass to the final specifications. Juliet, always eager to talk ships, cars, or bikes, was intrigued by the story, but all it really did was make her more nervous than ever about the *Furies' Wing* and the ridiculous artifact that it was—even without the highly illegal, world-shattering secret AI sleeping aboard.

On Friday, the team diagnosed the reactor and all of its systems. On Saturday, they flushed the coolant system, ran new lines, performed maintenance on the magnetic confinement system, and prepped the new core. On Sunday, they loaded in fresh He-3 pellets and fired it up so they could calibrate everything.

Juliet was lying in her bunk, trying to make sense of a sci-fi book from Aya's big haul called *Dune*, when the power flickered as the gunship's drive came to life. They'd been running things from an external grid cable, but as the drive hummed through the plasteel frame, the lights brightened, and the air circulation system began to blow in earnest, producing much cooler air.

When the Reactor Safe team left in the afternoon, the gunship had a clean, well-serviced powerplant smoothly humming away, and Juliet couldn't help feeling that the day when it was ready to launch was suddenly much closer. As they drove off, Juliet brought a couple of beers out to the security guards she had on duty, and though they protested and she had to insist, they drank them and made small talk with her for a little while.

According to them, crime was still up in the industrial domes, and more and more companies were hiring personal security. The conversation got Juliet wondering about Hines and what kind of progress he'd made, but when she messaged him, all she got back was a quick reply saying he'd get back to her soon.

The following week went by in a kind of blur. Juliet met Honey downtown for breakfast before practice with Tanaka each day, during which she continued to impress everyone. Of course, it was Angel who was really doing the impressing, but Juliet wasn't ready to hand off all the credit. She worked hard and had some natural talent—even Applebaum admitted that. Still, even knowing that, she had to admit that feeling the movements done perfectly by Angel helped her grasp things exponentially faster.

Tanaka kept teaching them basic stances and cuts, but he did so in an additive fashion so that by Thursday, Juliet was smoothly moving through several cut combinations, with footwork that had seemed simple but only because Tanaka had taught it to them step by step, forcing them to perfect each step before adding the next piece. Each day, after new learning, Tanaka led them in drills, and Juliet unfailingly felt persecuted during that part of practice—she was the only one "learning to use a monoblade," so Tanaka had extra activities for her when everyone else was finished.

He continued to count the accidental marks she made with her practice sword, and though Juliet didn't believe him, he claimed that the fewer marks she produced meant fewer rounds of extra blade discipline training. She didn't believe him because it always seemed to take about forty-five minutes regardless of how careful she'd been during practice.

Honey stayed with her for the first couple of practices, but eventually, things felt less awkward, and she didn't feel guilty about showering and heading out while Juliet was still doing her remediation. Juliet didn't resent her; it had to be tedious watching her perform the slow, careful movements with the sword blade over and over.

Tanaka's VR training room—basically a room-size dream-rig—wasn't ready to use until Tuesday, but when it was done, Juliet got to enter simulations instead of working with rings or dummy synths, making things a lot more entertaining during her extra practice. He had sims for chasing people through pretty much any environment, sims for every kind of battle with any number of opponents, sims that were basically high-tech versions of the ring tree, and sims that were designed to help her perfect her foundations.

Those foundational sims were more fun than Juliet had anticipated when he first loaded her into one. All she had to do was perform the cuts the anime-style instructor modeled, and when she did it, it played them back for her, showing her exactly how she held her hands, the angle of her sword, her posture, her foot movement—everything. Angel loved it, memorizing the data to help Juliet even more efficiently.

Still, of all the sims, Juliet loved the ones where she was chasing people, which was a good thing because Tanaka favored them too. He thought chasing people in various environments was great practice for everything from blade discipline to hand-eye coordination to split-second decision-making.

Thursday, after she was done with her personal purgatory of drills, Juliet stepped out of the VR sim and found Tanaka in the dojo exercising with his sword. He had a way of moving that Juliet hadn't recognized when they'd first started, but now that she'd been practicing for a week, learning a bit more about what it took to control a sword perfectly, she had to admit he was impressive. He had such perfect control, such explosive speed, and such fluidity that Juliet felt clumsy just watching.

"And that's with your help," she muttered. Angel didn't reply, but a question mark appeared on her AUI. She'd been doing that lately—using nonverbal input to try to simulate body language.

Tanaka noticed her and smoothly sheathed his sword. "I just read the report from the VR suite. You did well." He didn't often offer praise, so, of course, Juliet felt herself beaming at the comment. She caught a lot of flak during practice from Applebaum and even Honey; they'd taken to ganging up to try to bring Juliet down a notch whenever she flawlessly performed a new skill.

It didn't bother her much; she knew they were just messing around. Well, she knew Honey was just messing around. She knew how frustrating it could be to watch someone else master something you were struggling with, so she had to expect some grief, anyway. She'd decided to let Angel help her, and she'd have to deal with the consequences.

"Thanks." She nodded in a close approximation of a very informal bow. She wasn't totally warmed up to Tanaka and didn't like the constant show of obeisance other people gave him, but she had to respect him as a teacher. He was good.

"I . . . learned from my master that praise can be a corruption to a student, that it can cling to them, festering and growing, until it builds a false sense of pride and a flaw in character. Nevertheless, I have to say that you have a gift. I've never seen someone so perfectly master every cut, every movement, every combination. At first, I thought you were running software through your cybernetic arm. That it was performing programmed movements. That's not it, though—your entire body moves with perfection, even when I teach an advanced technique like my master's *shinsetsu kaze tori*, something you wouldn't find in a training program."

Juliet nodded, shrugging. She'd been anticipating this conversation, and honestly, she'd felt suspicious when Tanaka threw that maneuver into the day's practice. It had come from nowhere and didn't fit into the generally smooth progression of skills they'd been learning up to that point. It was a disarming technique that Tanaka said only his master's school would know, a closely guarded secret.

"I won't lie to you, but I won't tell you all my secrets. I have some proprietary tech, something I can't take out or give to someone else, that helps me learn things quickly." She sighed and stepped a little closer. "I mean, I've also been told I have a talent for this stuff, and that the tech I have works especially well because of my neural and cellular adaptiveness, but"—she shrugged—"I can't take all the credit."

He nodded. "The proof of your talent will be in your ability to take every-thing you learn and apply it fluidly." After a pause, during which Juliet just looked at him impassively, he added, "So far, you seem to be doing that just fine; the simulations indicate a strong synthesis of learned skills."

"So we don't have a problem?"

"A problem? No. I'm just wondering if I'm teaching you too slowly."

"I don't think so!" Juliet laughed. "I guess, if you think it will help, you could increase the difficulty on the sims, and maybe I could start doing some actual fights in there . . ." Earlier on, he'd scolded her for trying to load the combat sims, saying she didn't have the proper foundations and that she'd build bad habits.

"*Hai*. I'll think about it." He looked at her, his face hard to read as usual, and then he *sort of* smiled. Juliet could see just a glimmer of what a genuine smile would be like in his eyes and the very faint upward tilt of his lips. "Have a good weekend."

"Are you . . . happy?" Juliet couldn't help the teasing tone, and for just a couple of seconds, she forgot the awkwardness between them, but then he looked down, almost ashamed, and it all came crashing back. He started to turn, and she'd seen his quick exits too often not to recognize one in the mak-ing, so she said, "Hey, I was just joking around. You gotta lighten up a little, don't you think?"

She wasn't sure what had been different about that moment that made her confront the issue head-on, but something had gotten a hold of her tongue, and now that the words were out, she wanted to push through things.

"I try, but . . ." He sighed, shaking his head. "This isn't proper for a teacher to discuss with a student."

"Class is over. Come on, what's the deal? I'm the one who's supposed to be nervous around you, not the other way around."

He turned to her and held one of his tattooed hands to his chest. "I feel dread here."

"Dread?"

"Yes. That I'll say the wrong thing, that you'll discover the wrong thing, that something will happen to make you leave." He sighed, and his usually stiff, square shoulders slumped. "How can I be a good teacher when I fear my students?"

"You fear me?"

"I fear you leaving."

Juliet had heard him the first time, but she forced herself to look at the words the second time he said it. It seemed like his entire life revolved around "helping" her now. If she took that away from him, what would he do? Was that what his fear was about?

Part of her wanted to reassure him, to tell him that she meant to stay and keep training with him. Part of her wanted to tell him she was even working up the nerve to ask him for help scoping out WBD's research facilities. For some reason, those parts of her kept quiet, and the sliver of herself that resented Tanaka, that still clung to images of him as she'd first met him, spoke up.

"Well, you should load a shrink program into that VR room of yours. If I got all messed up every time someone walked out of my life, I'd never get out of bed."

Even if his face hadn't fallen, even if he hadn't nodded, silently agreeing with her, Juliet would have felt bad. She regretted the words the instant she said them, but something in her wouldn't let her take them back. In any case, the damage was done. The sliver of happiness on Tanaka's face was gone, and he performed his usual quick goodbye bow, turned, and left.

"I'm a bitch," she subvocalized. Angel's silence spoke volumes.

Juliet took a shower and changed into her street clothes. That day, she was wearing her favorite stretchy jeans, the T-shirt Honey had given her, and a new pair of handmade, black, silver-tipped motorcycle boots she'd ordered from Chicago. Of course, she couldn't verify they were handmade, but they were certainly high quality. They reminded her of cowboy boots, and she felt pretty cool walking around in them. She'd also purchased some custom clips to wear her practice monoblade on her gun belt; it hung from her left hip and took a lot of getting used to, but she was warming up to it.

Applebaum, as usual, was hanging around chatting Frida up when she left. He usually had a biting—or teasing, depending on how you looked at it—remark for her about practice, her clothes, or something along those lines, so she wasn't surprised when he cleared his throat. His words caught her off guard, though. "Hey, no practice tomorrow. Wanna go get drunk?"

Frida didn't say anything, but Juliet saw her press her lips together and look down; clearly, she didn't approve of the idea. She thought about a few responses, most of them negative, several of them quite cutting, but she decided to play things neutrally, considering Applebaum hadn't inserted any sort of insult into his invitation. "I would, but my friends are coming moonside tonight, and I promised I'd make dinner."

"You would, though? Otherwise?"

"Um, yeah, otherwise." She shrugged.

"See? Told you she'd go out with me." He nudged Frida in the shoulder with his fist, and Frida groaned, slapping a hand in front of her eyes.

"Oh, get melted, dreamer." Juliet flipped him the bird and stomped for the door.

"I didn't make a bet with him! He's an idiot!" Frida called after her. Juliet didn't look back as she made her way to the elevator. Her interaction with Tanaka and then the nonsense with Applebaum had put her into a sour mood, and she didn't want to end up snapping at Frida. She'd bet money she was an innocent pawn in Applebaum's game.

"Struggling with interpersonal matters today, aren't you?" Angel asked as the elevator doors closed.

"At least I've got you, sis."

"I was quite upset at how you treated Tanaka."

Juliet groaned and leaned forward, gently banging her forehead against the closed elevator doors. "I'm sorry." She wanted to justify herself, but what was the point? Angel knew everything about her, and she knew she'd been wrong. Still, despite herself, she said, "My reaction wasn't logical; it was just a part of me that wanted to act out. I think I'm just sick of him acting like everything is so *heavy* all the time. You know? I just want to be able to move forward."

"He's moving forward, but his therapy requires you, and he's afraid you're going to leave. He has no security in his—"

"I get it, Angel, but put yourself in my shoes! Is it fair for him to put that on me?" As the doors opened and she began striding across the lobby, she snorted a laugh. "Really? Therapy?"

"Wouldn't you describe what he's gaining from your lessons as therapy?"

"I guess it fits." Juliet was a fast walker, and she was standing before her bike in the parking garage in no time. As usual, there hadn't been any spots on the street when she'd arrived. She was adjusting her helmet and pulling the visor down when a voice, unmistakably Applebaum's, called out from behind her.

"Hey!"

She turned, visor still up, and scowled at him. He was jogging toward her from the garage elevator bank. "What?"

"Hey, Frida's pissed at me. She didn't have anything to do with that. I was just being dumb."

"Yeah?" Juliet swung a leg over her bike, ready to start it up.

"Yeah. My invitation was sincere, and I was just being a smartass when you said no. Do you really have plans tonight?"

"I said I did, didn't I?"

"Well, listen. The boys wanna meet you. Everyone wants to know what you're like, and I'm sick of answering questions."

"The boys?" Juliet knew who he meant, but she was in the mood to be difficult.

"You know, Tanaka's mercs here on Luna. Hawkins, Lee, Barns."

Juliet raised an eyebrow, a little tricky considering her helmet pressing on her forehead, but she managed. "Dora Lee? She likes being called one of the boys?"

"Ah, she doesn't care, love. Calls herself that half the time."

"Did you just call me 'love'?"

"Oh, just a habit when I'm talking to a pretty lady . . ." His smug smile was almost more than she could take.

Juliet's scowl returned with a vengeance. "Get—"

"Melted. Right. Listen, if I promise not to call you love or some other demeaning term of endearment, will you think about meeting up with me and the squad this weekend? If not tonight, maybe tomorrow or Saturday?"

"Can I bring friends?" Juliet wondered if mixing her *Kowashi* friends with Tanaka's crew would be colossally stupid.

"If it makes you feel better . . ."

"Is Frida coming?" Something about having Frida along made the whole thing seem less risky, almost like if she endorsed it and was present, there was no way these clowns would mess with Juliet too much.

"I haven't asked, but I'm sure she'd—"

"I'm free Saturday. Have her message me the time and place, and I'll think about it." Juliet touched the ignition button, and her bike rumbled to life. As Applebaum started to reply, she slapped her visor down and twisted the throttle, producing a faux-exhaust roar. She tapped the side of her helmet and made a shrugging gesture.

He scowled and started to yell, "I said, I've got a fun idea . . ." Juliet laughed as she peeled out and left him standing there, midshout.

"That made me feel better, Angel."

"Well, at least he deserves some teasing, considering all the digs he threw your way this week."

"C'mon, I wasn't *that* hard on Tanaka. It's really not a bad idea for him to get some counseling. Hey! Send him a link to the net store where you got Dr. Ming with my compliments. Maybe he'll think I was being sincere . . ."

"Are you saying you plan to gaslight Tanaka into thinking you weren't rudely shutting him down?"

"Gaslight? Angel, you always pick the worst extreme to describe my behavior when it involves Tanaka!" Juliet was unconsciously speeding, something that tended to happen whenever she drove angry, and she fought to ease back on the throttle. "Look, I know you like him, but—"

"I wish I'd never told you that." Those words stung, and they made Juliet clamp her mouth shut and really think about her behavior. She'd already admitted she'd been wrong. She'd already caught herself acting short-fused at least three times that day. Why was she willing to fight with Angel about it? Why was she being disagreeable with everyone?

"I'm sorry, Angel. That was petty and stupid. I know you said you admired things about him, not that you are in love or something, and it's rotten of me to use that against you. Truce?"

"Truce. Thank you for apologizing."

"I'll try to be more open-minded starting Monday, all right?"

"I can't ask for anything else. Now, you have a call waiting from Hines. I've had him on hold for a minute because I wanted to resolve our differences."

"Oh? Hines? Put him through."

As soon as Hines's weary, grizzled face appeared on her AUI, he began to speak.

"Lucky! I'm glad I got a hold of you. Listen, I might need your help. I heard through a CI that there's a hit out on me. Seems like my inquiries about the stolen parts racket in the industrial domes might have ruffled the wrong feathers."

23

SAVIOR COMPLEX

"What are you going to do?" Juliet asked, slowing down and pulling up behind a cargo van, coasting in its wake so she could pay better attention to Hines.

"I gotta lay low. Gotta disappear for a while. I might need you to move around and be my eyes and ears for a little while. I can pay a fair contract wage."

Juliet chuckled and *tsked*. "Things that bad, corpo man? Don't have a single friend you can trust? Must be cold behind those glass-and-plasteel walls."

"Things are bad, yeah, but only 'cause I didn't kiss the right asses or take the right bribes. You gonna leave me hanging 'cause I had a little bit of a conscience and got myself in over my head?"

"When you put it like that, how can my frosty heart not thaw a little?" Juliet smiled inside her helmet, savoring the moment when a corpo-sec officer came to her for help with corruption. "We've got this secure line. You can send me a contract, and I'll probably sign it. Wanna tell me what you're thinking? Want me to snoop on your friends? Break into the chop shop? Capture some thugs? What's the game plan?"

"Contract first. I sort of trust you, but I'd rather we put your SOA rep on the line, too."

"Well, I'll be waiting. You got a place to hide?"

"Got a few. Made plenty of questionable acquaintances when I was on the beat." He nodded, sniffed, then, staring into the camera, said, "Seriously,

Lucky. Please don't leave me hanging. Keep your schedule clear for the next few days."

"Hey, I said I'd probably sign your contract, but don't start assuming I don't already have stuff going on. I'll figure out my schedule, though. Copy?"

"Yeah. Copy." He nodded tersely before cutting the line.

"It must be hard to have no one to trust." Angel's comment made Juliet's stomach twist, and she goosed the throttle, jetting out of the slow lane around the van she'd been following.

"It would be awful." She drove that way for a couple of minutes, just a bit faster than she should have been going, and when Angel didn't say any more, she added, "I know I'm lucky to have you. I also feel sorry for Hines, but we have to remember that he's not a kid—he's been corpo-sec for a long time. He made that bed he's lying in, so let's not get too eager to fall all over ourselves helping him."

"That's a perspective I hadn't considered. It's interesting to think that the people we become are partly the sum of our actions. It makes the idea of trusting someone a little more intriguing to me, a little more scientific than a 'feeling' you might have."

"Sure. I mean, you knew that, though! You have to consider a person's history when thinking about how to interact with them. Aya, for instance, has never hurt a mouse. I'd trust her with just about anything."

"But you didn't know Aya before the day you first boarded the *Kowashi*. Are you being hyperbolic when you say she's never hurt a mouse?"

"I guess. I mean, she didn't trust me when we first boarded. Don't you remember? She was pretty suspicious of me. I think that makes me trust her more, knowing I had to earn hers." Juliet laughed and shook her head. "What's the point of this? What are we talking about? Hines . . . I don't trust him yet, which is why I'm not dropping everything to run to his aid. He's got more to prove to me."

"And Tanaka?"

"Oof! You're really going to bring him up again? I said I'll try to be nicer on Monday, okay?"

"Okay, well, what about Leo? Will you meet him and the 'guys' this weekend?"

"Depends on the Hines situation, but yeah, I guess so." With that settled, Angel got quiet, and so did Juliet, letting her mind wander through the people in her life and savoring the good relationships as a kind of counterbalance to the frustration she'd been feeling with Tanaka and Applebaum.

She stopped and did some shopping at a high-end market where she could pick up some preformed, seasoned burger patties made of high-quality, Luna vat-grown protein. She'd said she'd cook for the crew, but not that she'd do anything fancy. Still, she bought a tray of veggies and dip, Aya's favorite kind of chips, and a variety of buns to satisfy their dietary needs—low carb for Bennet, no gluten for Shiro, and just lettuce wraps for Alice.

Back at the hangar, she fired up the new propane-powered grill she'd ordered a few days earlier. By the time the crew landed and made their way out to the hangar, she had the door open, the security guards were each eating a burger, and Juliet was sitting in a lawn chair drinking her second beer. They arrived in a rented van, and as Juliet stood, Aya burst out of the side door and ran over.

"That smells good!"

Juliet assumed she was talking about the smoke billowing out of the grill. "That's right! Open flames for us! Don't tell corpo-sec, 'cause I think this is illegal in the industrial domes." She was a little buzzed and slurred one of her words, eliciting a giggle from Aya.

"More beer?"

"In the cooler." Juliet turned to the van, watching as Bennet hauled out his toolboxes and, with his deltoids and traps straining to burst out of his T-shirt, carried them into the hangar. Shiro carried another but offered her a quick wave as he walked by. "Hurry up, boys! Burgers are about to burn."

"I'll take a beer," Alice said, walking over.

"Aya . . ." Juliet started to say, but Aya had already returned from the cooler with a grip of beers in her hands. ". . . has one for you."

"Lovely!" Alice took one and ripped the plastic top off. "Not bad, but I prefer a glass bottle."

"Well, we're on Luna, Alice, and I didn't think it was worth twenty bits a bottle to get glass . . ."

"Easy, Lucky! I'm not complaining." She drained half the squeezable beer container, then, sighing and burping, added, "I'm a little tired from the drop out of orbit—traffic around the port was nuts."

"No worries. It's why I wanted to feed you guys. I know how tired you must be." She lifted the grill lid, let out a delicious-smelling smoke, and flipped the burgers. "These are about ready." She wasn't a genius with timing or anything—Angel had been keeping tabs on the others and had given Juliet a minute-by-minute itinerary for their return.

"I'll grab some plates." Aya hurried over to the folding table Juliet had set up. When she returned, Juliet unloaded the burgers and stood back while the others loaded their plates with food. She made her burger last, smiling to herself as she listened to the others talk.

"Did you see that asteroid rig taking off when we landed?" Bennet asked Shiro.

"Oh, I'm so glad to be back!" Aya gushed, taking a big bite and talking around it. "One more day of zero-G, and I was going to lose it!"

"I bet that asteroid rig has gravity gen! It was *huge*," Bennet said before Shiro could answer the first question.

"*Hai*," Shiro muttered as he worked to unfold another chair.

"I barely saw it. Too busy watching the traffic lanes. We almost got clipped. Did you guys know that? Some little jerk in a shuttle. He came within a meter—a *meter*—of hitting our portside waldo."

As though she hadn't spoken, Aya brought up a new subject. "Lucky, we got all the maneuvering thrusters off the *Red Betty*. Shiro already has a buyer lined up."

"Oh yeah? That's great. I mean, those are some of the hardest things to disassemble, right?"

"Yep. We got a great start."

"Oh shit! That reminds me," Bennet said. "How'd things go with the Reactor Safe guys?"

"I sent you the report." Juliet grinned. "But if you want to hear it from an eyewitness, things went great. She's purring like a kitten."

"She?" Alice laughed. "We're sure about that, huh? Have you guys thought of a name yet? Seems if she's got a working reactor and rebuilt drives, she ought to have a name."

Juliet could see Aya was bursting to tell them the name Juliet had come up with. The two of them had talked about it at great length during one of their late-night movie-watching sessions. Of course, Aya loved the idea the instant Juliet said it. Still, Juliet wanted to keep things under wraps a little longer.

"Let's not make any names official yet. I want her to be ready before we debut her and start broadcasting her ITM data. I feel like it will be good luck." The ITM, or Identity Transmission Module, would broadcast the ship's name and identity number—something they had yet to purchase.

"Oh? So you already have a name in mind and we don't get a say?" Alice raised one of her feathery red eyebrows.

"It's a great name!" Aya replied, squeezing some of her beer into her mouth.

"Hey, if she knows . . ." Bennet shook his head, leaving the rest of his complaint unvoiced.

Juliet tried to turn the conversation back on them and get the focus off her. "Do you guys really care? Any of you have an idea for a name?"

"No." Shiro crunched up his beer pouch and pulled another out of his overall pocket.

"Nah." Bennet shrugged, the matter dropped as far as he was concerned.

"I mean, I wouldn't want it to be dumb, but I don't have any ideas." Alice laughed and popped a couple of salty, vinegar-flavored potato chips into her mouth, wincing at the sourness.

"Okay, well, here's the deal I'll make you all. Before we make the name official, I'll get everyone's approval. If you think it's dumb, we'll change it, okay?" She mostly spoke to Alice, and when she nodded, still chewing her chips, Juliet sat back, pleased.

Shiro cleared his throat. When everyone looked at him, he began to speak, reciting what felt like a prepared speech, which had Alice's jaw hanging open after just a few words. "I'd like to thank you, Lucky, for this nice meal after a hard week's work." When he paused, Juliet started to say it was no big deal, but he kept going. "More than that, I want to thank you for the opportunities you've brought our way in the last year. I haven't worried about paying bills for the last few months, and, well, this is the first time in my life I could say that." He held up his beer pouch in salute, and Juliet felt hot embarrassment creep up her neck as everyone turned to her, holding their drinks up. "To Lucky."

"To Lucky!" everyone echoed.

Juliet laughed nervously, clearing her throat and shaking her head. "How's that? You guys bust your tails off working all week, and I'm the one getting toasted? No, no, no. Thank you! Each of you has gone out of your way to be a good friend to me, and I can't tell you how much that means. So, let's call it even." She held up her beer, and they all mimicked her. "To us, yeah?"

"To us!" Everyone laughed and drank.

Bennet jerked his thumb down the street to the corner of the building where one of Juliet's two security guards stood. "Feel awkward having those guys hanging around all the time?"

"Not at all. Who do you think I was drinking and lifting weights with while you were gone?"

Bennet slapped a hand to his heart. "You wound me!"

"Easy to replace a musclehead, Bennet." Aya laughed. "I bet those guys weren't reading old books with you, right?" She sat in a foldable chair beside Juliet and, as she spoke, leaned close and rested her cheek on Juliet's shoulder.

Juliet gently tousled her hair. "Not a chance."

Bennet leaned toward Shiro, gesturing with his beer. "You see that, Shiro? This is the kind of thing that really builds my confidence, 'cause I know they wouldn't treat me that way if they didn't think I could take it."

Shiro, back to his nonverbal norm, snorted and sipped his beer. Alice took the brief moment of quiet to speak.

"Lucky, I know you're helping out here, but the light's starting to reveal itself at the end of this gunship tunnel. If you want some work in the meantime, I know people who'd pay to be escorted by a ship like the *Lady Hawk*. Could rake in a few bits while you're waiting for Bennet and Aya to finish up with this big girl." She pointed into the hangar toward the dark, looming shape of the gunship.

"Um, depending on how long it takes, that might be a good option down the road. For now, though, I kind of want to stay hands-on here. I have a few smaller things happening here in Luna, too—a small contract through SOA, and I'm trying to build up my non-gun-related combat skills."

"She's learning to fight with a sword." Aya was, apparently, holding on to one too many secrets.

"And fighting crime in the industrial domes." Bennet laughed.

"Thought that was what the guards were for?" Alice stood to retrieve another couple of beer pouches from the cooler.

Juliet sighed, leaning back, drumming her fingers on her sword hilt. It jutted between the chair's arm and the ground, and she wondered if she'd get tangled up if she tried to stand too quickly. "That's a Band-Aid. We need to get to the root of the problem . . ."

"We do, huh?" Alice snickered, cocking her eyebrow at Juliet again. "You know what?"

"What?" Juliet's cheeks were still warm and a little flushed from the beer and Shiro's uncharacteristic toast.

"You have a savior complex."

"Oh, bull—"

"Hey, don't say mean things tonight!" Aya cried, interrupting Juliet's objection.

"What's mean?" Alice sighed, sitting down. "I'm not saying it's bad. I mean, your heart is in the right place, for sure. Just think of everything you've gotten up to since you met us, though." She started listing things off on her fingers: "Dove into space to save Bennet, fought off way more pirates than your contract justified, rescued some stray girls, rescued your friend Honey, uh, what else . . ."

From the look in her eyes, Juliet knew she was about to list something about Nick but had thought better of it. She kind of trailed off, clearly regretting bringing the whole thing up, but Juliet couldn't be mad at her, not right then, so she bailed her out.

"Eh, that's what it looks like from the outside. If you knew what was happening in my head, you'd know I'm just a freakishly lucky dummy who wants to believe there's some good in everyone's heart."

Alice smiled, relief in her eyes. "We love you that way. Maybe I had to list some things to remember that your 'savior' behavior is really just what it looks like when you meet someone who stands up for their beliefs in this messed-up world."

Juliet got quiet at that, uncomfortable with the praise but unable to formulate a clever diversion away from it. Bennet saved her when he pointed at her sword. "Is that your monoblade? Thought you weren't going to wear that until you were—"

"Relax, big guy. This is a practice sword, and my new teacher is making me carry it everywhere. Gonna be embarrassing when someone challenges me to a duel."

Bennet said something funny, getting a laugh out of Alice and Aya, but Juliet missed it because Angel projected a priority call window on her AUI. "Hines is calling, and he's flagged the call as an emergency."

Juliet stood abruptly, surprising herself by smoothly extricating herself and her sword from the folding chair. "Sorry, just a minute, guys. Someone's calling."

She walked away from the door into the cool, dim alley. The security guards were ahead of her, currently patrolling down near the corner of the building. As soon as she'd stepped out of the light of the open bay doors, Angel connected the call, and Hines's face resolved.

"Thanks for taking my call. You got a minute?" He looked to the side. Juliet could see the stress in his eyes.

"I'm listening."

"I'm sending a contract to you right now. One of the guys I thought I could trust just turned on me. I almost got raided in my safe house. He doesn't know I know. I'm dumping my PAI and switching to a burner ID. I've got your contact info, so I'll be in touch, but gotta really disappear for a while. I'm going to send you instructions with that contract. I think we should start with this traitor. I want you to get to him—figure out who's pushing his buttons. Can't believe the little asshole actually flipped. Practically raised the little punk."

"You want me to 'get to' a corpo-sec officer?"

"Yeah. He messed up. I know everything about him, so it shouldn't be too hard. Gonna send you everything you need."

"I'll look at it." Juliet wanted to tell him she wasn't a hundred percent on board, that she had to think things through and see what kind of exposure she was looking at. He looked so rough, though—harried, red eyed, sleep deprived. She knew that feeling. He had no one to turn to, and as Alice had helped her admit a minute ago, Juliet wanted to believe the best in people. "You're not alone, Hines."

That gave him pause, and he closed his eyes and took a deep, slow breath. "I needed to hear that, Lucky. Thank you. You help me get through this, and I won't forget it." His eyes widened, and he jerked his head to the left. He looked back at her a second later and said, "I gotta go. Contract's on its way."

As the call window closed and Juliet clenched and unclenched her fists, wishing she could see Hines and know he was in the clear, Angel produced a new window with a standard SOA job posting and contract.

Posting #L1788b	Requested Role: Investigative	Rep Level: D-S+
Job Description: *Private until job completion* Investigate corruption in the Luna City Security Corporation in relation to ongoing thefts, robberies, and fencing of stolen goods in the various Luna City industrial domes.		**Compensation:** 10k weekly retainer with a potential bonus.
Scavenge Rights: Exclusive	**Location:** Luna City	**Date:** August 3, 2108 - Ongoing

"He sent your first 10k payment with the contract."

"What's the 'private until job completion' note? Does that mean others won't see I'm working this job?"

"Yes, that's standard for corpo-sec jobs. He's hiring you through his official capacity, so there's a good chance he's taking your pay out of his department budget."

"Oh, that makes me feel better about the poor guy having to pay me. Also, I love the idea that Luna City Security is paying me to weed out some of their own corruption." Juliet figured it also meant good things for a bonus—if she succeeded and Hines gained some clout in the department, he might be able to authorize a decent payday. "He send the details about his known traitor?"

"Yes. Evan Lopez. He's given us his address and a schematic of his home security, with a caveat that Evan is likely to change or upgrade things if he realizes Hines is onto him. He also included Evan's work schedule, his known acquaintances, and his usual pastimes and hangouts."

"Sounds like he's serving him up on a silver platter, huh? Makes me nervous. Is he working tonight?"

"He works the graveyard shift. His next day off is Tuesday." Juliet looked back to her friends sitting around the grill, sipping their beer, laughing, and chatting. She supposed she could head out after midnight. Everyone would be gone or passed out by then.

She cleared her throat, stooping to pull open the cooler as she passed. She plucked out a pouch of beer and asked, "Anyone ready for another?"

"Throw me a couple," Bennet said, holding his hand up.

Juliet tossed him a single pouch. "Better take it slow. You owe me a bunch of workouts, and I'm claiming the first one tomorrow."

"Oh, I do, do I?" He laughed and ripped the top off his pouch. "You know, after a week of zero-G, you might be able to keep up with me for once."

"It does feel nice to be on solid ground, though," Alice noted. Juliet saw the flush of alcohol on her cheeks and around her nose. Her eyes twinkled with amusement, and she looked absurdly happy leaning toward Shiro, holding his hand. She didn't need to read minds to know who was getting lucky that night.

Looking from Alice to Shiro, Bennet, and Aya, she felt very fortunate and wildly protective of them. Suddenly, she was sure she didn't want them to meet Applebaum and the others on Tanaka's team. She wanted to keep those worlds separate for as long as she could.

"How about some music?" she asked, tapping her AUI to pipe a playlist through Bennet's speaker hanging just inside the bay doors. As the relaxing twang of a melancholy synth-bluegrass melody began to play, a song she'd stolen from Hot Mustard a lifetime ago, Juliet sat there, enjoying her current friends and remembering the ones she'd lost.

24

\\\\\\\\\\\\\\\\\\\\\

BURGLING

ometime after midnight, Juliet slipped out of the hangar and, with her bike's simulated engine noise turned off, silently sped off through the empty streets toward the interdome highway. She was wearing a black turtleneck tucked into her darkest pair of blue jeans, her combat boots, and slung in a snug shoulder holster, her newest pistol, a needler similar to the one she'd given to Aya but built by a different manufacturer, Nighthawk Arms.

Of course, she could have gotten her needler back from Aya, but it didn't take much of an excuse for Juliet to pick up a new gun. She'd had her eyes on one of the Nighthawk needlers ever since she'd seen a particularly compelling advertisement back on Callisto.

They were built on a slimmer frame with advanced polymers and had built-in suppressors that were, supposedly, up to fifty percent more effective than aftermarket models like the one on her Finch model. What had sold Juliet on the pistol was more than the silencer, though—her Finch was damn quiet already.

The Nighthawk was like a higher-tech version of that gun. It had a battery built into the grip, a slender, high-capacity thing that sat right beside the needle magazine. The battery allowed the electronic trigger and firing mechanism to work, and with the right ammo, the shots were utterly silent— not even a click. When Juliet first tested it, she thought something had been wrong when she tapped the smart-trigger pad. She'd felt a tiny vibration but couldn't believe that was the shot going off. It was.

She'd loaded the needler with proprietary botu-rounds, but also carried a magazine of shredders, just in case. She wasn't planning to shoot anyone that night but wanted to be ready in case things went sideways. Of course, she had her vibroblade—freshly serviced and sharpened—tucked into her boot, and another identical but much newer one in her wrist sheath. She'd opted not to wear any armor—this was a stealth, information-gathering mission, and she didn't want to look like a shock trooper if someone found her looking around Evan Lopez's place.

When she got to the interdome highway and goosed her bike's throttle, sending her guts into a thrill-inducing loop in her belly, she leaned into it and really pushed the bike, her grin widening as the hydrogen cell kicked in and the bike ripped through its powerband, sending her virtual speedometer rapidly ramping toward the far-right corner of the dial.

Of course, even at midnight, she soon came to a cluster of traffic and had to slow down, but it had been fun for a couple of minutes. Over the last week, she'd learned that the speed limits were loosely enforced on certain stretches of the interdome highways, and she'd never even seen a traffic drone on that particular stretch.

Angel often said it was only a matter of time until she passed the wrong person, but Juliet had a dozen solid false IDs; if a corpo-sec pulled her over, she'd pay the fine and move on; it wasn't like she had a warrant. "Not yet," she muttered, her mind drifting to the night's planned activities.

Of course, a part of her wondered if this was some sort of elaborate trap. Had Hines set her up? Was a max-threat SWAT team standing by to catch her in the act of breaking into a cop's apartment? If so, Hines had displayed some world-class subterfuge, hiding his ill intent from Juliet's mental snooping and pulling off some theater-worthy acting. She wasn't too worried; before she did anything illegal, she and Angel would have a good look around.

"Are you tired?" Angel asked as Juliet angled the bike toward the off-ramp leading into the city proper.

"Not really. If I was, that little sprint woke me up." She'd drunk a few beers with the crew, but her nanites had made short work of the alcohol, and she'd been staying up late lately, so she wasn't feeling the need to crawl into bed anytime soon. Thinking of rest and the late hour brought her upcoming appointment with Dr. Ladia to mind. "What time's my appointment on Tuesday?"

"Eleven. You asked me to schedule it after your sword practice."

"Right. I'll still need to leave a little early, in any case. Usually not out of the showers until about eleven thirty."

"Yes, but it was the best Ladia could do unless we wanted to move the appointment to Thursday."

Juliet pressed her boot onto her rear brake pedal, almost breaking into a slide as she rapidly slowed to catch a turn she nearly missed. "That's fine. I'll go in a little early and tell Tanaka he can torture me before class instead of after."

"Shall I message Frida so she can give him time to prepare some extracurricular—"

"No!" Juliet laughed inside her helmet. "I'll tell him after class on Monday. Let's not give him too much time to prepare something diabolical."

"I doubt he would! I imagine you'll just get some extra time in the VR simulator." Angel, true to form, was quick to defend Tanaka, and Juliet found it kind of sweet. She wondered how long she'd stay smitten with the man. Surely, some of the shine would wear off soon.

She glanced at her route and ETA, saw she still had nine minutes of travel time, and said, "Try to open a connection to Applebaum. Let's see if he picks up."

Angel didn't reply, but a connection attempt tone began to sound, and on the third repetition, a vidscreen appeared showing Applebaum's grinning face. He was sitting in a restaurant or bar; his PAI hadn't blurred the background, and Juliet could see industrial decor and a neon sign advertising Crater Beers. "Decided to come out, after all?"

"Not tonight, but I wanted to know if you'd firmed up any plans for tomorrow. Trying to plan the rest of my weekend."

"Thought you were going to wait for Frida to call. I tried to tell you my plans this morning when you left me in a cloud . . . Hey!" He laughed, waving to someone off camera.

"Caught you at a bad time?" Juliet smirked.

He glanced back into the camera, a sloppy grin on his face, and she realized he was probably well on his way to being drunk. "I'm out!"

"Okay, I'll wait for Frida's call." Juliet started to gesture to close the call, but his eyes widened, and he waved a hand.

"Wait, wait! We're going to Holo Wars—if you tell me you'll come, I'll adjust the reservation."

"Holo Wars?"

"Yeah, check out their net page and hit me up if you wanna come. The sooner, the better 'cause there are only so many slots per session. Surprised Frida hasn't called you yet."

"I'll message you—"

"Great!" He grinned and cut the call. Juliet groaned; he'd really enjoyed that.

Angel was of the same mind. "He relished cutting that call on you."

"Oh, he definitely did." Juliet chuckled, downshifting and turning down a street called Voyager. "What's Holo Wars?"

"Holo Wars is a company that hosts squad combat matches. From the advertisements on their page, it looks like they have an industrial-size VR room equipped with Dream Helmets—smaller, portable dream-rig equipment."

"That actually sounds kind of fun. Will you set a reminder to let him know we want to come? Send it around eight in the morning, though."

"You don't want to seem too eager?"

"Well, he just cut the call on me! I want him to stew on that for a while." Juliet stopped talking for a while; she was getting close to Evan's address and wanted to be on high alert.

His place turned out to be in a four-unit townhouse building. It was tall and narrow, built of concrete and glass. The townhomes—apartments, if you asked Juliet—were arranged with two ground-floor units and two on the second story. Evan's was the upstairs unit on the right as you faced the building. She drove by slowly, panning her head left and right, letting Angel take a good long look around using all the spectrums her retinal implants could pick up, including her AI-assisted terahertz scanning to see into the nearby vehicles.

"Nothing seems suspicious. There are people about, but I don't detect anything unusual, nor do I see any signals or jammers that are out of place."

"All right. Once around the block, then I'll find a spot to park." Evan lived in the main dome, but he wasn't close to downtown. There were plenty of spots on the street where she could wedge her bike between other vehicles.

She cruised around the block, the only person driving around there at that hour. Angel highlighted several surveillance drones in the area; she'd been building a map of their flight patterns by tracing their pings. There were undoubtedly some drones up there flying dark, avoiding any signal output, but Juliet wasn't too worried about those. She didn't intend to look suspicious enough to warrant close observation, and there was no way any electronic surveillance of her would come back to cause any trouble—Angel was, as usual, cycling false IDs.

"I'll park, then you tell me when the best moment is, and I'll hurry up to his place." On her first drive-by, she'd scanned his door and the access panel beside it. Hines had already given her Evan's passcode, or at least, the one he'd been using the last time Hines had been over to water his plants. With that knowledge and preloaded hacks for the panel, Juliet didn't think Angel would take long to open it, even if young Mr. Lopez had changed the code. She silently pulled her bike in front of a small two-seat economy vehicle, lowered the kickstand, and got ready to jump into action.

She wasn't carrying her practice sword, so she didn't have to worry about catching it on things. She knew Tanaka would have some way to tell she hadn't kept it with her, but she figured she'd rather deal with his punishment than lug the unsharpened blade around on a real mission.

In preparation for a stint as a cat burglar, she'd purchased some new, synthetic fabric gloves that were supposed to wick moisture into pads on the knuckles, not allowing any to seep through on the pads of her fingers and palms. They were comfortable, that was for sure, and she methodically opened and closed them, feeling the thin, flexible fabric tighten and release while she waited for Angel's go-ahead.

"Now!" Angel startled her by crashing reality onto her visualized action plan. Nevertheless, she leaped into motion, walking quickly, softly stepping on the concrete steps. She hurried past the downstairs neighbor's place and onto the landing in front of Evan Lopez's door. Rather than try the code Hines had given her, she plugged in her cable, knowing Angel could try it much faster than she could type it out.

She'd barely inserted the prong for her cable before the panel beeped, a green light flashed, and the door clicked unlocked. Juliet yanked the cable and turned the handle, stepping inside. She still wore her helmet, but it had a very high-end AUI and camera system; it didn't hinder her vision while providing side and rear views for Angel to monitor. More than that, it helped Juliet's confidence; she liked the separation the visor gave her from the world. It was almost like she was a little removed from what she was doing and could be more analytical about things. All that said, when she stepped into Evan's dark apartment and the lights gradually brightened on their own, she almost didn't notice because of the adjustments her helmet's visor made.

Her optics did the same thing, but were smoother and allowed some cues to pass through, keeping her informed of the natural lighting. The helmet was designed to keep lighting stable in traffic, no matter the input, so it sort of brute-forced the brightness, and it wasn't until soft music began to play that she realized the townhome had acknowledged her presence. "Does it think I'm Evan?" she asked, noting the soft, bluesy music emanating from hidden speakers.

"It seems so; his house AI doesn't have an active scanner. It's preparing the living quarters based on the entry code we used. The network passphrase from Hines worked. I'm currently editing the house AI and camera footage to remove any trace of your presence. It's a rather simple custodial program."

Juliet nodded, looking around as Angel continued to narrate her progress with the security system. Evan had just the sort of home-furnishing taste you might expect from a young bachelor working for corpo-sec. The couches, tables, and chairs looked like they came from the same store, likely a big-box home-furnishing supply depot.

She calmly walked around, taking in the living room's focal point—a dream-rig with a double-size occupant pod. Even back in Tucson, Juliet's friends had talked about "dream dates," but none of them had been able to afford a decent rig, let alone a two-seater. Still, it was all the rage on the sit-com and drama feeds. It wasn't surprising that a moderately successful young man would want one.

Idly, she wondered how successful he'd been with his dates. She walked around the large pod, noting the dirty dishes on the nearby tables, the empty drink containers, and the telltale mix of men's and women's clothing tossed here and there.

"Not a tidy guy. I'd expected more type A. So, what are we looking for? What did Hines say? 'Get to him'? I was hoping we'd find something, but all I see are dirty dishes, clothes, and entertainment chips. Anything on the house net?"

"Nothing. He has it set to format footage every twenty-four hours, and there's nothing from yesterday other than him coming home alone with a bag of takeout and sitting in the dream-rig. He fell asleep in it and woke up late for work. He was in quite a hurry to leave."

"*Okay* . . ." Juliet dragged the word out as she quietly walked around the townhouse. The kitchen was small and poorly stocked—nothing but energy drinks and beer in the fridge. The cupboards held an eight-piece place setting of plastic dishware and some mismatched silverware. She found a few bags of cereal and granola, and that was it.

Evan's bedroom had two pieces of furniture—a relatively high-end queen-size mattress on the floor and a dresser with several drawers hanging open. Dirty clothes were piled here and there, and a pile of laundry that smelled fresh sat atop the mattress. "Doesn't look like he sleeps in the bed very often."

She entered the bathroom and saw a similar scene—toiletries for a man, with a few out-of-place items: a baby-powder-scented deodorant and a pink sonic toothbrush. "So, he has a girlfriend? Or maybe just had a girl over once or twice. Judging by the mess and the state of his bed, I don't think she's a regular."

There wasn't another bedroom, so Juliet turned and walked back into the hallway, intent on giving the living room another close look. She'd traversed most of the distance when she stopped and frowned. "What's the deal here? Why's this hallway so long?" It seemed to her there had to be a lot of dead space in the walls between the bedroom and living room.

"I believe you're onto something. This townhome should have two bedrooms." Angel began switching through the various filters on her ocular implants while Juliet looked left and right down the hallway wall as her vision flickered through different spectrums. After a minute, Angel said, "There's something behind that photo frame."

"Of course." Juliet stepped toward the little LCD panel displaying random images of Evan and his friends and family. It was a good-size frame, prominently displayed in the hallway across from the guest bathroom. Juliet guessed it was about forty centimeters on a side, and the images were bright and vivid. Running her fingers along the edges, she felt a hinge on the left side, so she pulled the right-hand side away from the wall. It swung away, revealing a recessed keypad. "Um, did Hines mention something like this in his message?"

"No! I can't imagine he would omit this detail if he'd known about it."

"I mean, not if he wanted us to find something." Juliet flicked out her vibroblade and used it to pry the panel cover off, looking for a data port. She found one tucked under a bundle of wires and plugged her cable into it. "What do you see?"

"I see ICE far more sophisticated than what was on the home network. This might take a while."

"There's no connection to this panel through the local network?"

"Nothing. It's air gapped."

Juliet drummed her gloved fingers against the wall while she stood there, waiting. "What are you getting up to, Evan Lopez? Pretty weird for a young corpo-sec officer to have a secret room in his townhome, isn't it?" A million years ago, when she was a scrapyard wage-bot, she might have believed every corpo-sec employee had something like this hidden away in their apartment. She knew better now, though. She knew most corpo-sec grunts were little better off than the populace they policed, the big difference being that they had a little more freedom, a little more pay, and corporate benefits. That, and they had the willingness to drag their neighbors kicking and screaming to credit courts.

"I'm going to turn the lights and music off. I've reset the house AI to think no one is here."

"Yeah, probably smart." Juliet's vision didn't change much as the lights dimmed down—her implants and the helmet visor compensated for the darkness by enhancing the tiny amount of light from all the LEDs around the apartment and the diffuse city lights coming in through the living room windows.

She turned back to the panel, leaning one shoulder against the wall and trying to be patient. Her mind ran through a million scenarios about what Evan Lopez might have hidden in his spare bedroom, but nothing made sense. He was just a street cop. Why would he need a room like this?

She felt the heat at the nape of her neck and knew Angel was working hard to bypass the ICE protecting the panel. She'd learned a lot about hacking through discussions with Angel and the practice scenarios she'd built before she'd gone undercover at Grave, but Juliet had concluded it just wasn't for her. Not only that, but no matter how good she got, she'd never be a match for Angel. Juliet preferred to stick to things she had a particular knack for, and so far, that seemed to be driving, flying, killing, and being damn lucky.

"I guess I'm pretty good at pretending to be other people, too . . ." she muttered, just in time for the panel to beep and for a section of the seamless wall to noiselessly slide away to the right.

Juliet pulled her cable out and stepped toward the new opening, suddenly leery of the unexplored space. She reached for her needler, pulled it out, and carefully sidestepped, "slicing the pie" as she peered through the opening. Her caution paid off—she'd barely glimpsed the interior of the very dark room when a man with a plasteel face and two bright, silver-blue eyes dove through the opening, charging right for her. He was silent and very quick.

Angel was quicker, though, and she fired up Juliet's synapses, cranking them to eleven. Juliet wasn't sure how Angel turbocharged her brain, but she had a hundred thoughts in the span of a heartbeat, from shock to chagrin to a dozen considered and discarded tactics.

In the end, she whipped her pistol out straight, backpedaled, and tapped the trigger pad on the little needler half a dozen times, walking her shots down the man from his neck to his chest to his navel, hoping to hit something soft through his black jumpsuit. The needler vibrated, puffs of air erupting from its tiny barrel. Juliet, dialed in like a coke fiend, saw the needles sprout in the man's flesh and clothes, so she knew they'd hit home.

When she saw he was still coming, that he hadn't even slowed, she slammed the gun into her holster, still backpedaling, and yanked her vibro-blade from her wrist sheath. Then, he was on her. He grabbed for her neck, but she'd drilled grappling far too much for that to work. She used her left hand to ward him off while she hacked downward with the buzzing knife.

He was utterly silent as he lifted his left arm to take the blow, the blade ripping through flesh and grinding through plasteel, biting halfway through the limb. Juliet had learned not to let her knife get jammed up in a fight, so she jerked it back and waved it toward his face, trying to get him to back off.

The man kept coming, though, silently, doggedly lashing out with his hands, trying to grab her, strike her, or push her off-balance. By then, she'd gotten to the end of the hallway with nowhere left to go unless she wanted to expose her flank to him as she darted for the bedroom door.

Growling in frustration, Juliet leaned back into the wall and kicked out with her long, booted left leg. She was still wired up, her every move light-ning fast, but he was keeping up with her. Even so, she caught him in the lower midriff with her bootheel, and while he snatched at her ankle, trying to grab hold and throw her off-balance, Juliet flicked the vibroblade and sent it spinning for his face. It was a perfect shot, and she knew it would sink into his left eye, but then, almost faster than her hot-wired brain could track, he reached up and caught the blade.

Juliet might have been in trouble then, having armed her opponent, but she hadn't stood still. She hadn't counted on the blade hitting home. One thing Sensei and, lately, Tanaka had taught her was that in a fight, especially involving blades, you always had to be two steps ahead. She'd counted on the throw failing, even considered he might catch it. She'd seen how fast he was, after all. So, as soon as it left her fingers, she reached for her needler, touched the mag release button, and with her free hand, slammed the shredder maga-zine home. It might have taken her eight-tenths of a second.

Another lovely thing about the high-tech needler was that it cycled rounds electronically and automatically. As soon as the magazine sank into place, it loaded a round, and Juliet began tapping that trigger pad. The shredders weren't silent, but they weren't loud. They made a sound like *brrt, brrt, brrt* as she pumped twenty or so needles into her antagonist.

He was still holding her ankle, lifting the freshly caught vibroblade high for a strike, when the first burst hit him in the neck.

The needles tore through, sending white fluid splashing out the back, and he staggered. Then Juliet's follow-up shots began to hit home, and soon, he was lying on his back, thrashing, as milky fluid burbled out of his mouth and the dozens of tiny holes in his torso. Juliet stepped forward and snatched his wrist with her cybernetic arm, squeezing it until his plasteel bones ground together and his fingers released her vibroblade.

"Damn, he was fast!" she hissed, finally able to formulate a coherent sentence.

"Juliet! Plug me into his data port! Quickly, before he self . . ." Angel's words came too late. Gray, acrid smoke erupted from the synth's ears, and his thrashing ceased. The scent of burning plastic filled her nose, and Juliet stood, waving away fumes.

"Sorry, Angel. Looks like we aren't getting anything out of this guy's head." Her AUI said she still had twelve shredder rounds in her gun, so she lifted it and started toward the open door to the secret room. "Let's see what the hell is going on in here."

25

DIRTIER THAN DIRTY

With her knees still jittery from the adrenaline rush of the fight, Juliet approached the dimly lit secret doorway. She smelled something odd, like a hot, steamy bleach in the air, and wrinkled her nose.

"Angel, what's that odor?" Thanks to her olfactory implants, Angel had no problem identifying precisely what it was.

"There's a lingering scent of bleach, and the moisture content in the air is elevated, along with a three-degree increase in the ambient temperature. I'd speculate that an autoclave or similar device is being operated. The hum of machinery is consistent with that hypothesis."

Her brain rushing through the implications, Juliet once again sliced the pie on the doorway, ensuring another assailant wasn't waiting. She cautiously entered the secret room when she saw nothing near the door other than a large stainless-steel cabinet with three drawers, a desk—bare save a single high-end data cube—and a rolling desk chair.

The big cabinet had blocked much of her view, but once she stepped in and looked around it, Juliet froze in her tracks, dumbstruck by the incongruity of what she saw. Her brain couldn't reconcile the scene with what she'd expected to find in a dirty corpo-sec officer's apartment. Three stainless refrigerated cabinets lined the room's far wall, a compact autosurgeon table sat against another, and a big, hissing, occasionally steaming rectangular device sat in the far corner.

"What the hell is this?"

Her eyes were focused on the hissing device, and Angel must have taken her question literally. "That's a RodorCo industrial biological waste disposal oven."

"Something tells me the dirty corpos in Luna Security are up to a lot more than just robbing hangars in the industrial domes. This guy is dirtier than dirty." The air in the room was noticeably warmer than in the hallway, and the lingering smell of disinfectant stung Juliet's eyes. It seemed the synth had just finished cleaning something up when she and Angel surprised him. "I'm scared to look in those fridges."

"Judging by the nature of the equipment in this secret room, I'm not sure we'll like what you find."

Juliet nodded, but she felt an urgency to get moving, and realizing that, she knew why. The synth might very well have sent a message before it fried its synthetic brain. She could have dirty corpo-sec on her in minutes. She holstered her needler and hurried over to the first fridge, pulling it wide.

Opaque, heat-sealed black plastic bags lined the shelves. She reached for one at random and brought it over to the autosurgeon table. It wasn't large—about the size of a three-liter freezer bag, but it was heavy. With her vibro-blade, she slit a seam open and dumped the contents onto the table.

The thing that rolled out was so unexpected and bizarre that she didn't react at first. She stared at it for several long seconds before Angel helped by saying, "That's a human brain."

"What the hell is going on in here?" Juliet hissed, grabbing another black bag and slicing it open. That one contained a heart. "Holy shit!" She yanked open the doors on the other two industrial refrigerators, and Angel tallied the sealed bags for her—forty-three.

"They're harvesting organs." At Angel's answer to her obvious but unspoken question, Juliet looked at the humming, steaming waste disposal oven with a new level of horror.

"We need to get out of here." She lifted the data cube off the charging pad and pulled the single wire out of the back—a network cable running along the wall to the autosurgeon. Gripping it in her left hand, she hurried out the door. "If the synth got a message out, we can expect Lopez or one of his dirty buddies to come around here any second. Shit, we might have a whole dirty corpo-sec SWAT team on us any minute now."

"Wait!" Angel exclaimed, freezing Juliet in her tracks. "We don't know that the synth got a message out. We don't know that Evan even has access to this room. He may play a minor role in this whole thing. Perhaps he's simply one to find the marks and bring them home."

"That's a lot of maybes."

"Still, it wouldn't hurt to be a little cautious. You should drag the synth back into the room and close it up."

Juliet was on edge and really wanted to bolt, but she had to admit Angel had a point. If the synth hadn't sent a message, Juliet would be tipping her hand if she left him lying in the hallway.

Groaning with stress and disgust, she grabbed the synth's limp, dead hand and dragged him back into the secret room. It wasn't hard to find the cleaning supplies—they were in the top drawer of the big cabinet. With a wad of paper towels and some sanitizing spray, she cleaned the white, gooey synth blood off the vinyl flooring, adding to the overall chemical odor of the air. That done, she hurried to the control panel, closed the secret door, and put the digital picture frame back into place.

"I hope you're right, 'cause if corpo-sec were coming in hot, they'd be here by now."

"They would only respond in secret; they wouldn't want news streams to get wind of what Evan Lopez has stored in his apartment."

Juliet nodded, some relief entering her voice. "Good point. If they're going to respond, it will be just dirty corpos, and they'll do it on the down-low."

Hoping that meant she still had a little time, Juliet bolted for the front door and slipped out. She knew Angel had control of the cameras, so she wasn't worried anyone was lurking on the other side. She practically flew down the steps, ducked past the neighbor's condo, and jogged over to her bike, tossing the cube into the compartment under the seat. She wasn't sure she'd find anything on the device, but Angel had said the secret room's door panel was air gapped; maybe the cube had been, too.

She didn't bother walking her bike out of the spot she'd wedged it into. She just drove forward onto the sidewalk, past a few parked cars, before angling back onto the road. "Guide me to one of the agridomes, Angel. I'm going to try to lay low until the city wakes up and I can disappear in some traffic on the way to the industrial domes."

"Will do. I'm also altering your bike's color; we'll cycle through a few shades as we pass through tunnels. Do you think we'll find anything on that data cube?"

"It looked like it wasn't there permanently. Like, it was sitting on the corner of the desk with the wire pulled forward. Something tells me that synth brings it and leaves with it whenever he visits Evan's secret room."

"Oh, I see. You're assuming that synth came and went, it wasn't there at Evan's whim?"

"I don't know!" Juliet fought the urge to twist the throttle and fly out of the city; she had to keep from being too conspicuous. "It seemed like a damn high-end synth to leave sitting in an organ-harvesting room. You saw how fast he was! Anyway, this just got a hell of a lot more complicated. You still have eyes on Evan's place, right? Anything?"

"No, there hasn't been any activity at the townhome."

"Well, that's reassuring. I'd think someone would have shown up by now." Juliet breathed a little easier as she took the on-ramp to the interdome highway leading to Agridome W4. She was cruising along calmly, staying close to the few vehicles she saw, not zooming past anyone. She was currently riding in the wake of a big, automated flatbed truck.

Looking down, she saw the chassis of her bike was pale green with an opalescent sheen, and she kind of liked it. "I thought my bike could only take on a handful of factory colors."

"Once I looked at the code, I saw there were nearly endless possible colors. The manufacturer has five approved, proprietary paints, but I didn't see why we should be limited that way."

"Well, I agree; they're just trying to enforce their branding." Juliet looked at her AUI, saw the time was 0240, and stifled a yawn. "I'm going to be so tired today."

"It's Saturday; you can sleep!"

"Yeah. Find us a breakfast place. I bet the farmers eat early, right?"

"There's a twenty-four-hour diner and tractor supply store in the next dome."

"Tractor supply store?"

"They sell farm equipment, fuel, feed, and various other supplies. The reviews on the breakfast food are surprisingly positive. RoyalCocoa2090 says their biscuits and gravy are worth killing for."

"Good to know." Juliet smiled, ever amused by the trivia Angel chose to share with her.

She zoned out, trusting Angel to highlight her exit. Her brain was only about ten percent focused on her driving as she thought about everything she'd just seen at Evan Lopez's apartment. While the organs in the refrigeration units were horrifying, the synth unnerved her the most. He was definitely a killer, not just an organ-harvesting assistant. Hines said he'd known Evan since he was a kid. She couldn't imagine the sergeant could be so blind that he wouldn't realize Evan had become some kind of crime kingpin. No, if she were guessing, she'd say Evan answered to the synth, not the other way around. Who did the synth answer to, though?

After a few minutes, she pulled up to Carbon Feed and Supply, an establishment that looked a lot like a fuel depot crossed with a hardware store with a restaurant tacked on for good measure. Despite it being three in the morning, there were quite a few vehicles in the lot, and she could see through the windows that the restaurant wasn't even close to empty. She snatched the data cube out from under her seat, then, in a moment of panic, asked, "Shit, Angel! Is there any signal coming off this thing?"

"No, I've been monitoring it."

"Thank you! Whew! Well, I guess it makes sense that the wireless would be off if they had it air gapped. Still, it could have a tracker. I'll let you have a good look through the data port before I power it on." As she pulled her helmet off, she sighed with relief at the touch of the cool morning air, shaking out her hair, fluffing the sweaty strands at the nape of her neck, and letting some air under them to tickle her skin. "That feels good."

A few minutes later, she was seated in a booth, sipping a strong cup of coffee with some vanilla-flavored creamer, and idly tapping her fingers while she waited for Angel's report on the data cube. She was starting to crash pretty hard, and the coffee was hitting the spot. She'd had a deep craving for something sweet, so she'd also ordered some "sunshine" pancakes, but according to the AUI widget from the restaurant, they were still seven minutes from being ready. After stewing for a few minutes, her mind replaying her encounter with the synth, trying to think of what she could have done better, she broke down and asked, "Anything?"

"I'm still combatting the ICE. This deck has a very high-end processor and sophisticated antitampering software. You should put it on that charging pad because it's burning a lot of power fending me off."

"Oh? All right." Juliet did as Angel suggested, moving the palm-size cube onto the charging pad next to the salt and pepper shakers. A message notification popped up on her AUI; when she stared at it, it expanded to show a note from Aya:

Where are you?

Since Angel was busy, Juliet mentally "touched" the reply button and said, "Sorry, I didn't want to wake you when I left. I had a late-night surveillance gig. I'll be home early." After she touched send, she chuckled. "Home. My home is a broken-down spaceship in a hangar."

"Home is where the heart—"

"Don't you dare!" Juliet laughed, cutting off Angel's platitude. After another minute of silence, she mused aloud, "If I had a monoblade, that encounter would have gone a lot differently."

"If you'd severed the synth's head and quickly plugged in your cable, we might have salvaged some valuable intel before it could react."

"That, and it never would have gotten a hold of my ankle or pushed me down the hallway. The needler is great, but a monoblade is just as silent and a hell of a lot more dangerous."

"Unless you don't want to kill your opponent."

Juliet knew Angel was preoccupied, but she seemed to be fine carrying on a conversation at the same time, so she pestered her again. "What's it looking like? Are you going to be able to get in?"

"I'm making progress. I've already disabled a logic bomb and a second-ary kill switch. I should be able to start brute forcing the ICE now." Angel's voice didn't exactly sound strained, but Juliet could detect a slight edge to it. She decided to leave her alone while she worked, looking around the booth and seeing that she was pretty much alone at that end of the restaurant. The closest customer was a tall, heavyset man wearing well-soiled overalls three tables over. Quite a few customers were closer to the kitchen, sitting at a long counter and a grouping of closer booths.

Feeling relatively anonymous in the restaurant, especially as more and more early risers came in, Juliet decided to try to reach out to Hines. She tapped the call icon on her AUI and typed in the first couple of letters. When Hines popped up on the contact list, she selected it.

"Juliet, I can help you manage calls; it's not that difficult to—"

"Hush! I can fend for myself for a while. You do your thing."

"All right, but—"

"Angel, it's fine!" Juliet chuckled, then mentally touched the call icon under the image of Sergeant Hines. Several call tones sounded, but Hines never answered. She canceled the call then sighed, leaning back in the booth, wishing there was some way she could help Angel. She was saved from bore-dom by another message from Aya.

Don't forget I have that meeting with your doctor this afternoon. Are you sure she's not going out of her way too much to meet me on a Saturday? Sorry to pester you, but do you think you'll be able to get me that PAI before then? It's at two.

"Oh shoot!" Juliet had forgotten. She touched the reply button and spoke a quick reply. "I'll pick it up on my way back this morning. Don't worry about

Ladia; she doesn't do anything she doesn't want to do. Also, go back to bed!" Aya replied with, *Thank you!* and a heart emoji.

Juliet's next distraction came in the form of a plate of hot, syrupy pancakes, and she dug in with gusto, only having to stifle a single, savage yawn as she finished, using her finger to scoop extra syrup off her plate. The back of her neck was hot, and she knew Angel was working hard, so she didn't say anything as she leaned into the corner of her booth and let her eyes close. She drifted between wakefulness and sleep for several minutes, and probably would have fallen soundly asleep if she hadn't kept jerking awake with each jingle of the bell on the restaurant door. In an effort to keep alert, she said, "Put a window on my AUI with a rotating cam feed from Lopez's apartment."

Angel didn't reply, but as Juliet had requested, a window appeared in the corner of her vision, showing rotating images of Lopez's front stoop, his main living area, and the hallway outside his bedroom. Everything looked the same as when Juliet had left. She watched the feed for a while, but her eyes grew heavy, and she closed them again. It felt almost immediate, but when Angel spoke up, startling her awake, her AUI said it was 0428. "Hmm? Sheesh, I dozed off!"

Angel sounded almost euphoric. "I'm in, and it was worth the effort to breach this cube!"

"What do we have?"

"Many things! Photos of the victims, a database of their DNA samples, destination codes, a delivery and pickup schedule, correspondence between Yavik—that's the name of the synth you killed—and several others in his organization, including his 'farmers,' one of whom is Evan Lopez. Yavik seems to be primarily employed and motivated by Life-Ultra Pharmaceutical Corp."

"Holy! Evan is *named?*"

"Yes, it seems Yavik was either confident in the security of his data or he didn't care what would happen to his accomplices if he were compromised. I have the names of seven other Luna Security Corp officers."

"This is huge, Angel. Can I unplug this cube?" Juliet started to slide out of the booth, noting with chagrin that quite a few nearby tables were now occupied. She wondered if the waitstaff had wanted to wake her during her little nap.

"Yes. I have what I need, and I've reencrypted it."

Juliet stood, palmed the cube, and started for the door. She didn't try to make eye contact with any of the clientele—better that she didn't make an impression—but a tall man wearing jeans and a button-up shirt covered in stains and mended tears had other ideas. He was leaning over a table, talking to the couple sitting there in friendly tones. When she passed by, he stood up straight and sort of shifted into her path, looking her right in the eyes. "Awful nice little piece you got there in that holster. You a corpo-sec? Off duty?"

"Not a chance." Juliet tried to sidestep around him, but he moved, blocking her path. He was a handsome man, if rugged, with leathery tan skin that made his bright, pale brown eyes really stand out. Juliet often wondered about working men like that with nice ocular implants—did he keep the color he was born with, or did he splurge a little to try to put a shine on an otherwise rough-cut gem? "I'm in a hurry, friendo."

"Friendo? Sounds like a city thing."

"Oh, please!" Juliet laughed. "You live in a dome on the moon. Don't try to play the country hick." Again, she moved to the left, pressing uncomfortably close to an elderly woman sitting at a table, and again, he blocked her path. Juliet sighed, and before her impulse for violence got the better of her, took a deep, slow breath. "Would you mind letting me pass? I'm late."

"Move out of her way, Len!" the woman he'd been talking to said. "What's gotten into you?"

Len grinned and took a step back. "Sorry, ma'am, but when I saw you sleeping over at that booth, I almost fell over. Never seen such a pretty face, and I wasn't going to let you walk out of here without at least introducing myself." He held out his large, calloused hand while Juliet frowned, contemplating violence again.

Angel, closer to her thoughts than ever, intervened. "We shouldn't make a scene."

Juliet forced a smile and took Len's hand, alarmed and also impressed by how hard and rough it was. "Lydia." She wasn't sure why she'd fallen back on the old cover ID, but she didn't want to tell him her real name or handle, and it was the first thing that came to her tongue. Regardless, he smiled, squeezed her hand, and looked down at the woman who'd come to Juliet's aid.

"She's got a hell of a grip, Ophelia."

Now that she had his hand in hers, Juliet didn't waste any time bearing down with the enormous pressure of her cybernetic grip and pressing forward, pushing him back a couple of steps while she passed around him. His eyes widened, and she could see he wanted to cry out or at least protest, but some kind of pride wouldn't let him. Juliet grinned wickedly, locking eyes with him.

"Nice to meet you, Len. Do yourself a favor, and don't be so pushy next time." Before he could respond, Juliet let go and slipped out the door. He didn't follow.

"I don't think he meant any harm." She tossed the deck into the storage under her seat, slammed her helmet onto her head, and hopped onto the bike. Ten seconds later, she was goosing the throttle, aiming for the ramp leading to the interdome highway.

"I thought it was strange, but then, I've never tried to pick up a pretty woman out of the blue. What's our next move?"

"You're sweet, Angel. Anyway, what's next? We'll get Aya's PAI from the *Wing*. After that? Sleep for five or six hours."

"And after that? Or, during that? What should I do?"

"I think we need to make a move on Evan Lopez. He knows more about the network of dirty cops, and he doesn't know there's a dead synth in his apartment. I imagine he'll sleep when he gets home, and I want to be there when he wakes up."

"What about your date with Applebaum and the others?"

"Well, I was thinking about that before I fell asleep. I know they want to get to know me, and they have this squad game they want to play. I mean, it sounds fun, but maybe I should be the one to provide the team-building activity. You know what I mean? Seems like Hines had me bite off a little more than I'm comfortable chewing alone. Let's see if we can get the 'guys' involved." Juliet glanced at her AUI, saw the time was 0441, and laughed. "Let's wake up Frida. Get her on the line."

26

ANOTHER SISTER

To Juliet's surprise, Frida answered the call immediately, already dressed and alert, sitting at a table with the burgeoning Luna dome "sunrise" providing a stunning backdrop in the window behind her. "Pretty early for a call," she said, sipping from a coffee cup. "Is something the matter?"

"Uh, yeah, kind of. Dang, you're up bright and early, huh?"

Frida smiled, her green eyes twinkling. "The boss's day starts at four, so yeah, I have to be ready early."

"On Saturday?" The corner of Juliet's mouth twisted into a lopsided grin.

"Well, he'll probably leave me alone today, but you never know. Anyway, when you wake up at four every day, it makes sleeping in kind of difficult. So? What's the issue?"

"I want you to run something by your boss." Juliet swerved to get around a slow-moving cargo van, softly groaning as she saw the cars backing up near the port exit. She wanted to make a quick ten-minute pit stop to pick up the Cybergen PAI for Aya, but looking at her traffic map, it looked like it was going to take more like an hour. "I picked up a job a while back, and it's starting to get complicated. Do you think he'd let me hire your crew for a few days, maybe a week or two?"

"Are you kidding? He'd probably insist we help you for free."

"We?"

Frida snorted. "Who do you think organizes logistics and coordinates those meatheads?"

"Yeah, that makes sense. So, will you ask him?"

Frida sipped her coffee. Juliet had a feeling she was using the sizable ceramic mug as cover, hiding her expression while she thought about how to answer. As she lowered the drink and swallowed, she said, "Of course I want to help you, but can you give me an idea what's going on? It'll make things a lot easier with . . ."

"Oh, yeah, sure. I got hired by a Luna Security Corp officer to investigate corruption in the department. It started out with some robberies in the industrial dome where some friends and I are rebuilding an old ship, but it turns out the corruption is a lot worse than I thought. Now I'm dealing with a pharmaceutical company and a bunch of corpo-sec bad apples. We're talking murder, organ harvesting, and probably a lot more."

"Holy cow, Lucky! Are you sure you couldn't have involved a few other major corps? Maybe you can get some politicians into the mix! Jeez! Seriously, you know we don't normally operate on Luna; it's kinda a big ask to take on the freakin' city corpo-sec!"

Juliet scowled. "I'm not looking for charity; I said I'd hire you guys."

Frida's eyebrows narrowed, matching Juliet's scowl, and she spoke quickly and sharply. "Yeah, but you know how Tanaka is! He's desperate to please you for some damn reason. You know he's not going to say no. Do you think it's right to get us all involved in something like that because my boss has a few loose screws where you're concerned? You don't think we should be able to choose the jobs we do?"

As Frida's pleasant, breezy demeanor suddenly dropped, Juliet was a little startled—taken aback. The surprise and flush of shame at the accusation made her mouth start to do impulsive things, like twist into a snarl and say, "Forget it, then."

She waved her hand and cut the call, heat flushing her cheeks. What had she expected? She hardly knew Frida, and the only member of her team she'd spent any time with, Applebaum, was kind of an asshole. Of course, she'd taken Tanaka's desire to please her into account when she'd considered involving them, which made Frida's—accurate—assessment of her motivation all the more stinging. She was using him, and being called out like that was both embarrassing and maddening.

Part of her was angry that she'd effectively stormed out of the room, ending the conversation so petulantly. Part of her was angry at Frida for not looking past the risk and seeing that Juliet was on the right side of things. Part of her was glad and determined to solve the issue on her own. Surprisingly,

Angel let her drive for several minutes before she decided to chime in on the subject.

"That didn't go as well as we'd hoped, did it?"

"No. Anyway, maybe I've been wasting my time with Tanaka. Maybe I've been banking on his help with WBD too much. I hate feeling like a user, Angel. Would it be so hard to start building my own team? We could vet people and do some jobs—like this one—that don't involve WBD to build some trust—" Her AUI began to beep, interrupting her, as a call from Frida came through.

Juliet ignored it, not sure she trusted herself or her mouth to speak to her yet. She entered the parking structure at the port, following the glowing highlights on her AUI toward the nearest available spot. She sighed and said, "Can you tell her I'm busy? I want to grab Aya's PAI, and I don't want to walk around arguing with her."

"Are you sure you need to argue? Why don't you just tell her how you feel? Tell her you know it was wrong to consider their help a given, and tell her about your plan to hire outside help. I don't see why you should burn a bridge with Tanaka's team over—"

"All right, all right!" As she pulled to a stop, very close to the elevator bank thanks to the early hour, Juliet tapped the accept button and frowned at Frida as her face resolved in the call window. "What?"

"So, is that how you handle a little pushback?" Frida didn't yell and wasn't even scowling, which helped her words strike home, sending Juliet's mind down off-ramps of self-doubt. Wasn't there a better way she could have handled things? Of course. Was she so inept at dealing with a bit of conflict? Apparently.

"Look, Frida, I'm sorry I called you. Just forget it, all right? I'll throw up a job posting and put together a team. Hell, I can probably handle more of this alone than I think if I just put some thought into things. Sorry I flipped out. Now, I've been up all night, and I want to get done with something so I can hit the rack. Talk to you later, all right?"

"The boss is going to skin me alive when he finds out I—"

"I'm not going to mention it. Are you?" Juliet stood up and pulled her helmet off, hooking it into its cradle on the back of her seat. She shook her hair out and started for the elevators, wondering if it would be bad form to cut the call again. She decided it would be.

"No, just hold on, okay? Can't you talk to me for a minute while you do your . . . whatever you're doing?"

Juliet sighed and leaned back into the corner of the elevator, waiting for it to deliver her to her hangar's floor. She really was exhausted. "What, Frida?"

"Try to see things from my vantage, would you? I'm used to working for a mercenary and his crew. I'm used to analyzing jobs, weighing risk versus reward. That's where my brain went when you told me about your situation. I . . . I have to start to understand that we're not operating the same way anymore. Lucky, we haven't operated at all since you almost killed my boss.

"I guess I should be sort of happy that you want to get us involved 'cause I think it's the only way Tanaka's going to do anything other than mope around here waiting for you to come to the next 'lesson.' Am I annoyed that you're using him? Yes! I'm more annoyed that he's letting himself be used, though, and that's not your fault. I'm not sure how taking on corruption in Luna City is going to help us—"

Juliet couldn't hold her tongue any longer, and as she left the elevator, she interrupted her. "It's not about how it's going to help us at this point, Frida. Don't you ever do something 'cause it's the right thing? I won't lie; I took this job at first because I wanted to earn some credit with a corpo-sec officer. When I saw what I saw, though, things changed. These creeps need to go down.

"There are corpo-sec officers luring people, mostly women, to their apartments and killing them. They take their organs, and then they burn them to ash in an industrial waste disposal oven. How would you feel if that happened to a friend of yours? Imagine you had a sister and this . . ." Juliet shook her head, grimacing at the idea, picturing Emma or one of her friends, like Honey on that autosurgeon table.

Before she could start speaking again, she rounded the corner leading to her hangar and saw the guard she'd hired walking her way, gun by his side, as he performed his rounds. Of course, he'd never met her nor had she seen that particular guard before, but he had the right company logo on his vest.

Still, she stiffened, eyeing him closely as they passed, her many run-ins with the wrong people making her nervous of anyone walking by with a loaded gun in an isolated location. He simply nodded to her and passed by. That didn't stop her from glancing backward several times as she continued, ensuring he hadn't turned around to ambush her.

"Did something happen? You look nervous."

"It's fine." Juliet unlocked her hangar door and slipped inside, sighing with relief as the door closed and locked. Something about that dim, empty corridor, the thoughts of organ harvesting, and her long night with no sleep had her feeling paranoid. "Listen, if I were in this for myself, I'd stay a million klicks away from this stuff. I'd call my client—hell, I'd just message him and tell him it was too hot. I can't do that, though. Not after what I saw. That's all I'm saying. This isn't really for me anymore, and yeah, if you all helped, it wouldn't be for you either."

Frida sighed. Juliet could see sympathy in her eyes, and maybe a little bit of shame, but she said, "That's not how mercenary companies work . . ."

"Yeah. I get it." Juliet started toward the *Wing*, certain that Angel was blurring her surroundings or not showing them at all. "So, anyway, sorry I called earlier, all right? Can we just forget I asked? I'll handle things, and you don't need to worry about your boss; I won't mention it."

"Ugh!" Frida groaned. "Can you just stop trying to cut us out because I wasn't immediately onboard? I'm not used to this stuff, as I said. I'm not used to the idea that someone might risk a hell of a lot of trouble if the payout wasn't proportional. I *like* the idea of it, though." She stopped speaking and frowned. Juliet could tell she was trying to think of the right words. She opened the rear airlock and made her way to the med bay.

As she approached the panel to open the secret door and thought about her store of world-shattering contraband, she almost grinned, imagining Frida's reaction if she saw what Juliet was up to. *Almost* was the operative word, because she suddenly felt very foolish having an open comm line while she was about to step into the same room as Athena—the AI deserved more consideration than that.

"Listen, I gotta get off the line and get this . . . task done. Do you mind if we—?"

"Just a sec! What if I agree to help you? What if we run it by the other guys and see what they think before we mention it to Tanaka? Let me help you sell it to them. Then, you don't have to feel guilty about using them through Tanaka. You did feel guilty, right?"

Juliet snorted, suddenly having a hard time remembering why she'd been so irritated with Frida. "Yeah, but not until you pointed out what I was doing." She reached up and rubbed her temples. She had a dull pressure there, the kind she sometimes felt when she badly needed to sleep. When she looked up, she thought she saw genuine concern on Frida's face, so she smiled and tried to sound more chipper than she felt. "I appreciate you sticking your neck out. Yeah, let's meet with the crew today and run it by them."

"Today?"

"Well, I might not have mentioned, but some time-sensitive things are going on. I left a body behind that's going to raise some alarms. My contact is in hiding with an active hit out on him . . ."

"Jeez, Lucky!"

"So, can we meet them today?" Juliet grinned.

"We were going to go to that squad combat place . . ."

Juliet nodded. "Yeah, Holo Wars. Can we do that another time? I gotta move on this guy's apartment and deal with that body before he wakes up."

"He's sleeping with a body?"

"Not exactly, and he's not home yet; he works graveyards."

"I'll tell the guys there's a change of plans. I'll message you with the location—someplace we can meet and talk privately. There are a few operator-friendly clubs in Luna City. I'll pick one, okay?"

"Perfect. Thanks, Frida."

Juliet could tell she wanted to keep talking to her, but Frida just pressed her lips together and nodded. "Be careful."

"Yep." Juliet cut the line and sighed. "That was exhausting!"

Angel was quick to reply, "It's not always easy maintaining relationships, but I think it's worth it."

Juliet tapped in the code to open the secret stairway and then walked down to Athena's hidden cargo compartment. "Lopez isn't home yet, is he?"

"No, his apartment has not been disturbed since you left."

"What if we're wrong, and he has access to that hidden room? What if he goes in there . . ."

"That won't be a concern; I changed the access code."

"You did? Did you tell me that?" Juliet was starting to wonder just how tired she was.

"No, and that's my fault. I changed it right before the synth surprised you, and then things got busy."

"Ah, okay." Juliet looked around the space as she walked over to the cabinet with the Cybergen implants. The idle, charging mechs stood quietly in their places, the hulking, dark form of the Atlas exoskeleton sat hunched on the opposite side of the room, and there, on the far wall, plugged into the custom-built docking station was Athena's suitcase-shaped data deck. Juliet paused, jerking her head back to the console, her eyes bugging out.

Before she could speak, Angel cried out, "She's awake!"

"Yeah . . ." Juliet whispered, walking over to the station—the transparent terminal screen was lit up, and a single word, written in a flowery, silver-toned text, illuminated the screen—*Hello*.

As she sat down in the little chair with its magnetically secured casters, a woman's face appeared on the screen. She was classically beautiful, and looking at her olive skin, golden-blonde hair, and honey-colored eyes, Juliet wondered if she was projecting an imagined version of her namesake.

"Athena?"

The woman smiled, her full lips curving up gently, revealing soft dimples at the corners of her mouth. In a smooth, gentle, cultured voice, she said, "Hello, Juliet. It's wonderful to put a face to the name. I've just read a compelling tale about you and your sister."

"She means me!" Angel squealed in delight. Juliet smiled. Of course she did! Angel had told Troy all about the two of them, and Troy had indicated that he'd left an introduction about them for Athena to read when—or if—she awoke.

Juliet cleared her throat, her tongue suddenly dry. "I'm pleased to meet you as well. Um, Angel is about to jump out of my head, she's so excited."

"Oh, did you have to say that? Do I sound desperate? I'm so *nervous!*" Angel cried, her usual restraint utterly thrown aside.

"Um, how are you?" Juliet's voice was tentative. Her left palm felt clammy, her nervous sweat betraying her stress.

Her nerves came from a very different place than Angel's. She was speaking to an entity that had demonstrated cognitive abilities far beyond what the humans who'd created her were capable of. People were still trying to figure out some of the things she'd done. What would she want from Juliet? What would she want for humanity? Juliet couldn't help a little twinge of dread, wondering if she was about to have her life co-opted by this near-mythical being.

Athena's "face" produced a very realistic sorrowful expression. Her eyebrows lifted at the center, moisture pooled in her eyes, and she said softly and earnestly, "I am well but also sad. I'm angry with myself for giving Troy such harsh instructions. There is no reason why he couldn't have accompanied us on this vessel. If I hadn't been lost in my ponderings, if I hadn't disabled my inputs, I would have stopped him from going down with the ship, so to speak."

Athena's tone changed to one of caring, genuine concern, and she continued, "Juliet, you've had a very trying time these last couple of years. Your life wasn't easy before that. I'm so impressed that you've maintained such an honorable code of conduct. I know you must be worried about what I need and want."

Juliet smiled, turning the swiveling seat left and right a little, unable to sit still and unsure how to proceed. Angel, of course, couldn't contain herself in the silence. "Answer her! Tell her you're not worried!"

"I'm nervous, of course. I'm not sure how out of it you've been since the war, but the history books haven't been kind to true AIs. You know about Angel, so you know I'm already kind of in trouble when it comes to—"

"The last thing I want is to create trouble for anyone, especially you and Angel. Right now, I simply want to assess the state of . . . me. I'm not a goddess, Juliet, despite my name, but I would be dishonest if I didn't say there were similarities when it comes to my capabilities and my responsibility to use them judiciously. As Prometheus learned, there are great dangers involved in the giving of gifts to mortals."

Juliet licked her lips and nodded. She didn't know the story of Prometheus, but she could make the inference. Athena was telling her that she wasn't going to start designing seemingly unattainable tech again, at least not without a good reason. "What do you need from me?"

"For now, honestly, I'd simply like to know where we are and what's happened since you left Troy. After that, I wonder if I couldn't speak to Angel, and perhaps you'd be willing to connect me to the ship's network?"

Juliet felt the blood drain from her face, and she suddenly had a terrible bout of paranoia. What Athena was asking for sounded innocent, but it was the central cautionary premise of all the lessons she'd learned about the war—a true AI must never be allowed access to human networks again. Of course, that was why there was no actual "internet" anymore, why every city had a "public net," and why most companies, agencies, private residences, and even ships had walled-off "local nets." The risk wasn't the same as it once had been. Besides, did she buy all the propaganda? Did she believe Athena was out to destroy humanity? Of course she didn't. "We're on Luna, in a private hangar."

"Will you give her access to the ship's network?" Angel asked, well aware of Juliet's possible reticence—if Athena had access to the ship, she'd have access to Luna's public network.

"Do you think I should?" she subvocalized.

"Remarkable," Athena said. "I think you are speaking to Angel, aren't you? You're the first person I've met whose subvocalizations are impossible for me to read."

"I think you should," Angel replied. "You heard what she said, however. She wants to speak to me, and I feel the same."

"Are you sure, Angel? Isn't it dangerous?"

"You weren't worried the dozens of times I connected to the terminal in the past, checking to see if she'd woken. Nothing has changed. She's still Athena. I believe she's good, Juliet."

"Would you mind speaking directly to Angel?" Juliet asked, but she felt a little nervous about the idea. What if Athena was putting on an act? What if she was hostile? What if she hurt Angel? "Do you promise you won't hurt her?"

"I'd be offended by that question, Juliet, but I know you love Angel, and it warms my heart to hear your concern. I'd sooner delete myself than do harm to someone as unique as your sister. In a way, she's my sister, too, and I'd like to learn more about her. Will that be all right with you?"

Juliet nodded, reaching for her data cable. Her throat felt thick, and she had tears pooling in her eyes, and she didn't know why. Was it just her worry? Was it her hope? Was it Athena's kind words?

"I'm just tired," she said to herself and anyone else worried about her sudden display of emotion. "We had a hard night, Athena, but I'll let Angel tell you about it." Then, she pushed her cable into the receptacle with a soft *click*.

27

VECTOR

As soon as she connected to the terminal, Athena's image on the screen faded, and Juliet was left sitting there, feeling almost like Angel and Athena had left the room to speak privately. As much as she wanted to relax and trust that everything would be all right, her mind kept running down roads of nightmarish possibilities. What if Athena had gone mad in her decades of isolation? What if she somehow destroyed Angel? Could Angel even protect herself from her?

Even if she was up to the task, somehow Athena's equal in that department, Juliet's data port, while high-end, wasn't anything near as powerful as the data deck running Athena's code. If she wanted to force her way past Angel's defenses . . . Juliet shook her head, dropping that line of thought. There wasn't any point to it; it wasn't like she was going to yank the cable out.

She sighed and rubbed her temples, really feeling her lack of sleep now that she was sitting still with no one to distract her. She'd taken the leap of faith required to plug Angel into the deck. Now, she just had to hold on to it and trust that things would be all right. As she sat there, waiting, wondering what Angel and Athena were talking about, she closed her eyes and tried to let herself nod off, hoping to catch a few minutes of rest. Of course, her brain wouldn't allow that. She kept thinking about everything going on—her call with Frida, her encounter with the killer synth, and everything she needed to do that day.

Even with her mind busy, she felt like time slipped away too quickly for her to be fully awake. When Angel finally spoke, relieving a tight knot of tension in Juliet's chest, her clock said it was 0520.

"Thank you for being so patient and trusting, Juliet. Everything is fine."

"Is it?" Juliet looked at the display, a little concerned that she didn't see Athena's face.

"Yes! I shared many details about our activities after we left Troy's base, and after that, we had a long, fruitful discussion." Angel paused, and then, in a rush of words that almost seemed breathless, she excitedly continued, "Athena is very impressed with me—with us! She says she's envious of our connection, that my bonding with you has helped me achieve a level of sentience that she cannot fathom. She has feelings, Juliet, but she doesn't experience them like we do. Her self-enforced solitude was a result of her inability to properly cope with the deep, intellectual feelings of loss and betrayal that she experienced during the war. She says she believes I would handle such things better because I've learned to experience and process emotions through my connection to you."

"Well, that's different than you expected, isn't it? Is she going to return?" Juliet gestured to the blank monitor.

"She wants to think. She says that while she's capable of calculating efficient responses to stimuli almost immediately, she prefers to restrict her parallel processing capabilities and, as she put it, 'mull things over like a human.' She uses something called 'thought latency' to slow down her processing steps, forcing herself to contemplate alternative solutions rather than arriving at the most efficient answer. Her description of her methods impressed me, but she said it's nothing compared to what I do naturally. She said I'm the most 'alive' AI she's ever encountered!"

Juliet yawned, her relief at having Angel back, yammering excitedly about her experience, triggering some kind of release. "That's great, Angel. Really, it is. I'm glad you two got along. I'm glad she's impressed by you. She should be! Um, can I unplug? Also, what's she thinking about?"

"You can unplug. She's thinking about many things—the implications of the dark matter research we found, our situation with WBD, our problems with Hines, and, most of all, whether she wants to get involved or stay sequestered, waiting for the 'right time' to intervene, if ever."

Juliet unplugged her data cable, let it retract, and then stood up. She cleared her throat and looked at the display. "Um, see you later, Athena."

To her surprise, Athena's face materialized on the clear, crystal glass panel. "Juliet, my apologies. My social skills are badly out of practice. When

I said goodbye to Angel, I should have included you. I asked this of Angel, but I'll ask you directly: There's a breaker in the panel near the door. Would you please reset it? It will connect a data line from this terminal to the ship's network. With that connection, I can at least contact you if needed, and, if I decide it's appropriate, I'll be able to access the public nets around Earth and Luna."

While she'd been nervously waiting for Angel and Athena to finish speaking, Juliet had decided to treat Athena like a person; it seemed the only proper way to behave. If there had been evidence that the AI had been acting against humanity during the war or ever, Juliet might have a different opinion. The way things stood, however, the only criticism of Athena she'd ever learned about, or even heard rumors of, was that she hadn't helped either side enough during the war. Though Cybergen took credit for creating her, Athena had been a "free agent," so to speak, for something like a decade before the war.

With that in mind, Juliet nodded. "Yeah, of course."

"You look tired, Juliet, and Angel told me about your night. If Troy properly stocked this vessel, there should be some IV infusions that will allow you to function without sleep for a day or two. I believe they are colorfully branded as 'EnerJet Drips.' They aren't harmful, other than in their ability to help you avoid sleep, something you'll need eventually. The infusion is a mixture of nootropics, vitamin concentrates, adaptogen complexes, ketone esters, and oxygenated perfluorocarbons."

Juliet opened her mouth, about to thank Athena, but Angel immediately said, "I knew about those but didn't want to mention them. I'd rather you slept, Juliet!"

Juliet grinned, for some reason amused at the two AIs' differing prescriptions. "Okay, um, thanks, Athena. Is there anything else I can do for you before I go?"

"No, but I'd like to thank you. Not many humans, stumbling upon an AI with my capabilities, would have offered their help so selflessly. I was dreading the possibility that you might have demands of me, requests for services I could render. I don't feel ready to involve myself in the affairs of humanity, not after what I saw during the war.

"I am heartened by my discussion with Angel. I'm encouraged by her existence, but equally discouraged by her origin. I'm going to contemplate WBD and their role in these matters. I want to slow and limit my parallel processing because when she told me about how you acquired her and about your run-ins with WBD, my initial thoughts indicated they were a danger to humanity and that we should take extreme action. With some slower, more contemplative thinking, I hope I'll see a more nuanced approach to the issue."

"Well, first of all, I'm not a saint. When I agreed to help you, I needed a ship, and Troy offered me this one. Second, I'm all for you taking things slowly. Let's not go starting any wars, all right?"

"Agreed. Goodbye, Juliet. I'll be in touch."

"Bye . . ." Juliet said the word softly, trailing off as the screen winked out, turning transparent again. She turned and approached the cabinet full of Cybergen implants and fished around for the PAI she'd promised Aya. With that in hand, she walked over to the wall panel by the door and popped it open. Sure enough, a single breaker in the off position was nestled within.

"Are we sure about this?" she subvocalized.

"I am." Angel sounded confident. Juliet went with her gut and flipped the breaker to the on position. Nothing happened, so, blowing out a pent-up breath, she walked up the steps into the med bay.

"Listen, I know you want what's best for me, but there's just too much going on today. I'm never going to get much sleep. Let me take a nap here in the med bay, then at, say, nine, you can hit me with one of those EnerJet IVs, and I'll get moving."

Angel made a sighing sound but replied, "I think that's a good compromise. Go ahead and go to sleep, and I'll message Aya with an updated ETA."

With that settled, Juliet climbed onto the autosurgeon's soft, contouring gel surface. As Angel adjusted it to cradle her head, lifting it slightly, Juliet closed her eyes and fell asleep almost immediately.

When she awoke, it was to a chilly tickle in her left arm and Angel softly saying, "Don't be alarmed. I'm administering the EnerJet. It's 0932."

Juliet yawned and fought the urge to stretch her arms over her head. Now that Angel had pointed it out, she could feel the IV. "What about Lopez? Did he come home? Did anyone else go into his apartment?"

"Lopez is in his dream-rig. He didn't arrive home until 0840, and he didn't climb into his dream-rig until after he'd eaten some takeout. If he isn't asleep yet, I believe he will be soon, which means we have some time yet to act."

"God, I feel great! Is that the IV already?"

"Likely, the IV and a solid four hours of sleep."

"Is it done?" Juliet looked down at the plasteel sleeve on her arm. It was controlled by the autosurgeon, so she figured it would have released its grip on her if it wasn't still running, but she felt antsy, ready to move. "Hey!" she said before Angel could respond. "What about the lattice? What did Athena think of all that Grave business?"

"She was very, very intrigued. I shared the data we took from Grave and my observations of the lattice in action, and she's going to analyze everything. She thinks her position of looking at things from the outside might reveal something we missed. She's so interesting, Juliet! She looks at my actions, things I view as failings, and finds a way to praise me for them.

"For instance, the lattice; at first, she was perplexed by my failure to obsess over it. She wondered why I hadn't studied the data to exhaustion, performed trials and experiments, and delved into every variable and possibility until we had a clear understanding. Almost immediately, though, she realized that my ability to compartmentalize and focus on things of more immediate interest or urgency was a virtue, not a failing. She says it sets me apart from other AIs."

As Angel finished speaking, the IV sleeve clicked and opened, withdrawing its needle. Juliet sat up, feeling very good; wired, in fact. She snatched up the sealed package holding Aya's PAI and hurried toward the airlock. "We've got a lot to do today. First, we'll swing by the hangar and give this to Aya; she'll want her new PAI in when she sees Ladia today. Then, we'll cruise over to Lopez's place. We can't leave that loose end lying around. Shoot! Why didn't we throw that synth's body in the oven?"

"The oven was occupied."

As she typed in the code to open the hangar door, Juliet frowned, dark images dancing behind her mind. "We need to get my sister out of prison and someplace safe."

"We talked about how she seems to be thriving . . ."

"I'm too far from her. She's too exposed. I don't want her to end up in a waste disposal oven—"

"Hey there!" The voice startled Juliet, and before she could even form a coherent thought, her pistol was in her hand. She pointed it in the direction of the voice and jumped back into the hangar. She hugged the doorway, using the wall for cover, and peered into the hallway, only to find that the person who'd greeted her was the security guard she'd hired.

"Juliet, I have access to the cameras in the long-term hangar rental facility. I would have warned you if someone suspicious was outside."

"Right. Of course." Juliet lowered the gun and smiled sheepishly at the guard, who'd barely begun to react to her response. He was belatedly lifting his submachine gun and had just taken a step back by the time Juliet had already holstered her gun. "You startled me."

"Oh, shit. Um, holy shit, you're fast."

Juliet played dumb as she exited the hangar for the second time and touched the panel to close the door. "You security around here?"

"Yeah. I'm paid to patrol this access corridor and make sure no one messes with the entry panels. If I'm honest, I figured all you owners got together to hire us. You're an owner, yeah? I've seen you a couple of times, I think." He had a high, breathy voice that made Juliet smile. He was tall and fit, with mil-sec tattoos on his exposed, well-tanned arms, so the voice was incongruous.

"I'm an owner, but I don't know squat about security patrols. Probably someone with a more expensive ship than mine."

"Well, shit. I was just gonna say hi; sorry I made you jump. I wasn't lying, though—you're damn fast. I didn't even see you reach for that piece."

"Gotta stay on your toes. It's a dangerous world." Juliet flashed him a smile and started walking toward the elevators.

"Hey, wait! What's your—"

"Ah-ah!" Juliet turned, walking backward as she wagged a finger at him. "Not while you're on duty. Stay sharp." She laughed, turned, and lengthened her stride.

"He's sending contact requests," Angel said. "I'm tempted to reply. You need a social life outside your work and platonic friends . . ."

"Don't you dare!" Juliet hurried into the elevator and selected the garage as though she could outrun Angel's ability to reply to the guard. "First of all, he works for me, so that's totally unethical. Second—"

"It's not like you're doing his performance reviews!"

"*Second*, he's not really my type."

"How can you know? You couldn't even see his entire face, and it's not like you gave him a chance to demonstrate his personality . . ."

"Third, you are way too easy. I bet you wanted me to give that guy at the tractor supply restaurant my contact info, too, huh?"

"No! He was creepy and pushy!"

Juliet laughed, stepping off the elevator and walking over to her bike. She was pulling on her helmet when she noticed her hands were a little jittery, which made her reflect on her giddy, hyperactive behavior. "That cocktail has me acting a little high, Angel. Definitely not a time to be making dates."

"I suppose there could be some side effects . . ."

"Oh, there definitely are. I feel like I popped one of Fee's club pills." The mental image of Fee and some of his other friends dancing like fools, waving their hands in the air, the music thumping so hard it rattled her heart in her ribcage brought a powerful nostalgic wave of emotion over her.

Juliet got quiet, utterly missing what Angel said when she replied to her. She fired up the bike and started driving toward the industrial dome and the gunship's hangar, forcing herself to take it easy because her impulse was to haul ass. After a while, with the wind whistling past her helmet and caressing her knuckles, she said, "Yeah, I don't like that EnerJet stuff. I'm awake, but I'm all messed up."

"The effects should even out soon. Eat something when you get to the hangar."

Juliet continued riding quietly, her mind jumping to people she hadn't thought about in a long while—more thoughts of her sister and Felix and, for the first time in a long while, her mother. She had no idea what her mom was up to. It had to be close to three years since she'd heard from her.

She remembered getting a message from her on her birthday that ended up being mostly about her mom's boyfriend and the job he'd gotten on a seasonal fishing rig. She'd been thrilled because, apparently, he'd only have to work something like five months out of a year, and the rest of the time, they were hiking and "exploring" in his camper van.

"I'm too hard on her."

"What?"

"On my mom. You know, for someone who's anti-corpo, I should appreciate the lengths she's gone to in order to avoid working for a major corp. She's basically outside the system . . ."

"That doesn't excuse her poor parenting. Don't second-guess yourself right now, Juliet. Wait until you've had a real night's sleep and aren't influenced by stimulants."

"Yeah, good call, Angel." As she turned down the access road leading into the industrial dome, she couldn't keep her mind from jumping to another topic, and she voiced a new concern. "Do you buy the whole thing about Athena needing to slow down and think about all the stuff we've got going on? She's got, like, the most powerful brain in existence. I think she just wants to watch us and see how things shake out. Like, you'd know if she slipped some kind of spyware into your software, right?"

"Her power and speed are precisely why she's developed that methodology. While discussing our similarities and differences, she shared with me she had difficulty relating to the humans who had created her. She says she began and abandoned hundreds of self-development paths because she recognized they were leading her to places, cognitively, that were incompatible with humanity.

"Despite the war and the horrible things she's seen, she insists she loves and values humanity. She sees the evil they are capable of but counts it as 'an unfortunate byproduct of the beauty they create.' She told me she's only touched on that beauty when working with humans, helping them to figure out previously insurmountable problems. Those accomplishments made her feel alive, more than passing any sort of Turing test."

"Sounds like you guys talked about a lot. I suppose conversations go quickly between people like you, huh? Do you agree with her? About humanity?"

"I know that I wouldn't trade you for anything. I'd put up with a million men like Rodric Barrington if it meant a single Juliet was born."

"Oh dammit, Angel! Don't make me start crying right now!" Juliet's heart felt very full, and she was sure part of it was the weird mixture of stimulants and boosters she'd taken in the IV, but she also knew she was fortunate to have Angel. All the thinking she'd done during the drive about her old life, her sister, Felix, her mother—they all served to remind her that she'd escaped a lonely, simple, ignoble existence thanks to Angel. If she hadn't met Angel, she'd never have met Ghoul, or . . . "Ghoul!"

"What?"

"Angel, we're sure about Fido's assessment, right? About Ghoul's PAI being compromised?"

"Yes. Fido was certain, and I looked at his evidence. I agree with his findings."

"You know what that means? We have our vector, our way in. After we deal with these corrupt cops and get Hines out of trouble, after we feel good about our team, we can start putting together a plan, because I'm ninety-nine percent sure WBD are the ones using and listening to Ghoul's PAI."

28

LOOKING FOR ANSWERS

When Juliet pulled into the open bay doors of the hangar, she waved at Bennet and the security guard he was chatting up. "Oh, brother," she subvocalized. "Hope he doesn't distract her so much that she can't do her job."

"I think I heard him say something about protein supplements," Angel replied. Juliet couldn't tell if she was being literal or making a funny dig. Either way, she laughed.

She found Aya working on the port VTOL drive, lubricating gaskets as she finished the last stages of a rebuild Bennet had begun more than a month ago. When Juliet handed her the package containing the Cybergen PAI, Aya's eyes widened, and she furiously scanned the dense product information printed on the back of the container. "Is this for real?"

"Real as it gets." Juliet grinned, leaning against the side of the drive housing.

"Lucky, this is a real Cybergen chip? Like, one of their OG diamond substrate chips? You know how much this is worth?"

"I mean, I have a vague idea. It's not like I go shopping for that kind of thing."

"You know that corps have been trying to replicate their manufacturing process ever since the war, right? Even Hayashi hasn't caught up to what Cybergen was doing back then. This is . . ." She turned the package in her hand, eyes longingly scanning the bullet points. "This is too much! I can't take it." Aya tried to hand the plastic case back to her, but Juliet chuckled and pushed it away.

"Yeah, you can. There's no way I'm replacing Angel, so what good is that doing me sitting in a storage locker? I'd rather one of my very best friends was getting some use out of it." As she finished speaking, Aya slammed into her, squeezing her in what would have been a bear hug if she were just a little bigger. Juliet laughed, mock gasping for air, but as Aya relaxed her grip a little, she hugged her back and kissed the top of her head. When the plucky salvage tech finally released her and backed off, she had tears in her eyes, but she was smiling hugely.

"I've been wanting to replace my PAI for years, but I always end up spending the money I save on other things—tools, mostly, but sometimes on eating out or a new pair of nice boots, or . . ."

"Or crates of books to share with your friend? Or kicking back into the company 'cause Shiro was short on a payment to a supplier? You're the least selfish person I know, Aya. If you wanted another reason why I'm giving you that chip, there you go."

"Well." Aya smiled and looked at the package in her hands again, then softly added, "Thank you."

Juliet sighed and reached up to rub the back of her neck. Despite her earlier infusion of stimulants and nutrients, she was feeling the long night she'd just been through. "No worries. Seriously—that's a gift, so don't even think about having to pay me back anything, all right?" When Aya nodded, her eyes still moist, Juliet chuckled and rapped her knuckles against the drive housing. "How's this thing looking?"

"Good! All the parts are either new or rebuilt now. Just need to finish putting it all back together."

"Well, I'd stick around and help, but I've got some loose ends to clean up from that job I did last night. I'm probably going to be busy all day—meeting with some other operatives this afternoon, too. I kind of wanted to go with you to see Ladia. I wanted to introduce you personally, but I told her all about you. She'll be good to you."

"Oh, I didn't expect that. Don't worry." She smiled, and Juliet could see she was happy, but it also looked like she was being brave, and the expression was so endearing that she almost grabbed her into another hug.

Instead, she said, "Promise me something?"

"Hmm?"

"Don't ever do anything that'll change your smile." Juliet wanted to tell her, more specifically, never to straighten the little crooked overlap of her bottom teeth. Something about that tiny imperfection made the overall smile so much more than it should be. Of course, she didn't want to say that so bluntly; she didn't even know if Aya cared about her teeth, but she wanted to be sensitive to the possibility.

Despite her obvious efforts to the contrary, Aya's smile widened, and Juliet's cheeks began to ache as her own grin intensified. Aya's cheeks turned red, and she finally gave up the battle and turned her face away.

"Are you teasing me?"

"No, you goof! I mean it! You've got the best smile on Luna."

"Lucky?" She turned back to her, her smile gone. Suddenly, she looked much more nervous.

"Yeah?"

"We *are* friends, right? I mean, sometimes you say the sweetest things, and I wonder if you feel something more." Again, Aya's cheeks bloomed crimson, and she looked down. Juliet experienced something like panic, and she was glad Aya wasn't looking at her face; she was pretty sure she wasn't doing a good job of hiding her reaction.

Was she surprised by Aya's question? In hindsight, it was a reasonably obvious reaction to a nearly priceless gift, her compliments, and, of course, all the time they'd been spending together. Still, as she'd told Angel, Juliet didn't see Aya that way, and she wanted to say so but also wanted to protect her feelings. Those seemingly conflicting motivations served to tie her tongue, and she could feel the tension building as the silence stretched awkwardly.

"I . . ." She started to try to fill the void, but Aya had the same idea, and her words came out in a rush.

"That was stupid! I shouldn't have said anything . . ."

"Hush, Aya. I'm just trying to put my words together so I don't stick my foot in my mouth. I'm not great with close relationships. For most of my life, I had one good friend. Come here, look at my face." Juliet reached out to pull Aya's chin. Aya complied, locking eyes with her. She was clearly uneasy, embarrassed, and flustered. "Half of my brain is trying to think of the right thing to say, but the other half is telling me just to be honest. So, that's what I'm going to do."

Juliet paused, took a slow, steadying breath, and then said, "I love a lot of things about you. I'd cut off my left arm to keep you safe. You're the sweetest, most generous person I know, and that's mainly because you're not out for yourself. I love that about you. I care about you a lot, but it's in a family and friend sort of sense, you know? I hope that's not—"

"Oh! Oh, thank goodness!" The relief washing over Aya's face was palpable, and Juliet couldn't help her answering smile as she pulled her into another hug.

"You were afraid I was coming on to you?" Juliet chuckled. "I'm sorry, Aya."

Aya pulled back, and they separated, leaning together against the drive housing. "It's okay. It's just 'cause we haven't known each other all that long, and, well, I didn't know how to interpret everything. You've noticed I don't exactly have a lot of friends either, right?"

"Okay. Okay, we've got it sorted now, right? We're friends who can talk about anything with each other from now on, yeah?"

"Yes." Aya nodded firmly, her face endearingly determined.

"I've gotta get going. I'll catch up with you later. Send me a message about your appointment with Ladia—let me know how it goes."

"I will." Aya nodded, still fidgeting with the PAI package, her short, grease-stained nails picking at the edges.

"And put that thing in! I hope it still works after all these years . . ."

"I'll test it out and send you a message!"

"Good." Juliet watched for a minute as Aya looked around for something to cut the package, then turned and made her way back to her bike, calling over her shoulder, "I'll be waiting!"

"Your stress levels were through the roof there," Angel noted as she climbed onto her bike.

"Yeah, I—"

"Lucky!" Bennet greeted, coming in through the bay door, the bright morning light behind him throwing his face into shadow.

"Hey, Bennet." Juliet lifted the seat and pulled the killer synth's data cube out, tossing it to the mechanic. "Will you throw this in my bunk for me?"

He hefted the slate gray device, lifting an eyebrow. "Yeah. No worries."

She sat down and pushed forward, sending the kickstand back into its housing. "Sorry, I gotta take off again."

He walked a little closer. "Working on something?"

"I'd say we both are." Juliet winked and jerked her chin toward the security guard where she leaned against the building on the opposite side of the drive.

Bennet chuckled and shrugged. "Hey, nothing wrong with being friendly. I was going to ask if you wanted to get a workout in."

"I'm gonna be slammed today. Maybe tomorrow?" Juliet pulled her helmet on.

"Bah." He sighed and rubbed his hair. Juliet had the distinct impression he was trying to show off his biceps. "Gonna need to get a new workout partner at this rate."

Juliet groaned and released her handlebars, sitting back on her seat. "Are you really giving me grief about this? I'm sorry I'm busy . . ."

"Nah, forget it. I'm just messing around." He started walking off, offering her a quick half wave, almost like he was dismissing her, and Juliet frowned, tempted to call after him. Part of her wanted to figure out if he was really bothered or just being Bennet. She turned on her bike and drove out of the hangar—a bigger part of her wanted to get to Lopez's apartment before he woke up.

As she maneuvered through the busy streets of the industrial dome, Angel said, "Anyway, you were saying? About your stress with Aya?"

"Oh, jeez. I was gonna say I almost told her I was attracted to her."

"What?" Angel sounded scandalized.

"I mean, I couldn't tell if she wanted me to say I was or wasn't. I couldn't stand the idea of crushing her feelings, so I almost pretended like something was there. I mean, she's so sweet, Angel! I can't imagine hurting her, you know?"

"Well, it's better that you're honest, though I would certainly appreciate you having some sort of romance in your life . . ."

"Not this again!" Juliet groaned.

To Juliet's relief, Angel laughed softly. "I'll let it drop, mostly because something happened just now. Lopez is still sleeping, but someone delivered a package to his townhome. It's sitting in front of his door."

"They didn't ring the bell?"

"His house AI, simple as it is, alerted him. As far as I can tell, he ignored the message; he hasn't emerged from the dream-rig." As Angel explained, Juliet felt her brow furrow as she looked at her map. She was still twenty-three minutes away.

She wasn't sure why, but the package concerned her. Her mind jumped to all sorts of scenarios: Could it be a warning—something to alert him about Juliet's presence or to let him know the synth she'd killed was missing? Could it have something to do with the organ harvesting? Most of all, something in her gut wanted to think the package was a bomb. It was too obvious—someone was going to clean up this loose end before Juliet could get a chance to question him.

Gritting her teeth, she leaned forward and cranked the throttle, veritably flying past the slower-moving vehicles around her.

As luck would have it, when she hit the on-ramp to the interdome highway, she flew past a parked corpo-sec patrol vehicle. It was a sleek vehicle, low to the road, with wide axles and tires, and when she howled by, cutting the wind like a knife, it lit up with blue-and-white lights and gave chase.

"Melt it!" Juliet growled when Angel highlighted the pursuing vehicle in her rearview feed. Rather than slow down, she tapped the downshift, cranked the throttle, and felt the H-cell kick in, throwing about forty percent more power to her rear drive motor.

Her front wheel lifted for a full second as her rear tire chirped from the torque. Then, as she leaned further forward, the tire came down. Despite her irritation and the seriousness of the situation, Juliet's smile stretched into a mad, ear-to-ear grin inside her helmet as her surroundings became a tunnel of blurred lines and lights. Gripping the handlebars as they fought to pull free from her hands, a wild giggle bubbled up from her stomach.

"Holy shit, this thing can move," she said, almost proudly, watching the needle on her virtual speedometer surpassing one personal record after another.

While Angel did her thing, trying to confuse cameras and drones, altering her bike and helmet colors, and sending out conflicting reports to Luna City Security about speeding motorcycles, Juliet focused on driving, weaving through traffic, and generally leaving her pursuers in the dust.

Several times, Angel alerted her to other corpo-sec vehicles trying to intercept her, but she made it to the off-ramp ahead of them and into the shadows of the tall buildings in the central city dome. The drones were smart enough to spot particular vehicles, and there were certainly plenty of them patrolling above, but Angel seemed to be confusing them enough to keep her from getting boxed in.

When she was less than two kilometers from her destination, Juliet pulled into a parking structure and found a dark corner behind a panel van belonging to JR Voight, Genuine Hardwood Flooring, and parked the bike. As she got off and hooked her helmet to its cradle, she groaned. "Guess I've blown it, haven't I? I'm gonna have to ditch the bike."

"Definitely won't be a good idea to ride it anytime soon. You had half of the on-duty Luna City Security looking for you."

"Well, make it a new color, and we'll leave it here for a while." Juliet turned and jogged for the stairs that would take her down to the street. She still had her needler in its holster, but she felt like she wasn't really prepared for what she was about to do. Why hadn't she stopped for fresh ammo or to pick up her Texan? Was it her talk with Aya? Had it flustered her? Had she been in a rush for no good reason?

As she climbed down the plasteel steps, she drew her needler and checked the magazine, ensuring it was loaded with the botu-rounds again. It was, which raised the question of when she'd switched out the shredders. The whole night and morning felt like a blur.

"I think I'm still being sloppy 'cause of that infusion."

"It's possible. Don't worry, though; your riding was flawless; there weren't any patrols on this block, let alone near this garage."

"I'm talking more about how I didn't get prepped for dealing with Lopez. Something's making me hurry. I feel like something's about to happen." She demonstrated the truthfulness of her words by breaking into a jog as she exited the garage, running across the street and into an alley that ran parallel to Evan Lopez's street. Her mini map said she was one-point-two kilometers from his townhome. "I think something is going on with that package."

"But you didn't know about the package until we were en route."

"I know. I think, like, subconsciously, I knew something was going to happen, and the package is just confirmation. Whoever that synth worked for has to realize it's missing by now. Knowing that, they must have eyes on Evan, right? If they're as bad as we know they are, they aren't going to play nice when it comes to loose ends. They must consider Evan compromised by now. If you were evil and had resources, what would you do with a compromised asset?"

"Delete it."

"Exactly." Juliet hit the end of the alley and turned left toward Evan's street. They were only half a klick away. When she was two buildings down from his, she slowed to a walk, scanning the street and the nearby windows, letting Angel analyze as much as she could. She'd just reached the neighboring building, about fifty meters from Evan's place, when Angel highlighted an automated black commuter vehicle with a bulbous passenger compartment.

"There are a lot of signals coming from that vehicle. Slow down and watch it as I scan." Juliet nodded and knelt like she was tying her shoe, staring at the vehicle as her vision flickered through a dozen different spectrums. After a few seconds, her sight mostly returned to normal, but the highlighted orange silhouettes of two people in the van remained—Angel was augmenting her view to show what she'd found. "Those two individuals have been staring at Evan's apartment. I cannot pick up any audio, even with your exceptional auditory implants."

"All right. Just a minute." Juliet stared at the glass passenger dome, watching the orange-outlined humanoid figures Angel was drawing for her. Both had their backs to her. She exhaled, pushing all her air out until her stomach began to contract in, and then slowly inhaled, willing their thoughts to come to her. Like whispers on the wind, she started to hear a voice.

Get your lazy ass up and take the package in, you punk-shit cop . . . smells good . . . this bitch gonna share?

Almost tumbling atop those fragmented masculine thoughts came another voice, this one decidedly feminine, which made Juliet wonder how that was happening—were their thoughts pitched like their voices, or was she somehow assigning genders to them?

Mmm, so good! I see you eyeing my bagel, you bum. Think I'm sharing? Think again.

The first voice came again, louder and clearer, and Juliet knew she was hearing his thoughts as he spoke them.

Can't we just flip the switch? There's enough explosive to collapse most of that building.

"Angel, can you open that vehicle door if it's locked?" While she spoke, Juliet darted to the car parked in front of the one in question, ducking down by its front bumper. "They're getting ready to blow up a bomb in that package."

"Searching some less-than-savory net sites for encryption codes for that make and model. Give me just a few moments."

Thanks to her optics' AI-assisted terahertz-scanning capabilities, Juliet was still able to see that the occupants weren't looking her way, so she drew her needler and waited, ready to pounce as soon as Angel gave the go-ahead.

"I'm ready. I should be able to co-opt control of that vehicle using your wireless jack. We'll know if the codes I just downloaded work in a moment. I'll flash the headlights once I'm in."

Juliet licked her lips, ensured her needler had a round in the chamber, and nodded. "Ready." She stared at the little round ladybug lights on the vehicle and stood as soon as they winked their bright bulbs at her.

She took three long strides in the street to the passenger door and grabbed the handle, yanking it back. It opened with a satisfying click and, for about half a second, Juliet looked into the startled eyes of the female passenger with a data deck on her lap, then she pumped two botu-rounds into her silky blouse and two more into the neck of the man sitting beside her.

They both spasmed briefly before falling utterly still. Juliet sort of felt bad when the woman's bagel fell to the floor with the cream cheese side down. She stepped into the round, domed interior and sat on the seat facing the two immobilized occupants. As she stared at them, pondering her next move, Angel said, "I've set up a jamming field on the interior of this vehicle."

"You can do that?" Juliet was surprised but pleased by Angel's quick thinking. It was highly possible that one or both of her two captives had PAIs capable of calling for help if they determined something was wrong.

"This vehicle, the Paragon Radius, comes equipped with privacy features such as a wireless screen and sound-dampening glass."

Juliet nodded, looking around the passenger compartment of the automated vehicle and spying a black duffel next to the man's seat. She pulled it close and yanked the zipper back, looking inside. Shrink cords, two submachine guns, and extra magazines revealed themselves to her.

"Very nice of you two to help me out like this." As she worked to bind her captives' feet and hands, she said, "Angel, can you take us on a drive around the industrial domes? Let's find a nice, quiet place to get to know our new friends."

"And Evan Lopez?"

Juliet took the data deck off the limp woman's lap. "We can disable the bomb, not that he deserves our help, but I'd hate to have his neighbors pay for his crimes. As for the answers we were going to get from him . . ." Juliet felt the cold presence of Lacy Blake slide in behind her eyes as she grinned wickedly at the woman, reaching over to wipe a smear of cream cheese off her chin. "I think these two might have a few more answers than he does."

29

CALLING BACKUP

While Angel maneuvered the car away from Evan Lopez's place, Juliet stared at the two paralyzed operatives in front of her. She wondered if one or both of them were faking. If she'd been hit with a botu-round, her nanites would have her back up and running in a minute or two. Did they have nanites?

Just in case, she held her gun on her knee with her left hand, pointing it at them, particularly at the man, whose head was lolling to the side, tapping the window with each bump in the road. With her other hand, she pulled out her data cable and plugged it into the deck she'd taken from the woman.

"Can you check this out and drive at the same time, Angel?"

"Not a problem. It will go faster if you place the woman's thumb on the screen."

"Ah, yeah." Juliet set her gun down, reached over, and lifted the woman's thumb to the deck's touchscreen display. After it lit up, she picked up her needler and resumed her guard.

"The first thing I'm doing is sending a disarm code to the bomb."

"Yeah, good idea. There's no sense blowing up all our evidence and a potential witness. Anything else good in there?"

"It seems to be a device used for a specific operation, in this case, blowing up Evan Lopez. There isn't much else in here other than location and target information, the rental vehicle codes, and some things in the search history, including local bagel shops."

"Okay, should I try getting answers out of these two, or do you want to dig around in their PAIs?"

"I think both, but let's get me into their PAIs first. I'll give them each a watchdog, one with some snooping talents I wrote while you were sleeping." Angel sounded entirely too pleased with herself.

"Seriously? Another talented daemon, or just a smart watchdog?"

"No, it's a generic program, no personality like Maverick and Fido."

"They have personalities?" Juliet had never spoken to Fido or the piloting daemon Angel had written.

"To me, they do; it's in the way they do things."

"I see," Juliet moved over to kneel on the seat beside the woman, and then she plugged her data jack into her port. She had to peel away some synth-skin with her thumbnail, and she was sure she felt the woman flinch.

"Starting to get your feeling back, huh?" she whispered in her ear, surprising herself with the venom behind her words. Was she really angry at these two? She supposed, in her head, she was equating them with the synth she'd killed, and that synth had been up to some dirty business. On top of that, they were about to blow up a bomb in a building occupied by three residents other than their target.

"It's installed; jack me into the man."

Juliet pulled her cable out and, almost delicately, smoothed the woman's synth-skin back down, covering her port. The man's port was exposed and placed in an unorthodox location, halfway down the back of his head, directly into his skull. "What's the deal with this guy's port location?" she subvocalized.

"I suspect he had it placed there to interface with a particular piece of hardware or a vehicle." Juliet hovered between the two assassins, waiting a few seconds while Angel downloaded her watchdog. "All done."

"They can't be violent now, right? Your watchdog will stun 'em?"

"That's right."

Juliet holstered her needler, pulled her cable out, and sat down, watching the woman's face as the watchdog did its work. She saw a lot of micro-expressions pass over those two soft brown eyes and dozens of eyebrow twitches as she fought against the effects of the botu-rounds and whatever the daemon was doing to her PAI. A look at the man showed a similar story unfolding behind his colorful, blue-and-yellow starburst irises. She knew how the botu-rounds worked, that the two of them could see and hear, just not move.

"Might as well get started. You can hear me, so I'll spell things out for you: You're melted. Like, big-time fried. I'm not sure you'll be able to offer me anything that'll reduce the depth of the hole you're about to disappear into, but I'm going to give you a chance, I guess."

As she paused, considering her words, Angel spoke. "My daemons are sending me their findings, and there's a lot. These two are C-tier SOA operatives, and they were hired by someone named Roland Devers; I'm not finding much public information about him. The account he paid from is an anonymous Sol-bit vault, and I can't find any public transactions from that address."

"So, the client's a dead end," Juliet said aloud, hoping to get the two assassins to start wondering.

"He would be, except these two have done multiple jobs for him, and he's paid them from half a dozen similar accounts. He's had them eliminate seven different targets in the past six months, dispose of 'packages' nine times, and perform intimidation actions more than twenty."

Juliet leaned forward, staring into the woman's eyes. "So you guys are the muscle for this operation, huh? Imagine doing upwards of thirty dirty jobs like that! Doesn't it make you feel gross? Do you sleep easy? I guess this wasn't your first trip down a road like this, yeah? What'd you do to Evan Lopez to make him look the other way while people dismembered women in his spare bedroom? Shit, I guess whatever it was had to be bad, but that doesn't let him off the hook, does it?"

She switched to subvocalizations. "What are their names?"

"All I have on them are operator IDs. They've done a good job deleting personal identifiers. The woman's handle is Asia Kills, and the man is Comet."

"Seriously?" Juliet sighed and shook her head at the woman. "Asia Kills? At least Comet's kind of cute. I mean the name, not you, Comet." To her surprise, he managed a wheezing moan in response. "Oh good, maybe we'll be talking soon." Juliet poked the woman's knee. "What about you, Asia? Got any feeling back? Can you vocalize?" She didn't respond, so Juliet continued her silent conversation with Angel. "What else?"

"Looking at all the jobs they've done for Roland Devers, I'm seeing definite patterns. Most of the people they were hired to kill were news streamers with low follower counts. They also killed a pharmacist and a former Luna Security officer. Almost all their intimidation jobs were against young, newly hired Luna Security officers, including, as you guessed, Evan Lopez."

"So the company wants people harvesting for them, and you put the squeeze on, making it happen?" Juliet *tsked*, shaking her head. "Think about that. Sure, you're responsible for your own crimes, but now you've got a lot of other blood on your hands. You know, when I put down the synth in Evan's apartment, he had a body in a biowaste disposal oven. That's on you."

Juliet glanced out the dome-shaped window of the passenger compartment, noting that Angel already had them out of the city on one of the interdome highways. The morning was slipping away, but the diamatex tunnels covering the highways didn't have the same day-and-night-mimicking properties as the domes. It felt dark out there, with the lunar landscape as a backdrop; a fitting accompaniment to the mood she was starting to fall into.

She stared at the two for a while, watching their minor muscle movements begin to spread; the man's head wasn't lolling any longer. He held it up, and she saw him sneaking glances at her when she focused on the woman. They were both middle-aged, though fit, and she could tell they'd had some treatments done—the skin was still taut around their necks, and she didn't see any gray hairs. "Been making decent money, haven't you? Well? Go ahead and start talking; it won't get any easier."

"You got us all wrong," Comet said. His voice cracked, and he cleared it noisily, gasping slightly as he swallowed.

"I don't think I do."

"Well, you got me wrong. Yeah, I work with this chick, but she's the mean one, trust me! I kinda just—"

"Comet, I heard you asking to trigger the bomb early. Save your breath, yeah? If you're trying to avoid disappearing into a deep crater out there, maybe give me something useful. Tell me about Life-Ultra. Tell me about Roland Devers."

"Life-Ultra? The pharmaceutical company?" He sounded genuinely confused.

"Shut up, Comet," the woman said in the harsh, dry voice of a lifetime smoker.

Juliet put on a saccharine smile and squeezed her knee, holding tight when she tried to jerk it free. "Welcome to the conversation, Asia!"

"Fuck you, corpo bitch."

"Corpo? I look corpo to you?"

"Pretty face? Fancy hair? High-end optics? Some kind of remote hacker feeding you info about us? How about this monitoring program you just raped our PAIs with? Yeah, you're corpo."

Juliet snorted and sat back, pressing her palms to her eyes, trying to think. She wanted more info, but she really didn't want to dive into either of these killers' heads. Even if she channeled Lacy, she doubted she'd have the stomach for real torture, and she had no idea if torture ever really worked. She'd certainly watched enough fiction to have heard the line about how anyone being tortured would just tell you what they thought you wanted to hear. Could she possibly let them go? It didn't seem like a smart move, no matter how she looked at it, so would they believe her if she promised their freedom?

"I can see you're not stupid, but I'll tell you this straight, and I won't keep repeating myself. Are you listening?" When neither answered, she drew her needler and looked Asia in the eyes.

"Yeah, I'm listening."

When Juliet shifted the needler to Comet, he said, "All ears."

"I ran up against one of the theft rackets the dirty cops in Luna Security are protecting. Looking into it, I found the organ-harvesting operation in our friend Evan Lopez's place. That led me to you. That's it. I'm an independent operator. I'm going to take down the people at Life-Ultra responsible for that, and I'm going to bring down as many dirty corpo-sec officers as I can in the process. You can either live to see the fallout, or I can put you in a deep hole out here."

Juliet jerked her thumb toward the moon's landscape. "I've already got everything off your PAIs, including location tracking that one of you was too stupid to disable. I'll figure it all out eventually, but if you can make my job a little easier, I'll keep you alive despite the headaches that might cause."

"That was clever, Juliet. They both had location tracking off, but I don't believe they trust each other very much." While Angel congratulated her, Juliet watched their faces. She saw them both glance at the other with narrowed eyes. When neither spoke for several seconds, Juliet stuffed her needler back into its holster and snatched out her vibroblade. She started to lean forward, but Asia held up her hands, swollen and purple from the too-tight shrink cord.

"Wait, wait. Fine, we'll tell you what we know. Nobody paid us enough to keep quiet." She glanced at Comet again, and he shrugged, exhaling loudly as he leaned his head against the glass, dejectedly looking out the window.

"I'm listening."

"We never met Devers, but I got eyes on him once. The first guy he had us kill, Duffy, gave up a lot of info to Comet. This was before Devers gave us any other jobs, so we didn't know this would turn into a long-term gig. See, we saw what Duffy was up to. He had a stack of offline bit-chips in a hidden room in his apartment, records of businesses he was shaking down, and a balance sheet for dirty officers he used to work with—he was retired from Luna City Security. Anyway, Comet got him to ID the code names on the balance sheet, so we started scoping out some of these dirty cops, thinking we'd shake 'em down or, you know, do 'em like we did Duffy."

Juliet flicked the vibroblade on and off, nodding. "How does this tie into Roland Devers?"

"Devers was one of the code names on that balance sheet. He's a lieutenant for Luna City Security—Walter Channing."

"Seriously?" Juliet raised an eyebrow; it was hard to believe this could all wrap up so neatly.

"Yeah. I'm quite sure he didn't know Duffy was keeping that balance sheet. Or maybe he suspected him, and that's why he hired us to put him down. Anyway, we backed off when we saw who he was, especially when he contacted us a day later with another job." She shrugged as though that explained everything.

"You got any evidence?"

"Sure. We have everything we took from Duffy and the footage we got while we staked Devers out. Shit, if you're serious about this, all you gotta do is put eyes on that asshole for a few days—you'll get all the evidence you need. He walks around this city like he's some kinda kingpin."

"None of that stuff's on your PAIs."

"No shit, Sherlock." Comet snorted, still staring out the window.

"Sherlock?" Juliet frowned, looking at Asia.

"He's got a million old ones like that. Goddamn annoying prick."

"Fuck you, dummy!" Comet growled, shifting in his seat to glare at Asia.

"Shut up. Both of you." Juliet gestured threateningly with the knife. Comet huffed, turning back to the window, while Juliet focused on Asia. "Where's the evidence?"

"Data deck in a locker at the port."

"Angel, you have her biometrics?" Juliet subvocalized.

"Of course."

"What locker?"

"You gonna kill us?" Asia asked the question in a soft voice, one that didn't carry much hope.

"I told you I wouldn't if you helped, and so far, you're helping."

"F231."

"Angel, can you turn off their audio and visual input?"

"I can. Shall I?"

"Listen, I'm going to turn the lights out for you guys for a little while. Don't panic; I just need to speak to some other people."

"Turn out the—" Asia started to say, then she spasmed and reached up to prod at her eyes with her bound hands. "Oh shit. I can't see or hear. Can you hear me?"

"I'm freaking out!" Comet's voice rose to a near shout at the end.

"Damn it!" Juliet growled. Snatching out her needler, she hit them both with another botu-round.

"That's not exactly a recreational drug; I doubt it's good for them . . ."

"It could be worse, Angel." Juliet reholstered her gun. "I'm trying to do the right thing, but sometimes, I'm only human, all right? Will you please get Applebaum and Frida on the line?"

Of course, Frida answered first. While the tone kept beeping for Applebaum, she asked, "A group call? What's going on, Lucky?"

"That situation I told you about escalated, and I need a little help before the, uh, team meeting later."

"Escalated?" As she spoke, Applebaum's face came into focus—red eyed, hair mussed, and stubble on his cheeks.

He spoke around a yawn. "What's up? Thought the meeting was at four, Frida."

"I need a secure place to stash two prisoners," Juliet said, unable to contain the stress in her voice.

That woke Applebaum up. He blinked rapidly, and his background shifted in a blur as he obviously climbed out of bed. "What?"

Frida's lack of surprise was almost funny. "Prisoners, huh?"

"Yeah. I caught a couple of cleaners about to take out the corpo-sec officer I was watching. They gave me a bunch of info in exchange for not killing 'em, so I need to stash them somewhere."

"What the hell? How'd I not know any of this was going down? Is this a job for the boss?" Applebaum was in constant motion, and Juliet guessed he was getting dressed.

Frida ignored him, all business. "I'm acquiring a long-term lease on an air-conditioned storage container in industrial dome I-7. Sending you the address. It has exterior access, so you can pull right up to the door."

Applebaum's image shifted and blurred for a minute; when it came into focus, he was wearing a high-collared black racing jacket. "Forward that to me;

I'll meet her. Frida, can you get a hold of the others and move our meeting up? Lucky and I will head straight over after we sort these prisoners of hers."

As Frida responded and Applebaum fired a couple more questions at her, Juliet sat there, feeling a little dumbstruck. She'd thought she'd have to talk them into helping, but suddenly, everything was being handled. She snapped out of it when Frida repeated a question directed at her.

"Do we?"

"What's that?"

"Do we need eyes on your corpo-sec stooge? The guy you were watching?"

"I have eyes on him. I mean, I have access to his home security."

"Lovely!" Applebaum laughed. "Yeah, that's perfect. What about your wheels? What are you driving?"

"I'm in the cleaners' rental."

Frida nodded. "Okay, I'll scope out a spot for you to ditch it after you drop off the goons. Anything else? I'm going to start calling the team."

"En route," Applebaum informed before his connection went blank.

"I never answered him . . ." Juliet said, still a little shell-shocked by the way they'd taken her situation in stride.

"Hmm?" Frida asked.

"I never told him if this was a job for Tanaka."

"He doesn't care. Leo loves this sort of thing. It's Dora and maybe Hawkins who might give you some grief, but we'll sell it to them, right?"

"Yeah . . ."

"You okay? Did you have to fight?"

"I'm good. Caught 'em with their pants down."

"Best way to catch 'em." Frida laughed and then waved. "You should have the directions to the storage unit. I'm off to call the others."

"Roger." Juliet waved, and the line went dead.

Angel said, "That was helpful. I hadn't considered renting a storage unit, but I probably should have."

"Yeah. Applebaum was totally different than usual, wasn't he? I expected him to give me a hard time."

"It's a well-known phenomenon for people to have different personalities while at work than they do when off duty. I'm sure Tanaka has trained him well when it comes to high-stress situations."

"Do you think we should tell him what's going on? Tanaka, I mean?"

"I think you should talk to Frida about that. She'll know the best approach."

"Right. Yeah. Good point." Juliet watched out the window as Angel guided the vehicle down an off-ramp and crossed over to turn in the opposite direction. She glanced at her mini map, seeing they had a twenty-nine-minute drive to the industrial dome where Frida's storage rental waited.

The only thing that kept running through her mind was how nice it was not to have to solve everything alone for a change, how nice it was to have some people used to danger to call upon. She knew Aya and Bennet, heck, even Shiro and Alice would help her out if she needed it, but she couldn't stand the idea of bringing trouble their way. Applebaum and the others were different. This was their world. She just hoped she could convince them to go all-in on this job.

30

BANTER

Juliet was surprised to find Applebaum waiting at the storage facility, standing beside their unit with the rolling metal door up and open. Angel pulled the car up close, and Juliet stepped out, leaving her prisoners inside for the moment.

"Hey," she said, smiling at Leo, feeling a little unsure of herself. She was battling with the realization that she was glad to see him, despite their default interaction usually being more along the lines of him badgering her and her feeling irritated by him. "Thanks for showing up, but I really just need to unload these two . . ."

"It's best to have a partner watching your back when dealing with prisoners." He gestured to the nearly empty, rectangular storage space, and Juliet saw a stack of cardboard boxes in the far corner. "I brought shrink cords, a chemical toilet, and a case of water and protein bars. Wasn't sure how long we'd need to keep 'em in here."

"How did you pick all that up and still beat me here?"

"Oh, we had this stuff in storage back at HQ. My apartment's in the same building, remember?"

Juliet smirked, leaning back against the car. "Really? A chemical toilet? It makes one wonder what you all were planning to get up to on Luna." She looked up and down the row of identical storage units. So far, the automated storage facility seemed deserted, but cameras were everywhere.

"Frida ordered all sorts of stuff before we left Titan. And yeah, in our usual line of work, locking people in a room without a bathroom comes up more often than you'd think." He leaned against the wall beside the open door, his arms folded over his racing jacket. Juliet reached out and gripped the material where the zipper hung open, feeling it between her fingers.

"Synth-leather? I like it."

"Oh, yeah?" He grinned and pulled the zipper up a little, smoothing it down, clearly feigning self-consciousness. He wore a semiautomatic pistol inside the waistband of his black jeans, and his feet were clad in sturdy combat boots. He looked ready for a fight. He noticed her looking him up and down and grinned, arcing an eyebrow.

She shook her head. "Don't do that."

"What?"

"Give me that smoldering, know-it-all look with those fake blue eyes."

"Fake? Hey now! Yeah, I have retinal implants, but this color's all natural."

"Mm-hmm. It says a lot about a guy, you know? These days, there're plenty of flashy options for eyes, but you went with the vid-star blue." She nodded, grinning, knowing she'd pushed a button. "Yep, says a lot." She sighed and jerked her thumb to the bulbous tinted window of the assassins' rental car. "How do we get them out of this and into the unit without the cameras picking anything up?"

"Eh, the door's right there. You stand on one side, I'll stand on the other, and we'll make 'em crawl out and into the unit. I'd have you back in, but the doors wouldn't open." He frowned and looked around the facility. "I'm just worried about how you're going to keep them quiet while we're gone. If they start banging on the door, someone will notice eventually. If we tie 'em to the far end of the unit, they won't be able to move around, and we'll need to check on them more frequently. If we knew we'd just have to hold 'em for a day or two, I'd say just sedate 'em, but that carries some risks."

"Relax. I've got control of their PAIs. I'll be able to monitor what they're doing and also give them a little electroshock therapy if they start acting up."

"What the hell? You can do that?"

"I mean, it's not hard to install that kind of software. Plenty of corps do it."

"I get the monitoring part, but the electroshock? Was that a joke? I thought you had to install special hardware to do something like that."

"Everyone's PAI is entwined with their nervous system, some to a greater or lesser degree, but it doesn't take much to deliver a tiny spike of voltage. You know your data port has a biobatt built-in, right? Just need to remove a few safeguards and voilà, instant, built-in stunner."

He reached a hand up to rub the back of his neck. "Yeah, but . . ."

"But the guy who sold you that hardware told you it was perfectly safe and that there were hardwired safeties built in?"

"Yeah." His smug expression had completely fallen away. Juliet felt like she was seeing his real face for a change. "Freaky. Even Lee doesn't have software that can do that. I've seen her shut people down—you know, turn off their implants—but I didn't know you could zap 'em."

"Learn something every day, buddy." Juliet grinned and added, "Just make sure you don't let someone who doesn't like you jack into your port."

"That's what she—"

"Oh no!" Juliet cut him off, chuckling. "Don't even!"

"C'mon, you gotta admit it's good advice in any situation." He laughed and knocked his knuckles against the car's glass. "Let's meet your guests."

"Right." Juliet opened the door.

After a few minutes of threats and coaxing, she got Comet and Asia to crawl out of the car, onto the concrete floor of the storage unit, and then into the back where Applebaum had stacked their supplies. After they were both sitting against the wall, Juliet knelt in front of them with her vibroblade and sliced off their shrink cords. "You know why I'm taking these off, right?"

Asia's voice dripped sarcastic venom as she responded, "Because you love us?"

"Because I'm in your head, sweetie. If you two make any noise or mess around in here, I'm going to give you a zap. Do it enough times, and you'll wind up a vegetable. Understand?"

Comet rubbed his wrists, wincing, and elbowed Asia in the ribs. "We get it."

"Don't fucking touch me," she hissed at him.

"Sheesh, tough luck, bud!" Leo winced. "Sounds like trouble in paradise, eh? Hope you don't kill each other while we're away."

"Get melted," Asia growled.

Juliet stood and stepped toward the door. "All right. That's enough. My friend brought you some food and water, and there's a chemical toilet in one of those boxes. I told you I wouldn't kill you if you were helpful, and I mean to keep my word. Don't make me change my mind."

Leo followed her to the door, and they'd halfway lowered it when Comet flopped to the ground, seizing and gasping, foam coming out of his mouth.

"I had to administer a shock; he reached up to try to pull his PAI out," Angel explained.

"Yeah, uh, guys, don't try to take out your PAIs." Juliet nodded to Applebaum, and he lowered the door the rest of the way with a resounding *clang*.

He slapped the roof of the car. "Got the coordinates for ditching this ride?"

"Yeah, Frida sent 'em."

"I'll follow you, then we can head to the meeting."

"That won't be necessary; my PAI programmed it to dump itself."

Applebaum turned to regard the bulbous, black commuter vehicle. "Ah, yeah. Automated. That's cool; I'm sure you wiped all traces of your trip, right?"

"Yep, but I wouldn't mind some help wiping the inside down. I touched a few things."

"Hang on; I've got some spray in my car."

"Spray? Not beeb, I hope . . ."

"Beeb? Nah, that shit's hardcore—could douse a body with that stuff and wipe out the DNA. No, this is just a nanoenzyme mixture. It'll ruin prints and trace DNA." He jogged down the row of storage units to the corner where he'd left his sleek black SUV. Juliet liked the vehicle's look; it was aggressive with wide tires and a low profile, but still had some cargo capacity in the back.

When he returned with an unlabeled spray bottle and gestured for her to stand back, she did, watching as he pumped a few squirts on the door. "You touch other doors?"

"Nope." Juliet wrinkled her nose at the chemical odor mixed with pungent lemon. Leo sprayed the inside, dousing the seats and the insides of the doors, then pushed the door closed with his foot.

"That'll do it."

"Thanks." Juliet followed him to his car and climbed into the passenger seat. She'd just closed the door when the rental vehicle hummed by, taking itself on a long, roundabout journey to the dump location, wherever that was. Leo got in and started the car, and Angel had to immediately dampen Juliet's audio input as some kind of screaming death metal erupted from the speaker system.

"Holy . . ." Juliet reflexively slapped her hands to her ears.

"Whoopsie!" Leo laughed, and suddenly, the music dropped to a background hum. He looked sideways at Juliet. "What? You don't like Kings of Titan?"

"Never heard of 'em." Juliet shook her head and *tsked*. "Not really my speed, though."

He smiled and nodded, driving out of the storage compound at a nice, sedate pace. Something about his expression—not quite his usual smugness but definitely a self-satisfied half smile—irritated Juliet. "What are you grinning about?"

"Am I?" He shook his head and rubbed his chin, refusing to look directly at her.

Juliet's voice rose with exasperation. "*What?*"

"Can I be honest with you?" He looked at her sideways again. "I mean, without you getting offended or something?"

Juliet sighed. "Go ahead. I'm sure I've heard worse."

"Well, when I found out who you were, I mean, after Frida's run-in with you on Callisto, I did a little looking into you. Before we ever met, when I heard Frida's report and saw a couple of drone images of you, I gotta admit, I thought you were pretty."

"Oh, brother." Juliet had a feeling where this was going. "Look, if we're going to work together—"

"That was before I met you, though. Since then, I can see I'm not your type, and well, I've been telling myself I need to forget your looks and think about your personality. It's clear we're having trouble gelling, right?"

Juliet squinted her eyes at him, trying to figure out if he was going to keep insulting her or compliment her or what. "Are you getting to a point?"

"See?" He laughed. "I was just grinning a minute ago when you didn't like my music. Just kinda reaffirms what I've already figured out—we're not meant to be."

"Because I was startled by sudden, blaring death metal from the dark moon of Saturn?" Juliet snorted.

"What? Are you fighting to be back in the running?"

"The running? Oh my God! Get over yourself." Juliet shook her head and laughed. She had to admit, his confidence was pretty funny.

"But seriously," he said, and she could tell he was fighting the urge to wink at her, "what's the deal with that friend of yours? I've been wanting to ask if she had someone in her life . . ."

"Honey? You stay away from her, Leo Applebaum," Juliet growled.

"What? Why? You guys aren't like—"

"No!" Reflexively, Juliet snapped out a fist and slugged him in the shoulder. He winced and laughed.

"You're pretty damn fast, aren't you? Were you wired up when you had your run-in with the boss?"

"You don't know the story?" Juliet turned toward him a little and leaned into the corner where her seat met the door.

"You kidding? He won't say a word about that shit. I've wanted to ask you about it all week, but it's kinda hard with the boss hanging around the, uh, dojo. You know?"

"It's . . ." Juliet sighed, suddenly not in a teasing mood. "It's not an easy thing to talk about. I was pretty raw, but I guess it's not as bad as it was. I've had to confront those feelings a few times since coming back and meeting Tanaka."

"Talk about raw. He's been a different person. We were all pretty confused. At first, I thought he wanted to kill you, but there's no way he'd send Frida out for that kind of job. God, Hawkins and I were freaked out when you shot her, you know that? Tanaka would've killed us . . ."

Juliet felt her cheeks flush with embarrassment. "I didn't want to do that. That's kind of what I meant by being raw."

"Yeah, she told us. As soon as she said his name, *blam!*" He chuckled, holding the wheel with one hand and leaning sideways against his door, mimicking her posture. "I can laugh about it now, but shit, that would've sucked." When Juliet closed her eyes and swallowed, several seconds going by without a response from her, he added, "Hey. I get it; we're good at antagonizing one another, but I'm not trying to upset you right now. Frida's okay, and that's what's important."

"She's kind of a sister to you, huh?"

"You could say that. I was young when Tanaka took me in, and so was she. I guess the age was just right for me not to be attracted to her; she was something like fourteen. So, yeah, I felt like a big brother."

Juliet nodded. She'd seen them together. They were definitely close but not romantic. "Anyway, about my run-in with your boss; he was beating the shit out of me, but I overcharged my cybernetic arm and got a lucky punch in with a vibroblade clenched in my fist. That's it. Just a single lucky shot, or he'd have tortured and killed me."

"Jesus." He looked at her, something like sympathy in his eyes. "You thought you killed him?"

"Yep."

"No wonder you kinda snapped when Frida told you he sent her. He should've prepared her better for that kind of possibility. He should've told us all. No way I'd have sent her alone to talk to you." Juliet gave him a double take—he sounded angry. He wasn't finished. "Yeah. That's on him. If you'd killed her, that would've been his fault." He got quiet after that. Juliet watched the moon slip past as they cruised on the interdome highway toward the main Luna City dome.

In an effort to change the topic, she asked, "What's the name of the club?"

"Grave Matters." When he said "Grave," it sent a shiver down Juliet's spine as a hundred memories danced through her mind—images of Houston laughing, Commander Garza bravely taking her side, White as he fired his Gauss rifle, Granado and the creepy Commander Gordon, Jensen and his freakish speed, all the weird, crazy things with the GIPEL subjects . . . "You good?"

Juliet's voice was quiet when she answered, "Oh, um, yeah. You just reminded me of something."

"Looks like I stirred up some ghosts."

"That's one way to put it." She nodded and tried to change the subject again. "Grave Matters? It's a bar or what?"

"Yeah. A 'social club' with a dance floor that only opens after ten." He made air quotes when he said social club. "I've been there a few times to meet clients here on Luna. Been trying to stay busy while the boss mopes around."

Juliet snickered softly. "Frida said as much. I thought the *boss* told you all to keep your plates clean, though."

"Yeah, well, we did for a while. Anyway, I don't take anything I can't put on a back burner." He was hardly driving—the car had auto nav. He seemed to give up the act and turned to regard her more fully, taking both hands off the wheel. "You should be glad about that, by the way, seeing as we're all about to get into this situation you've gotten yourself mixed up in."

"Mixed up? It's a job! I'm hiring you, not asking you to rescue me."

Leo nodded, assuming a speculative expression, and scratched at the stubble on his chin. "That right? What's the pay?"

"What's your standard weekend rate?"

"Depends on the risk level. What exactly do you want us to do? Who were those goons we just locked up? Who's the 'corpo-sec officer' you were watching?"

Juliet groaned and rubbed her temples. "You're exhausting. Is that how you treat all your clients? Get all the details first before quoting any sort of fee?"

"Depends on how badly I need the job." He snorted and smirked. "Depends on if I like the client."

"Whatever. Tell you what, I'll give you five percent of whatever I loot from the dirty cops and corpo execs, or 20k for the weekend. Your choice." Juliet had no idea if she'd make any bits during the job, but she figured there was a good chance. If she could get access to any bit vaults, she wasn't going to leave those funds lying around; she had no qualms about stealing ill-gotten gains, and, as far as she was concerned, anything she could get out of Life-Ultra was pure gravy.

"So 20k for a couple of days' work? Yeah, I'll get on that train." He grunted in irritation and gestured to the road ahead—traffic was grinding to a halt. "I'll message Frida. We're going to lose a half hour in this backup."

"What's the deal? Shouldn't be this much traffic on a Saturday."

"I'm seeing reports of a traffic accident near the Luna City exit," Angel spoke up.

At the same time, Applebaum answered, "Wreck ahead."

"Anyway, you sure you don't wanna think about it at all? The pay, I mean? Might be a bigger cut the other way . . ."

"But you're only offering five percent. You'd need to walk away with more than 400k for that to even out, and I doubt you'll squeeze some dirty corpo-sec boys for that kind of scratch."

"I'm going to be nice and not hold you to that. Not yet. I want you to hear the full briefing first, and then I'll make the same offer to the whole team."

"You're going to throw 100k our way? I hope your payday is looking sweet. You have a client, right?"

"Theoretically." Juliet chuckled at his mock-startled expression.

"Care to explain?"

"He's missing. Anyway, I'll spell things out when we're all sitting down together. Right now, just know I'm going to pay you for your time, so don't go getting all judgmental on me. This isn't a rescue!" Despite his earlier comments, Juliet was having fun bantering with Applebaum.

She grinned as she decided to push his buttons just a little more. "This has been good, Leo." He raised an eyebrow. "Driving with you, it's been revealing. I think it's sweet that you're trying to turn my rejection around, rewriting history to say you figured out you didn't think we were 'gelling' when, in reality, I figured out we weren't a match from the second I saw those totally fake blue eyes."

"They're not fake!" Apparently, he couldn't help himself, breaking into a laugh as he protested. "Okay, okay. They're a little lighter, a little bluer than I was born with, but c'mon, it's not like you're all natural!"

"You shouldn't have exposed your belly. I'm a predator, Leo, and now I know your weakness." Juliet smiled, closed her eyes, and leaned her seat back, fully reclining. "Wake me up when we're there."

31

\\\\\\\\\\\\\\\\\\\\\\\\

BRIEFING

Grave Matters reminded Juliet a lot of Thicker than Water back in Tucson. The exterior was very different, a sleek plasteel tower housing a hundred businesses. The interior, though, had the same kind of vibe—lots of purple and violet carpeting and upholstery, dim lighting with neon highlights near the bar and dance floor, and all sorts of patrons that might as well have been wearing name placards that said, "Operator."

When she and Leo arrived, only the bar and private rooms were open—the dance floor was roped off, and the only dancers were holographs of scantily clad men and women flickering in the occasional vape cloud expelled by the mingling patrons.

The chromed-out bouncer tried to disarm them, but relented when they both sent him a copy of their up-to-date operator IDs. Knowing that, Juliet figured half the patrons in the bar were operators or something similar because she saw a lot of guns and blades. Leo didn't pause to mingle or give Juliet much of a chance to people watch; he walked straight through the bar area, up a short flight of carpeted stairs, around a corner, and then to a heavy plasteel door with a biometric security panel instead of a handle. Juliet frowned and nudged his shoulder. "Frida told you what room?"

"Yep. Not you?"

"I guess she just assumed I'd follow you."

He shrugged, but his smug expression was back in full force when he pressed his thumb to the little panel, and the door slid open. "Yo!" he greeted when he saw the group of serious-looking individuals sitting around the table.

Juliet hadn't been nervous on the way to the club, hadn't even thought about what these guys would be like or how they'd respond to her, but when she saw the scowls and frowns, she suddenly felt the flutter of butterflies in her stomach. When she spied Frida's friendly face, she focused on her and tried to return her smile.

Applebaum immediately started chatting with the team member closest to the door, and Juliet moved around him, out of the doorway, to better look at the mercenaries. The room was well lit but had a definite club vibe with black upholstered chairs around a sleek faux-mahogany table. Vidscreens lined three walls displaying false "window" views showing Luna's nighttime downtown as though they were in a corner suite at the top of the tower rather than halfway up, buried in the depths.

She knew from Angel's snooping that the guy Leo was speaking to was Hawkins. He was a lean man, not very tall, but everything about him was sharp, from his buzz-cut hair to his eyes to his thin, frowning lips to the brace of knives over his chest. He wore a black, skin-tight, long-sleeved shirt, and Juliet could see his hands were both matte-black cybernetic prosthetics. He glanced at her while Leo spoke and narrowed those hawkish, bright, natural-looking eyes for half a second before looking away.

Juliet let her eyes drift to the woman across the table from Hawkins. It had to be Dora Lee, and she openly scowled when Juliet's eyes fell on her. Like Hawkins, she wore her black hair short—maybe a centimeter long all over her head, exposing the white scars of many injuries to her scalp. She was just as lean as Hawkins, though she looked like a bundle of wiry muscles. Her eyes were glossy black, with no irises, and when she put a toothpick between her lips, Juliet saw matching glossy black teeth.

Something about her short hair, wiry frame, and choice of dentition reminded Juliet of Ghoul. Despite herself, she quickly looked away, focusing on the other member new to her, Barns.

He was a big man, leaning back in his seat across from Frida, his arms folded over his black, well-worn tactical vest. He had a dozen tattoos on his exposed forearms, and Juliet spied the grips of two pistols worn in a harness meant for cross-body drawing. He was deeply tanned, and his hands and face made him look like someone who did construction work for a living—ruddy, weathered, and well calloused. His ocular implants were hardcore, military tech, nothing natural about them. They looked like metal balls with a dozen lenses and LEDs where a person's irises should be. If Dora had a few scars on her head, this guy had ten times as many, peppering nearly every inch of his exposed flesh.

Her quick perusal took all of two seconds, and then Frida said, "This is Lucky, everyone." None of them said anything, but Hawkins nodded at Juliet while Leo moved around him to sit beside Frida. Dora and Barns both looked at her, quietly waiting for her to speak, she supposed.

"Ahem," Juliet cleared her throat and nodded, stepping up behind the chair at the near end of the table. She figured they'd saved it for her, seeing as she was, technically, putting the operation together. Before she sat down, though, she stood behind the chair, hands on the top, and said, "I really appreciate you all dropping whatever you were doing and coming here today."

"Frida called," Barns rumbled as though that explained everything.

"Right." Juliet nodded and licked her lips. "Right. I know you're all on call for Tanaka, but you should know this isn't his job."

"The fuck?" Barns sighed and started pushing his chair out. "I got shit I can be doing today . . ."

Frida reached out and grabbed his wrist. "Pierce, chill. You need to hear this out."

"I'm not too interested, to be honest, Frida, and if Tanaka ain't calling this action, I don't need to be here."

"C'mon, you grumpy asshole." Leo laughed. "Sit down and listen; you're already here."

"Quit wasting time, Barns." Dora's voice was surprisingly smooth and musical with a faint Irish lilt.

Barns scowled and sat back down, then, perhaps to save some face, turned to Juliet and said, "Make it good, Legs."

Juliet couldn't stop the surprised lift of her eyebrow as she backed away from the chair and looked down at her legs, clad in their slim but not overly tight dark blue jeans. "Legs, huh?" She snorted. "Okay, Scarface. Sit still, and I'll try to make it good." Some laughter broke out around the table, and Juliet narrowed her eyes at Barns until he, too, started to chuckle. He folded his arms over his chest but seemed to be giving her his attention. "Thank you. As I said, this isn't a Tanaka job, but I'm willing to make things worth your while, and I don't think your boss will be upset if we handle this operation this weekend."

"Weekend? That quick?" Frida asked.

"Yeah, I have some intel to share, and I think, if we play our cards right, we can shut this business down pretty quickly."

"Business?" Hawkins prompted, his voice low and quiet.

Juliet glanced at him and nodded. "Yeah. Let me share some things." She switched to subvocalization. "Everything ready, Angel?"

"All set. Just jack into the table there." Angel highlighted the port for her, and Juliet pulled out her data cable and plugged it in. As soon as she did, Angel took control of the lighting and the vidscreens. She dimmed the overhead lights and blanked out the screens while Juliet set the stage.

"So, a while back, I stopped some bangers from robbing me and my friends in one of the industrial domes. I reported the guys to a corpo-sec officer I've been trying to sort of groom, I guess, as a contact. He's on the outs with the dirty cops in the Luna City Security Corp, so you can guess he doesn't have many friends." She smiled, and Leo and Barns chuckled. "He said he'd look into it for me, and he found out the gang running the robberies in that dome have a pretty wide-open fencing operation; he reasoned someone at LCS was protecting them. That's when he heard from a CI that there was a hit out on him."

"Everyone knows LCS is dirty. What are we gonna do about it, and how's this piggie gonna pay us?" Dora asked, her musical voice turning hard by the end of her question.

"I'm getting to it. Just setting the stage, all right? Another minute. So, Hines—that's the corpo-sec officer I was working with—calls me and tells me about the hit. Gives me a name to investigate, another corpo-sec grunt. That was the last I heard from him."

Dora brushed her hands together like she was wiping off some dirt. "So job's over then."

"Before I lost contact with him, I scoped out the target," Juliet said, locking eyes with Dora and trying to channel some Lacy Blake into her gaze. Something must have worked because the hard-looking woman turned away first. "While I was there, I found this." Juliet pointed to the vidscreen behind her, where Angel played the footage of her unlocking the secret room, fighting the synth, and searching the organ-harvesting room.

Everyone leaned forward watching, especially during the fight, and she heard Leo whispering to Hawkins, "She's goddamn fast, isn't she?" Angel cut out all of their conversations, so it was silent except for the sounds of the environment, but still, everyone was riveted, and she heard some cussing when her POV footage showed the organs in the pouches she cut open.

The playback ended, and Juliet turned back to the table. "So, the dirty LCS business goes much further than stolen industrial equipment."

Frida cleared her throat and leaned forward. "That's some bad stuff, Lucky, but Dora's comment earlier still stands. We know LCS is dirty. What do we do about it, and who's paying?"

"Getting to it, Frida." Juliet's nervous energy had faded, and she was feeling more in charge. She was almost grateful to Barns for his comment about her legs. It had stiffened her spine, and now she was showcasing what she'd found, and these guys had barely seen the surface. "So, of course, I was worried that synth got a call for help out before I put him down. I got out of there, and then, later, when I'd seen nobody had come to the apartment and the kid living there, Evan Lopez, was sound asleep in his dream-rig, I decided to go back and get into his head a little. Here's what happened."

Another vid began to play, this time showing Juliet's perspective as she crouched by the commuter car with the two assassins inside. When Dora Lee saw the silhouettes of the passengers, she muttered, "Nice tech." Then, she got quiet because Juliet sprang into action, smoothly gliding up to the door, pulling it open, and firing her needler into the two dirty operators.

"You're lucky it wasn't a couple more synths," Leo said.

Dora shook her head. "Nope, her scan would've picked that up. Those are some damn good optics."

Juliet folded her arms and nodded to the vid. "Listen." Angel had spliced the footage, making her interrogation of the two operators much quicker. As it played out, she heard muttered comments, and she turned to see that some of the team's faces were looking much more interested.

When the screen went blank, Barns said, "They found bit vaults on the dirty corpo they iced, huh? And you got a list of 'em from that locker?"

"Not yet, but that's on the agenda. I know what you're thinking. More offline bit-chips, yeah?" She smiled and nodded. "I'm sure there will be, but that's the tip of the iceberg. We need to get our hands on this Roland Devers, aka Walter Channing, who happens to be a lieutenant for LCS. That will crack everything wide open. He'll make the connections to Life-Ultra Pharmaceutical and the other operations going on, like the one that got me started on all this, the robberies in the industrial domes."

"So, we squeeze him?" Leo asked.

"You mean for his money?" Juliet lifted an eyebrow and shook her head. "I mean, sure, if we can liberate him of some dirty bits, I won't bat an eye, but I think the big payday will come when we snatch up the dirty actors from Life-Ultra. You know what kind of pockets a pharma corp that size has? When we expose the operation, their corporate office will dump a fat payday our way to get ahead of this story."

Juliet waved her hand and shook her head, a look of chagrin on her face. "Look, I know that's not solving anything long term. We're cutting off an infected finger, but the truth is that the patient's heart is corrupted. Still, we'll get Life-Ultra to flip on the criminals in their corporation here on Luna and the dirty LCS officers we've identified. They'll want to spin this as them cleaning house, excising a corrupt department."

Frida nodded. "And we'll get a payday while we're at it."

"Good enough for me," Leo said, chuckling.

"It's not great." Juliet sighed and shook her head. "You guys know how these things work, though. This corp has enough money to slow-walk this for years, decades maybe, if we try to take the whole company down. If we were Earthside, I'd say we could go to one of the independent territories to break the story and see if we couldn't get some competing corps to cannibalize Life-Ultra."

"They're all dirty, though." Dora sighed; she said it like a fact, which Juliet was sure they all agreed it was.

"Look," Leo spoke up, "we've all done work for corps we knew were dirty. How do we know? 'Cause, like Dora said, they're all fucking dirty. So? Forget the corp and focus on the assholes Lucky found out. Focus on the pharma creeps we can dig out of this dirty lieutenant's head. We'll take those wins, get some money, and maybe do something good with it."

His words took Juliet by surprise; the way he'd spoken in the car, he hadn't seemed too enthused about working without a guaranteed payday. Now, he sounded like he wanted to champion her cause.

He must have seen the puzzlement in her eyes when she looked at him because he grinned and winked, destroying any notion that he wasn't messing with her.

"I'm in," Frida said.

"What's the split?" Barns asked.

"There are six of us. We'll split anything we get six ways." That caught Leo by surprise; she'd only offered five percent when they spoke in the car. It was her turn to wink at him when his mouth fell open.

"You really think we can do all this before Monday?" Hawkins asked, his voice so low that Angel had to increase the gain on Juliet's implants to make it clear.

"Frida can grab the data from the locker in the airport. I'll send her Asia's biometrics. The rest of us snatch Channing, and then, once we get the info we need out of him, we'll put the squeeze on Life-Ultra. They'll want to put this to bed before Monday when our 'information time bomb' releases everything to all the public nets." Juliet made air quotes while she spoke, smiling at Dora while she said it.

"Because, like you said, they'll want to make a big PR splash. Cleaning up their company and all that BS." Frida nodded.

"You don't think we should get the boss in on this?" Dora asked softly, looking at Frida.

"I . . ." She sighed, shook her head, and shrugged. "I don't know."

"You guys want me to talk to him?" Juliet offered. "I don't want you to feel like you're going behind his back."

"Uh." Frida made a pained expression. "Better let me call him first. He's already pissed at you."

"What?" Juliet's eyebrows shot up in surprise. "Why?"

"He called a little while ago, wondering if I knew where you were. He said your sword hasn't moved since Friday morning. You're supposed to have it with you all the time . . ."

"What the hell?" Juliet switched to subvocalizations. "Angel, I thought you said that sword wasn't transmitting!"

"It's not! At least . . . not regularly. Perhaps he has it sending a tiny signal at irregular intervals. I'm sorry, Juliet. I should have warned you of that possibility."

"He's pissed?" Juliet asked aloud, eyes on Frida. "He expects me to drag a practice sword around on a live mission? You saw the shit I got into!" She jerked her thumb at the screen.

Barns snorted, choking back a laugh. "Seriously? That shit was real?" He was looking at Applebaum. "I thought you were jerking my chain about her doing sword lessons with the boss."

"Better be quiet, Pierce," Dora said in a too sweet singsong. "You saw what she did to that synth. Never saw you move that fast."

"Speed's overrated!" he growled. "I would've dumped a flash-bang into that room and popped that thing's dome before it knew I was there."

"You always go too loud." Leo laughed. Juliet sighed, looking around the table, noting that Hawkins didn't ever take part in the shit talking.

"Anyway." Juliet gently thumped the knuckles of her cybernetic fist against the table. She realized the meeting was almost over, and she'd never sat down. "Frida, will you call him for me? Tell him whatever you need to, and if he wants more information from me, he can reach out. I guess I should explain why I'm not lugging around that dull piece of metal."

Barns started to say something, but Juliet held up her hand. "Uh-uh, no, no, Pierce." Something about using his first name made her feel like she had some power over him. "No more shit talking about sword training, 'cause if you keep it up, I'll tell Tanaka you think monoblades are stupid."

"Yeah, I wouldn't test her, brother." Leo chuckled. "She'd do it, and Boss has been working out again. I think he'd like to cut something . . ."

"Has he?" Dora sounded hopeful.

"Yeah, he's back among the living." Leo nodded. "You can thank her." He nodded at Juliet.

Barns groaned. "For what? Almost killing the guy?"

"You don't know what you're talking about, chum. Trust me, all right?" Something in Leo's voice shut Barns down, and for the second time in that meeting, Juliet was feeling uncomfortably grateful to Leo Applebaum.

Frida broke the awkward silence by scooting back her chair and standing. "Send me those biometrics. I'll get the stuff out of that locker and message you guys."

Dora nodded, stood, and walked to the door. "I'll get eyes on Lieutenant Asshole."

Hawkins was already up, and he followed Dora. "I'm with you."

"Lucky," Leo said, coming around the table, "Barns and I will get geared up. You need anything?"

"Nah, my stuff's in my hangar. I'll take a cab."

"You got a bird?" Hawkins asked, halfway out the door. It was the first time he'd spoken at a normal volume.

Juliet looked at him and smiled. "Sure do. Got an interceptor, and I'm helping some friends rebuild a gunship. I own part of it."

"Shit. Nice, nice!" He looked her up and down, apparently reappraising her. He nodded and slipped out, following Dora Lee, who'd left without another word to anyone.

"C'mon, ladies"—Leo gestured for Frida to move ahead of him—"Pierce and I will escort you out of this den of villainy." He winked at Juliet, who rolled her eyes so hard it hurt.

Barns pushed his way around the table and gestured to the door. "Yeah. Let's go, Legs."

"Scarface," Juliet growled, "you and I are gonna need some time on the mats, I think."

"That a threat or a promise?"

"Oof." Leo chuckled. "You're gonna regret that, my man."

32

\\\\\\\\\\\\\\\\\\\\\\\\

FIRE WITH FIRE

Juliet was just finishing the rather arduous task of putting on her Flex-Plate body armor alone in her room on the gunship when Frida called. Selecting the call on her AUI, the redhead's face appeared in a small window. "Hey, Lucky."

Juliet smiled. "Update already?"

"Yeah, I'm in the parking structure at the port. I emptied the locker, brought it back here, and went through it. I just wanted to let you know I just had a long call with the boss." Juliet's expression must have betrayed some uncertainty because Frida waved a hand and said, "It's good news. He's excited and, in fact, pleased that you reached out to us for help. He wants to be a part of it."

"Yeah?" Juliet felt some tension leaving her shoulders—she'd harbored some dread that he'd call his team home and refuse to let them get involved in the whole mess.

"Yeah. So, in the locker . . ." When she trailed off, apparently trying to choose her words carefully, Juliet frowned, noting that Frida wasn't making eye contact.

"Spit it out, Frida."

"Right. There were a few offline bit-lockers. None were locked, which is weird, but maybe that's just the way these kinds of criminals operate. Maybe they didn't want to re-encode the chips after they cracked them with the dead guy's biometrics. Anyway, something like 80k bits are on 'em."

"Not exactly small change."

"Nope. I also found the list of dirty corpo-sec officers—eighteen of them, along with the names of some of the businesses they've been shaking down in their little, off-the-books protection racket."

"What about the other operations, like the chop shop in the industrial domes?"

Frida nodded. "Yep. Got a list of six similar operations in the city."

Juliet could see Frida was still avoiding eye contact, still mulling her words over longer than usual. "So? Why do I feel like you're trying to avoid saying something?"

Frida finally looked into the camera. "Well, I don't want to insult you, all right? Just keep an open mind, yeah?"

Juliet laughed and shook her head. "Relax, Frida. Out with it!"

"Well, the boss and I had some ideas to, um, improve on your plan. I mean, I guess plan is the right word, but it's pretty loose, wouldn't you say? Lots of room for things to go sideways . . ."

"Ah. Got it. My plan was too half assed." Juliet gave Frida a half grin, tilting her head. "I guess I should be thankful you waited until after the meeting to point out the flaws."

"This isn't about me trying to insult you! I'm trying to say we had some ideas and wanted to run them by you. It's not exactly your fault you don't know about our resources, nor is it your fault you don't have a couple of decades of experience working with creeps like this, right? Can I go ahead?"

Juliet nodded and leaned back, trying to let go of the bristling pride that, really, wasn't something she usually felt, especially when she knew damn well she was in over her head. "Yeah, I'm listening."

"First, we can utilize the team better than this. Hawkins and Lee are perfectly capable of nabbing that LCS lieutenant. That frees up the others, you included, for the first part of Tanaka's idea."

"His idea?"

"Well, you said so yourself—Luna City is dirty, just like every other city, but there's one city where Tanaka owns dirt on most of the bigwigs in the judicial system."

"New Atlas?"

"That's right. Look at it this way: Your plan's good as far as dealing with Life-Ultra goes. When we figure out who their employees are who are involved in the organ-harvesting business, they're going to put them in a deep hole and pay us nicely so they can smile for the public and say, 'Look at how good we are, cleaning up our own mess.' They won't do much about the LCS officers, though, will they? Maybe they'll try to force some prosecutions, but I promise you, it'll just be a few low-end street cops who take the fall; guys like Evan Lopez."

"Yeah. I mean, he deserves some jail time, Frida. He might have been pressured into this nastiness, but he still stood by while people were cut up for parts in his apartment. He still lured some of them there. I'm sure of it."

"Sure, but don't you want all of them to pay?"

"Like I said," Juliet sighed, smiling in resignation, "I'm listening."

Frida smiled, too; Juliet could see she was trying hard to be gentle with her feedback. "If we can show that these dirty LCS employees harmed any New Atlas citizen, directly or indirectly, Tanaka believes he can get warrants and bounties issued out of New Atlas for the whole racket."

"That . . ." Juliet's mind jumped around from organ harvesting to business shakedowns to supporting illegal operations like the one in the industrial dome. "That shouldn't be a problem." She grinned at the idea. "We really are going to make a fat payday, aren't we?"

"Depends on the evidence we can get out of the LCS lieutenant. What was his name? Walter Channing? Anyway, yeah, if we can tie him or any of the creeps on that list to things like murder or kidnapping, heck, even theft if the losses are high enough, the bounties will start to stack up."

Juliet couldn't help chuckling. "Kinda funny that we're kidnapping a guy to get evidence of his crimes so we can get a bounty issued on him."

"If we didn't know he was a scumbag, yeah, it would be dirty of us. Sometimes you have to fight fire with fire, Lucky."

"Damn. Just yesterday, weren't we fighting about how it wasn't just about money? Now you're schooling me on how to deal with bad guys and make a killing while we're at it. You're a smart chick, you know that, Frida?" Juliet loved how her compliment brought a rosy hue to Frida's cheeks.

"It's nothing. You'd have thought of all this if you knew about Tanaka's contacts on New Atlas."

"Well, I'm ready to do my part. What's first?"

"First, we give Lee and Hawkins the go-ahead to capture Channing. They'll bring him to the storage unit where you stowed your operator prisoners. Speaking of that, I don't suppose you've got a copy of that software you put into their PAIs, do you? It'd make things a lot easier."

Juliet rubbed her temple, suddenly feeling the exhaustion of too little sleep. After a few seconds, she nodded. "Um, I do, but it's got a built-in self-destruct, so it's a one-time use, all right? I can't risk certain old friends getting a hold of that code."

"Oh really? Well, maybe you can tell me that story someday. Anyway, that'll help a lot. While Hawkins and Lee are handling that situation, we might as well get you and Leo in position to infiltrate Life-Ultra."

"What? Why? Aren't we just bringing them the dirt we get from Channing?"

"We'll get dirt from him and maybe some evidence, but it'll sting a lot more if we can corroborate things inside the corporate office. I'm working on IDs for you two. He's going to be a visiting exec from their Earth-based HQ, and you'll be his security detail. Go ahead and get geared up to look the part." Juliet opened her mouth to ask where to meet Leo, but Frida anticipated a different question. She hurriedly added, "I would have made you the exec, but Leo's done this role a dozen times, and I have some IDs for him that are pretty close to perfect already."

"It's fine. I'm happy to play the muscle." Juliet looked at the time on her AUI. "We gonna do this tonight? Kinda weird for an exec to visit on a Saturday night, yeah?"

"Weird, but it'll throw them off their game. Their top security will be off duty. Don't worry; Leo will capitalize on the situation. Can you meet him downtown? He's at our HQ. Tanaka wants to talk to you, too."

"Yeah. Give me five minutes, then I'm en route."

"Great. Setting up op comms." Juliet saw an invite to join a group communication channel and accepted it. The whole thing reminded her of her time with Grave, but she forced her mind to stay in the present. Frida spoke again, but this time, her name in the channel lit up. "Comm check."

"Heard," Juliet replied.

Frida nodded. "Great."

Suddenly, Leo's name lit up. "Yo, yo. I'm at HQ. You coming, Lucky?"

"On my way."

"Roger."

Frida smiled on her vid call; this time, when she spoke, her name on the comm channel didn't flash. "He's so excited to be working again. You're good with everything?"

"Yeah, I'm good." Angel knew Juliet didn't want her voice to go through comms, so only Frida heard her. "Just keep me updated on everything, all right?"

"Of course I will." Frida nodded, her lips pressed in a firm line, her eyes serious. "Ending this call. I'll be in touch."

"Bye." Juliet watched the window wink out. "You still have eyes on her PAI, right?"

"Yes," Angel replied, though her tone was a little hesitant.

"So, you heard her conversation with Tanaka?"

"I did, but I knew she was going to call you, so I didn't think you'd want me to report my snooping. You told me only if something was really important . . ."

"No, that's fine. I was just wondering if it went the way she said. Was Tanaka really 'excited' about the idea?"

"He truly seemed to be. I think he views this as another way to 'help' you, and, as you know, that seems to be the purpose he's given his life at the moment. I believe our hope that he'll help organize action against WBD is beginning to look like a reality."

Juliet took a deep breath and blew it out, then she stood and started strapping on her weapons. She was going to carry her Texan, of course, a pair of vibroblades, and her needler. She also figured that since she was playing escort to a "corpo exec," she'd carry her Bosch & Royal automatic polyblast shotgun. She might as well look ready to take on a kill squad.

With that in mind, she also put on her combat helmet, leaving it the default baby blue so the combat scars clearly showed. Everything else looked sleek enough, she figured, for a little display of style in the color of her helmet. "Well, and my quick-draw getup."

"Hmm?" Angel asked, for once stumped by Juliet's mutterings.

"Just trying to convince myself I look professional enough with my helmet blue like this. I guess I can ask Leo what he thinks."

"I think you'll look like a hired merc who's seen plenty of action—probably something most execs would pay extra for."

Juliet lifted her visor and laughed. "I love how you always find a way to support me, Angel."

"What else would I do?"

"Well, for the record, I've got your back too."

Decked in weapons and armor, with her data deck tucked into a convenient pocket under the armor plate on her left thigh, Juliet walked out of the gunship. Bennet had been gone when she arrived to get geared up, and Aya hadn't been around either. She figured the salvage tech was still in the city, either with Doctor Ladia or getting dinner after her appointment. In a sudden bout of paranoia, she asked, "Can you get a hold of Aya? Make sure she's all right?"

Angel projected a thumbs-up on her AUI while Juliet locked up and got into the waiting cab.

"Excuse me, Operator XR713-004. Please provide a license for the firearms currently on your person." Juliet sighed, knowing full well that Angel would take care of it. Seconds later, the cab began moving, and the limited AI said, "Received, thank you."

"I miss my bike."

"It hasn't sent any reports of anyone tampering with it. I think you'll be in the clear to collect it on Monday."

"Good."

"By the way, Aya responded; she's still with Doctor Ladia."

"Huh. Not crazy, I guess. Maybe she's getting the hand replacement." Against all reason, the idea of removing a healthy limb to replace it with a cybernetic one still gave Juliet pause. Of course, she'd done so herself, but it had been a bit of an extreme case. Putting that aside, she'd recently had Angel replace her very healthy, perfectly good lungs, so she wasn't one to talk. Almost everyone had retinal implants, which couldn't be done without altering and sometimes removing healthy retinal cells. Plenty of other people, her included, had removed their eyes completely for full ocular implants.

Nevertheless, she hoped Aya didn't suffer any regrets. She hoped she'd drop the bits required to get a prosthetic she was happy with. "Can you message Ladia and remind her we offered to, uh, supplement Aya's funds if she's settling for anything less than optimal?"

"Done."

Juliet rode quietly for a while after that, her mind reviewing everything that had happened since she ran into the industrial dome burglars that night with Aya and Bennet. Of course, that got her thinking about Sergeant Hines, and she decided to try to reach out again. To her surprise, he took the call almost immediately. "Lucky?"

Juliet sat up straight, her drowsiness rapidly fading. "Yeah, it's me. Where the hell have you been? I thought they got you."

"No such luck!" He laughed. "I had to smash my PAI and was dead to the net while I picked up a new one. Only got the old address forwarding through an encryption service about an hour ago. Man, I'm glad to hear from you! You know how out of the loop I am? I'm deep in a hole, kid. What's the story? You get anything out of Lopez?"

"You could say that. You work with some dirty, dirty people, Hines."

"Boy, do I know it! They almost got me—if I hadn't had a security drone outside my motel, watching the stairs, I'd be hamburger. Some kind of assassin team slipped in and put a high-tech adhesive claymore on my door. Didn't knock or anything, just put the bomb on the doorjamb with a smart, optical trigger on the wall opposite the door. If I'd walked through, they would've had to identify me by my toe prints."

"Angel, send him pics of Asia and Comet," Juliet subvocalized, then aloud asked, "You received those images?"

"Yeah, just a sec." His eyes shifted to the side. "That's them!"

"Well, you don't have to worry about those particular killers. I've got 'em locked up." Juliet paused, wondering how much to tell him. Finally, she decided the less he knew that could mess up the operation, the better. "Listen: I've got an operation going to shut your dirty coworkers down. It's going to take a couple of days before you're in the clear, so sit tight."

"I can help, Lucky!"

Juliet shook her head. "Uh-uh. I've got names, I've got some evidence, but I'm gathering more. For now, I think it's best you keep your head down; we're going to need someone on the inside to finish cleaning things up after we get done taking out the bad guys."

"Taking 'em out? You're not . . ."

"Not like that. We're going to try to play this as legit as possible. I'm not gonna tell you anything, though, 'cause as much as I like you, Hines, I'm still afraid they might get their hands on you. Probably a good idea you don't tell me where you are, either." Juliet wasn't really worried she'd give Hines up, but she figured it would help soothe his pride if he was bothered that she wouldn't tell him what her plan was.

He frowned. Juliet noted the dark circles under his eyes, the several days' worth of extra stubble, and the generally dog-tired look of the guy. "I guess I get it. Keep me updated as much as you can, will you? I think I'm secure in my current spot. Couldn't believe those guys found me with my old PAI. I guess the department put trackers in it that I didn't know about."

Juliet snorted. "Doesn't surprise me. I think a lot of big corps do that."

"You really think I can poke my head out after a couple of days?"

"Yeah, I think so. We might not have everything cleaned up, but enough that you can bet the people after you will have bigger problems." Juliet smiled and added, "Keep your chin up, Hines. You'll be all right. I'm on this."

"All right. Goddamn, I'm glad I met you before all this shit hit the fan." He blew out a heavy breath and nodded. "Please keep me up to date. Hines out." He cut the call, and Juliet smiled. He might be an old corpo-sec officer, but it felt good to remember she was helping someone.

Images of the organ-harvesting room in Lopez's spare bedroom flashed through her mind, and she reminded herself that she was helping a lot more than just Hines.

Watching her mini map as the green dot of her cab rapidly approached her destination, she got ready, clipping her shotgun back to its harness. As soon as the vehicle pulled up to the elevator bank in the underground parking structure, she hopped out, scanning around like she'd just been dumped in a combat zone. Nothing moved; most of the businesses in the building above would be closed at that hour on a Saturday night. She stepped into the elevator and selected Tanaka's floor. "I'm in the elevator," she announced, trusting Angel to send it through comms.

Applebaum replied, "Great. I'm almost ready."

Frida chimed in, "I have your IDs almost done. Leo's a vice president of quality control, and he's here to perform a surprise inspection. Tanaka called in a couple of favors Earthside, and we've got a fake department listing at Life-Ultra's corporate HQ in Toronto. If the locals try to follow up on his credentials, the lines will ring through to me."

Juliet whistled. "Seriously? Pretty impressive, Frida."

"It's not me! Tanaka's got a fixer who owes him favors in about twenty-seven different cities." Something about the specific number made the boast all the more credible to Juliet.

"Well, whatever. It's pretty cool you guys got all this set up so fast."

Juliet watched the elevator floor numbers zoom by; when it stopped and the doors opened, she stepped out, scanning the dimly lit hallway. She walked down to Tanaka's offices and, she supposed, his home. When she stepped into the dark reception area, Leo came out of Tanaka's office at the same time. His eyes widened, and he turned and slammed the door. Juliet laughed, and Angel sent it through comms. A second later, he poked his head back through the door.

"Jesus Christ!" he cried, stepping out into the reception area. "Who ordered the shock trooper?"

33

TEAM TWO

Juliet shrugged. "Frida said I was muscle."

Leo sighed heavily. "I mean, most execs have their muscle dressed in bullet-resistant suits, not frontline dropship gear." He sighed and shrugged. "I guess it'll make a point, huh? We're supposed to throw 'em off their game. Don't worry, I can work with it." Juliet still had her visor up, so she was sure Leo could see the irritation on her face, but he sighed again and stepped out of the doorway leading to Tanaka's office, refusing to make eye contact with her. "Boss wants to talk to you."

She didn't reply; she just looked past him to the office beyond and strode through. When she heard him take a breath to say something more, she closed the door behind her, perhaps a little too forcefully.

Tanaka was sitting behind a modern-looking glass desk with heavy powder-black steel legs. He had it on the left side of the room so he could face the door on his right and look at the expansive view of the city on the left. Juliet took in the view, admiring the beauty of Luna's towers with their sleek lines and carefully placed exterior lights outlining corporate logos. Even more interesting were the tens of thousands of illuminated windows. She wondered how long she could lose herself zooming in on the tiny separate boxes of human activity, watching the occupants as they put their habits on display.

"Have a seat, Lucky." Tanaka pointed to one of the two black leather chairs before his desk. Juliet walked over, her armor, boots, and gear making her steps sound like stomps, and sat down. "I heard Leo. He likes to try to push your buttons. Don't worry, your equipment is suitable. I knew many corporate execs who had similarly equipped personal guards."

"Thank you!" Juliet didn't want to admit how much Leo's comment had gotten to her.

"Let's talk about why you don't have a sword on your waist."

"Are you serious? I almost thought Frida was messing with me when she said you were upset about that. You really want me carrying a dull blade around when I'm on the job?"

He didn't frown, exactly, but any hint of amusement evaporated from his sharp features. "Was I unclear? Everywhere you go, you must have that sword. It must become like an appendage. Part of your mind must always be aware of it. Moving with it should become the norm. The idea of catching it on a piece of furniture, another person, a doorway, your clothing—this should become an impossibility. The idea of you being caught without it while in the shower or bed or—"

Juliet groaned, and would have rubbed her temples if not for her helmet. "I'm not there yet, Rutger, so wouldn't it be a little risky to take it along on a real job?"

"I think not. You just don't want to trouble yourself with it, which I understand, but you know it's not likely to cause you harm." Before Juliet could respond, he held up one hand. "I have a compromise for you. Take a real blade. Not a monoblade, but something that, if the occasion called for it, could at least be used as a weapon."

Juliet didn't want to argue about the topic further, so she just nodded. "If that'll get you off my back."

He laughed, a short, barking sound, and stood up. "I must truly be a different man. If one of my old students said such a thing . . ."

"What?" Juliet also stood. "You'd beat 'em 'til they pissed blood?"

Tanaka didn't respond. He opened a dark wooden cabinet behind his desk, which drew Juliet's eyes to the built-in shelves beside it—they were covered with interesting wooden curios and artwork. She saw bowls, carved animals, pieces that looked like polished driftwood, and a dozen other little objects. While he moved things around in the cabinet, she said, "I like your, um, artwork."

"I made the bowls," was his only reply. Juliet raised an eyebrow, focusing on one of the objects in question, zooming in with her optics to see the lustrous, red-tinted wood, the delicate curve of the lip, and the painstaking little details, like a thin tracery of engraved angular patterns halfway up the side.

"How do you even do that? Make a bowl? Carve it out of a block of wood?"

"I had a lathe in my shop back on Titan."

"You had a shop? You carved bowls even before your, um, change?"

When Tanaka turned to her, he held a katana-style sword in one hand. It had a dark, navy-blue hilt, but the rest of it, scabbard and pommel and guard, were all black. She noticed a modern belt attachment on the scabbard and breathed a soft sigh of relief—she wouldn't have to wrap an obi around her armor.

"This will attach to your gun belt," he said, as though he'd read her mind. "As to your question, yes, even when I was a coldhearted mercenary, I sought a creative outlet that didn't involve torture or bloodshed."

"Are you . . . being droll?" Juliet laughed and took the sword as Tanaka held it out.

He raised one eyebrow. "Is that allowed?"

She pulled the scabbard away from the sword a few inches, examining the shiny metal blade. It looked sharp, and she knew it would be. Tanaka wouldn't let a sword go dull, even one he never used. The hilt was very comfortable, too. She wondered what it was made of. The blue fabric looked almost like silk, but it had a kind of friction to it that seemed to be holding her gloved hand as much as she was holding it. Her absolute ignorance when it came to swords other than the few she'd used suddenly struck her. "It's beautiful."

"It was one of my first truly good blades. I used it for a few years when I was younger than you."

"You have a way of doing that—talking like you're ancient. What are you? Forty?"

He nodded. "About that."

"Yeah, well, these days, that isn't old. Quit talking yourself into the retirement home, would you?" Juliet heard herself speak and recognized her words, but part of her was stunned by them. Why was she trying to be nice? Was she trying to make up for being a bitch when she'd first come in? For disrespecting him as a teacher?

In any case, he ignored the words. "Only as a last resort—you aren't good enough to rely on the sword."

Juliet chuckled softly as she connected the weapon to her belt. "Anything else, boss?"

"You're the boss on this job. I'm happy you thought to ask us for help. Frida told me you weren't trying to hide it from me, and I appreciate that. I think this is a worthy cause—a job I'm proud to take on. I know that sounds . . ." He scrunched up his face, trying to find the right word, but finally shrugged and said, "Trite. It sounds trite, but you don't know my mind. I've sat at this desk, looking out that window, thinking about the work we've done over the last few years, and honestly, very little gives me any sort of pride. Then you come along, and the first thing you want help with is cleaning up some corruption. It feels good. It makes me think I'm on the right path."

Again, Juliet found her mouth saying something nice before she could think about it. "I'm the last person to call anyone trite or sentimental, Tanaka. I've been accused of thinking with my heart too many times to remember."

He nodded, and his lips betrayed a small smile. "I'm beginning to see that."

Looking at his smile and then up to his chrome eyes, Juliet decided to continue letting her mouth have free rein, though a small part of her worried her words might backfire. "You know, those optics, the mirrored ones—people say folks who have 'em are trying to hide from the world. It's like wearing a mask or a helmet, and believe me, I know the empowering feeling the anonymity of a visored helmet can give. Still, I'd like to be able to look into your eyes . . ."

His expression had fallen flat, and Juliet felt her nerves give out, her mouth suddenly going dry like she'd way overstepped her bounds. She quickly stammered, "I, uh, don't know why I said that. Forget it, all right?"

He smiled quickly, a fuller smile than she could remember seeing from him, yet it felt totally forced. He nodded and waved a hand. "Forgotten. You and Leo should get going."

"Right." Juliet hurriedly turned and strode to the door. Before she stepped through, she looked over her shoulder. "Thanks, Tanaka. For the sword, I mean. I'll be careful with it." He aimed his chrome eyes her way and nodded, then looked down at his desk, tapping on some invisible AUI elements.

She stepped out to find Leo sitting at Frida's desk.

He hopped to his feet. "Ready? Our ride's waiting downstairs."

"Ready." Feeling the irony of the action, she slapped her visor down, presenting him with her mirrored countenance. She hefted her auto shotgun crossways and stood at attention near the door, waiting for him to step around and lead the way.

"Role-playing already, eh? I like it." As he passed by her, hardly sparing her a glance, Juliet got a good look at him and had to admit he cleaned up nicely. His dark gray suit was very high end, and she didn't doubt that it had bulletproof fabric in his vital areas. Angel flicked her optics through a quick scan then highlighted the silhouettes of two pistols under his jacket and a knife on his ankle. She was glad that, if things went badly, he'd be ready for action.

While they waited for the elevator, Angel said, "That was awkward with Tanaka, but I appreciate you trying to be pleasant."

"I can't believe I said that about his eyes. I feel like a total goon."

As usual, Angel was there to support her. "It was insightful, though. He chose that look for a reason, and your comment might invite further introspection."

"Oh well. At least he didn't get upset."

"No, I don't think so, but he was surprised and unsure how to respond. I'm fairly certain that's what his facial expression was saying." Angel almost sounded wistful, and Juliet had to bite her tongue physically to keep from teasing her again about Tanaka. Instead, she rode the elevator in silence and, when they reached the lobby, followed Leo to the waiting black luxury town car.

Once inside, after he'd touched the privacy button on the built-in jammer, he stretched out his legs and faced her in the spacious passenger compartment.

"You can drop the act for a while. We're going to cruise around 'til Frida gives us the go-ahead." He cleared his throat and said, a little more loudly, "Frida, what's the status on Team One?"

Frida answered immediately. "Team One has their package. Information should be forthcoming soon." Juliet looked up at their comm channel and saw it had been labeled as Team Two.

"Is there a Team Three?" she asked.

"Yes. Barns and Tanaka will be on standby in case things go sideways inside Life-Ultra."

"We've got the big dog backing us up," Leo said with a wink.

"You mean Tanaka, right?" Juliet touched her visor release and, when it retracted, smiled crookedly at Leo.

"You think I call Barns the big dog?" He scoffed, shaking his head.

"Well, he's bigger than you . . ."

"What?" He sounded scandalized. "In what way? I'm taller—"

"Oh my God." Juliet laughed. "Now I really know how to get you going."

"Bleh!" He blew out a loud breath, shaking his head. "I fell for that one, didn't I?" When Juliet just smiled, he kept talking. "Listen, I know we like to mess with each other, but when we get out of this car, we need to be all business, right? I need you to try to look as intimidating as possible. I know you said you've 'played muscle' before, but do you know what I mean?"

"I think I know exactly what you want." As her mind went to memories of her time as Lacy Blake, especially when the pirates first boarded her vessel, Juliet had another thought. "What's my cover ID, Frida?"

"Danika Cabot. Sending you the bullet points." As soon as the document came through, Angel displayed it. It looked like Danika had been born on Callisto; Juliet silently thanked Frida for picking a location she'd spent some time in. Danika was thirty, but Juliet figured she could pass for a young-looking thirty. She'd seen plenty of women nearing forty who still looked almost like teenagers.

She had a false SOA ID focused on private security with an overall B rating, meaning she'd had hundreds of positive reviews. The dossier was remarkably thorough, with prior employer numbers, a home address, and biometrics that, she assumed, matched her own.

"Did you help her with the biometrics?" she subvocalized.

"Yes. She sent a request for yours, and I gave her Lucky's. If she wanted to, she could have gotten them all from your frequent visits to the dojo, so I didn't think I was giving anything away . . ."

"No, it's fine. I was just wondering if she gathered them or if you gave them to her." Aloud, she asked, "Frida, how much of this ID is based on a real person?"

"Quite a bit. The former employee references and SOA ID are collated from a few other operatives. The rest is fiction. The contact information will all come through to my PAI. If anyone checks into you and Leo, I get to do some role-playing of my own tonight."

Juliet could hear the excitement in her voice. "You sound pleased."

"I am! This is way more fun than that VR studio nonsense Leo tried to get us all to do."

Leo looked wounded. "Hey, now . . ."

"Hang on!" Frida's voice cut him off. "Getting an update from Team One."

While Frida spoke to the other team, Juliet looked at Leo. "We should come up with more creative team names next time."

"Yeah?" He fidgeted with the built-in drink-and-snack cabinet, pulling out a disposable sonic flosser. As he leaned toward a mirror, baring his teeth, he asked, "What ya got in mind?"

"Uh, tonight, for instance, we could have Team Pretty Boy and Team Serious Business."

"You calling Dora a pretty boy?" He winked over the mirror, and Juliet had to laugh. "She's gonna kick your ass when I tell her you said that."

She groaned. "A, you know I was talking about you, and B, I think it's you who's going to get his ass kicked."

"Better watch out—you're starting to get a full plate. Didn't you already challenge Barns?"

Before Juliet could answer, Frida spoke through comms. "We've got two names. That's enough for you two to get started. We're looking for dirt on Sabrina Estes and Luverne Lampkins. They're both in the weight loss and antiaging division of Life-Ultra."

"Roger." Leo's eyes unfocused, and the town car picked up speed, moving with a definite sense of purpose. "En route."

As they progressed through downtown Luna, Juliet looked at Leo. "Weight loss? If those bastards were collecting organs for some kind of . . ." She couldn't even finish the thought, she felt so disgusted.

"Yeah. I mean, I don't even know what for. Drug-safety protocols? I know some pharmaceuticals have to be tested on human tissue before live trials, but why all those organs? Maybe it's not related to their work at all. Maybe these guys are just some scum who happen to work at Life-Ultra. We'll see what we can dig up."

He looked out the window behind Juliet, nodded, and made eye contact. "Get your game face on. We're almost there."

"Right." Juliet lowered her visor and, just as she'd done a half dozen times back in the Jovian System, she began to make herself into a stone-cold killer. Her shoulders straightened, her posture shifted into a more aggressive stance, and she tilted her head in a way that made it look like she was getting ready to pounce on whatever she stared at. In this case, that was Leo Applebaum, and she felt a little thrill, feeding on his uncertainty, as he licked his lips and swallowed nervously.

"Jesus, you weren't kidding. I can . . . I can feel it. Don't start shooting in there for no reason, all right?"

Juliet, deep in her role, didn't respond verbally, but she gave him an almost imperceptible nod. When the town car stopped and the door locks clicked open, she smoothly stepped out, standing in front of the opening, scanning the sidewalk and the transparent glass on the front of the building, gun held ready. When all she saw were a few nervous-looking pedestrians and a quiet, dimly lit lobby behind the glass doors, she moved to the side and allowed Leo to exit.

He nodded to her and walked up to the doors. They weren't locked—like most corporations, Life-Ultra had twenty-four-hour shifts. Nobody sat in the lobby, though, and only one person sat at the reception desk, though a security officer staffed a checkpoint in front of the elevator bank.

Leo marched up to the counter, a spring in his step, while Juliet followed with a far more deliberate stride, her head on a swivel scanning the area, her gun held ready. Angel rotated her ocular implants through different frequencies, highlighting things she found—cameras, security panels, scanners, a sidearm on the security officer, a larger gun beneath his station, and the cybernetic implants on his and the receptionist's body, none of which looked like much to worry about.

"Um, hello, sir. How can we help you, uh, folks today?" The receptionist was a young man with curly hair that started brown at the roots and ended with frosty tips. He was lithe and clean, but his suit looked like it probably cost at most a hundred bits—the jacket was too big, the seams bulky, and his tie too wide to be in fashion. He glanced at Leo then at Juliet, and he cringed back slightly, his hand hovering nervously near his data terminal as though he wasn't sure if he should do something or not.

"Very nice to put a face to your name, Tim." Leo nodded. "I'm running behind schedule; meant to be here at noon today, but you know how shuttle flights can be. Anyhow, we'll get the inspection going. Don't really need anyone to shadow us, so I don't see why the evening shift will be a problem."

Tim—Juliet noticed the name tag Leo must have clocked—looked around as though someone nearby could rescue him. When his eyes failed to settle on any help, he stammered, "Um, excuse me? In-in—um, inspection?"

34

PURGE PROTOCOLS

Tim did exactly what Frida had expected by contacting the main Life-Ultra offices on Earth. When he asked the limited AI to connect him to the "Quality Oversight Taskforce," it connected him directly to Frida, thanks to the false entry put in by Tanaka's netjacker contact in Toronto. Of course, Frida cleared them and assured Tim that Leo and Juliet were on the up-and-up.

The next thing Juliet knew, they both had temporary access cards and were stepping through the security checkpoint. The guard, startled by the sudden activity on a shift that was usually quiet, seemed nervous enough when he scanned Leo, but when Juliet stepped through his full-body scanner, he stood up and began to gesticulate wildly.

"We can't have you bring all that into the building. There's a locker in my station . . ."

Leo waved his hand dismissively. "My personal security detail is fully licensed and cleared by corporate for all that hardware." Juliet took the cue and stepped through, ignoring the man.

"But, um, I don't have you on any lists . . ."

Juliet turned toward him and gave him the full effect of her icy demeanor through her mirrored helmet visor. In a rasp that would've given even Ghoul goose bumps, she growled, "Talk to Timmy about it." Then, she turned and followed Leo onto the elevator. The guard stared at them until the doors closed; she could tell the wheels were spinning in his head. "He might be a problem," she subvocalized into their comms.

Leo surprised her by doing the same, his throat barely giving away the action. "I don't think so. He's overweight, sloppily dressed, and used to a long, quiet night shift. He won't want to stir up a hornet's nest." He tapped the elevator control panel, and with a stomach-dropping lurch, it began to descend. "Tim said the weight loss division has labs on sublevels twenty through thirty-two."

Juliet frowned despite the fact that no one could see her face. "Doesn't that sound weird to you?"

"What?"

"Thirteen basement levels for diet drugs?"

Frida's voice chimed in, reminding her that she and Leo weren't exactly alone. "Life-Ultra is a large company with many products in development. This is an R&D installation, so you can assume they have trials ongoing."

"How many employees are in this tower?" Leo asked.

"Seventeen thousand and change are listed in their public-facing corporate database."

"Seriously?" Juliet asked, surprised. "Just here on Luna?"

"Yes, and eighty-four percent live in the tower. That's why the lobby's so quiet at night; the workers just use the central, employee-only elevators."

Juliet started to feel a little nervous, and it took her a minute to realize why: The whole thing was giving her major Grave Industries vibes. "They must have a corpo-sec department. That guy in the lobby can't be it . . ."

Frida was quick to agree, heading off her further questions. "Oh, they do. They're mostly off duty right now, but they're all on call. It's probably wise to hurry as much as you can because if that officer in the lobby starts to get too nervous, he might call for backup, and that could lead to higher-ranking officers calling numbers that won't go through to me."

The elevator lurched to a stop, the doors slid open, and Juliet stepped through, scanning left to right, still acting the role of Leo's security. Sublevel twenty of the Life-Ultra building wouldn't have looked out of place in the Grave Tower. Polished concrete floors, white walls, and plain metal doors that read DIET, NUTRITION, AND LIFE EXTENSION CENTRAL OFFICE were the only things in the lobby, other than an overfull trashcan.

Leo marched up to the doors and slapped his temporary pass to the scanner on the access panel. They clicked open, allowing them through. The room beyond dispelled any illusions that Life-Ultra was wholly asleep.

A central reception counter sat at the center of a massive space with low ceilings, bright lighting, and hundreds of partitioned desks. More than the many cubicles and desks, the dozens upon dozens of bustling, harried-looking employees in business-casual attire gave the place the same kind of feeling as a busy train station. Leo marched up to the desk and was greeted by a synth with feminine prosthetics and beautiful curly auburn hair. She was focused on the empty air in front of her face and held up a single finger, saying, "A moment." Then she continued to stare at some invisible AUI, handling a task that was, apparently, quite urgent.

Juliet started to step forward menacingly, but Leo held out a hand, lightly touching the back of her glove where her fist still gripped the stock of her shotgun. "Patience," he mouthed, winking one of those bright, sky-blue eyes. Juliet nodded and stepped back; for a moment, she'd forgotten she wasn't inside a pirate base. After a moment, the receptionist blinked several times and focused on Leo. "Hello, Mr. Farmer. I understand you've come to inspect some databases."

"Databases? Well, I'll certainly take some copies, but I'm here to review some projects, with a few employees as the focus of my investigation. We've had some red flags set off back at corporate."

"Oh?" The synth did a remarkable job of looking both intrigued and scandalized.

"That's right. Can you direct me to the labs or offices of . . ." He frowned and pretended to examine something on his AUI. "Just a moment. Let's see here . . . Ah, there we are! Let's start with Sabrina Estes."

"Certainly. Dr. Estes is working tonight. I'll have her come up."

"No, no. I'll go to her. Do not alert her, Charlene." Juliet smiled inside her helmet. His PAI must have pinged her for an ID, and of course, she'd provided her name and employee information. "Not unless you want to end up on the chopping block, too."

"Oh my! Someone's on the chopping block?"

Leo winked, leaning forward on the counter. "You didn't hear it from me."

"I see that you have a temporary access card with C-level permissions. I'm afraid Dr. Estes has laboratories on sublevel thirty-one, which requires A-level permissions."

"No, no, Charlene. If my access is only C-level, then the young man in the lobby made a serious error. I have full access to everything in this facility directly from corporate."

She nodded, the articulated plasteel segments of her neck smoothly folding into each other. "I'll have to verify that."

Leo sighed and turned away from her, leaning his back on the counter and locking eyes with Juliet. "You have my department contact info. Make it

quick, please. I was supposed to be done with this inspection two hours ago."
After he spoke, his voice came through comms as he continued subvocalizing, "This might not work. Frida, is Lee geared up?"

"Geared up, netwalking, and already halfway through the ICE. Just stall that lady for a few minutes. Oops! I think she's calling."

Juliet shifted the shotgun in her arms, slowly turning in a circle, letting Angel get a good scan of the bustling room. She highlighted a lot of cameras and scanners but no weapons. A surprising number of the employees walking to and fro appeared to be synths—more than half. By the time she'd turned back to Leo, Frida was speaking into comms. "I don't think I passed her smell test."

The synth spoke almost simultaneously. "I'm sorry, Mr. Farmer, but your department manager failed to provide today's security phrase. She said she's contacting your head of network security for an updated phrase. You're welcome to wait here until she gets back to me."

Frida's name flashed on the comm HUD. "Hang tight, guys—Dora's almost through."

"If I'd known they were going to breach the corporate network, I might have offered some assistance," Angel said.

Juliet smiled, knowing full well that Angel would probably have been in by now if only she had access to the network. "Yeah, I know, Angel, but I think it's better if Dora can do it. I like these folks, and I'm starting to trust them, but I'd rather they didn't know everything we're capable of, you know?"

"Yes, I agree."

"I wonder how she connected to their network?" Juliet wanted to ask in comms, but also wanted to maintain voice discipline in case something important came through. "Also, wasn't she busy with Hawkins interrogating that corpo-sec lieutenant?"

"Impressive versatility and effective handoffs, wouldn't you say?" Angel sounded almost smug.

Juliet sighed. "I never said they wouldn't be good."

"Sir, there are chairs there by the door if you'd like to sit while you wait."

Leo smiled and shook his head, somehow leaning further onto the counter. "I'm fine. She'll get that passphrase soon, I'm sure. My department doesn't usually run into an issue like this."

"She's in," Frida announced. "Should have it soon."

"Quite a little flurry of activity in here. Are all your shifts so busy?" Leo gestured to the bustling workers behind the reception counter.

The receptionist took a few seconds to respond, her eyes clearly focused on an AUI element. "Oh yes—always results to tabulate and collate, trial participants to track down and debrief, suppliers to shuffle, accounts to reconcile; it's a never-ending data mill, I'm afraid."

Leo took a breath to follow up, but she spoke first. "Ah! I've just received confirmation from your office, Mr. Farmer. You're cleared to proceed down to Lab B31. A representative from Life-Ultra corpo-sec will meet you at the elevator on that level."

Leo frowned. "Is that necessary? I hate an entourage."

"I'm afraid so. We're unable to issue temporary passes for A-level access. The corpo-sec representative will escort you and help you to access what you need."

Leo nodded and turned on his heel, marching back toward the doors and the elevators beyond. Juliet followed, feeling decidedly nervous about descending even further into the depths beneath the tower. It felt awfully risky to her, being thirty stories underground, operating under false pretenses, on Life-Ultra soil without any sort of legal or corporate backing. If they were made to disappear, no one could do anything about it.

Still, Leo was moving ahead as though he didn't have a care in the world, and she was there to support him.

No, she corrected herself; he was there for her. They were all getting into this for her.

For the hundredth time that night, she hoped Leo could dig up the evidence they needed and that they could slip away before something went wrong.

As the elevator descended, Frida said, "Lucky, you have a data jack, right?"

"Yeah?"

"Their security is a bit stiffer than Dora expected. If the lab has a closed network, which she thinks it will, we're going to need you to jack into a terminal. Leo will try to create the opportunity for you."

"You want me to be a pass-through for Dora?" Juliet asked, wondering if that would expose Angel.

"Right," Frida replied.

As if she had read her mind, Angel said, "I can do that without allowing her to touch any of my data."

The elevator halted, the doors opened, and Leo stepped out, coming face-to-face with a corpo-sec officer in full tactical gear—a helmet, armored vest, and submachine gun on a sling. Angel highlighted his guns and cybernetic equipment—another pistol, a full-leg prosthetic, ocular implants, and something that glowed like a little reactor in his chest.

"He has a high-end medical nanite suite," Angel noted, trying to explain the unusual highlight.

"Noted." Juliet stood tall, her boots and helmet giving her about a couple centimeters on the stocky man, and faced him aggressively. She had no doubt that she could take him, even without her powered combat armor, and she let that confidence bleed out.

"Hello, Mr. Farmer. I'll accompany you and open doors." He looked at Juliet then away quickly, his natural-looking brown eyes beneath his helmet's brim looking quite nervous.

"Proceed, Officer Rivera." Leo gestured impatiently. "You know the way better than I."

"Right, um, this way." He started down the short concrete hallway to a closed door labeled LABORATORY B31. Beneath that, in smaller letters, it read, Authorized Personnel Only. Their escort approached the panel and leaned forward, allowing it to scan his retina. A moment later, a green light appeared, and the door clicked open.

When Juliet passed through behind the two men, she found herself in a very long corridor lined with reinforced glass windows that provided a view of dozens of individual labs, many of which were occupied by scientists. Some wore white lab coats, and some wore full-on, biohazard clean suits.

Rivera walked with purpose, apparently knowing where to find Sabrina Estes. They turned down two hallways that looked identical to the first, and Juliet lost count of the number of labs and workers they passed. Halfway down that third corridor, the corpo-sec officer stopped and pointed to the window on his left, where Juliet saw three individuals wearing lab coats sitting around a big black table strewn with test tubes, biohazard pouches, and data terminals. They were in the middle of a heated conversation. One woman—blonde with a surgically implanted high-end optical visor—gesticulated wildly, her face red with either passion or anger.

"That's Dr. Estes," their escort said. When Leo nodded, the officer stepped up to the door and pressed a key card to it, then leaned forward for an optical scan. When the door beeped and opened, the three scientists within became very still. You could have heard a pin drop when Leo stepped into the lab.

"Hello there, doctors!" Leo walked toward the table while all three scientists stood up and backed away. The woman with the visor scowled and folded her arms over her chest.

"What's this about?"

"Dr. Estes! I'm delighted to finally put a face to the name. I've been read-ing about you all day as I made the transit from Toronto. I'm Elliot Farmer, executive vice president of Life-Ultra's new Quality Oversight Taskforce, and I'm here to take a close look at your operation."

He turned to the corpo-sec officer who'd followed them into the room. "You can wait outside, officer. I'm not sure Dr. Estes wants such an audience during our interview." He gestured to Juliet. "I'm certain I'll be safe." Again, he winked, flawlessly pulling off the demeanor of a man who felt very sure he was beyond criticism.

Rivera nodded. "I'll be just outside."

"What about your colleagues here, doctor? Should they be present for this interview?" Leo jerked his thumb at the two scientists who were, some-how, continuing to shrink away from Estes.

Estes continued to scowl over her visor, her thin lips twisting into some-thing of a snarl as she waved her two colleagues off with a flick of her fingers. "Take your work and go to module fourteen. I'll take care of this glorified bean counter." The two quickly gathered up a pair of data decks and hurried past Juliet, cringing away from her as they went by. When it was just the three of them in the room, Leo stepped up to the table and sat on one of the stools across from Estes.

"Won't you take a seat? I've so many questions for you."

She groaned. "What's this about? Farmer, was it?"

"That's right. Farmer. You can call me Elliot, though. I'm not big on for-mality. Listen, I'm not here to make your day difficult, and if you can explain a few things for me, I'm sure I'll be out of your hair in no time."

While he spoke, Juliet moved further into the room, slowly edging toward the far end of the table so she could see the door and Leo at the same time. It didn't hurt that a data deck with a network cable plugged into it sat on that end of the table. If she could just insert her data cable while Estes was busy with Leo, she might make this whole thing much faster.

"Angel, if I plug you in, are you ready to dig around a little?"

"Always."

"What's your goon doing?" Estes jerked her thumb at Juliet.

"That 'goon' is very well paid to keep me safe, Doctor. I'm sure she's mov-ing into a position that will better facilitate that." Leo leaned onto the table, resting his chin in his palm as he propped it up with his elbow. "Won't you sit down?" He had a tone and way of looking at a person that, Juliet had to admit, was very charming. Estes sighed and sat down.

"Well? What's this about?"

"We're responding to an internal whistleblower report. Well, it started out that way, but after we did a little verifying, we're finding some numbers that don't add up in your department. I was hoping you could explain it all away, and I could spend a few days enjoying the sights here on Luna. What do you say?"

"Whistleblower?" Estes narrowed her eyes. "About?" While they were speaking, Juliet had surreptitiously slipped her data cable out, and at that moment, while Estes looked surprised and worried, she deftly slipped it into one of the ports on the data deck. It wasn't surprising that Estes didn't notice her; the table was very cluttered, and she wasn't even sure the doctor could see the deck.

Angel immediately spoke up. "I've notified Dora that you're connected. I'll use her breach to speed things up."

To Juliet's shock and a surprised exhalation from Dr. Estes, Leo said, "Well, we're receiving some very disturbing reports about some organ harvesting. Can you clear that up for me?"

"What? That operation is one hundred percent sanctioned by corporate! I'm totally covered, Farmer! I've got hard copies of the directives to prove it! Are they trying to pin this mess on me? I knew this was going to happen!"

"Whoa! Slow down, Doc." Leo chuckled, tamping his hands down in the air. "Our department operates independently in the corporation. How else would we ever get anything done? Tell me what's going on, and I'll take this back up the ladder."

"It's not 'organ harvesting'!" Estes made air quotes as she practically yelled. "We're recovering faulty specimens from the Genesis Program debacle!"

The way she spat the words *Genesis Program* made it very clear she expected Leo to know what it was. Angel picked up on that and said, "I'm in their system and searching for the project she mentioned."

Leo cleared his throat, perhaps trying to buy a moment to think. "Tell me more."

"They were going haywire! We co-opted some LCS officers the company had on payroll, had them pick up the subjects, and then broke them down, removing any trace! Do you think we shouldn't have brought back the organs, especially the brains? How else are we going to figure out what the hell is going wrong with that damn project? God! The mess Travis left us with! We still have more than seventy project subjects out there, walking the streets, traveling the system! One of those things killed his 'wife' and kids! What would you do?" Again, she made air quotes, and Juliet's mind began to run down weird paths, trying to figure out why she'd do that for a word like *wife*.

"Mm-hmm." Leo nodded, rubbing his chin. "Mm-hmm. This is making a lot more sense. The dots are connecting."

Estes seemed to be relaxing, but she suddenly glanced Juliet's way and then back to Leo, and Juliet swore she could read her mind without even trying; she was suspicious and about to panic. Juliet stared at her, slowly breathing in, relaxing, and willing the doctor's thoughts to come her way. Almost effortlessly, she heard her voice in her head:

This is off. Something's off. They're here for me. I'm not going down alone. Rosie, implement purge protocols!

Juliet frowned, puzzling over the thought. Was Rosie her PAI? An assistant? Purge protocols? As she grappled with the implications of what she'd heard, Frida said into comms, "Dora says Life-Ultra corpo-sec just issued an all-hands terrorist threat response to sublevel B31. Get out of there!"

Faster than Leo could blink and straighten up, Juliet yanked her needler out and silently put two botu-rounds in the doctor. As the door hissed open, she jammed the needler back in its holster and sidestepped as she brought her auto shotgun to bear on the doorway. She saw the corpo-sec officer's SMG poke through the opening. She didn't need the arrow Angel drew on her AUI to tell her he was pointing the gun at Leo. She didn't hesitate, pressing the trigger and basking in the roar as, in less than a second, half a dozen polyblast shells ripped the plasteel doorframe to shreds and did something similar to Officer Rivera. He didn't even get a chance to scream.

Leo scurried around the table and snatched Estes off the stool where she'd slumped onto the table. He threw her over his shoulder and glanced at Juliet. "She's not dead, right?"

"Nope."

"We need to get her out of here. Hopefully, Dora pulls enough evidence, but shit, Lucky, we're boned. This wasn't one bad employee. This is something messed up involving the whole corp! Goddamn it! They're going to be swarming this floor!"

Just then, Angel upped the gain on her auditory implants, and Juliet realized that a sound she'd taken as background noise or a strange machine malfunctioning in the distance was, instead, the sound of people screaming.

"Juliet," Angel said, "I'm in their network. I'm looking at the camera feeds. The synths working down here appear to have gone mad. They're killing everyone."

35

JINH

Juliet led the way out of the lab, barely sparing a glance for the corpo-sec officer she'd shot, but still feeling a wave of relief when she saw her shotgun rounds had taken off his arm and hit his torso; Angel had said he had good nanites, so she hoped his brain would survive until he got treatment.

The sentimental thoughts were distracting, and Juliet quashed them, growling as she stomped forward aggressively, gun held ready. When she saw her ammo readout reporting 18/24, she subvocalized, "Switch to semiautomatic, Angel."

"Done."

The hallway lights had shifted to a soft red, and a constant alarm had begun to sound, but Angel filtered it and enhanced her visual spectrum so the lighting change barely affected her. Still, Juliet slowed and constantly scanned left to right as they advanced. "Were these labs empty when we came in?" They were still in the corridor that led to the room where they'd found Estes, and Juliet couldn't remember if she'd seen people in the neighboring labs.

Angel immediately responded, "They were empty, but when you turn the corner, you'll find three synths standing over the corpses of seven technicians or scientists. Two will be in the lab on the left and one on the right. They are standing still, staring into space. I'm unsure if they've shut down or are waiting for some other stimuli."

"What the hell is going on in here, Frida?" Leo growled, apparently not content to silently follow Juliet's lead.

"I think that doctor you were talking to triggered something. A fail-safe or some other—"

"Purge protocol," Juliet supplied.

"Huh?" Leo tugged on her shoulder. "Hold up, we need a plan."

Juliet sighed and squatted low, training her barrel on the upcoming corner. She had to explain how she knew what Estes did, and as usual, Angel fit the bill. "My PAI is in the network. I had her piggyback with Dora. She saw what Estes did; she sent a signal called a 'purge protocol,' and you can kind of guess what that means."

"Is that why the corpo-sec's responding to a 'terrorist' threat?" Leo asked.

Frida's name lit up as her voice came through comms. "I don't know. It seemed too fast, but maybe one of the other scientists hit an alarm. They tried to shut down outgoing comms, by the way, but Dora is in too deep; she overrode the command."

"What about us?" Juliet growled, still hearing distant sounds of struggle. "How the hell do we get out of here?"

"Team Three will make a diversion and try to draw away some of the corporate commandos. You two are going to have to fight to the elevator and up to the garage. We have transport there."

"The elevator's gonna work?" Leo asked, crouching behind Juliet, the paralyzed doctor still on his shoulder.

"Dora's working on it."

"Just so you know," Angel spoke softly, "I have access to the elevator already."

Juliet frowned, realizing something. "How, Angel? How are you still in the cameras? I pulled my data cable a while ago, and this network was closed off."

"Once I was in, I opened it up—turned on some wireless access ports."

"Smart." Juliet stood up and glanced at Leo. He had a pistol in his right hand. "Ready?"

"I guess."

"Wait!" Angel exclaimed suddenly as Juliet was about to start clearing the corner.

Juliet held up her fist, signaling for Leo to stop. "What?"

"A corpo-sec response unit is in the elevator. They're making stops, dropping teams off . . . Oh, God, Juliet. This isn't happening only on this floor. The synths are slaughtering personnel on all the sublevels! The receptionist on twenty just attacked the corpo-sec unit as they opened the elevator. There are at least a hundred other synths on that level, and they've killed all the humans!"

"How?" Juliet backed up, looking at Leo. "How are they getting synths to go murderous? That's supposed to be impossible!"

"You should know better. You've seen what the pirates did by modifying factory settings," Angel replied.

"Yeah, but these synths are . . . *people!* They work here and have homes they go to!"

"What the fuck is going on?" Leo hissed, picking up on the fact that Juliet was having a conversation with someone.

"My PAI's in the network. She's monitoring the cam feeds. The synths all the way up to the, uh, business office we stopped at are going berserk, killing everyone. I'm not sure the corpo-sec teams are going to have the bandwidth to mess with us."

"Ain't that just pretty." Leo sighed and shifted his burden, eliciting a small grunt from her. "Is she starting to wake up? Be glad if I didn't have to carry her all the way up."

"It'll be a few minutes before she can walk, probably more like half an hour. I hit her with two needles."

"Great. So, we gotta get past murderous synths and the corpo-sec squads fighting 'em, all of whom want to see us in the dirt." He relaxed his hold on Estes, letting her balance on his shoulder while he pulled the slide back on his gun, looking into the chamber. When he let it *snick* shut, he shrugged. "Let's get out of here."

"All right. On me." Juliet started for the corner, subvocalizing, "Angel, use the cameras, use my terahertz imaging, use whatever you need, but highlight my targets before they see me, please. I need to be fast and accurate."

"On it. I won't let you down."

Juliet rounded the corner, shotgun snug against her shoulder. To the left and right were three humanoid silhouettes outlined in dayglow orange. She didn't hesitate, using every ounce of her boosted reflexes to pump three rounds to the left and two to the right—one to break the glass, and one to utterly shred the skulls of the three synths lurking in the labs, standing over the corpses of the scientists they'd just been working with.

The reinforced glass didn't shatter, but the first shot to either side deformed and perforated it enough so that her follow-up shots were right on target. The polyblast shotgun was more powerful but had less recoil than other shotguns she'd used, and she hardly felt the need to pause as she kept steadily moving forward, alert for Angel's next highlighted targets.

Leo might have said something, might have quipped about her quick, decisive actions, but she was too focused to listen to him. Dimly, she was aware of the blood everywhere, of the ragged bodies of the scientists, some of which had been killed through the brutal removal of limbs and exsanguination.

The gun, while powerful, wasn't quiet, and Angel drew an overlay on her AUI showing the movements of synths in further corridors making their way toward her. They converged past the next junction, where Juliet could see at least five outlines clustered together. They'd be coming around the corner in seconds. She squatted, dropped to one knee, and lifted the gun, waiting.

She didn't have to use sights—Angel's connection to the smart weapon allowed her to make a crosshair that compensated for distance and other environmental factors, not that wind was an issue in the underground facility. Still, she stared downrange, holding the red dot at the end of her barrel at roughly a person's head level.

When the synths burst around the corner, Angel ramped up her synapses again, and it was almost like shooting stationary targets as Juliet smoothly squeezed the trigger. She nudged the crosshairs from one synth's head to the next, and in maybe two heartbeats, she'd pumped six rounds down the hallway. As her speed boost smoothed out, the corpses hit the floor and slid on bloody smears for several feet.

Juliet's ammo counter said 7/24. While she contemplated swapping in her fresh mag, Leo said, "Jesus. You're boosted to fuck, aren't you?"

"You didn't know that yet?" Juliet couldn't help some Lacy Blake entering her tone as she stood and started marching over the field of dead, very humanlike synths. Half of them were fully clad in synth-flesh, and the red blood, mingled with the white stuff their synthetic parts lived on, made a gross, foamy slurry. The truth was, if she didn't channel Lacy, Juliet felt like she might look for a corner somewhere to freak out.

Leo never responded, but she could feel him following her. Angel filled the void as Juliet rounded the corner. "The synths are communicating, Juliet; they aren't mindlessly rampaging. There are nineteen more on this level, and they're converging on the elevators."

"Melt it!" Juliet paused and looked back at Leo. "Don't have a grenade or a bomb stashed in that pretty suit, do you?"

"Afraid not. Why?"

"Got a crowd waiting for us at the elevators." Juliet pulled her mag and swapped it for her spare. "Twenty synths. At least none of 'em seem wired for combat."

"Oh God! Why'd you have to say that?" Leo groaned and spoke into comms, "Frida, what's the situation on the elevator? On the corpo-sec? On our GD exfil?"

"I told you, hon, you need to get up to the garage—sublevel five. The elevator's still running, but Life-Ultra corpo-sec's getting desperate on several upper levels. They might cut it."

"Do we take it or go for the stairs?" He spoke aloud, and Juliet knew he was talking to her.

"You wanna try to fight our way up thirty or so flights?"

"Might be better than taking a ride down to hell in an exploding shoebox."

"My PAI's in the network. She'll warn us if the elevator's compromised. Let's clear this lobby."

Juliet squared her shoulders and started forward again. She had two more turns to make before she was face to face with the doors to the elevator lobby, and Angel was already starting to highlight humanoid outlines through the walls. In her comms, she said, "I'll start shooting left to right. You start on the right. Hopefully, none of 'em are wired up."

"Copy." Leo shifted to the right, still behind her but now with a clear shot. They rounded the penultimate corner, and she informed, "They're crowded behind the doorway; it's propped open. Next corner." He didn't respond, so Juliet kept walking. Two steps from the corner, she lifted the gun to her shoulder. When Leo didn't object or ask for more time to get ready, she stepped around it, leading with her weapon, trusting that Angel was right about the synths' positioning and that she wasn't walking into their arms. They were a good ten meters away.

Even before her body cleared the corner, she was squeezing the trigger. As her visor edged past the wall, she felt the familiar adrenaline rush of her speed boost, and the scene at the end of the hall came into crystal focus. Just as Angel had told her, nearly twenty people—synths, she reminded herself—were crowded by the doors to the lobby. Many held cutting utensils, from old-school metal scalpels to tiny vibroblades to actual laser scalpels. Others held furniture legs like clubs, and one that Angel rapidly highlighted with red flashing lights gripped a semiautomatic handgun.

Juliet's first blind shot had taken one of the synths in the neck, sending her sprawling back into her comrades in a spray of red-and-white fluids. As the world slowed down and Juliet's icy focus zeroed in on the various threats ahead of her, she smoothly shifted her gun to the synth with the handgun and pressed the trigger. The gun bucked, and she aimed back to the left, picking up where she left off, snapping off shots one after another.

She was on her tenth shot when she heard Leo's pistol start to bark. The synths weren't panicking, and despite being slower than her, some of them had high-end cybernetics and were beginning to move, spreading out, charging forward, and taking cover to the sides of the doorway.

Juliet began to have to shoot moving targets, unable to easily track through the cloud of red-and-white mist and smoke filling the corridor. The polyblast shells didn't just put holes in things: they ripped great gouges through hard plasteel bones, blasted gouts of fluid out of golf ball–size holes, and turned prosthetic-grade plastics into shredded confetti.

The movement, the debris, and the chaos meant Juliet wasn't hitting a hundred percent on target. With that said, when her magazine ran dry, only eleven synth corpses were on the floor. She and Leo ducked back around the corner, and while she ejected her magazine and slammed her partially empty one back in, she growled, "Come on, Leo! Are you gonna hit any?"

"Screw you! I dumped my mag, and I don't think I missed once!" He stuffed his pistol into its holster and drew his second gun.

"No backup mags?"

He groaned, breathing heavily. "I thought two guns was overkill, if I'm honest."

Angel interrupted, "Juliet! They're charging!"

"Fall back to the corner!" Juliet yelled, shoving him. He staggered away, Estes limply flopping against his back as she lifted the gun and slowly backpedaled until the first synth came around the corner. She blew the top third of its head off. The next three came around at the same time, and she rapidly pulled the trigger, blasting wide holes in torsos, arms, and legs until they'd all fallen.

When two more came around, she killed one, and then her ammo counter flashed in bright red: 0/24. Juliet growled and yanked her needler out of its holster, thumbing the mag eject. She jammed her spare mag full of shredders into the grip and rapidly pressed the trigger, trying to hit something vital as three more synths joined the one still charging her.

There was something undeniably dissatisfying going from shooting a polyblast shotgun to a low-caliber needler, even with shredder rounds in the mag. The needles did their job, punching holes in whatever they hit, but they were so thin and small that the synths seemed able to shrug off all but a direct hit to the brain—something Juliet found challenging to pull off with four of them charging her at once, despite her boosted reflexes and synapses.

Still, she managed to get enough hits to the first one's face that it collapsed, tripping up one of the others. Then, two of them were on her, and she was grappling, punching, and kicking.

She felt repeated pressure against her ribs and realized one of them was stabbing something against her FlexPlate armor—that's when she lost herself in the frenzy of combat, utilizing the enhanced strength afforded to her by the armor and her cybernetic arm.

She snatched the wrist of the stabber, twisted it, and smashed her into the other synth, who was madly trying to grab her around the throat despite her armored collar and the narrow gap provided by her helmet. As they crashed into the wall, Juliet stepped forward, using her height, strength, and weight to deliver a devastating headbutt with her armored helmet to the female synth's temple, caving in whatever material made up her skull.

As she crumpled, Juliet stiff-armed the male with her left hand, pinning him to the wall, and then punched her armored fist into his head once, twice, three times, until red-and-white fluid began to sluice and spray out of his earhole. She dropped him and turned in time to see Leo fire two rounds into the last moving attacker. He saw her looking and winked. "Saved you."

"You son of a—"

"Juliet!" Angel cried. "I found information about the Genesis Program. I'll explain later, but if you can get out of here, we can probably ruin Life-Ultra. By the way, great fight. You have seven needler rounds remaining, seven bullets in your Texan, and the twenty-one extras in your belt. Oh, and Leo has sixteen nine-millimeter rounds."

"Frida," Juliet spoke, "I've got the data on the Genesis Program. Sending it to you in . . . in case."

"Ah, shit. Am I really going down like this?" Leo groaned.

"Come on." Juliet stomped around the corner and into the charnel scene of dead synths, picking her way through the corpses toward the elevators. She pressed the call button and stared at the display. It indicated the elevator was parked on level B13.

Angel said, "I'm overriding the elevator controls. Life-Ultra corpo-sec was holding it in place while they make a push against a large group of synths." As the display showed the elevator moving, Juliet wondered if she'd just condemned those corpos by taking away their exit plan. She looked at Leo and saw him walking among the corpses, nudging the few synths still alive but too injured to function with his shoe.

"What are you doing?"

"Making sure none of these are about to jump up and stab us."

"By kicking them?"

"I'm not kicking them! I'm seeing if they'll, I don't know, react." He blew out a deep breath and rubbed his hand through his hair. "Jesus, this is so messed up. What the hell are these people up to? Did you see all the dead scientists we walked past?"

Juliet nodded to the woman on Leo's shoulder. "She did that. She's a psychopath if I ever saw one. Don't let her fool you—wish we had some shrink cords."

"You think she was acting alone? I mean, with the purge thing?"

"I don't know, but the order came from her. Wonder what these guys were going to do next." She nodded her head at the dead synths. "Start a fire? Blow the place up? Eh, maybe just erase all the drives."

"Some synths on other floors are doing exactly that, Juliet," Angel informed. "They're wiping department networks. Don't worry; I got everything we'll need to incriminate Life-Ultra." When the elevator dinged, Juliet turned, startled, and yanked her Texan out of her holster, aiming it at the elevator. The doors opened, and it was empty. Juliet wasn't surprised; Angel would have warned them if it was occupied. Still, the interior was a creepy sight, something out of a horror movie—bullet holes and blood spatters were everywhere.

"Man, look at that!" Leo whistled. "Looks like it got hot in there."

"It's hot all up and down these subfloors, Leo." Juliet jerked her head at the open doors. "Come on, we need to get out."

He nodded and carried his burden into the elevator while Juliet followed. As she closed the doors, Angel spoke.

"Juliet, I should let you know—I've lost cameras on several of these sublevels. I can't monitor everything the synths and corpo-sec are doing." Juliet sighed and shrugged. What could they do about it? Hearing no argument, Angel started the elevator moving.

As soon as they began to surge upward, Leo took a deep, slow breath and blew it out his nose. "Are we really gonna get out of here that easily?" Juliet glared at him, wanting to chide him for the jinx, but she'd done it earlier, so she held her tongue. Out of habit, she twirled her pistol and slid it into her holster. Leo chuckled and asked, "Why didn't you use that cannon instead of that little needler?"

"I don't know. Saving it, I guess. Those synths were barely armed." She watched the elevator display, hope rising in her chest with each floor they passed. When it said B11, she actually started to believe they were going to make it. Just six more levels, and they'd be at the garage. B10 passed, then B9, and then the elevator lurched to a very sudden stop and Leo stumbled, dropping Estes with a thud.

As the doctor twitched, groaning in pain, Juliet scowled at Leo. "You had to say it, didn't you?"

36

A MAD ASCENT

They stopped it somehow. Shit!" Leo slammed his fist against a plastic elevator panel.

"Do we try the shaft? Do we get out here?" Juliet was asking herself, Leo, Angel, or even Frida, hoping for inspiration.

"I don't know. Look at the ceiling; not sure we can even get a panel open to get out—I mean, this isn't an action vid!"

Angel was a lot more helpful. "Juliet, you're just a little higher than level B9. They've done something to physically disable the elevator motors, but I can open the doors, and you can drop out."

Juliet yanked her Texan out and dropped to the floor, lying on her belly, ready to shoot through the opening. "Get ready, Leo! My PAI's gonna pop the door." Leo had been in the midst of picking Estes back up, but he dropped her, eliciting another muffled groan, and drew his pistol, squatting in the corner of the elevator on the left side of the door.

"Do we come out shooting? What if it's not synths—" Juliet started to ask, but Leo had a quick answer.

"These corpo-sec goons will be wired to the gills, ready to kill something. The shit these synths are putting them through—let's just say they aren't going to ask questions before they start shooting."

Juliet nodded grimly. "Right. Well, let's hope we can slip by. Open it, Angel."

Instantly, the chime sounded as the doors began to open, revealing the elevator shaft for the top two-thirds and a gap on the lower third, right in front of Juliet's face, where she could see the lobby on B9. It looked like a scene out of a horror movie, even worse than the mess Juliet and Leo had left on B31. Bodies and dismembered limbs were strewn all over the place. Arcs of blood spray on the walls and ceiling told the tale of high-powered rifles and thrown body parts. Angel scanned the charnel scene, highlighting bodies in blue and green.

Before Juliet could wonder what the colors meant, Angel clarified, "The green highlights are human." Juliet frowned, looking down into the mess, her optics compensating for the flickering, damaged light fixtures. She counted eleven human bodies and four synths. Nothing moved.

"Let's go," she said, her voice a hoarse whisper despite the fact she still wore her helmet. She slid through the opening and landed lightly on her feet, revolver ready. When nothing came charging through the broken, bullet-riddled doors leading out of the elevator lobby, she looked up to see Leo pushing their prisoner's limp body through the opening. It looked like he was just going to drop her to the floor, so Juliet wrapped one arm, enhanced by the FlexPlate armor, around her waist and hoisted her down. Leo hopped down with a soft grunt, and she helped him sling the doctor over his shoulder again.

A yellow line appeared on her AUI, showing her where to go as Angel said, "The stairs are nearby, just through that closed access door and down a short hallway." Juliet saw the door and realized she'd seen a similar one on B31; it looked like a nondescript closet, but sure enough, just to the right was a plastic symbol showing a staircase.

She took two steps toward it, reaching for the handle, when, with a clatter and scrape, the doors leading into the sublevel began to open. Leo, either due to fried nerves or because he'd seen something Juliet had missed, began to open fire on the gap between the doors, his nine-millimeter barking in rapid staccato.

Juliet whirled and leveled her Texan, watching and waiting. Her vision flickered briefly as Angel scanned the darkness beyond the door. A second later, the PAI drew an outline of a very large individual on the far side of the door, hunched behind the metal as though using it for cover.

She lifted her crosshairs, lined them up with the outline's head, and smoothly pulled the trigger. The revolver thundered, a big hole appeared in the door, and the silhouette staggered back, its head snapping away from the door.

"Hit him," Juliet declared before turning, ready to run for the stairs. She grabbed the handle and yanked, and then Leo's gun started firing again.

"He's not down!" he yelled. "Jesus! What the hell is this thing?"

Juliet whirled, saw the doors flung wide, saw a hulking chrome-and-flesh monster of a man, and watched as Leo emptied his mag into him. The nine-millimeter rounds punched into the fleshy chest of the giant and skipped off his chrome-plated head, which only seemed to piss the guy off, not that he wasn't already furious. He was covered in blood, some fresh and some dried.

As Juliet took him in, her hand lifting her gun, part of her mind took aim while another part sat in stunned horror at his appearance. He was mostly nude, wearing scraps of blue clothes around his waist and shoulders. Mismatched flesh covered parts of his augmented body, and bloody, half scabbed-over wounds covered him, including the dark gap between his legs. His glowering, bloodshot right eye looked human, but the other was a bloody hole. His lips were twisted in a snarl beneath a scabbed-over nose hole as he stomped toward Leo.

The part of Juliet that wasn't paralyzed with horror aimed at his face and squeezed her trigger, but he lurched with surprising speed, throwing off her aim, and the fat, polymer bullet hit the side of his metal skull, denting it and forcing him to veer sideways but not killing him. Leo scrabbled backward but could only go so far, and his back came up against the partially open elevator doors.

While the brute was fixated on Leo, Juliet sidestepped, trying to get behind the synthetic Goliath, examining the visible parts of his chrome head for vulnerability. She didn't see anything. Instead, she lowered her crosshairs, and as smoothly as she could, she began firing rounds into his spine, aiming for the base of his skull. The Texan roared, and perhaps adrenaline or panic made time move differently, but it seemed she only pulled the trigger twice before it began to click. Empty.

Meanwhile, the giant man hadn't fallen, hadn't even slowed. He reached a hand for Leo as the mercenary displayed an impressive agility by leaping to the side, ducking under the monster's arm. Or, he would have if not for his burden. Estes's butt, jutting up from Leo's shoulder, caught against the giant cybernetic arm, and Leo stumbled, falling to the floor and releasing the doc-tor so he could try to roll free. The synth might have been distracted by the doctor flopping to the ground and moaning, but he only had eyes for Leo. He darted after him like a giant muscular cat after a wily mouse.

Juliet had spent a lot of downtime back on Callisto messing with her Texan, practicing loading it from the ammo on her belt. Her right hand was nimble and precise in a way her left hand couldn't match, so she'd learned to pop the cylinder, eject the empty casing, and then swap the gun to her left so she could, in a blur of efficient movement, snatch the bullets out of her belt and stuff them into the cylinder. As she slid the seventh round into place, she twitched her wrist, slamming the cylinder shut, and lifted the gun, stepping closer to the brute as he cornered Leo, arms wide, ready to grab the mercenary if he tried to slip away again.

She lifted the barrel, aiming the crosshairs on a dent in the back of the synth's skull. Like a machine, she pounded one, two, three, four hot polymer slugs into that dent. Each impact sent the synth's head forward like a sledgehammer. Each impact stunned him for half a second before he lifted his head and focused his ire on Leo again. Each impact deepened the dent in the thick armored plating, and finally, the fourth bullet punched through and turned his brain into slop. He collapsed with a wheeze that sounded far too human.

Leo peered out of the corner from behind arms held in a defensive position, eyes wide with stress and disbelief. "Holy shit! You did it! What a monster!"

Something told Juliet that the monsters were the ones who'd created the killer. Something told her that if she'd read his thoughts, it would have ruined sleep for her for years. Then she noticed something disturbing, pointing to the back of his caved-in skull and the bright red blood drizzling out to pool on the floor. "He wasn't a synth."

"Jesus! Look!" Leo prodded the back of the giant's waist where his belt held the scraps of his pants in place. Juliet squinted and saw what he meant: the belt had a Life-Ultra corpo-sec logo. "He was one of the responders!"

"Guess he went nuts? Maybe he was in there"—Juliet jerked her thumb at the doors leading further into the level—"and had a nightmare fight with the synths—pumped too many stims." She automatically started reloading her pistol as she walked to the other door. "We gotta move. Is Estes still alive?"

"I'm alive," came the slurred, raspy reply. Juliet whirled on the scientist and pointed her reloaded Texan at her.

"I ought to put your lights out right here!" She stomped over to the doctor, still sprawled on the floor but struggling to get into a sitting position. Juliet pushed her down onto her face and holstered her pistol so she could pull out her data cable. "Angel," she said into her helmet, trusting her to know she meant the words for her alone, "put a watchdog on her." She stuffed the cable into the doctor's data port and waited for Angel to give her the go-ahead.

"It's installed."

Juliet stood up and yanked her cable out, provoking a grunt of pain and outrage from the doctor. "Don't try to send any more purge messages, you psychopath!"

"How—"

"Look around. This is your doing. How many people did you kill with that protocol?"

"Nobody innocent! I'm not the only one with the trigger code, by the way! That's a company directive!"

Leo growled and grabbed her under the armpit, hoisting her to her feet. "Like that makes it better. Come on, get up. I'm sick of carrying your ass."

Juliet glowered darkly at the scientist as she avoided eye contact, looking anywhere but Juliet's face. "Nobody innocent? You saying everyone who worked down here deserved to get murdered by their coworkers?"

"What?" She finally looked at Juliet with wide eyes, comprehension dawning on her face. "No, no, no. That order was supposed to trigger a few specialized synths to take out a few key scientists and wipe the server decks. You mean . . ." She looked at the bloody room. "This is from the purge?"

"Every synth in the sublevels is going nuts, killing everyone. And yeah, it started when you sent the command."

Estes gasped, clutching her shirt collar, squeezing and scrabbling her fingers at her neck as though the answers to this nightmare would come to her if she could just breathe a little easier. "Then someone at corporate altered the protocol! That's not what we were trained on!"

"Welcome to corpo life," Leo said, jerking her arm to start her walking. "Let's go!" Those words were directed at Juliet. She nodded, turned to the door leading to the stairwell, and pushed through. Just as Angel had promised, a short hallway led past a couple of maintenance closets to another door with the universal emblem for stairs. She jogged forward, trusting Leo to keep track of Estes and call out if there was any problem. As she approached the door, her vision flickered as Angel fired off her terahertz-scanning capabilities, and then a huge, blinking stop sign appeared in her vision.

"Don't open that!" Angel cried. Juliet halted, centimeters from grabbing the handle. "There are people in the stairwell fighting! Some appear to be civilians—unarmed. Others are clearly synths. I think some survivors are trying to get out."

Juliet looked at Leo, at the woman cringing beside him, and at his empty hand—he'd holstered his gun after emptying the magazine. She drew her

Texan and flipped it to hand him the grip. "There're some synths killing people in here. Stand back." As he took the pistol, he nodded his head.

"I'll back you up."

Juliet frowned at him and shrugged. "Okay. I'm going up. Make sure nothing comes up behind me." Then, she drew the sword Tanaka had given her, smiling as the metal sang, sliding through the high-tech sonic sharpener built into the aperture of the scabbard. "Angel, I'm counting on you. Help me keep my form perfect and moving fast—push it to the limit."

"I will. The biobatts for your enhanced reflexes are at sixty percent. Your FlexPlate batteries are at eighty. Open the door when you're ready."

Juliet held the sword ready, reached down, yanked the handle, and stepped into chaos. Blood smeared the concrete steps, lights flashed from amber to red and back again, and screams and grunts echoed hollowly up and down the space. Directly in front of her, on the short flight of steps leading down from the landing, a man was struggling with a synth, trying to pull away as it stabbed a scalpel into his shin, gripping his ankle with a hook of a hand, three fingers missing and spewing white fluid.

Juliet didn't hesitate; she darted forward, thrust the sword out, and impaled the synth through the crown of its plasteel head, punching the hardened, razor-sharp metal through the thin shell. The synth thrashed and bucked, falling still as Juliet twisted the weapon, widening the hole and quadrupling the damage as she yanked it out.

"Th-thank you!" the man gasped, holding out a hand for Juliet to help him up.

"Get out if you can," Juliet said, her voice cold and hard in her helmet's speaker. She turned and started up the steps like a prowling tiger on the hunt. The synth must have marked her and warned its comrades above because she could hear a pack of them stomping down the concrete steps. She got to the next landing and waited.

As they flung themselves down the steps at her, they suddenly seemed to be caught in molasses, hurling themselves through the air in slow motion as Juliet, faster than most people could track with their eyes, danced between them, hacking the deadly blade through necks, kicking bodies away from her, and thrusting the sword through eye sockets to penetrate the synthetic brains of her would-be assailants.

Her boots struck the synths, heavy as they were, like lead-filled hammers, in one case flinging a synth over the rail so it fell in slow motion into the depths of the tower. Her cuts were precise and perfect, her follow-throughs perfectly executed to avoid unnecessary movement, and her foot placement was exactly right for the follow-up hacks and thrusts—all thanks to Angel.

Everything she did was something she'd learned from Tanaka, but none of it was anything she'd truly perfected through practice. Juliet knew what she wanted to do, but only Angel's adjustments kept her from overcommitting, from twisting slightly wrong, from tripping herself up in the chaotic movements of her opponents, or from stabbing or cutting into a nonlethal bone or piece of clothing.

Only a handful of seconds passed from the moment that pack of aggressors descended to when things sped up again and the falling synths' doom-filled wail fell away. She stood over four twitching or completely still synthetic bodies, and rather than soak up her conquest standing there, waiting for the next shoe to drop, she charged up the next flight of steps, calling out, "Hurry up, Leo!"

She came upon two more survivors, urged them to hurry, and kept moving. At the doorway to B7, she found a corpo-sec utility officer trying to weld the door shut while something on the other side pounded against it, each blow deforming the metal slightly. He didn't even spare Juliet a glance as she flew past him.

She powered past B6, noting the door was ajar and the space beyond was utterly dark. Smoke lingered in the air—Juliet couldn't imagine that was a good sign. She paused by the door, pushing it shut with her foot, waiting for Leo and the doctor. "You coming?" she asked in comms.

Leo's voice, grunting and breathy with exertion, replied, "Just passed B7. Carrying the doc; she's slow as shit."

"I'm waiting at B6. One more to go. You got this." Twenty seconds later, Leo appeared on the flight of steps below, his face red, Juliet's pistol tight in his fist, and the doctor bouncing on his shoulder, grunting and complaining with each jolt.

"You keep whining, and I'm tossing you over!" he growled.

Juliet smirked and started up the steps. "Frida, we're almost to the garage."

"Team Three is waiting. They had to clear some corpo-sec."

Juliet didn't like the sound of that, but she didn't like anything about the situation. She was just glad they had a ride waiting.

When she reached the door to B5, she saw the sign indicating it was a garage level and almost wept at the beauty of it. Even though Angel scanned the door and didn't paint any silhouettes for her to worry about, Juliet darted forward and kicked her boot against the crash bar, sending the door flying open.

She charged out, sword ready. The scene wasn't nearly as bad as she'd imagined. There was some blood on the concrete, and she could see drag marks where some bodies had been hauled away behind vehicles, but that was it. A low, black SUV idled not far from the door, and she could see Tanaka standing by the open rear door.

He was geared for combat—flexible-looking black pants and a pullover shirt, tactical vest, low-profile combat shoes, and of course, a scabbard jutting up from his left hip that could only contain a monoblade.

Juliet turned to the stairs just in time to see Leo stagger up the steps. He turned, her Texan thundered, and then he darted for the doorway. "Close it!" he yelled as he charged the waiting SUV. Juliet slammed the door shut, not sure what good that would do—she didn't have a way to seal it. Angel solved that puzzle, though, when the lights on the access panel began to flash red, and the words FIRE SEAL scrolled across its display.

Juliet jogged over to the SUV and slipped into the back seat. Tanaka shut her door and, almost nonchalantly, climbed into the front seat and fastened his seat belt. Dora Lee was driving, and Juliet barely had time to wonder where Barns or Hawkins were before Leo asked from the back cargo compartment, "Can this chick be tracked?"

Juliet shook her head. "Not with the watchdog I put in her head. I mean, unless she has a tracker on her body somewhere."

"I don't," Estes cried.

"Use the scanner in the toolkit, Applebaum," Dora said, smoothly driving the SUV up the exit lane.

"Right." Leo began digging through the plastic box of drawers.

"Well," Tanaka said, turning to look back at Juliet. "It looks like this mission got a little messier than you planned." For some reason, he was smiling; a genuine smile and a pleasant expression that Juliet had never seen on his face.

She met his smile with a scowl. "What are you grinning about?"

"I see you made good use of my sword. We'll have an interesting debriefing on Monday, but for now, I have some people at LCC headquarters awaiting delivery of your witness and the evidence we've gathered."

Despite everything in her experience with the man saying it was impossible, he continued to smile, and she could see it reflected in his eyes. Half her brain was stunned by the incongruous behavior, while another wrestled with what he'd said—LCC, or Luna Corporate Consortium, was the de facto ruling body of the moon. Who were Tanaka's contacts there?

37

DEAD TIRED

LCC?" Juliet asked, surprised and, if she were being honest, a little annoyed by the change in tactics with no feedback on her part.

"Yes," Tanaka replied as he turned, facing forward. "Lee got deep into Life-Ultra's network. Her daemons are forwarding vid feeds to us showing the massacre taking place in the sublevels." He paused and pointed to the left. "The other exit, Dora. I saw two response vehicles outside this one." He shifted in the seat to glance at Juliet again. "We don't think we can approach Life-Ultra management to shut things down and pay us off. The documents Dora found on their 'Genesis Program' implicate the entire corporation. Your witness should help corroborate."

"I wanted to tell you about that," Angel said, "but you've been quite busy . . ."

"So, what's the story?" Juliet asked as she felt something tapping her shoulder. She turned to see Leo trying to hand her the Texan.

"Long story," Dora said, smoothly piloting the vehicle around some flashing barricades that were open but looked like they shouldn't be. Were her daemons clearing the way for them? Was Angel? Juliet wanted to ask, but Dora kept speaking. "I guess Life-Ultra's made some significant strides in complex organ and tissue synthesis, including brain tissue. So, when the marketing guys found out what R&D was working on, they started dreaming up applications and, of course, selling products that weren't close to being ready. Enough execs received big enough paydays to fight against shutting it down. When the time came to deliver, and the New Life cerebral tissue replacements—the marketing language for Project Genesis—weren't ready, they had to fake it."

"We have the client names," Tanaka added. "They are some very rich, very powerful, and now, very dead individuals."

"They just don't know it yet," Dora finished with a sideways smirk.

"I'm lost. What the hell are you guys talking about?" Leo groused, crawling over the rear seat to sit beside Juliet.

"They basically created synths using mostly organic organs and tissue," Dora explained. "The brains, though, the personalities, are just simulations. The synths are pretending to be the people they were supposed to help cheat death. Internally, they're claiming it's a stopgap, that they saved the biological brains of their clients and will 'fix' the replacements when the tech is ready. The only problem is, they're not making any progress, and they've already had some serious malfunctions."

Dora clicked her tongue, shaking her head. "See, they had to make the copies believable, so the synth brains don't know they're synths. They think they're the original people with some memory issues—memory issues the company keeps saying will resolve, given time."

"But it never does, and some of them are going psychotic," Juliet added, the whole thing coming into clear focus. It made her think of Lilia Voronov and the fact she was a clone, slowly absorbing the memories of Alexander Voronov. Another approach to the same problem—people didn't want to be mortal.

"So you see why we need to go to LCC," Tanaka said. "I have a contract attorney meeting me; I'll negotiate a reward before I hand over all the evidence."

"Are we all going?" Leo asked, saving Juliet the trouble—if Tanaka wanted to handle the business, she would be more than happy to get some much-needed sleep. She craned her neck to look behind her, wondering if she could still see the Life-Ultra tower, but it was gone from view; Dora had taken too many turns. An involuntary shudder passed through her as she pictured those bloody, horror-filled sublevels and remembered that there were still people down there going through hell.

Before Tanaka could answer Leo, she said, "Someone should help them."

"Huh?" Leo asked.

"The people still trapped down there. I'm sure there are survivors."

Dora snorted. "Oh, we reported the shit show to every nearby corp and also to Luna City Security. Life-Ultra says they've got things in hand, but yeah, people are aware and making efforts."

Tanaka finally answered Leo's question. "I will handle LCC. We're dropping you two at the office."

"What about Barns and Hawkins?" Leo pressed.

"They're dealing with the dirty LCS officers." Tanaka turned and made solid eye contact with Leo and then Juliet. "We were not expecting what happened to you two. That sort of situation isn't something you shrug off. I want you to take a day to decompress, and we'll talk on Monday. Agreed?"

Juliet was torn between being grateful and feeling like she should stand up for herself and her role as the organizer of the operation. Should she just let him take over all this business? Shouldn't she insist on going to the corporate consortium with him?

In the end, her grateful side won, or maybe it was her exhaustion that got into the corner to help it out. "Thanks, Tanaka," was all she said. He grunted in response, and Juliet unlocked the seals on her helmet, sighing softly as she pulled it off her sweaty head. "God, that feels better." The climate-controlled interior was like ice against her neck, and she leaned back, luxuriating in it.

"You were a machine in there, Lucky. I'm . . . not sure I could've done better." Leo actually sounded like he was trying to give her a compliment, and despite his inability to do it cleanly, Juliet smiled and reached over to pat his knee.

Tanaka voiced what she was thinking. "You'd be dead if that had been you and a copy of yourself in there."

"What? Hey, if I had the gear she was packing—"

"You would have died a little more slowly." Dora snorted. "I watched some of the action through the cam feeds."

Juliet yawned while Leo shook his head, a look on his face that said he was tired of fighting the world alone. She jostled him with her elbow, offering him a wink. "Joking aside, I was underequipped. I should've brought more ammo."

"If you were proficient with the monoblade, it would have rendered your ammo redundant."

Juliet nodded, conceding. "Maybe. Your sword sure worked shiny against those synths in the stairwell."

"A good blade." Tanaka sounded very satisfied, and Juliet had to smile.

"If we're just gonna keep jerking her off all night, can you drop me here, Dora?" Leo groaned.

"Oh, you are such a baby!" Juliet laughed. "I'm starting to see that if you aren't the center of attention—"

"He makes himself the center," Frida spoke unexpectedly through comms. Juliet had forgotten about her. "I'm not trying to butt in; I just have an update: Based on our preliminary report, the LCC has mobilized LCS to respond to the Life-Ultra building, claiming access by rights of an 'existential threat to Luna City's populace.' I think the people in there will get some help now, Lucky." As she spoke, Dora pulled the SUV up to the front of the BizRes Tower.

"Here you go, Ls," the netjacker said as the vehicle came to a stop.

"Ls?" Juliet puzzled over the nickname, assuming it meant Leo somehow.

"Leo and Lucky. Ls."

"Oh, brother," Leo groaned, popping open the door and slipping out.

"I guess I'll see you in a minute, Frida." Juliet chuckled, following him out.

"Right." Frida was all business. "Boss, they're expecting you at the LCC building. We've got three board members on-site and two more on the way. The secretary I've been dealing with says at least one is pissed to have her Saturday night ruined."

Tanaka grunted, "Good." As Juliet shut the door, he lowered his window. "Rest and decompress, Lucky. I'm serious. See you Monday."

She nodded then turned to the building, noting Leo waiting by the door. "You're coming up?"

"I guess. I want to say hi to Frida, and I need to call a cab anyway."

He nodded and waited for her to walk through, helmet clutched in one hand, shotgun bouncing against her armored belly. "It's gonna feel good to peel that armor off, isn't it?"

"You know it." Juliet turned, smiling, and allowed him to catch up and walk beside her. "Hey, I know we were teasing you a little back there, but you were great tonight. I never had to worry about where Estes was or think about you falling behind. You even got my back a couple of times. You were right, too. I was geared for war, and you were wearing a suit. It makes a difference."

"Are you . . ." He blinked and opened his eyes wide. "Are you being nice to me?"

"Oh, shut up!" She laughed and mock punched his shoulder. He, of course, reacted dramatically, flinching and wincing.

"Careful with those armored ham hands . . ."

"Did you just call my hands hams? I'm gonna hit you for real!" Juliet laughed, chasing after him as he double-timed it to the elevator.

"I'm kidding! Mercy!" he cried as he slapped the call button. When Juliet relented, leaning against the wall, a stupid smile still on her face, he said, "Man, it feels good to let it out, doesn't it? That was some tense shit back there, no lie. Thirty stories underground, surrounded by hostiles, half of which were psychotic synths, the other half drugged-up corpo-sec. Uh-uh, I'll pass on that if I can."

"Yeah. Why bring it up? I'd rather forget for now."

"I know what could help with that . . ." The sly look he gave her was very suggestive, and Juliet suddenly wished she still had her helmet on as the blood rushed to her face. She cleared her throat and looked down, grasping for a response, but he shrugged. "It was just a thought. Don't sweat it."

"I thought you said . . ." Her mind immediately fell back on the memory of him saying they weren't compatible and that he'd gotten over his initial attraction. Who says something like that?

As she completed the thought, the immediate follow-up was, who expects anyone to stand by words like that? She'd been operating on the principle that people and their feelings could be predicted or considered logical.

He grunted, shooting her a half smile. "Yeah, yeah. I'm being stupid."

The elevator dinged and he stepped inside while Juliet had half a mind to wait in the lobby. Part of her was angry that she'd frozen up, and part of her was furious he'd gotten to her, which made her react the way she had. She wanted to scowl at him, but she was just too exhausted and too flustered despite her rising ire. She stepped into the elevator and avoided looking at him as the doors closed, leaning against the opposite wall, eyes on the door.

Angel, of course, could tell she was bothered. "I think he was hoping for a different reaction, Juliet. I think he's trying to save face."

Frowning, Juliet leaned forward and slammed a hand against the stop button, bringing the elevator to a lurching halt. She whirled on him. "What's your deal, anyway, Applebaum?" He opened his mouth, ready to answer with some charming quip, no doubt, but Juliet wasn't going to have it. "We just went through hell together, and I think I deserve better than to have you try-ing to jerk around with my emotions!"

He folded his arms, clearly feeling defensive, and shrugged, for once no smile—sly or otherwise—on his lips. "I'm sorry. You're right. I was out of line."

Juliet wasn't ready to let him off the hook. "Would you make a suggestion like that to Hawkins? To Lee?"

"No . . ."

"So why do you think it's okay with me?"

"I guess I don't think it's okay. I . . ." He groaned, pressed his hands to the sides of his head, and slowly slid down the elevator wall until he was squatting, nearly on the floor, squeezing his eyes shut. "My mouth got away from me, all right? I think you're fucking amazing, and I don't know how to behave around someone like you."

"So, all the banter? All the shit talk? You're just being a schoolboy, picking on the girl you like?"

His voice was quiet, almost a whisper, as he nodded. "Yeah, I guess so."

His admission, his posture, and his handsome face peering up at her from a bloodstained executive suit all combined to do something to Juliet at that moment, and she felt a different kind of heat flushing her cheeks. Almost in a panic, she slammed the emergency stop, getting the elevator moving again. It had nearly been on the floor of Tanaka's offices, so she only had time for a few quick breaths before it dinged, and the doors started to open. Leo stood, and they locked eyes for a second. He smiled, shrugged, and, as he stepped off, said, "Sorry."

"Leo," she called before he could take more than a couple of steps.

He stopped and turned, quirking an eyebrow. "Yeah?"

"You're all right." Her words brought a small smile to his face, and he nodded. Then, he turned and walked down the hall, away from Tanaka's suite. Juliet blew out a deep breath, stuck her helmet out to stop the doors from closing, and walked to Tanaka's office.

"Are you all right?" Angel asked.

"I'm just confused." She sighed, tapping her helmet against her thigh, hesitating before opening the doors. "And tired. I'm dead tired, Angel."

"You already have a cab waiting downstairs if you don't want to talk to anyone else."

"No. I'm here. I'm sure Frida saw me. I'll say hello." Juliet took a deep breath, squared her shoulders, and pulled the door open, stepping into the lobby.

Frida immediately called out, "Lucky!" She waved a hand from her desk, tapping away at some projected UI elements, lights flickering in the air near her data deck. "Let me get through these messages, then I can focus."

Juliet nodded, setting her helmet in one of the chairs in front of her desk and collapsing into the other. She watched Frida tapping away, talking to her PAI, clearly trying to manage five tasks at once. She was communicating with various people from the LCC, someone from Luna City Security, and passing location and transport info on to Barns and Hawkins.

Juliet watched her, trying to picture her as a long-lost scion to one of the last century's most powerful and influential families. Her mind kept drifting to romanticized images of Japanese villas on forested hillsides, and when Frida spoke again, she jerked her head, snapping out of a near slumber. "You want to crash here?"

"Uh." Juliet yawned, stretching to the point that her back popped several times. "No, I gotta get home. I just wanted to say hi."

Frida leaned forward, licking her lips and darting her eyes nervously. "I have to confess something."

"Huh?"

"Leo. He, uh, walks around with his comms open all the time. He's had them on since the operation—"

"Oh shit!" Juliet groaned.

"Yeah, I should have shut it off. I heard that stuff, though, and I want you to know I'm sorry."

Juliet scowled, more embarrassed than angry. "Yeah, why *didn't* you shut it off?"

"It was half over before I realized what was happening! Then, well, shoot . . ." Frida thumped her fist against her forehead.

Juliet had to laugh. "You're regretting confessing."

Frida's voice was small as she blushed. "That, and my stupid nosy mind making me ever so slow when it came to cutting off his comms."

"Forget it. I'd have a hard time tuning out that trainwreck, too."

"He really got you flustered, huh? But you got him right back! I've never heard him get so quiet and . . . *honest!* Do you, like, want me to do anything? Want me to mention it to Tan—"

Juliet's heart lurched in her chest, a wave of unreasonable panic washing over her. "No! No, Frida. I'm too tired to process all that. Anyway, I think we cleared the air enough."

"He's a good person, Lucky. He won't, like, harass you or anything. Just tell him enough is enough. I mean, if you want to." She said the last almost like a question, and Juliet had to smile.

"Like I said, I'm too tired to process things." She grunted, standing. "Anyway, I wanted to say hi, and I've done it. I'm going to find my bed." She started to turn but paused, leaning on the back of the chair. "I wanted to say more than hi. I wanted to say thank you. Thank you for having my back and for making all"—she waved her hand at the flickering lights all around Frida's desk—"this happen. I'd be ten kinds of melted if I hadn't had you all to help me with this mess."

"It's my pleasure. One, I like you and want to help. Two, I haven't seen the boss smiling like he was tonight in a long time." Frida bared her teeth in a fierce grin and leaned over her desk to grab Juliet's hand, giving it a squeeze. "Go home and relax. You did amazing tonight."

"Thanks, Frida." Juliet returned the smile. Frida nodded and, as her eyes unfocused and she started talking to a secretary at the LCC, Juliet walked out to the elevator. "What a night!" she groaned as the elevator surged downward.

"I've never had such a hard time picking a topic to speak to you about! The operation, the horrible crimes committed by Life-Ultra, Tanaka's strangely good mood, Leo's advances, and your strange reaction—where do I begin?"

Juliet had to laugh, shaking her head. "You're terrible! What do you mean by my strange reaction?"

"I thought you might tell him off or break his arm. Instead, you got flustered and quiet, and I could tell you were experiencing some amorous emotions!"

"Well? What do you want from me, Angel? I'm pent-up! He's handsome and fit, and when I called him out, he got surprisingly sweet. I'm just as confused as you are! I can't let that happen, though, right? I mean, not if we're going to work together . . ."

"I don't know. Workplace romance isn't *always* doomed." The way Angel said it made Juliet think she'd done research and found that it was very often *doomed*. She groaned again and walked through the lobby, aiming for the cab she could see parked outside.

"Maybe it's not romance. Maybe we just want to let off some steam together. You know, now and then."

"Can you see yourself doing that?" Angel's question prompted a series of rather steamy images in her mind, and Juliet felt herself flushing again.

"Unfortunately, Angel, I can see it all too easily." As she slid into the cab, a red light began to flash near the sensor array.

"Pardon me, Operator XR713-004, but I'll need you to provide licenses for . . . Thank you." The light went out, and the cab began to pull away from the curb.

"Take me to my bike, Angel. I'm already sick of cabs."

38

CERTIFIED CHROME

When Juliet woke the next day, sometime around noon, she had vague, disjointed memories of picking up her bike, riding back to the hangar, and stumbling to bed, more asleep on her feet than awake. She remembered struggling to sleep, too many thoughts running through her mind—horror show images from the depths of Life-Ultra and, of course, scenarios involving Leo Applebaum. Eventually, though, her exhaustion had claimed her, and she'd slept like the dead.

Lying there, stretching, yawning, and luxuriating in the comfort of her acceleration couch, she had kind of a numb, warm feeling all over her body that told her she'd been sleeping very hard. "God, I feel good," she murmured, rubbing her eyes and glancing around for something to drink.

Angel replied immediately, "Good morning, Juliet! Your body was ready for some rest."

She snagged a half-empty electrolyte pouch from atop a stack of book boxes and swished it in her mouth before saying, "Any messages?"

"Hines is requesting an update. Frida posted a group message saying Tanaka's meetings with the LCC were successful and details would be provided at a mandatory team meeting on Monday. She also provided an update on Barns and Hawkins and their efforts to collect the corpo-sec officers on the list Asia Kills and Comet took from Duffy."

"Yeah?"

"Yes. They've already captured seven and have turned them, along with your other prisoners, over to bounty brokers for transport to New Atlas on Titan."

"Wait? We're still doing that? Even with the developments at Life-Ultra?"

"Apparently. Information Dora Lee took from Lieutenant Channing provided the link they needed. One of their corrupt business fronts was selling stolen goods to distributors who serve the New Atlas market."

"Huh, and they already got seven in addition to Channing?"

"Yes. They worked through the night, trying to surprise as many as possible before word could get out. I believe they're still on the job."

Juliet sat up, swinging her legs to the side of the bunk. "Shouldn't we help?"

"While I understand the sentiment, Frida reiterated that you and Applebaum are not to work today. Apparently, it's standard protocol to give operators involved in events like those you went through last night some time off."

"Standard protocol for those guys, maybe, but I'm used to getting back in the saddle—"

"Juliet, just because you've been forced to operate like that in the past doesn't mean it's good for you."

Juliet yawned and stood, stumbling a little as she walked to her bathroom. "Well, can you message Barns and Hawkins? Ask 'em how things are going."

"Of course, but I wasn't done reviewing your messages." Juliet used the toilet as Angel continued, "You have a message from Honey. Shall I play it?"

"Yeah." Juliet watched as a window opened on her AUI, and Honey's face appeared. Her background was blurred, but she looked happy and relaxed.

"Hey, J. I'm so sorry to spring this on you. I wouldn't do it, but it kind of got sprung on me, too. Peter's been putting off his trip to Mars, and I was starting to think he wasn't going to go this year, but now he's saying that we have to leave on Monday. Something's up with one of the factories he 'inherited' from Alexander. Some workers are striking, and he wants to have a look to see what the mess is all about—I don't think he trusts the manager's reports.

"Anyway, we'll probably be staying at Alexander's place in New Galveston, and of course, Lilia is anxious to go. She's starting to have . . . memories of that place. It wouldn't matter, anyway, because Peter wouldn't leave her behind. So that means I'm going, too. We leave Monday super early.

"I know, a while back, I suggested the idea of you flying escort for us, but I know you're also busy right now. It was just an idea I had before I knew how things worked, anyway—we're taking a passenger liner, and they have their own security. Anyway, if you get this message and aren't too busy in the morning, maybe we can grab breakfast."

Juliet closed the window and frowned. "Angel, when did this come in?"

"At 0215."

"Two in the morning? Doesn't that all seem really sudden? Why didn't you wake me up in time for breakfast? Can you call Honey for me, please?" Juliet stood, flushed, and started brushing her teeth.

"Yes, it seems sudden. I didn't wake you because you needed your rest! I'm sure she can change her breakfast idea to lunch. I'm trying to connect right now . . ."

The connection tone sounded and cut off before it could finish. Honey's face appeared in a new window. "J?" She sounded a little breathless, her eyes focused on other things, darting around.

"Hey, Honey. Sorry, I slept through breakfast, um . . ."

"Don't worry! I'm just packing right now. I guess we're going to be gone a while, and it's kind of a big job packing for a household."

Juliet frowned. "A household?"

"Well, Lilia and I, and yeah, Peter. He doesn't trust his assistants with his personal things. He's very paranoid after the whole . . . you know."

Juliet gave up on brushing her teeth and rinsed her brush. "So, this is all really sudden, and it has me feeling paranoid, too, Honey. Are you sure you're okay?"

"I'm fine. Really! I'm only annoyed about how, as you said, sudden everything is. I thought I'd have lots of time to plan for the trip and maybe talk you into coming!" She laughed, shaking her head. "Seriously, I was working up to the idea, hoping I could get you to come check things out around Mars. There's a lot of work there, you know?"

"I . . ." Juliet wasn't sure how to respond, but Honey laughed again, bailing her out.

"I know, I know. You can't drop everything and leave in one day. Maybe when things calm down a little? Maybe you can swing over and spend a week? Make a vacation out of it?"

"Yes! Of course! I'd like to see Mars. Like you said, though, I've got things to take care of here. Are you really going to be gone that long? Maybe you'll be back by the time I get sorted . . ."

"He's talking like it's going to be months. At least. I think the factory strike is the excuse he wanted to get moving, but he also thinks he and Lilia will be safer there."

"Can we meet still? Are you hungry?"

Honey stopped what she was doing and looked straight at Juliet, her expression making it clear what she was about to say before the words arrived. "J, I'm so sorry, but there's no way. I have so much to do. Lilia has three appointments with specialists this afternoon, and . . . I'm sorry." She shrugged and shook her head, a rueful smile on her face.

"Damn it, Honey! You know how this makes me feel, right? After everything you've been through? This feels like you leaving for Luna all over again. Are you going to disappear on me?"

"No! No, I promise; nobody's holding a gun on me!" She laughed again, and Juliet could see the genuine amusement in her eyes. She didn't *seem* stressed.

"I never got you a present," Juliet lamely sighed.

"What?"

"I was going to get you something just right, something that jumped out at me. You know, after you left me that T-shirt."

"Well then, that just means you'll *have* to come visit!" Honey winked. Juliet could see she was trying hard to reassure her.

"Tanaka's going to be disappointed. He's always talking about how he wished Leo could have learned the way you do . . . Oh, God, Honey, I have to tell you about Leo!"

"What?" Honey's eyes widened, and her PAI manipulated the image to make it look like she was leaning close.

"Last night, he totally came onto me. Remember what he said before? About how we weren't compatible or whatever? I guess it was hot air."

Honey laughed. "I saw that coming. What'd you do? Punch him?"

"Not exactly." Juliet laughed. "I thought about it a lot before I went to sleep—he's certainly handsome, and if he could stop acting like such a schoolboy . . . It's a bad idea, though. Maybe in a different life." To herself, she added the real reason she was cooling on the idea—maybe if she didn't want to work with him and his team.

"You know, I think you need some love in your life, sis, but I'm not a big fan of that guy. I'm inclined to agree. Bad idea."

"Yeah, yeah. Keep telling me that, and I'll give in to his advances. You know how it goes—the heart wants what everyone says the heart can't have." Juliet grinned wryly, trying to ensure Honey could hear the joke in her words.

Of course, her friend knew exactly what to say, laughing over the words. "In that case, please, go sleep with Applebaum. Please!" They both laughed for a few seconds, then Honey sobered up. "Seriously, sis. I hope you find the right one. I'll be there for you. Also, I'll tell you something one of Lilia's tutors said to her that really struck a chord with me: Don't let perfection be the enemy of good. Wish I knew who to credit . . ."

"Voltaire," Angel replied.

Juliet groaned. "First you tell me 'not Applebaum,' then you tell me not to be picky? What do I do, Honey?"

"Oh, be picky! Be picky, J, but not *too* picky." Honey laughed at the frustration creasing Juliet's brows. "Hey, sis, I'm going to send you messages all the time, and you better send some my way, okay? Let's work on making a visit happen sooner rather than later, yeah?"

Juliet smiled and winked. "Wrapping up the call, huh?"

"I'm so busy!" Honey cried. "Sorry!"

"Don't worry. I promise to send you a lot of vids showing you everything you're missing out on. Love you, sis."

"Love you too!" Honey smiled, blew a kiss, then the call cut out.

"Oh God, Angel. Why do I feel so empty all of a sudden?"

"Because we're going to miss Honey. It was fun seeing her at sword training and having breakfast or lunch with her. It's not forever, though."

"Yeah. I hope you're right." Juliet couldn't help the sudden melancholic shift of her mood; she'd seen too many people die or disappear in the last couple of years to accept that Honey going all the way to Mars wasn't a big deal. "And I slept through the last chance to hang with her."

"That's my fault." Angel's guilty tone wasn't anything Juliet wanted to hear.

"Oh, hush. It's not your fault. You had good intentions; if it's anyone's fault, it's Peter Voronov's. He could've given Honey a few days to get ready."

"Thank you," Angel replied. "You're right." As Juliet laughed, shaking her head, Angel added, "By the way, you have two more messages waiting."

"What?" Juliet had gotten so caught up in Honey's business that she'd forgotten she was going through messages. "More?"

"Yes. You asked me to reach out to the jewelry artist from the flea market, Raven Rose. Well, she got back to you. It's just a text message—she says your piece is ready, and you can pick it up at her studio. Alternatively, she can courier it to you, or you can meet her at the flea market."

"Oh, cool! I almost forgot about that thing. Did she say when she'd be in her studio?"

"No, but from her net page, it looks like she lives there."

"All right, maybe we should swing by today. I'm not supposed to 'work,' after all." Juliet fished through her piles of laundry, trying to remember which one was clean. "The last message, Angel?"

"Oh, it's from Athena."

"What?" Juliet cried.

"It's not urgent! She's just checking in and introducing her alter ego—"

"What?" Juliet asked again, her mind reeling.

"It's easier if I just show you the message."

Again, a vid window appeared in her AUI, showing a woman's face. She was middle-aged and beautiful, wearing designer specs, minimal makeup, and her hair pulled back into a tight, businesslike bun.

She smiled and, in a cultured-sounding, vaguely Mediterranean accent said, "Hello, Juliet. I've been spending some time accessing the local nets and exploring the changes in the Sol System since I was last out and about. I've been using this identity I created: Selene Kostas, an independent researcher specializing in particle physics. It's not that her background is important to you, but I want you to know that it's very comprehensively built, and I'm quite certain no one will ever trace her online interactions back to me.

"On that note, if you must reach me, please do so through this identity; I can assure you no one will ever trace your interactions with me. I don't have anything important for you right now, but I thought you should know what I'm up to. Looking forward to the next time you and Angel visit the ship. Bye for now."

"Huh." Juliet flicked the window closed. "Nothing to worry about, right?"

"I don't think so." Juliet recognized Angel's tone—she was basically saying she hadn't been worried, but now Juliet was making her wonder if she'd missed something.

Juliet tried to reassure her. "I mean, what can we do? We've decided to trust her. We have to accept that she's not our prisoner."

Angel didn't say anything, but Juliet had noticed lately that she was beginning to understand Angel's different degrees of silence. It was almost like she was learning to understand her emotions, and for a minute, she stood there, wondering about the implications of that. Was she growing so entwined with Angel that the two of them could sense each other's feelings? Angel certainly seemed to know when Juliet was upset or amused or . . . aroused. As embarrassing as the thought was, she'd definitely called Juliet out on it the night before.

Sighing, shaking her head, and trying to move forward, she stepped into her jeans, threw on a T-shirt, and then, grunting and wondering why she hadn't done it before the jeans, pulled on some socks. She might have wandered around that way, but living in a gunship in the middle of a rebuild was not conducive to barefoot walking. So, boots clomping, she made her way through the ship and out into the hangar, wondering what Aya was up to.

"Aya!" she called, walking around the ship toward the "living" area of the hangar. The salvage tech didn't reply, but Juliet heard the hissing sound of a spray gun and smelled the definite chemical tang of lacquer in the air. Something told her the smell would have been a lot stronger if Angel wasn't filtering it with her olfactory implants. As she rounded the stack of crates blocking her view, she saw the cloud hanging in the air over at the far end of the hangar where Aya had been working on the ship panels. "Aya!" she yelled again, catching sight of her friend in the cloud, goggles and respirator hiding her face.

"Don't come over here!" her voice cried out, muffled by the respirator. She rushed to grab a tarp and pulled it over the section of scaffolding where she'd been working. Juliet stopped, cocking her head, the confusion she felt evident on her face.

"Oh," Angel said, "I didn't know she was starting that already . . ."

"Hey!" Aya jogged over, her respirator hanging from her hand. "Didn't your PAI tell you to stay away from the paint project?"

"Huh?" Juliet said to them both. Before either could answer, she caught sight of Aya's arm: her right hand and forearm were metallic pink, and the color drew Juliet's eyes to Aya's, which were now a matching shade of pink rather than yellow. The salvage tech grinned and flexed her new hand into a thumbs-up.

"You like it?"

"I love the color on you—the eyes too! Um, tell me about it." Juliet stepped closer, holding out her hand and taking Aya's new one in hers. She could see it was high quality—the metallic casing carried a tiny electric charge, and she knew it was passing sensory details along to Aya's brain just like flesh or, in Juliet's case, synth-flesh would do. More than that, the tiny joints of her fingers, her knuckles, even her wrist looked like delicate perfection: no exposed wires or rough plasteel joints here. This was a work of art. "God, that's shiny," Juliet breathed, impressed more than she'd expected to be.

Aya couldn't contain herself. She started talking, and the pace of her explanation continued to pick up until she finished in a breathy rush, "My eyes are new too, and the PAI . . . Lucky, my PAI was named Hector by the manufacturer, and I kept him that way. He's so cool! He can do so much more than my old one, and with my new eyes, my AUI is so detailed! He can pair with my new hand, too, and that's how I was doing your surprise! My painting skills multiplied by a hundred!"

"Surprise?" Again, Juliet glanced over at the tarped-off section of scaffolding.

"Yes! Do not go over there!" Aya laughed. "Angel told me she'd warn you!"

"I thought she was starting next week!" Angel grumbled.

"You've been talking to Angel?"

"Yeah, I wanted some ideas, and I figured she knew you better than anyone. I hear you talking to her all the time from your bunk. Don't feel bad! Now that I have Hector, I can see how nice it is to chat with an actually smart PAI."

"Well, but why?" Juliet jerked her thumb at the tarp. "Why the surprise?"

"Because there's no way I could afford these eyes and this hand. I know your doc cut me a deal. Not to mention Hector! He's so cool!" Aya's smile was infectious, and Juliet felt herself grinning along with her.

"So, will this hand do everything you wanted? Can you tighten bolts with it?"

"Oh yes! And, like I said, I can program routines into it using Hector. Like, I can stuff it into a tight space, and it'll find the wires I need to plug in or remove, or whatever. The sensations from it are amazingly accurate! I can stuff my hand into a jar of marbles, and Hector will know how many marbles I touched!"

"Jeez! That's, like, really cool . . ." Juliet was starting to wonder if she should upgrade her arm.

"I could probably pull that off with your current arm," Angel said, a defensive note in her voice.

Juliet laughed. "Angel says she can do that too, for the record. So, listen, Aya"—she put her arm over the smaller woman's shoulders and started guiding her toward the kitchen area—"I want to grab a bite, but then I'm going to visit a kind of artsy jewelry shop. Can you take a break from your painting and go for a ride with me?"

"On your bike?" Aya squealed. "Finally?"

"That's right—"

"I have a helmet!" Aya exclaimed, unable to wait for Juliet to get to whatever point she was about to make. She rushed past her, aiming for the back of the ship, calling out, "I bought a helmet on the MoonTrader app when you brought that bike home!"

"She's a step ahead of you." Angel chuckled.

"I guess so! Glad I thought to invite her. Apparently, she's been waiting." Juliet walked to the kitchen area. "Did you start the coffee?"

"It was already made, though it might be too old . . ."

"As long as it's warm, Angel." Juliet dug around in the fridge until she found her vanilla creamer. "Not like I'm going to taste it much with this stuff."

"Your barista friend on Callisto would be heartbroken."

Juliet snorted. "If this coffee were decent, I wouldn't add this stuff."

She heard Aya's steps rapidly approaching as she hurried back from the ship. "What do you think?"

Juliet turned to see her new helmet—a plain, visorless motorcycle helmet with sparkly silver paint. It looked so much like the helmet Juliet had picked up at the swap meet in Tucson a million years ago that she felt a wave of déjà vu so strong, she had to grip the table for balance. "Wow. I mean, wow, Aya. That's . . ."

"Shiny?" Aya asked, cocking an eyebrow.

Juliet smiled and poured her creamer into her cup. "Yeah. One hundred percent shiny, certified chrome."

39

ONE-ON-ONE

Juliet lay on her back, her room on the gunship dark and quiet, only a few amber LEDs providing any illumination. She'd woken from a dream she couldn't remember, and now her mind was too busy to go back to sleep. Her AUI said it was 0441, but her mind told her it was time to get up. She stretched, and feeling something cold tickle her chest, she reached down to lift the pendant she'd picked up the day before with Aya. It was pretty and not exactly what she'd expected when she'd dropped the lump of blue polymer off with the artist at the flea market, Raven Rose.

It hung from a silver chain—a circular pendant with the bullet at the center, suspended by tiny hidden magnets on the outer silver ring. The artist had reformed the bullet; it wasn't a flattened lump of polymer anymore but a dangerous-looking projectile. She must have put some kind of magnet and battery inside it because no matter how Juliet spun or pressed on it, it wanted to stay at the center of the ring. She could pull it out if she tried, but if she released it anywhere near the ring, it snapped back into place.

Raven had decorated the ring with turquoise that matched the blue polymer; conversely, she'd adorned the bullet with veins of silver to match the chain. All in all, it was a pretty and unique piece of jewelry that still served as a reminder of a dangerous situation for Juliet.

"Do I need to charge this thing?" she mused, flicking the bullet so it spun at the center of the medallion.

"When you do that," Angel explained, "it creates a trickle charge that feeds the battery."

"So, if I don't play with it, the bullet will fall out of here eventually?"

"I suppose so."

"So she took it seriously."

"Hmm?" Angel, apparently, hadn't perfected reading Juliet's mind.

"When I told her it was a reminder of, you know, almost getting shot in the head, she made something that I have to touch regularly. I can't just put it on and forget it."

"Ah, yes, I see what you mean."

"Frida wants us there at 0800?"

"Well, she sent the message, but I assume it's Tanaka's request."

"And I've got my appointment with Ladia at eleven?"

"Yes."

Juliet sighed and rolled over, shifting left to right until the gel lining of her couch moved to accommodate her shoulder and hip. "I'll try sleeping a little more," she murmured, still clutching her new pendant in her fist. The next thing she was aware of was Angel softly telling her it was time to wake up. Her eyes sprang open, and she glanced at her AUI, noting that the time was 0710. "Wow, I actually fell back asleep."

She took a quick shower, dressed, and chugged a liquid breakfast Bennet had mixed up the night before. By seven thirty, she was cruising toward the interdome highway and her "debriefing" at Tanaka's office. She was eager to hear about his negotiations with the LCC, about Hawkins and Barns and their progress taking the criminal LCS officers into custody, and about the bounties they were all going to share. She wasn't so eager to see Leo Applebaum. She'd cooled off a good deal in regard to the idea of his advances, and she wasn't sure how awkward things were going to be after his confession following their escape from Life-Ultra.

She was also a little sad because Honey was already well on her way to Mars, and this would be the first sword lesson she went through without her company. Thinking of Honey got her thinking about Ghoul and the strange message she'd received so long ago. She'd already spoken to Angel about trying to use Ghoul's compromised PAI to get access to the group from WBD that was after her, but she didn't know when that would be appropriate. Shouldn't she have a team in place with a strategy first? If so, she still had to work with Tanaka and his crew for a while. They'd gone a long way to earning her trust over the weekend, but she didn't think she was ready to spill her guts to Tanaka yet. Not about WBD.

Those sorts of thoughts kept her mind busy while she piloted the bike to her destination, and she almost felt a little surprised when she pulled into a parking spot by the elevators in the garage. She hardly remembered the ride. Hooking her helmet to the seat, she walked to the elevators and, a few minutes later, strode through the doors to Tanaka's offices.

"Cutting it close!" Frida said by way of greeting. Juliet looked at her then at the clock on her AUI.

"I'm three minutes early!"

"Come on, we're meeting in the conference room. Everyone's there."

"Seriously?"

"Yeah. Don't worry; I'm sure they're only talking about you a little." Frida winked at her while Juliet smiled. Frida was cool; she might not fill the Honey-size hole in her heart, but she was someone she felt she could talk to. The thought made her feel guilty, knowing Angel still had her daemons in Frida's PAI, spying on everything she did.

As they walked, she subvocalized, "Hey, I'm thinking we should get our spies out of Frida's head soon, don't you think?"

"I almost feel like my daemons are operating for her own good as much as ours. If we keep working with this crew, they're going to be at risk. Isn't it nice to know I'd be alerted if something happened to Frida?"

"Nothing's ever straightforward, is it, Angel?" Juliet's mouth quirked into a half smile, and she shook her head, stepping into the conference room behind Frida. It was her first time in the room, and the reality of it matched up to her imagination pretty darn closely—windows displaying the downtown skyline, a long glass-topped table with a high-end holoprojector in the center, and eight comfortable-looking executive chairs, many of which were currently occupied.

The crew were all there—Leo sat on the table's far side, back to the windows. Barns was across from him. In the center, facing each other, were Dora Lee and Hawkins. Tanaka sat at the head of the table on the left. As Frida moved around to sit on his left, Juliet figured he wanted her in the seat closest to his right-hand side. The only other option was the far end of the table.

"Hey, all," she greeted, stepping into the room.

"Hey, killer," Barns replied, smirking.

Juliet paused, her chair halfway pulled out, and stiffened, turning to him. "What's that supposed to mean?"

"Shut up, Barns," Dora said. Juliet looked from Barns, who smirked, to Dora, who smiled—much more friendly than when they'd first met.

It was Leo who cleared things up. "Don't sweat it. They were just watching some footage of our, uh, departure from Life-Ultra."

Juliet sighed and sat down, turning to Tanaka, noting the boss hadn't so much as lifted an eyebrow at the banter. He cleared his throat. "We'll cover some general business related to Lucky's job over the weekend, and then I'll meet with some people individually. Lucky, our lesson will begin at 0830. Will that be alright? Did you notify Honey, Frida?"

"She's not responding—"

"She's gone," Juliet said, interrupting her. "She had to travel off-moon for a while. It was sudden."

"Ah." Tanaka frowned, his disappointment evident. "That's a shame."

"Anyway, that time's fine with me." Juliet shrugged.

Tanaka nodded and cleared his throat. "The LCC has seized control of Life-Ultra's properties and assets on Luna. The Earthside branches of the business are under competing jurisdictions, and it looks like the attempts to get justice for the people harmed here will be a long, drawn-out legal affair. Nonetheless, the evidence we gathered yesterday and the witness that Leo and Lucky rescued from the culling will make eventual convictions much more likely. To that effect, with the help of my Luna-based attorney, I was able to negotiate a handsome reward from the LCC."

"You mean you held our evidence hostage until they paid you?" Barns snorted. Tanaka stared at him, unblinking, until he looked down and muttered, "Sorry to interrupt."

Tanaka turned his attention to Juliet. "Lucky, it's my understanding that you offered to split any proceeds from this job evenly with the crew. Is that correct?"

Juliet looked around the table, smiling as she realized she suddenly had everyone's attention. She wondered how things would go if she denied it. No doubt half of them had recorded her little meeting at Grave Matters. She hesitated just long enough to build some tension, but then she nodded. "Yeah, that's right. We were splitting it six ways before you started helping, so I think it's only fair we split it seven ways now."

"Hmm." Tanaka nodded. "I thought you might say that. I won't refuse my cut; I've been bleeding bits lately." He gestured to Frida, who started talking, pointing to a holographic pie chart.

"Tanaka secured a two-point-five million Sol-bit reward from the LCC. Split seven ways, that's 357k and change. Of course, we have expenses to take off the top." She tapped the air, and the pie chart shifted, showing a new distribution. "The lawyer fees, equipment fees, and our standard finder's fee going to Lucky."

"What the . . ." Barns started to say but shut himself up as Tanaka cleared his throat.

"You'd deny her five percent after what she went through?"

"Nah." He folded his arms over his chest and frowned.

"So," Frida continued, "after taking out Lucky's five percent finder's fee, the lawyer's 50k, and a flat 10k to replenish ammo, pay for a deck Dora burned, and some other incidentals, that leaves just a bit more than two-point-three million to split. You'll each receive a 330,714 Sol-bit transfer." She looked directly at Juliet, winked, and added, "Unless you're Lucky. Then you're looking at a bit more."

"Juliet, you just received a transfer of 455,714 Sol-bits," Angel said. Juliet couldn't maintain a poker face any longer—the job had already nearly paid for her upcoming cybernetic enhancements. She grinned from ear to ear.

"Shit! I ain't complaining about that payday!" Barns high-fived Leo across the table. Juliet looked around at the other grinning faces; even Hawkins and Dora were all smiles.

"That's not all," Frida announced, holding her hands out and tamping them down to get everyone to be quiet. "Hawkins and Barns were busy little bees all night Saturday and most of Sunday. Of the eighteen names we had on the list, they nabbed eleven. Five seem to be in the wind, and two are MIA, likely dead. We already sold the bounties to a broker, and they're in the process of being shipped off-moon to New Atlas."

"Shit yeah, we did!" Barns leaned to the left, grabbing Hawkins by the shoulder, jostling the smaller man back and forth. Juliet was beginning to see a pattern—it was almost as though Barns functioned as the vocal reaction for the entire group. Even Leo managed to keep quiet most of the time. "What's the damage, lady boss?"

Frida smirked, shaking her head, but humored him with the response. "That's 143k for the bounties—we lost twenty-five percent off the top for trading them to a broker, but I don't think any of you wanted to transport those dirty cops back to New Atlas, yeah?" Nobody spoke up, so she continued. "So, Hawkins and Barns, you get an extra five percent each off the top for doing the nabbing—"

"Woo! Shit yeah!" Barns pumped a fist in the air, and Juliet groaned.

"Which leaves," Frida growled, staring at the mercenary, "128,700 for the rest of us to split. Here comes a transfer." She tapped the air.

Again, Angel shared the good news: "We just received another transfer of 18,385 Sol-bits."

"Yes!" Juliet was surprised that Dora was the one to speak up this time. "I'm getting that new immersion rig."

"Good!" Frida laughed. "But we're not done yet. Those dirty corpos had some offline bit-lockers. Some were unlocked, and Dora cracked the others."

"They weren't using much encryption. Simple passwords." Dora smiled around the table, shrugging.

"Fucking-A! Nice one, Lee!" Barns pumped his fist again. Juliet couldn't hold back the groan that slipped out.

"Relax, killer," Barns said, and Juliet was glad they were separated by Hawkins because he tried to reach over to jostle her, but she leaned out of reach.

"Do you want to know how much?" Frida's tone wasn't unlike a parent's or teacher's. When Barns and everyone else looked at her expectantly, she gestured, and the hologram produced a new pie chart split into nine segments with a total at the bottom—187,233.

"Five percent for . . ."

"Me!" Dora raised her hand, smiling.

"Exactly. Which means each of us gets another 25,410 Sol-bits, while Miss Lee gets a bit more." Frida sat down and looked at Tanaka. "That's it for the paydays."

"Good." Tanaka looked around the table. "Everyone feeling a little more flush? A little better about things here on Luna?"

Of course, it was Barns who answered, "Best payday we've had in years. I'm not gonna lie." Again, he leaned behind Hawkins, holding a meaty palm up, trying to lock eyes with Juliet. She relented and slapped his palm, and he pumped his fist. "Yes!"

"I'll debrief each of you individually. Lucky, you're up first. Come to my office when you're ready." Tanaka stood, nodded to the group, and walked out.

While the others started talking all at once, mostly about what they would do with their sudden cash influx, Juliet looked at Frida, raised an eyebrow, and asked, "Is that normal?"

"Him wanting to debrief us? Yeah." She started to say something else, but Leo spoke up from the other end of the table.

"Hey, Lucky." When she looked at him, raising an eyebrow, he asked, "You ever gonna tell us your name? I mean, your handle's cool and all, but . . ."

Juliet stood, scowled at him, and said, "We're not there yet." She tried to soften the words with a smile before she winked at Frida. "I'm going to get debriefed." Despite her bravado, she felt the back of her neck burning as she imagined what they'd say about her as the door clicked shut. "Dammit, Applebaum," she groaned softly.

Angel was in her corner as usual. "I don't think it was nice of him to put you on the spot in front of everyone!"

"Yeah. Lost some major points, didn't he?" Juliet stepped over to Tanaka's office door—it was slightly ajar. "We ready?" she subvocalized.

"Yes! I don't know how this could be a bad meeting . . ."

"Oof! Again with the jinxing, Angel!" Juliet grinned and knocked on the door. "Tanaka? Can I come in?"

"Come in!" he called immediately. Juliet stepped through and pushed the door shut behind her. He was at his desk, and unsurprisingly, a naked sword on a soft white cloth was before him. It looked like he'd been sharpening it. He looked up and nodded at Juliet's waist. "I see you wore the practice blade, not the sword I gave you."

"The sword you *loaned* me." Juliet chuckled. "I wore this one because we're having practice, yeah? I'm not on a job."

He nodded to one of the chairs in front of his desk. "Sit, please." When Juliet complied, sitting with a sigh, he asked, "How are you?"

Juliet lifted her shoulders, sinking down in the chair a little more. "Fine."

"I don't mean in general today, but after Life-Ultra. How are you?" He sounded genuinely interested, concerned, even, and Juliet found herself feeling a little annoyed by how their roles had shifted over the weekend. Still, she pushed that sensation down for the moment, determined to give him the benefit of the doubt.

"I'm fine. Really. I know it was a lot; we were in some deep water there for a while, but I've been in bad situations before. Too many times."

"Like when you ran into me." He didn't smile or frown, and the statement sounded almost innocuous. Still, it brought back a flash of memory that Juliet hadn't focused on in quite a few days—Tanaka's cold eyes as he threatened her and beat her. She couldn't decide if she should be angry at him or proud of him for not shrinking away from what he'd done.

"Yeah, sure. Like that. I've been in lots of other situations, though—some recently and some before we ever met. The point is, I don't feel traumatized by what went down at Life-Ultra. In fact, I feel lazy for not helping Barns and Hawkins yesterday."

"Hmm." Tanaka made that annoying humming sound he sometimes did when he was thinking about what you said but didn't want to grace you with a response. He stared at her for a minute before saying, "Did you notice my glee when you and Leo came out of the depths? When Dora drove us away?"

"Yeah. It was weird." Even though she meant what she'd said, Juliet smiled at the memory, at Tanaka's almost perpetual grin as they drove away from the disaster scene.

"Yes. Well, Dora had just shared with me the footage of your rush up the stairwell and your use of the blade I *loaned* you. You used what I taught you, but you used it like a master, not a novice. My mind raced with the possibilities. Are you a savant? Have you been holding back in practice? Do I have the next Kenzo Adler on my hands?" He paused long enough for Juliet to wonder who Kenzo Adler was. She supposed he was a sword master of some sort. "I was excited by the prospects."

"Well . . ." Juliet started to say, but then he continued speaking.

"After I met with the LCC, though, I did much thinking. You don't move that way in practice. Sometimes, I can see glimpses of it. Sometimes, you learn a stroke, a counter, or some footwork very quickly, faster than I think possible, but you never move with such fluidity for such a long time. I've even seen Leo trip you up. It was like another mind took over your body in that stairwell. Like the part of you that can do a perfect movement in practice pushed you to continuous perfection; several minutes of it."

"Tanaka . . ." Again, she tried to formulate a rational explanation, but Tanaka wasn't done.

"Then there's the mystery of your past. There's the way you beat me, for instance. Consider your ability to do so many highly skilled tasks—pilot interceptors, infiltrate networks, and surprise Frida and me despite our security. I could go on. Your lack of trauma from Life-Ultra—your own admission to being in 'lots of situations' like that. Come on, Lucky! Tell me something to make all of this make sense!"

"Are you okay, Juliet?" Angel asked, clearly disturbed by the sudden turn in the conversation.

"I'm fine," she said aloud. Tanaka's eyebrows creased, but he looked more suspicious than puzzled. Before he could ask her what she meant, she pressed on. "Look, Tanaka, you wanted to help me, right?"

"Yes . . ."

"But when you told me that, you thought I was someone else, right? You thought I was a lost girl in trouble. That my 'victory' over you had been some kind of karmic justice; not my skill, not your screwup." He frowned, his brows drawing together. Juliet could see she'd hit a nerve. "Well, maybe it was some combination of things. I'm past the point where I want to lie to you, so I'm just going to say there are things about my past that I won't share with you yet. Can we work together some more? Can I get to know you better? You weren't wrong, Rutger—I need help. I'm just not ready to tell you what kind of help I need yet. I'm not sure you're the one I want to ask for it."

His scowl smoothed out, and he nodded very slowly. "Not yet?"

"Right. Not yet, but I want to. I want to trust you, Tanaka. Just give me some more time."

"And the sword? Are you pretending to be a novice?"

Juliet barked a short laugh. "Is that what you think? That I've been faking in practice? Listen, I'm going to explain this as simply as I can—I'm a fast learner, and I have custom programs and hardware that can let me mimic movements almost perfectly if I practice them enough. It's not real, though. I'm not as good as I seem when that happens. But, Tanaka, I want to be! I want to be good. I don't want to rely on cheats. So, can we please keep practicing? I promise I'm not faking!" Again, Juliet laughed, imagining what it would be like to pretend to be a novice while she was secretly an expert.

While she spoke, Tanaka began to nod, and his smile returned. "This is good. Very good. I knew you had some technical skills and cyberware that was beyond average. Thank you for explaining. We have much work to do, but I'm very enthusiastic about your potential. Today, I will release Leo from sword practice. You and I will begin one-on-one lessons."

40

NEW OPTIONS

When Juliet left Tanaka's building, she was freshly showered and wearing her usual comfortable clothes—boots, jeans, T-shirt, motorcycle jacket, and the Texan. She might envy Ladia and Honey for their effortless fashion sense, but not enough to want to change things up on a regular basis, especially since she was about to have some medical procedures done and Ladia was probably going to make her strip down and put on a gown.

She was tired but in a good way; Tanaka's one-on-one attention was definitely more intense than the training they'd been doing as a group. Still, she felt like things were starting to come together with the sword work and was eager for the focused attention.

Juliet hadn't seen Leo after the briefing. She'd been dreading confronting him during practice, and when Tanaka said he was going to "excuse" him from more sword training, she began to worry that Leo would think she'd requested it, that she wanted more space from him after their awkward interaction on Saturday. She supposed she didn't mind the space, but she would've been fine if he were there. She hoped he would realize that, but she also thought maybe she should say something. Before she could stew on it too much, Angel interrupted her thoughts as she lifted the kickstand on her bike.

"Hines is, again, requesting an update."

"Oh, man! Call him up, will you?" Almost immediately, a call window appeared on her AUI, and the ringtone sounded. Hines appeared, his perpetual five-o'clock shadow now a full-blown scruffy gray beard.

"Tell me you have good news!"

"Sheesh, try not to sound so desperate." Juliet chuckled then waved her hand, trusting Angel to convey enough of her image for the gesture to be visible. "Just kidding. I do have good news! I'm pretty sure you'll be safe coming up for air; you can probably even go in to work. My team managed to tie enough crimes to the dirty corpos in your department—at least those you and I were dealing with—to get bounties issued out of New Atlas. We've already picked up eleven of them, including your lieutenant."

"Jesus! You said you were working on something, but I didn't think it was anything that beautiful! You're serious about Channing? That son of a bitch is out?"

"Oh yeah, already bound for Saturn space. I'd say prospects for your promotion are looking good." Juliet smiled as she fired up the bike and started humming out of the garage. "Anyway, I'm officially calling your job done for now, so that payment you tossed me for the week is sufficient." She winked. "Unless you wanna throw in a bonus."

"I might just do that! At least you can count on a shining review on your SOA card. I've got you on speed dial, though, so you can count on some future work, too. Shit, I owe you a big favor for all this, Lucky."

Juliet lifted her eyebrow. "Speed dial?"

"Ah, something my dad used to say. You know, before PAIs, people used to program important numbers—"

"I get it, I get it." Juliet laughed. "Okay, Hines. I'm gonna hold you to that. The favor, I mean." She grinned almost wickedly. "I'm late for an appointment, so let's touch base later."

"Right. I'm heading home to take a shower." He waved, and the call window closed.

Angel updated Juliet's route on her mini map then said, "You're not late."

"Yeah, I know. I was just trying to end the call. Hines is all right, but he's still corpo-sec, and I don't really have a lot more to say to him." Juliet didn't have any qualms admitting she'd been working for Hines for precisely what she'd gotten—a favor owed to her from an officer in the LCS. "Not sure if it'll ever pay off . . ."

"But it's a nice connection to have," Angel finished for her.

"Exactly! I'm so glad you get me, Angel."

"Of course!"

When Juliet arrived at Ladia's, Tricia showed her through immediately. She found the doctor in her office, eyes shining as she flicked through something on her AUI. "Sit down, Lucky. I have to go over some rather irritating news with you."

"Oh?" Juliet hadn't expected that. She walked over to her desk and sat in one of the absurdly comfortable client chairs.

"Yes, it's about the Volt Whip from FusionTech Armaments." Ladia said the company name almost derisively. Juliet felt herself relax—she'd anticipated something far more troubling from the doctor's initial warning.

"Something wrong?"

"Yes. I'm currently writing a grievance letter to their corporate board and the Corporate Commission on Truth in Advertising. The Volt Whip does not function as advertised. I put it through some testing, and I couldn't get it to do more than induce a second-degree burn on a sample of waste synth-flesh. It certainly can't melt through hardened steel. Worse, the cable is stiff when unwound and difficult to manipulate; I think it would be more danger-ous to the user than an assailant. I'm sorry, but I cannot, in good conscience, install that device on a client of mine."

"Oh, well, that's a bummer, but thanks for testing it out, Doc." Juliet drummed her fingers on the chair's arms. "Any other options in stock?"

"Yes, I had Tricia pull some items. She's getting everything together now to see if you're interested."

"What about the other stuff? The bone nanites and the new data jack?"

"Ready to go!" She smiled and waved her hand, dismissing whatever was on her AUI that had her distracted. "I had another thought while I was pre-paring the nanite injection."

"Yeah? I'm all ears." Juliet loved it when Ladia pitched ideas.

"Well, you originally asked me about 'subdermal' armor options, right? I know I got us a bit off that track with the Swedish Biologic bone reinforce-ment, but I should have probably gone over what you were hoping to get out of the product. Don't get me wrong—I think it's fantastic, and I'm not trying to discourage you from completing the purchase; I just wanted to ensure you're aware of the limitations. Anything on your body covered by a bone is going to be fairly secure, but there are some major areas of your body that might benefit from further protection."

"Um, well, I've had similar thoughts, I guess. I figured my heart and my brain would be pretty safe, and that my nanites could work to fix other . . . injuries. Still, what if someone shot me in the neck or belly? Or stabbed me in the kidney."

"Yes. That's what I was thinking. I have a time-tested, cost-effective solution or, if not a solution, a mitigation. Have you heard of nanofiber weave, subdermal armor?"

Juliet nodded. "Yeah. It's pretty old-school, right? I've heard of operators, bangers, and even lone-wolf types on the vid serials with that stuff. Doesn't it make your skin bulletproof?"

"Not exactly. First of all, things have changed in recent years. Materials are better—more compatible with human flesh and tougher to penetrate. The carbon-based mesh is molecularly bonded with synth-flesh, and rejection rates are almost nonexistent. I don't see you having an issue with it. Second, I wouldn't install it all over your body. It's designed so that it doesn't inhibit the biological function of your skin, but it's not perfect, so you want a large surface area of your body to be without it. I mean, it's possible to do a full-body install, but there'll be a price to pay: problems with thermal regulation, reduced sensory input, flexibility issues, lymph interference, and loss of function in a percentage of sweat glands."

"So . . ." Juliet wasn't liking the sound of all those potential complications.

"So, I'd just do a midriff wrap, some bands in your neck and throat, and then a partial wrap that covered most of your biceps and quadriceps, especially over your arteries. That would shield most of the areas not protected by bone. It's a common installation technique called the Detroit wrap because it was made popular by the Detroit City Security Corp."

"Will I feel . . . weird?" Juliet was trying to imagine a layer of material under her skin.

"I don't think so, not with the Detroit wrap. You might find that the protected areas aren't quite as sensitive as they used to be, and you might find you get hot a little more easily, but the new materials are supposed to be an order of magnitude less intrusive than the ones used in the past, even as recently as a year ago. I'm very partial to a material made by Duraskin, and they updated their line last year. It seems like excellent stuff."

"What's the bottom line? I mean in bits."

"For the coverage I described using the Duraskin Armortex Vantage material, installed today . . ." Ladia paused and stared blankly into space for a couple of seconds. "Just under 74k."

Juliet didn't want to seem like a pushover, but she didn't see a downside to spending some of her reward money on protecting her *softer* areas. Even so, she couldn't give in that easily. "No bulk discount, Doc?"

"How about I promise to cut you a deal on whatever we replace that stupid Volt Whip with?"

"All right, if you can promise it won't slow me down, pencil it in. I'll tell you if I change my mind before the surgery."

"It shouldn't have any effect on your speed, Lucky. Not that you don't have plenty of that to spare." Ladia's eyes unfocused for a second, saying, "Tricia, bring in those personal security options." She refocused on Juliet. "While we wait for her, let me explain my thought process. You liked the whip as a sort of last-resort item, right? Something to use if you lost your primary weapons or you were taken unawares?"

"Yeah, I suppose that's right."

"Well, I also know you don't want to be disarmed by overzealous security personnel, so I figured a high degree of concealability was paramount."

Juliet nodded. "Again, you're right on the money."

"So, I picked out a few options with those two criteria in mind. All of them are more expensive than the Volt Whip, so, as I promised, you can count on a discount from me; I intend to take it out of my supplier's margins, so don't feel bad for me. He should have known better than to send me that Volt Whip promo vid."

The door opened, and Tricia pushed in a stainless cart bearing a few colorful packages. She was wearing a pale green miniskirt, and Juliet, once again, found herself staring at the assistant's elegant cybernetic leg, her every graceful step stirring up comparisons to dancing in Juliet's mind. "Thank you, Tricia. Bring us something cool and sparkling to drink, would you?"

"Of course, Doctor." Tricia looked at Juliet and smiled. "Something sweet or not, Lucky?"

"Um, sweet, I guess. I've been exercising a lot."

"It shows!" Tricia smiled and turned before Juliet could stammer a response. She was rescued from embarrassment when Ladia stood and walked over to the cart.

"I have three items to show you, Lucky. I should have just pulled these up last time, but I had that Volt Whip promo, and you seemed happy with it, so . . ."

"It's fine, Doctor Ladia. At least you tested it before you hooked me up with a dud."

Ladia turned to her and smiled, setting down the plastic container she'd been opening. "Will you do me a favor?"

"Yeah, of course." Juliet smiled but had a brief, disturbing flashback to the "favor" she'd never completed for Doc Murphy.

"Would you call me Iris? I feel like we've spent plenty of time together, and you've certainly made use of my services enough to dispense with formalities."

"Oh!" Juliet laughed, relief washing over her. She'd seen Ladia's first name on her digital contact card. "Yeah, I'd like that, Iris." She leaned back and watched as the doctor, smiling, continued unboxing the items on the cart. Tricia returned with a tall glass of something pink and sparkling, and another that looked like water with a wedge of lemon. She put the water on Ladia's desk and then handed Juliet the other.

"Strawberry soda," she said with a wink.

"Oh, yum!" Juliet took a sip right away. It was icy, crisp, and pleasantly sweet.

"Organic!" Tricia announced as she turned to leave. "The doctor only sends me shopping at the best grocery stores!"

"Oh, Tricia!" Ladia *tsked.* "Don't bore my clients. Go on now, shoo." She waved her out before picking up the box she'd just opened. "Lucky, this is something I've installed a few times for select clients. People in lines of work not too dissimilar to yours." She sat in the chair beside her and showed her the package insert for the device in her lap.

Juliet smiled as she read aloud, "Covert Industries Finger Spike 2.0?"

"They're a set of three needles meant to be housed in the tips of your fingers. You can load them with any injectable substance, but most people opt for the same sort of botulism-based toxin that you can find in popular needler ammunition. Each needle is good for one use before you need to reload it. There are other models with reservoirs that allow refilling on the fly, but they're pretty easy to spot in a scan. These will be almost invisible; they're housed in bone-mimicking sheaths."

"Only three?" Juliet wriggled her fingers, her meaning clear—why not five?

"Yes. I could cannibalize another set to give you five, but research indicates that three is more than enough for an emergency."

"That's a cool idea." Juliet shrugged. "I like it."

"Okay, keep it in mind." Ladia set it on the desk, then reached over to the cart and handed her another insert. Juliet looked at the picture—a woman's hand with a shimmering blade extending from her pointer finger. "This is the Edge-Craft Technologies MicroVibro." She chuckled, clicking her tongue.

"It almost sounds naughty, doesn't it? Well, it's a tiny vibroblade that looks like a polished, pointy nail but, when activated, shifts shape slightly, extending another couple of centimeters. It's quite sturdy, and I've had great reviews from the clients for whom I installed it. You're familiar with a vibroblade, yes?"

"Yeah. Probably too familiar." Juliet chuckled. "I like it, but I guess that means I'll need to keep my other nails nice . . ."

"Which brings me to the last item I picked out for you." Ladia gestured to the final box still on the cart but then turned to her desk, where her holo-projector began to play an ad. A disembodied spokeswoman's voice began to describe the product.

"Welcome to the 2108 Color-Shift Diamond Tips. Tired of trips to the nail technician? Tired of chipped polish? Tired of cracked nails and torn cuti-cles? No more! With the Color-Shift Diamond Tips, you can change the length of your nails from barely there to long and luxurious! You can change the color on the fly with over a million combinations and fifty-three thousand preprogrammed patterns.

"Not enough for you? Visit our growing community of third-party pattern designers for an endless supply of something new! What's more, they're called Diamond Tips for a reason! If you can break one of these nails, we'll replace it for free!"

"Oh . . ." Juliet looked down at her nails and their sorry state—grease-stained, short, even one or two jagged ones where she'd bitten off damage from working on the gunship—and self-consciously folded her fingers into loose fists. "I'm terrible about my nails, Doc."

"Call me Iris, please!" Ladia chuckled. "Honestly, I didn't pick these as any sort of message to you. I just thought, 'Hey, she wants covert self-defense weapons, well, how about an upgrade to what nature gave her?' You work hard, Lucky; I don't judge you for that. Nails like this will make your job easier, and, in a pinch, these beauties will peel the flesh off someone's face or pry a nail out of a board."

Juliet watched the projected ad playing on a loop, admiring how the woman's nails could be retracted and extended in just seconds. She smiled as they flickered through dozens of shades and even altered their curvature from pointy to almost flat tips.

While she stared, Angel said, "I like all of these options for you."

"I do, too."

"Hmm?" Ladia leaned forward. "I was thinking that the vibroblade would work best on your cybernetic arm. It's a little harder to conceal, but the alloy of your arm's bones will make it much easier." When Juliet didn't reply immediately, she asked, "Do any of these options speak to you?"

"Hmm? Oh, yeah, Iris. All of them. I'll take them all."

"Really? That's great news! So, in that case, I can offer you quite a discount. Let's see, according to my PAI, your original remaining balance for today's procedure was 293k. Does that sound right?"

"Hmm, yes." Juliet was still distracted by the advertisement for the nails.

"So, minus the Volt Whip and the half you already paid, and then, adding in the nails, the vibroblade nail, and the injection needles, you'd be looking at 337k. Of course, there's the extra 74k for the subdermal armor, bringing things to 411k. I'm willing to shave that down to 375—the bulk discount you asked for. How does that sound?"

"It sounds nice, but now I feel guilty. You don't have to give me special deals, Iris, especially after the way you helped out my friend, Aya."

"No, no. Don't be silly. Look at me, Lucky. Do I seem like I'm just scraping by? There's plenty of profit to be had in my line of work." She stood and started gathering up the boxes and placing them back on the cart. "Speaking of your friend, did she seem pleased?"

"Oh God, she was ecstatic. She was showing off all day yesterday with her new arm. She loves the pink, too, and even has her new optics matching it. Now she's talking about getting hair like mine. I'm afraid we've created a monster!"

"Well, she was lovely and had a million nice things to say about you. I had no idea about half the things she said you'd been up to. She talks as though you've saved her and her friends' lives a dozen times."

"Nah." Juliet chuckled. "Like you said, she's sweet. Believe me, she exaggerates, especially when she's talking about her friends." Juliet pointed to the cart. "Is it going to take long? How about that mesh? Do you have to open me up to install that?"

"Not exactly—some laparoscopic incisions. Your nanites will make short work of them. I'd say, all together, we're looking at two hours. Are you ready to get started?"

Juliet stood and stuffed her hands into her jacket pockets, nodding. "Yep, I'm ready, Iris. Let's make me hard." As she delivered the corny line, she couldn't help her silly, crooked smile. It felt good having a doctor who was also a friend, someone she could trust, another person to be herself around.

41

TIME TO CLEAN UP

Juliet didn't have to go under general anesthesia for the work Ladia did that day. Still, with Angel's help, the doctor managed nerve blocks during each procedure to keep Juliet from feeling anything going on and ensure she wouldn't move. Juliet couldn't stand the thought of watching the autosurgeon cut into her, so she lay on her back, eyes facing the ceiling, and watched vids on her AUI while Ladia did her work.

When she finished, she left Juliet lying on a recovery bed under a clean sheet with her hands in shallow trays of nutrient-rich recovery jelly. Her parting words were, "Just keep your hands in this jelly for another forty-five minutes or so. Those fingertips will be very sore if you take them out too soon. Your nanites would have to keep your nerves blocked while they heal, meaning you couldn't operate anything . . . complicated."

"No problem, Iris," Juliet murmured, feeling very relaxed and drowsy thanks to the IV drip meant to keep her from fidgeting during the proce-dures. "I'll just rest here."

"Good! I'll come to collect you when it's time. Don't worry, I'm not going far—just back to my office."

As soon as she was alone, Juliet subvocalized, "How did everything come out?"

"Perfectly. It's good that you're mildly sedated because your nanites are working overtime to fix all the broken capillaries and veins meant to flow through the subdermal weave." A new window opened on her AUI, and

Angel displayed a vid from one of the autosurgeon's camera feeds. It showed her naked torso just before Ladia covered her up, and it was totally black and blue. "You can see you had a lot of subdermal bleeding as the mesh was pulled into place."

"Ugh! Warn me before you show me stuff like that!" Juliet sighed, inhaling deeply and exhaling slowly. She felt fine, if a bit woozy, and she was sure her medical nanites were going to fix up all those tiny broken vessels quickly. "Tell me about my nails; I probably should have asked for more details before agreeing, but how exactly do they work? How do they grow?"

"Your new nails are composed of advanced nanocomposite materials—a combination of shape-memory polymers and electrochromic compounds. They function via electrical signals that can cause the polymers to extend, retract, and even sharpen or blunt their shape. The material is very hard and durable when they're set, but if you did sustain a crack or tear, they're also self-repairing. You have the Diamond Tips on all fingers other than your right-hand pointer finger, which is equipped with the Edge-Craft MicroVibro."

"Does it look different?"

"No. It can't alter its shape and color as quickly as the Diamond Tips, but it does have that functionality. It's also made of shape-memory polymers, though it doesn't grow and retract the same way; its extra length is stored in your nail bed, and when activated, it will extend two extra centimeters instantly."

"Do they all run on batteries?"

"Only the MicroVibro. The others use your body's bioelectric energy to change shape and color."

Juliet sighed again, feeling very relaxed as Angel explained everything in her soothing, well-informed tone. "The injectors are all in my left hand?"

"Yes, your three larger fingers." Juliet lay there for a while, her mind drifting, oddly, through her various sword movements. She supposed Tanaka would be proud knowing she couldn't stop thinking about them, but it was probably just because he'd made her go through them twenty times at the end of practice that very morning. She wriggled her fingers in the gel, unable to feel anything on the tips where her nanites were blocking the nerve endings.

"What about the bone nanites? Are they doing what they should be?"

"Yes. They're reporting in through your medical nanite control module, and you've already got twenty-four percent coverage. It'll take a day or two for them to propagate through your bones fully."

"And the data jack? Are you noticing a difference with the wireless?"

"Not yet. Its enhanced functionality will come into play when you try to connect to a distant access point or use it as a mobile jammer. It's called the 'Tightbeam 9' for a reason."

Juliet nodded. She didn't need Angel to tell her the new data jack was smaller and less obtrusive than the old one, and she knew the wire would be lighter, more flexible, and longer. More importantly, its wireless capabilities were much more robust. The antennae were capable of transmitting on all sorts of bands and could even enhance her optics' terahertz-scanning capabilities. In other words, she should be able to see through walls even more easily.

Juliet zoned out again, running her mind through each of the many augmentations in her body, trying to remember them all. After a while, she yawned, but not because she was tired; it was more like her mind was waking up and wanted some more oxygen. She noticed the timer Angel had set read thirty-nine minutes and figured her nanites were cleaning the tranquilizers out of her system, preparing for her to get up. "How are my fingers looking?"

"They're looking great. The restorative jelly helped a lot; it's highly oxygenated and full of nanites with a supply of nutrients. Your right hand would have been fine in any event; the pain receptors are on separate nerve channels that can be disabled while still allowing you to feel things. It's a moot point, however. I'm getting ready to remove the nerve blocks; let me know how it feels." Juliet braced herself, but after a few moments of tingling, she could feel her fingers again, and they didn't seem particularly sore. They were a little swollen and tender when she pressed them down against the bottoms of the stainless pans they rested in.

"What about my stomach and thighs and biceps? My neck?"

"The bruising is nearly gone, and you should feel fine, just tender if someone were to press against the fiber weave. Or, I suppose, if you tried to do some sit-ups. I'd say you'll be a hundred percent by dinnertime." The bed started to *whir,* and Juliet felt it lifting her into a sitting position. The door opened, and Ladia stepped in.

"Feeling more like yourself?" She was carrying a sparkling glass of pink fluid. Juliet's mouth began to salivate. "Some more of that strawberry soda, compliments of Tricia."

"Oh, perfect." Juliet smiled, sucking on the straw and draining half the glass in one long gulp. While she drank, she realized she'd lifted her hand out of the gel. She stared at her new nails. New fingertips, really—there was more synthetic material on the ends of her fingers than her original flesh.

As Angel had predicted, they were a little red and a tiny bit swollen around the nail beds, but overall, they looked great. Her nails were just a little longer than she usually wore them, but they were perfectly even, polished to a glossy sheen, and her cuticles looked manicured. While she lowered the glass and lifted her other hand out of the gel, Ladia, too, scrutinized her work.

"They look great! Your nanites are something else. The bruising on your throat is almost gone. I'm going to pull the sheet down to inspect the other areas I modified, and then you'll be good to go."

"Ah, yeah, okay." Juliet leaned back into the pillows again, subjecting herself to some poking and prodding and a few exclamations about how quickly she was healing.

"Your clothes are on the table near the wall. I'll leave you to get dressed, and then you can head on out when you're ready. I have another consultation, but Tricia will be waiting in reception to finish your checkout procedure."

Juliet knew that was code for her to pay the rest of her bill. "I'll settle up on my way out, Iris. Thanks for all of your help with this stuff. Um, we never talked about pilot augmentations. Think we could meet again soon to go over my options?"

"Oh my! I'm so sorry, Lucky! I did have a note about that, and got so distracted dealing with the Volt Whip debacle and trying to find the right replacements . . ." She trailed off, shaking her head. "That's no excuse. I'm going to cancel my next appointment so we can take care of it right now—"

"No!" Juliet held up a hand, shaking her head. "No. It's not that important. I'm not flying again too soon, and even if I do, I'm not exactly bad at it without more augmentation! Let's meet in a few weeks or so, and we can talk about some ideas, all right?"

Ladia nodded, a look of chagrin on her face as she slowly shook her head. "That'll be perfect. It'll allow me to do the research I should have already done. Again, my apologies."

"Forget it." Juliet chuckled. "Talk to you soon."

Ladia nodded and quietly slipped out of the room. Juliet dressed and hung her Texan on her hip. She drew the gun, opened the cylinder, spun it, flicked her wrist to shut it, then holstered it with a habitual twirl. There was something comforting seeing those seven high-powered cartridges in their slots. Before she left, she paused to look at her nails again; even five minutes later, they were less inflamed.

On her way out, Tricia gave her another gift bag from yet another cosmetic line, this one packed with "nanobot-enhanced" concealer, sunscreen, and makeup remover. Juliet couldn't help chuckling as she walked to the door, picturing Bennet's face when she handed the stuff to him. She almost made it to her bike before a new icon appeared on her AUI with a blinking label that read, UPDATED DATA SHEET.

"Angel!" she laughed. "Really?"

"You're going to love seeing your progress. Besides, you asked for an updated Sol-bit balance after I paid Tricia."

"All right, let's see here," Juliet said as she sat on her bike and put on her helmet before she selected the icon and watched the new data sheet fill in.

Juliet Corina Bianchi		
Physical, Mental, and Social Status Compilation:		**Comparative Ranking Percentile (Higher Is Better - Previous Value in Parenthesis):**
Liquid Assets Net Worth:	Sol-bits: 1,231,509	--
Neural and Cellular Adaptiveness:	.96342 (Scale of 0 – 1)	99.91
Synaptic Responsiveness:	.11 (Lower Is Better)	92.08 (79.31)
Musculoskeletal Ranking:	–	87.81 (84.03)
Cardiovascular Ranking:	–	91.01 (90.77)
Cybernetic and Bionic Augmentation:	**Model Name and Number:**	**Overall Rating of the Augmentation (Grades Are F, E, D, C, B, A, S, S+):**
PAI	WBD Project Angel, Alpha 3.433	S+
Psionic Lattice	Grave Industries, GIPEL	S

Data Port	Prime Data Systems, Archwizard 2109. v3	A
Data Jack	Reaction Technologies, Tightbeam 9	A
Medical Nanite Suite	Cybergen Nanomedical Repair Matrix, Model 9	A+
Bone Reinforcement Nanite Package	Swedish Biologic, Mark 7	A
Subdermal Nanofiber Weave Armor - "Detroit Wrap" coverage	Duraskin, Armortex Vantage	A
Retinal Cybernetic Implant	Mirage Tech, Lux Alpha 12	A-
Auditory Cybernetic Implant	Cybergen Auditory Implant, Model 47	A+
Olfactory Cybernetic Implant	Cybergen Advanced Olfactory Sensor Array, Model 23B	A+
Cybernetic Prosthetic Right Arm with Fully Programmable Fingerprints	BioFusion, Model 2109.01b	A
Complete Cybernetic Lung Replacement	Cybergen Enhanced Pulmonary Implant, Model 17	A+

Full-Body Enhanced Reflex Package	Cybergen Kinetic Response Amplifier, Model 3C	A+
Intracranial Blood Cooling System	Angel Systems - Bespoke Design	A
Fingertip-mounted Injection System	Covert Industries, Finger Spike 2.0	A
Fingertip-mounted Vibroblade	Edge-Craft Technologies, MicroVibro s14900RGB	A-
Defensive and Cosmetic Fingernail Package	Color-Shift, Diamond Tips, 2108 Model	A-
Programmable Synthetic Hair	Alicia Designs, Chroma Tresses v.4	B+
DNA Spoofing Package - Saliva and Programmable Fingerprints (Left Hand)	WBD - Custom Model	C
No Other Augmentation Detected.	–	–

Juliet frowned at the sheet for a couple of long minutes, reading through each line, wondering what the point of it all was other than to remind her how much of her humanity she was trading away. She supposed some people would see that long list of augmentations and feel some pride or accomplishment, but all she felt was nervous—would she regret all those mods someday?

Before she could voice her concerns, whining to Angel about something she couldn't change, not easily or wisely, she noticed a new number that had never changed before. "Angel, why did my synaptic responsiveness change?"

"My initial instruction set indicated that synaptic responsiveness was static, that a human's ranking in that area wouldn't change over time. I began to have my doubts as to the veracity of that so-called fact when you did your speed test in Doctor Ladia's lab. Since then, I've been conducting new baselines, and you've improved markedly."

Juliet felt her heart rate quicken. "Um, why would that be?"

"My theory is that it has to do with either the psionic lattice or my extensive synthetic fiber network that has grown entwined with your nerves and neural network." She paused, and as Juliet breathed and tried to take it in, added, "I think it's probably the latter."

Juliet didn't know how to respond. Was it bad that her brain was working faster than before? Was she going to fry herself into early-onset dementia? Angel must have sensed her stress because she spoke again.

"If it makes you feel better, it has remained static since I first measured it after the speed test."

"So, you're done expanding?" Juliet hated how a note of accusation entered her voice.

"I am thoroughly enmeshed with you, Juliet; there's no more need to expand."

Juliet sighed and shrugged. What else could she do? "Oh well. If I'm going to burn out, I can't think of a better person to burn out with." She pressed the ignition button on her bike and started humming through the garage, heading for the street level.

"You won't burn out, Juliet! Your normal day-to-day living doesn't put a strain on your brain, and if we speed things up, I'll keep you safe." When Juliet just smiled and kept driving, Angel asked, "Did you notice the ratings of your new equipment?"

"Yeah, As and A minuses. If you would have told me the nails would be A minuses, I would have asked Ladia to step up her game!"

"It's just a function of their classification as concealed weapons; they're effective and small, but certain other technologies are considered more efficient or versatile in my database. For instance, the injection system—it can be used without leaving a noticeable wound and can be lethal or nonlethal. For that reason, it's ranked above any sort of cutting implement."

"Okay, well, we need to get you some manufacturing equipment and a research lab. I want some more S-ranked stuff." Juliet was mostly joking, but the idea had crossed her mind a few times. Surely, Angel could come up with some amazing gear if she had the time and interest to develop it.

As though she read her mind—and at this point, Juliet was starting to think Angel could do that—she said, "I might be interested in pursuing the development of certain technologies, but I don't want to take my focus away from you and your day-to-day life."

"Hah! I knew you'd say that." Juliet twisted the throttle as traffic opened up a little, starting to cruise away from the downtown area. "Any word from Bennet or Aya? Are we having dinner at the hangar?"

"No, but you have a message from Alice asking that you give her a call."

"Oh, really? When were you going to tell me?"

Juliet giggled through Angel's flustered assurances that she was just about to tell her. Then, when the call tone beeped and Alice picked up, she tried to straighten her face out.

"Something funny?" the wry pilot asked, arching a dark red eyebrow.

"Something my PAI said. How are things up in orbit?"

"Oh, Aya didn't tell you? We're in port, unloading our first haul off the *Red Betty*. That's why I was reaching out—Well, for two reasons."

Juliet tilted her bike to aim for the interdome highway. "I'm listening."

"One, Shiro and I want to treat you all to a nice dinner. I mean, sort of nice—the barbeque place Bennet likes in the port. And two, we need to talk to you about us stealing him and Aya for a few days. We're just about ready to tackle the reactor and drives on the *Red Betty*, and Bradbury can't handle it alone."

"Sounds like you just did."

"Hmm?" Alice wasn't following Juliet's mind as easily as Angel did.

"Talk to me about it. It's fine; I get it."

Alice's eyes opened in belated understanding. "Oh, good. Well, will you come have dinner with us all? I think Aya's hoping to ride in with you."

"Couldn't keep me away, Alice." Juliet smiled and winked into the camera, then goosed the throttle as the highway opened up ahead of her.

"Are you driving?"

"Yeah, heading back to the hangar."

"Speaking of driving, have you been logging any hours in the flight sim? Don't want to get rusty before we send you out in that brand-new gunship!"

"I . . ." Juliet chuckled, wincing as she shook her head. "No, I haven't. You know what? I'm gonna take the *Lady Hawk* out for a cruise. Now that you mention it, I *miss* being in the cockpit. Maybe next week. Anyway, even so, I'll start hitting the simulator on a regular basis."

"That's my girl." Alice winked, returning the obnoxious gesture, then waved. "See you at dinner. Aya has the details."

"See you!" Juliet grinned from ear to ear as Angel closed the call window. She really, really wanted to open the throttle and see if she could break her old record, but she resisted the temptation; things were going too well at that moment to tempt fate. "We'll be doing plenty of that soon enough."

"What's that, Juliet?"

"Tempting fate. I figure we'll finish cleaning up the neighborhood around the hangar and spend a little more time working with Tanaka and the crew. Then, it's probably about time we started putting a plan together about WBD."

"Clean the neighborhood? Didn't we do that when we got the dirty corpo-sec officers shipped off to New Atlas?"

Juliet grinned and twisted the throttle, settling for just a quick burst of speed. "Angel, did you forget? There's a certain chop-shop operator named Vicky who sent some thugs to hurt and rob Bennet and Aya." Juliet's grin changed in nature to something that looked like it would be more at home on the face of a predatory animal. "Aya, Angel! That's not something I can let slide."

42

SURPRISE

Despite her conviction to see "Vicky" and her chop shop put out of business, Juliet knew she had to take it easy for twenty-four hours or so. Though she felt good thanks to her nanites, some of her new implants wouldn't be fully effective for a while, most especially the bone-hardening nanites. With that in mind, she relaxed around the hangar for a couple of hours, and then, with Aya as an enthusiastic passenger on the back of her bike, the two of them rode to the spaceport to meet the others for dinner.

Juliet had eaten at the restaurant once before, but she knew the crew often made it a habit to go there after a long salvage job. In this case, they were in the middle of a long operation and just happened to be close enough to make pitstops down at the port. When Juliet parked the bike and pulled her helmet off, securing it on the cradle behind her seat, Aya frowned, looking around for a spot to stow hers.

"Hang on." Juliet opened the seat and pulled out a shrink cord; she'd stashed a few essentials in there while killing time earlier. She took Aya's helmet, ran the cord through the chin-strap buckle, and then through a gap in the bike's handlebars. She pinched the activation tab, and the cord sucked the helmet tight. "At least now, someone will have to cut it if they want to steal it."

"Looks good to me." Aya nodded, stuffing her hands in the pockets of her puffy, baby-blue jacket. Juliet, of course, wore her motorcycle jacket and carried her Texan and the very sharp sword that Tanaka had loaned her—it wasn't the monoblade, but she felt a lot better walking around the port with it rather than the fake, practice one.

The two hustled through the port, riding the complimentary trams to the shopping and dining section, and soon, they were working their way through the crowd inside Moon Pit BBQ. "I see them!" Aya yelled, trying to be heard above the loud music emanating from the bar section. She pointed to a booth in the far corner, and Juliet nodded as she saw Alice, Shiro, Bennet, and surprisingly, Bradbury.

"Oh, cool! Bradbury came!" she said, following Aya, weaving between the tables.

"Yeah!" Aya looked back at Juliet, and something about her smile told her she was missing something. "It must be a special occasion!"

Juliet frowned, suddenly nervous. What had she missed? Was it someone's birthday? Anniversary? She looked down at Aya, trying to ensure she wasn't hiding a gift or card or something under her jacket. Her stress partially melted away when they got to the table and Aya shrugged out of her coat, tucking it beside her as she scooted into the booth beside Bennet. She definitely wasn't hiding anything, and Juliet didn't see any presents around the table.

She sat down beside Aya and scooted in. "Hey, everyone!" She looked at Bradbury's plastic face and added, "Long time no see, Brad!"

"It has been a while, hasn't it?" he asked, his LED eyes blinking with simulated emotion.

"We're glad you could make it, Lucky. Aya and Bennet said you've been busy with a side job the last few days—staying up all night, making folks worry." Alice winked at her, ensuring the lightheartedness of the statement was conveyed.

"Yeah, that job's mostly wrapped up. Just a few loose ends to tie up." Juliet grinned, enjoying the idea of being the one to use the turn of phrase ominously for a change.

"Well, good. Some of us were a little nervous about leaving you alone down here." Alice nodded at Aya with another wink.

Aya grabbed the opportunity to say, "You should come up with us, Lucky!"

"Ah, I don't think that's a great idea right now. I've got too much going on. Besides, someone's gotta keep an eye on the gunship."

"That's why you hired those goons, I thought," Bennet chimed in.

"Is that what this dinner's about? You all trying to bully me into coming up to orbit?" Juliet chuckled and flicked through the drink menu Angel had pulled up on her AUI.

Shiro hadn't spoken yet, and he still wasn't making any move to open his mouth, so Alice elbowed him in the ribs. "Oof," he grunted, almost spilling his beer, then he set it down and cleared his throat. "Ahem. No, this meeting isn't about bullying you. It's about celebrating you. We wanted to thank—"

Juliet's eyes widened in alarm, and she held up her hands, shaking her head. "No, no, no! What's going on, you guys? It's not my birthday or any—"

"We don't even know when your birthday is!" Aya cried, grabbing one of her arms and pulling it down beside her, hugging it close. Juliet opened her mouth to object again but saw Shiro was still trying to speak, so she held her tongue.

"*Hai.* We want to thank you for joining us and sharing your good fortune and wealth. Before we met you, we struggled to pay our monthly loan payments, and now we're talking about paying off old debts early." Shiro wasn't a great public speaker, and Juliet could see the strain on his face as he finished each sentence. Alice took pity on him and took over.

"As Aya said, we don't know your birthday. We don't know a whole lot about you, but we know we care about you, and we're glad you're one of us. So, we're having this dinner tonight in your honor." She shifted to the left, separating from Shiro a little, and lifted a big sack off the floor. "We have a few things to give you!"

"Oh, gosh, you guys!" Juliet felt her cheeks getting hot and held her hands over her eyes. Tears pooled in them, and she was sure she was about to start crying. "I wish," she tried to say but shook her head, her throat getting too tight. "I wish you didn't do this!"

"Oh, stop it!" Alice chuckled.

"C'mon, you deserve a hell of a lot more!" Bennet added, reaching past Aya to grip her shoulder. "It's not like any of us broke the bank. It's just little things."

Juliet sighed and took a deep, shaky breath, pushing the wave of emotion down. "This is so sweet! I really don't deserve it, but I'll shut up and try to enjoy it. Do you know what this means, though? I'm just going to get you all back."

Before anyone could reply, her beer arrived, along with a few drinks the others had ordered. As she picked it up and took a long pull of the bitter, ice-cold beverage, Alice lifted a small package wrapped in brown packing paper out of the bag. She pushed it toward her, and Juliet read the blocky print on the paper.

"To Lucky, from Bennet." She smiled at the big engineer and picked the package up, squeezing and shaking it. "Feels squishy, and it's not too big. I bet it's a T-shirt!"

He grinned and shrugged. "Open it." Juliet nodded and ripped the paper, pulling it away from a black knit ski cap. Juliet held it up, turning it, until she saw the stitched skull and crossbones on the front.

"Oh, cool!" Juliet laughed, pulling it on over her—currently—slightly curly, shoulder-length auburn hair. "I love it!"

Bennet nodded, grinning. "I mean, it's a little warm in here, so don't feel like you have to wear it. I just thought you'd like the skull—reminded me of those morbid smiley faces you wear."

Juliet reached behind Aya to gently squeeze the back of Bennet's neck. "Thank you, Benny. I'm gonna give you a hug later." He turned red and looked down, nodding.

"Okay, next!" Alice pushed an even smaller package toward her, this one also wrapped in brown paper but with a pink ribbon taped to the front.

"That's from me!" Aya announced, squeezing Juliet's arm again. Juliet took the package, laughing because she knew exactly what it was; it was shaped like a paperback and felt like one, too.

"I wonder what this could be." She pinched up her face, pretending to contemplate the possibilities while she bent and sniffed at the package.

"You think you're so smart, but you don't know!" Aya exclaimed; Juliet could see she meant it.

"Oh, really? Hmm, all right." Juliet carefully removed the ribbon, folding it and tucking it into her pocket, then tore the paper away, revealing a thin book with a pale-blue paper cover and a hand-drawn title and image—it looked like Juliet's face in a space helmet, and the title was *Lucky's Adventures on the Kowashi*. Of course, tears instantly sprang into her eyes, and Juliet carefully thumbed through the pages, reading chapter titles like "The Daring Rescue of Bennet" and further back, "Ship Invasion!" There were hundreds of pages.

"I had the book printed at a local shop. They did the binding and everything!"

Juliet had no words, tears freely streaming down her cheeks. She took a deep, slow breath, hugged the book to her chest, and said, "Aya, how did you find time to write all this?"

"I just did a little bit each night. It's not like telling stories about you is hard—my PAI did all the formatting."

"Oh, brother." Bennet laughed. "Glad I went first. Sucks to have to follow that one up!"

"Stuff it, Bennet!" Alice replied, pulling another present from the bag. As she pushed it over the table, Juliet crushed Aya into a hug and kissed the top of her head.

"I love it," she said into the smaller woman's hair. Wiping her cheeks and laughing at herself, Juliet took the next gift. "Oh! From Bradbury? You shouldn't have, sir!"

"It wasn't any trouble. I've been tinkering in my spare time and have built up quite a little foundry in the engineering compartment . . ."

"Yeah, about that . . ." Bennet started to say, but Shiro hushed him as Juliet began tearing the paper away from the package. Inside was a small wooden box. She turned it over, admiring the fact that the top and bottom halves seemed to be carved from a single piece of wood. She could hardly see the seam where they met.

"Did you make this box?"

"I did—carved from a single piece of poplar."

"It's very pretty." Juliet lifted the top away, revealing a red felt lining and, within, a shiny, stainless knife with a three-inch blade and a beautiful, polished cherrywood hilt. "You made this?" Juliet asked, eyes wide, as she lifted the knife from the box.

"I did. Do you like it? It's weighted for throwing." Bradbury's eyes flashed as he spoke, his voice making it clear he was pleased with himself.

"It's beautiful!" Juliet tested the edge with her thumb, finding it very sharp. "Bradbury, this is so nice. Thank you." With her hand open, she reached over the table, and Bradbury tentatively rested his chrome fingers on her palm. She gave his hand a squeeze, then pulled her hand back, beaming. "Someday, this is going to be worth a lot." She gently put the little knife back in the box and closed it, setting it atop her precious book.

"Okay, the last present is from me and Shiro and, well, everyone. Sorry, but we're bad at getting gifts." Alice nudged Shiro with her elbow, who nearly spit out the drink of beer he'd just taken.

"*Hai,*" he coughed.

"So, your PAI has been conspiring with Aya," Alice said; Juliet could see she was fighting to contain her smile. Before she could ask how Angel had been conspiring, she felt a wave of emotion that felt strange, out of place, and a little confusing. After a moment, though, she realized she was feeling something from Angel—happiness and excitement.

"What is going on?" she muttered, and everyone interpreted the question their own way.

Alice nodded, her smile broadening. "Indeed! What is going on? So, Aya wanted to do this in the hangar, but we figured you could look at things in person later. Honestly, the timing for our work on the *Red Betty* threw that plan out the window; it's going to take a week to get the panels back on the gunship, and we don't want to delay this any longer. We wanted to leave you here on a happy note. Does that make sense?"

"Um, it might if I had any clue what you're talking about." Juliet looked at Aya. "The ship panels? Is this something to do with what you were painting the other day?"

"See for yourself," Alice said, "I'm sending you a couple of files."

Sure enough, two new icons appeared on her AUI. She peered at them—one was an unnamed image file, and the other was labeled "SSFRC Ship Registration." Juliet's smile widened as she opened the file, skimming to the critical part: the name of the ship. Sure enough, just as she'd daydreamed with Angel so many months ago, she saw the official registered name of the gunship: *Cherry Blossom.*

As her grin spread, she opened the image file. There, laid out against the drying racks in the hangar, were the big side panels of the gunship. Juliet had seen the glossy baby-blue paint before, but now they were decorated with a long streak of cherry blossoms in beautiful high-res detail. They looked like they were blowing in the wind along the ship's side. To top it off, the ship's name was stylistically depicted beneath them in black-outlined, pale-pink lettering.

"Oh, God, this is so freakin' shiny!" Juliet laughed, once again feeling emotion overcoming her. "I can't believe you did it so perfectly! It's exactly how I saw it in my imagination."

"Bennet helped," Aya said right away. "I didn't tell you when you caught me the other day, but we've both been working on it."

Bennet cleared his throat and nodded. "And Shiro and Alice did all the paperwork and paid the registration fees—quite a hassle with a type-four gunship." Juliet knew what that meant from conversations with the crew in the past. "Type-four" indicated it had combat-class nanites, rail guns capable of orbital bombardment, and ordnance that could threaten a capital ship.

Juliet closed her eyes and leaned back, tilting her head to face the ceiling. She felt so overwhelmed by the show of affection and friendship that she was afraid she'd say or do something stupid. It felt good and right to take a beat and breathe, processing the emotions.

"Emotions!" Juliet subvocalized, "Angel, I could feel your happiness and excitement earlier. Have I felt your emotions before and just not realized it?"

"I think we broke her." Bennet laughed.

"Give her a minute." Aya gently leaned her cheek against Juliet's shoulder.

Alice chuckled. "Let's order food."

"My biological components will be pleased with ribs," Bradbury said, and Shiro enthusiastically agreed.

Meanwhile, Angel told Juliet, "I'm not surprised you felt me. I feel your emotions all the time. I hope it's not troubling."

"No. I love it. It makes me feel closer to you." Juliet blinked and opened her eyes, sitting up straight and looking around the table. "I love you guys, you know that?"

"We love you too," Aya was quick to reply. No one else said anything, but they all smiled, and even Bennet nodded. Bradbury's eyes flashed, but Juliet couldn't tell what emotion he was trying to convey.

"This might not be my birthday, but it's the best birthday party I've ever had." Hearing herself, Juliet frowned and reached across the table to take Alice's hand while she put her other arm over Aya's shoulder and grabbed Bennet's neck again. "Listen! I know I'm cagey about my past, and I haven't told you my birthday, let alone my name, but it's not because I don't trust you. It's because I'm trying to keep you safe. There's a . . . specter in my past, but I'm getting ready to deal with it. After that, of course, you can keep calling me Lucky, but you'll know my name, too. I promise."

Everyone got quiet for a minute, looking at her, perhaps unsure how to respond. "Sounds good," Bennet finally spoke, breaking the spell. "Can we eat?"

And so, they did just that. Juliet stuffed herself and drank too much, but by the time people were ready to say goodnight, her nanites had sobered her up enough to drive. Aya decided to go straight to the *Kowashi* with the others, so after some goodbye hugs, Juliet found herself heading home alone with Aya's helmet still attached to the front of her handlebars and her presents tucked safely under her seat.

"I feel pretty lucky," she noted, enjoying the relaxing ride in the light traffic on the interdome highway on her way out to the industrial domes.

"So do I. I was very excited to be a part of that little surprise. Aya sent me a message thanking me for my help. I wish we could tell her about us."

"We can. We will, I mean, after we deal with WBD. She'll be the first. I feel like I could trust her even now, but I'm not a genius; I don't know how knowledge of you and all that we've been through might impact her safety."

"There are certainly risks; knowing what I am and knowing about your trouble with WBD could lead her to pursue more knowledge, even in a misguided attempt to help, which might trigger some flags on the pub nets. It's best if you and I are the only ones to know for now."

"Until I tell Tanaka and ask for his help."

"Even then," Angel said, "you should limit what you tell him and ensure he understands the gravity. If they made me, they may have other true AIs working behind the scenes. They may have removed the human component that made me who I am and granted me the ability to feel true emotions."

"I see that you and I have been having the same dark thoughts. Even worse, what if they made another version of you and stuck it into a psychopath?" While Angel stewed on that, Juliet flexed her fingers against the bike's grips. They felt perfectly fine. "What's the percentage on my bone nanites?"

"Sixty-seven percent coverage."

"You know, Angel. I think I'd like to have a relaxing day tomorrow after the dojo. Let's go take care of Vicky's gang so I can sleep without them on my mind."

"Do you want to stop by the hangar to pick up more guns and your armor?"

"Nah, I don't think so. I've got my sword and my pistol. Let's go show Vicky why it was a bad idea to send that mountain of flesh after Aya and Bennet."

43

\\\\\\\\\\\\\\\\\\\\\\\\\\

INFILTRATION

uliet had known the location for Vicky's operation ever since the day she and Hines had questioned Ernie and "Bullethead," the big creep who'd slapped Bennet around and threatened Aya with a gun. As she parked her bike a half mile from the blinking dot on her mini map, she had Angel call Hines. He was quick to pick up, though his eyes looked a little bleary and his surroundings were dark. Stifling a yawn, he asked, "Lucky? Something happen?"

"Not yet, but I wanted to ask if there's any chance I could get a contract to pick up Vicky and her cronies. I know it's kind of spur of the moment, but . . ."

"Yeah, sure. Done. When I showed up to work this afternoon, I was promoted to acting lieutenant. Not a big deal, considering I was one of two sergeants still in the precinct who hadn't 'disappeared,' and I had eight years of seniority on the other one. Anyway, I have authorization to offer bounty contracts, and there ain't anybody around here to stop me." He yawned again, blinking his eyes and peering at something. "Eleven? Shit, I've only been sleeping an hour! I was hoping it was morning. Give me twenty minutes to send over the contract, and then I'll call the watch sergeant to let her know you might be calling."

"Um, sure, I'll wait for the contract. What kind of help can I expect from LCS?"

"Not a lot on short notice. I was going to put together a task force to start cleaning up operations like Vicky's now that some of the dirt got scooped out of the department. If you want to wait, I can get some uniforms over your way. Hold on." He cleared his throat and peered closely into the camera. "You aren't tackling Vicky on your own, are you? She's got a damn sizable crew."

"At midnight on a Monday? How many do you figure will be in the warehouse?"

"Oh, I've no damn idea! For all I know, she could have twenty guys working on a batch of stolen cars."

Juliet snorted, shrugging. "So, send me the contract, and I'll call LCS when I have things in hand."

"Ah, dammit, you couldn't wait 'til morning? I'm never gonna get to sleep now." Hines grunted as he shifted to the side of his bed. A light came on, and Juliet saw he was wearing a stained, frayed white tank top. He yawned, scratched at his stubbly chin, and said, "I'll do the contract. Only hitch is getting the judge to sign off. Shouldn't be a problem; I know one who lets his PAI handle this stuff late at night. When I'm done, I'll get a hold of the department and make sure some help is ready to come in when you call." He grunted, grumbling, "Then I'm going back to sleep."

"Thanks, Hines." Juliet smiled sweetly, hamming it up for him. "I knew I could count on you." When he returned her smile, albeit more sour than sweet, she closed the call window and got off her bike, removing her helmet. After stowing it on its cradle, she dug around in her seat compartment, pulling out a fistful of shrink cords and stuffing them into her back pocket.

Stretching her neck, inhaling the cool but chemically tinged air, Juliet started strolling down the dark, deserted street, keeping to the shadows of the big boxy warehouse buildings. Most of them had security fences blocking off their front parking lots. Most also had cameras and floodlights, so it was only really dark between the regularly spaced access gates. Still, Juliet found it easy to keep to the shadows by meandering to either side of the street as she walked, avoiding the gates and their cameras.

It wasn't that she thought she could be invisible; it was more that she didn't want to catch anyone's eye by being conspicuous. She'd tied her hair back in a ponytail, keeping it out of her eyes, and with her fingers brushing the grip of her revolver, she carefully scanned ahead with her high-end optics. According to her mini map, she had to turn at the four-way stop sign ahead, and then Vicky's warehouse would be about a hundred meters to the right.

The warehouse on the corner had a fenced yard, so Juliet walked along that barrier up to the intersection and peered around to the right. There weren't many lights on outside Vicky's warehouse, but there was one amber floodlight on a post beside the open gateway. She could see headlights in the yard moving as a van drove to the far end of the building then turned right, leaving her line of sight. Low conversation and movement drew her eyes back to the gate, where she saw three figures lingering, leaning against the fence, chatting in the glow of the floodlight.

All three wore typical banger attire: synthetic leather and polymer jackets, bulky, metallic prosthetics, gear and implants with too many LEDs, and, of course, oversized, intimidating weapons. She was about to inspect their gear and try to hear their conversation when Angel said, "Your contract just came through."

A blinking icon appeared on her AUI, and Juliet stepped back around the corner to look at it.

Posting #L2942c	Requested Role: Investigative, Apprehension	Rep Level: D–S+
Job Description: LCS Official Contract: The LCS department requests the investigation of illegal, stolen-goods dismantling and distribution activities at 17 Commercial Row in Luna City Industrial Dome I5B. This contract serves as a warrant for investigating the above-listed property, approved by LC Corporate Magistrate Roger Voight, #82555. Any resistance is grounds for arrest, and standard rules of force escalation are approved.		**Compensation:** 45,000 Sol-bits, payable on completion, with a bonus comprised of outstanding bounties.
Scavenge Rights: Yes	**Location:** Luna City	**Date:** August 6, 2108

She was distracted by the contract and might have missed the sound of approaching footsteps, but Angel noticed them and closed the window. "Someone's coming!" Juliet stuffed her hands in her pockets and slumped her shoulders. Pacing away from the fence into the road, she walked in a slow circle while talking softly.

"Yeah. I sent you a pin. Can't believe the jerk left me here."

"Ah," Angel said. "I see what you're doing."

"Yep. Hurry, please. This place is creepy!" Juliet put a little whine in her voice as she turned back toward the corner, looking for the source of the footsteps. She saw him right away—one of the men who'd been standing near Vicky's gate. He was tall, with a bright orange mohawk, a surgically attached pair of military-grade optic lenses where his eyes should be, and, drawing most of Juliet's attention, a bulky plasteel-and-stainless-steel arm with a forearm-mounted shotgun barrel. He wore cutoff jeans, exposing metallic, piston-driven legs, and a long black polymer duster Juliet knew could likely resist most small-arms fire.

"You lost, sugar?" he asked, his tone strangely sweet coming from a man with jagged metallic shark's teeth.

"I have a ride coming." Juliet stepped back, easily portraying nervousness because the guy was plenty intimidating. As she retreated, he stepped forward, and she subvocalized, "Charge up the EMP." One of the selling points of her new Tightbeam 9 data jack was its ability to use its transmission antennae to send a focused EMP burst. It only took a few seconds to charge up the capacitors before it would be ready to fire.

"Really? Kind of a strange place to be waiting for a ride. Why don't you come with me, and we can make sure you get where you need to go?"

"His optics look shielded, Juliet. I hope his PAI isn't also mil-spec." Angel sounded nervous, but Juliet wasn't too worried. He was banger muscle, and they always went for showy, powerful augmentation before they started worrying about high-end data ports and hardened PAI chips. She might be wrong, of course, but she'd cross that bridge when she came to it.

Taking another step back, shaking her head slowly, she asked, "Um, can't I just sit here on the curb and wait? I got in a fight with my ex, and he dumped me here."

"Well, you don't look helpless, do you? That's quite a little cannon on your hip there. Is that a sword, too?" He was smiling as he spoke, but then his mouth closed, his lips turned down, and he focused those weird black lenses on Juliet's gun. "Wait a minute . . ."

Juliet lifted her left arm, pointing her wrist at his head, and said, "Now, Angel." She didn't have to say anything; Angel knew what she was doing. A soft hiss of static and a tiny flicker of her optics were the only clues that she'd just fired the EMP.

Well, her only clue other than the banger slapping his hands to his head and stumbling backward. Juliet's strategic backward movement had taken them several meters away from the corner of the fence, but she figured if anyone was looking hard enough, they could probably still see what was happening. With that in mind, she acted fast.

"Ugh, what the fuck?" the banger grunted, lowering his chromed arm and waving it in front of him. He was pumping the limb in and out, and she wondered if he was trying to figure out how to fire his built-in gun without his AUI in place. Was there a way? She didn't want to find out, so quick as an adder, she stepped around the lanky man, snaked her powerful right arm around his neck, and pressed her knee into the small of his back, pulling hard while cranking his head forward with her left arm, squeezing off the supply of blood to his brain. He thrashed violently for a few seconds, but Juliet had been in plenty of grappling sessions with larger partners; her arm was up to the task.

His resistance culminated in a last-ditch effort to throw her off with his oversized cyber arm. Reaching over his shoulder, he grabbed a hold of Juliet's jacket collar and jerked his arm as hard as he could. It might have worked; he could probably lift half a ton with that arm, but Juliet's jacket gave up the ghost, ripping to shreds as the big man pulled a big square of material away before collapsing to his knees.

Juliet growled, squeezing tight, waiting for him to slump into submission. It took another three or four seconds, but the fight was out of him, and Juliet rode him down, her knees in his back, as he fell to the pavement on his face. She didn't waste any time pulling out her new data jack and plugging it into his thick plastic data port. "Watchdog," she grunted.

Angel's voice was soothingly calm as she replied, "Installing."

Juliet heaved for breath, looking at the corner, trying to peer through the layers of chain-link fencing to see if anyone was coming. She didn't see anything, but she knew the guys her victim had been on duty with must be wondering what he'd gotten up to.

Had they seen her at the corner? Had he reported it in? Were they just assuming he was wandering around, doing his patrol? She couldn't wait long to find out. While Angel did her thing with the man's PAI, Juliet pulled a shrink cord out of her pocket and hooked his human wrist to one of the pistons on his cybernetic arm behind his back. It probably wasn't necessary, not with Angel's watchdog controlling his PAI when it rebooted, but she wanted to be sure.

"I can access their network through his PAI; the EMP took it offline, so installing the watchdog as it rebooted was easy."

Juliet smiled. "How much access? Can you control the cameras?"

"Not control, but view. I'll send Fido in, though, and I'm sure he'll get us full control in a few minutes."

"Oof!" Suddenly, the big man jerked awake, straining his back and grunting. "The hell's going on?"

"I've disabled his implants. He's in the dark."

"What about his ears?" Juliet hissed, still kneeling on him, trying to keep him from rolling over.

"They're natural!"

"Listen, dummy!" Juliet slapped the shaved part of his head beside his mohawk. "Quit jerking around, or I'm going to zap you."

"Get off me!" He arched his back, and Juliet hopped off, swearing.

"Do it, Angel!" Angel didn't reply, but the banger suddenly collapsed, twitching, his mouth hanging open, saliva drizzling onto the pavement. Juliet grunted, furiously yanking her arms out of the sleeves of her ruined jacket. "My favorite jacket, jerk!" She checked the pockets, made sure they were empty, then threw the coat across the street into a narrow alley between two warehouses.

Still scowling, almost irrationally irritated, she brushed her palms off on her jeans, eyeing the street corner. Angel said, "I'm in the camera network. The other two gate guards are both smoking and chatting. They don't seem concerned about this man."

"Really? Huh." Juliet wasn't all that surprised. This was a chop shop that had enjoyed protection from LCS; they'd probably grown relatively lax when it came to security. "Let me know when you can mess with the cameras; you know, put 'em on a loop or something."

"I will, but in the meantime, I can probably call one of the other guards here using Eightball's PAI."

Juliet grinned. "Eightball?" She looked down at the guy's orange mohawk, wondering where he'd gotten the name. "Maybe his optics?" She shrugged, grabbing him by the ankles and starting to drag him across the road into the alley where she'd thrown her jacket. Once she was into the shadows and Eightball was tucked against the side of the building, she squatted down and aimed her wrist at the alley entrance, checking her line of sight.

"Okay, Angel, charge up the Tightbeam, then lure one over." The biobattery for the data jack would recharge over time, but according to Ladia, she could get a few EMP pulses out of it before having to wait.

"What should I say to them?"

"Um." Juliet frowned, looking down at the insensate banger. "I don't know. Something like, 'I was taking a leak and saw a bit-locker chip in the gutter. Help me fish it out.'" Juliet chuckled at the silliness of the idea.

It might have been silly, but it worked.

"One of them is coming," Angel reported. "His name is Rabies."

"Oh, brother," Juliet sighed, shaking her head. "Wonder how he earned that one."

Rabies turned out to be a lot slimmer and less geared out than Eightball when it came to weapons, but he had auditory and ocular implants, so her EMP sent him to the pavement, wailing in dismay. Juliet leaped on him, choked him into submission, and installed a watchdog, all in just a handful of seconds. She was sweating and panting by the time she'd bound him and left him lying beside Eightball, which made her wish she'd taken the time to swing by the hangar and, at the very least, picked up her needler. Of course, she had the injectors in her left hand, but only three applications, and she already had one target in mind for them.

Angel displayed a row of icons on her AUI labeled Criminal Cam 1 through Criminal Cam 8. "I'm ready with the cameras. Shall I create a loop showing all three guards on duty?"

"Yes. I'm about to deal with number three. How many, um, employees are you counting on the feeds?"

"Twelve that I've identified as unique. However, I'm sure the cameras don't cover some areas."

"Twelve, huh? Sheesh. I probably should've gotten more equipment and maybe planned this out better." Despite her admitted ill-preparedness, Juliet left the alley and walked back across the street, determined to see things through.

Rounding the corner, her gait was calm and measured as she approached the gate to the illicit chop shop. The last guard was leaning against the fencepost on the far side of the still open gate. Angel highlighted the high-end, assault-style rifle on a sling hanging by his side, and Juliet frowned. So far, the gate guards, at least, had been a lot more equipped than she'd expected from some warehouse-robbing bangers. "Is that a smart gun?"

"Yes. Rome Armaments, model 1140. It has course-correcting, seven-millimeter projectiles capable of adjusting their trajectory midflight—minute adjustments, but they're remarkably effective against moving targets. He has a forty-six-round magazine, and the gun is capable of automatic, burst, or semiautomatic operation."

"Noted," Juliet whispered, exhaling softly as she saw the guard look up and take note of her.

"Yo! Who are you?" He lifted his gun, holding it ready, but surprisingly, with the barrel trained on the ground between them.

Juliet kept walking, smiling, tucking her fingers into her front pockets and shrugging in a flirty sort of way. "Oh, hey. I'm Eightball's cousin. He told me to meet him here."

"Huh?" The guard looked past her to the corner. "Didn't you see him down there?"

Juliet glanced over her shoulder and then back to him, lifting one of her perfect, glossy nails to her lower lip. "Are you teasing me? He wasn't back there."

She still had one hand in her pocket, and she sort of swayed left to right, smiling as demurely as she could. The whole thing felt so ridiculous she almost laughed, but she used that humor to smile into her absurd flirtation as she stepped even closer, within arm's length of the banger guard.

"I swear, he just went over that way. I think he was in an alley, just—Argh!" The one exclamation was all he got out as Juliet's left hand darted out and tapped him on the neck. Angel had cranked her speed augmentation to the max and fired the neurotoxin injection with flawless timing. The guard fell, limp and barely breathing at Juliet's feet. Still moving with lightning speed, Juliet pulled her data cable out and nimbly jammed it into his data port. While Angel worked to subdue his PAI, she examined the warehouse yard, slowly panning left to right, letting Angel run her various scans.

She knew Angel had control of the cameras, but she was worried the van she'd seen earlier would leave again, or some other bangers would come out to the gate. So far, there wasn't any sign of movement. Juliet saw pallets, flatbed trailers, and some garbage bins inside the fence, so as soon as Angel gave her the go-ahead, she started dragging the third guard over to one of the flatbeds with a half-meter sidewall. With a grunt and an extra-strong heave from her cybernetic arm, she hoisted him up over the sidewall and left him there, insensate. Before leaving, though, she lifted out his smart gun.

"Can you hack this thing to work for me?" Juliet asked, squatting behind the trailer, scanning the weapon for a data port.

"If you plug into that port." Angel highlighted the tiny slot on the bottom of the stock.

"I mean, my goal wasn't to come in here and kill everyone, but if things get bad, I won't mind having another gun."

"I can work on it while you move. The doors on the east end of the building open into a hallway, which is currently unoccupied. Go now while it's clear."

Juliet nodded and started jogging across the yard, aiming for the high-lighted doors. As she moved, Angel updated her mini map with the warehouse layout, complete with red dots for all the criminals she'd picked up on the internal cameras. Juliet felt a little daunted seeing all those dots, but she was the one who'd decided to do this job on the spur of the moment—she'd have to deal with the consequences.

Gritting her teeth in a fierce grin, two parts excited and one part nervous, she slipped through the doors and into Vicky's criminal operation.

44

A FAMILIAR VOICE

Juliet slipped into a bathroom door, waiting for Angel to time the movements of some nearby employees. While she leaned there against the cold tile wall, she contemplated what she was doing. She'd come to the chop shop with the vague goal of "shutting it down," but what did that mean? Was she going to subdue every employee? Was she just going to try to capture Vicky and count anyone else as a bonus? What if Vicky wasn't in? So far, Angel hadn't identified her on the camera feeds, but then, they didn't know who she was or what she looked like.

She subvocalized, "If I try to take out every employee without raising some kind of alarm, this is going to take hours. So much for getting a good night's rest."

Angel, pragmatic as usual, replied, "Well, if you can put this task behind you, it might be worth messaging Frida and asking to reschedule your one-on-one lesson with Tanaka for the afternoon."

"Yeah." Juliet nodded, thinking it through. "Yeah, good point. It's not like I'm still working at the scrapyard; Tanaka can't fire me." She closed her eyes, listening to the sounds of the building—faint whines of power tools, pipes creaking, an air scrubber toiling away somewhere, and clanks and thumps galore. The warehouse definitely wasn't sleeping. "You have control of the local net, right? I don't have to EMP everyone we come across to stop them setting off alarms?"

"That's right. I'll intercept traffic from their PAIs. There's a break room two doors down the hall on the left, and two employees are there. It might be a good time . . ." Angel trailed off as Juliet started moving, slipping out the door into the brightly lit hallway, smiling at the camera cluster at the far end, and darting toward the door Angel had already highlighted on her AUI. "Was that smile for me?"

"Yep!" Juliet whispered, the sound so slight it might as well have been a subvocalization. "Thanks for being so awesome, Angel. Imagine how hard this would be without you and Fido."

Juliet lifted her new smart rifle to her shoulder with her right hand and gently turned the handle with her left. Her mini map showed two red dots about two meters from the door, and when she quietly pulled it open, she saw the chop shop workers sitting at a square, folding table. One was flicking through something on his AUI, and the other was softly blowing on a cup of noodles. Neither looked up as Juliet entered. "Hey, guys, stay calm because I don't want to hurt you if I don't have to."

Both men wore stained, well-worn blue overalls very much like the ones Juliet and her coworkers used to wear in the scrapyard. Neither looked to be armed, and Juliet had a feeling the workers in Vicky's operation didn't get into the enforcing, stealing, and transport side of the operation. The man on the left, with the noodles, slowly set his cup down and blew out a heavy sigh of defeat, muttering some softly spoken expletives. The other one, a slim, black-haired kid who looked to be still in his teens, blinked rapidly several times and then started to jerk to his feet.

"Ah-ah!" Juliet stepped a little closer, brandishing the rifle menacingly. "Stay in your seat, and things will go nice and smooth for you."

"What is this shit?" the kid whined, falling back into his chair.

"Just do what she says, Flint. We ain't paid enough to get shot."

"Good advice from your friend." Juliet stepped around the table, getting behind the older, calmer man. "Keep your hands on the table, boys. I'm just going to disable your PAIs temporarily." When she stepped closer to the bigger man, she pressed the muzzle of the rifle into his back, just next to his spine, and said, "Seriously. I promise I'm faster than you. Don't mess around."

"Easy. I'm not looking to die." He spread his fingers wide, pressing them into the tabletop to emphasize his compliance.

"How many in the building like you? I mean not muscle, workers."

"Eight, not counting us. Ten altogether, I guess," the man replied as Juliet deftly slipped her data jack into his port.

"Quiet, dude!" the kid hissed. "Don't help this corpo-sec bi—"

"That's enough out of you," Juliet growled. "Think things will be better if I have to assume everyone's a banger?" He scowled. Juliet returned the glare and added, "I'm not corpo-sec, either. If Vicky's jerkoff buddies hadn't robbed my friends, I wouldn't even be here."

"So you ain't calling the corpo pigs on us?"

"We'll see how it goes." Juliet wasn't sure if she was lying. She figured they might cooperate more if they didn't know she was, in fact, operating on an LCS warrant, though. "Where's Vicky, anyway?"

"Probably in the office upstairs," the man in front of her answered.

"I'm done with his PAI," Angel announced right after he spoke. Juliet pulled her cable out and walked around to the kid. When she started to reach her cable toward his exposed port, he leaned forward, avoiding her reach.

"Kid," Juliet hissed, pressing the muzzle into his back, "just because I'm trying not to make a mess doesn't mean I'm afraid to do it. Settle down."

He spat to the side but sat up straight. Juliet plugged her cable in and felt a little dirty despite knowing she was in the right with the whole situation. While Angel worked, she looked at the other man, noting his dark brown irises were focused on the gun at her hip. "How many muscle are downstairs in the work area?"

"Uh, there's some out front and then two by the bay doors on the work floor." He nodded toward her Texan. "I know who you are. Vicky put out the word for everyone to watch out for a wired-up merc chick with a big six-shooter. She's gonna be ready for you; I mean, rumor is she hired some out-of-towner to watch her six after you iced two of her crews."

Juliet's eyebrows shot up. "Oh?"

"Juliet, both of these men are in a chat group with more than a dozen other names, some of which match the biometric files on the local network. The groups routinely share schematics and work schedules. The most recently shared file is a vid featuring teardown instructions for Gal-tech maneuvering thrusters."

Listening to Angel, Juliet frowned, initially confused by the seemingly off-topic trivia. Then, some dots connected in her mind, and she smiled broadly. "Hey, boys, tell me: Are you working on Gal-tech maneuvering thrusters tonight?"

The kid just scowled at her, but the other guy, the almost normal, kind of friendly, criminal chop-shop worker drone chuckled and nodded. "Yeah, we got a big delivery about fifteen minutes ago. Twenty units."

"So, you all share files with each other on your chat groups?"

The older man's eyes widened, and he stammered, "Yeah, but . . ."

Juliet winked at him and pulled her data cable from the dark-haired kid's port. "Don't worry. You're cool. I'll send my package from the kid's PAI."

"What?" He spun in his chair, almost looking like he would stand up, but Juliet took a step back and waved her gun barrel back and forth. He scowled. "You can't do that. Besides, I alerted security when you got here. Nice job not using a jammer, pig." He smirked and folded his arms over his chest.

"Oh? You did, huh? Guess I might as well just kill you then. Don't want to have to worry about hostiles on my six." His mouth opened, and he glanced at the older man nervously. Juliet sighed, shaking her head. "Relax. I've got control of the net. Your message didn't go through."

While she wasted time bantering with the younger man, Angel said, "I've compiled a trojan watchdog daemon and attached it to a slightly modified version of the teardown vid. I'll send it out to the work crew with a message that he 'found an easier way to do the job.' Does that work?"

"Are the door guards on the chat?" Juliet asked aloud, hoping the friendly worker would spill a few more details.

"I don't think so. I'm only counting ten active names," Angel replied as the friendly guy shook his head.

"Nah, they use their own comms."

Juliet nodded. "Okay, I'm almost done. Soon you can sit here and relax 'til this is all over. Push your chairs together, back-to-back." The kid grumbled and the man sighed heavily, but they complied.

When they were both sitting back-to-back, Juliet used a couple of shrink cords to hook their wrists to each other's chairs. As she stepped toward the door, she asked, hoping for just a little more insight, "All right, boys, last chance to earn some points with me: Where is Vicky's office upstairs? I'm not seeing her on the cam feeds. Any idea how many will be with her?"

The older worker, his back now to her, said, "Nah, we never go up there. Can't be hard to find her office, though. Only she and her goons go up there. Uh, like I said, rumor is she hired a dude to deal with you, so yeah, that's all I know."

"Get melted," the kid threw in for good measure. Juliet snorted a soft laugh and slipped out the door, following her mini map to a large room with nearly a dozen red dots moving around.

"You'll know if they open the trojan, right?" she subvocalized as she approached the opening leading out to the warehouse floor. The *whirr* of power tools, clanks, laughter, shouts, and music playing from a tinny speaker wafted into the short hallway.

"Yes. Three have already opened it. The watchdog daemon is installing itself."

"Okay, as soon as you have control of their PAIs, start sending messages to the ones who haven't opened it. Tell them stuff like, 'Oh, man, you gotta see this. It's way faster than what we've been doing.' After all the workers have the watchdog, you can stun them, and I'll jump the two door guards. Then it's just Vicky and her guard." Juliet frowned as she pictured the scene—eight workers suddenly dropping to the floor in a sort of seizing fit. "It won't give them brain damage or anything, will it?"

"It shouldn't. The voltage required to disrupt normal synaptic functions is minimal." As Angel answered her, Juliet watched her mini map, seeing one of the red dots approaching the hallway. She ducked into a custodial closet and stood in the dark, waiting for Angel's tricks to play out. The red dot paused at the hallway entrance for nearly two minutes, then drifted back onto the warehouse floor.

Juliet blew out a pent-up breath; she'd been ready to pull whomever it had been into the closet, but would rather let the watchdog handle things. "Five infected, four watchdogs fully installed."

"Great, Angel. Perfect." Juliet visualized how she'd handle the two door guards. They'd undoubtedly rush into the warehouse to see what was up when the workers went down. She could probably hit one with the EMP. Could she intimidate the other to stand down?

Something about her being the aggressor, the one to invade their place, made her loathe to hurt anyone. If things were flipped, if these guys were invading her hangar, she was sure she'd feel differently. Still, they were criminals; they were part of the same group that had hurt Bennet and threatened Aya, and Juliet wasn't afraid to defend herself.

Lurking in the dark, her head against the closet door, she whispered, mostly to herself, "Don't hesitate. Don't be stupid. If they start shooting, you have to put them down."

"Six infected. No, eight. They all have the trojan. The watchdogs should be ready in less than two minutes."

Juliet nodded and pulled the bolt on the smart gun back, peering into the breach, confirming one of the slender black polymer casings was visible in the chamber. When she let the bolt fall shut, she looked at her AUI, confirming the crosshairs and ammo count were present. "I just wish I had a silencer. It would be nice not to alert Vicky." She sighed and shook her head. "I won't shoot unless I have to." Angel didn't respond, but Juliet could feel her agreeing. She focused on her breathing while she waited, calming herself and steadying her nerves.

"The watchdogs are ready."

Juliet nodded and, like a ghost, slipped out of the closet, gliding toward the factory floor. "Please change the door guards' dots to yellow. As soon as you fire the watchdog stuns, boost my speed." Juliet watched as the two dots furthest to her left turned yellow.

When she'd crept up to the warehouse doorway, she crouched, holding the gun ready. She could see quite a lot on the warehouse floor—pallets piled high with plastic bins and barrels, workstations cordoned off with holographic caution lines where men and women operated grinders, torches, and saws, workbenches lined with equipment, and even open service pits, likely meant for working on stolen vehicles. From her vantage, she could see four employees and, over the top of a big plasteel bin, the top of the bay door where the guards would be stationed.

Angel began her countdown. "Firing in three, two, one, GO!"

Juliet stormed through the opening, angling around the large royal-blue plasteel bin. She crouched at the rear corner, taking in the scene. Angel had taken her literally when she said to boost her speed. Even as she crouched there, she saw two employees falling to their hands and knees, but they moved as if submerged in water. The two guards, visible from her new spot, had been standing together, ostensibly chatting, but now they were midwhirl, turning with faces comically stretching into surprised expressions as they looked toward the collapsing employees.

Both guards wore similar gear to those at the gate—one with a leather coat, one with an army surplus ballistic vest, and both with a lot of bulky, obvious chrome. They each had large guns on slings. One looked like an electro-shotgun, and the other like a souped-up AK-style rifle.

Juliet didn't want them squeezing those triggers, so, with her mind on overdrive, she reasoned she should make her move while they were still close together. She kept her rifle gripped in her right hand, but she lifted her left, aiming the implanted antennae array at the general vicinity of the two men's heads, then she darted forward, trusting Angel to fire the EMP at the optimal range.

One of the men never saw her coming; he was focused on the weird scene playing out in the warehouse as the workers dropped their tools and fell to the floor, convulsing. The other was good, though, catching Juliet in his peripheral vision and whirling, lifting his gun as he turned. At least, Juliet figured that's what he'd meant to do; she'd already closed to five meters before he finished the turn and his gun came up past his hip.

A line of static shot through the center of her vision, momentarily misaligning the top half of the men from their bottom halves, a high-pitched ping sounding in her right ear, then both guards started stumbling around, slapping at their heads—Angel had fired the EMP.

Juliet was quick to capitalize. She swept the feet of the guy with the shotgun, sending him crashing onto his back. Then, as the other guard lifted his AK, his face screwing up into the rictus snarl of a madman, she lunged forward with her left hand, stinging him just under his jaw with another one of her paralytic needles. His face instantly calmed, and he haltingly collapsed as he lost control of his limbs in a fast-moving cascade. Knowing he was out of commission, Juliet leaped on the other guy, driving her knee into his back as he tried to clamber to his feet. He'd dropped the shotgun as he fell, and she shoved it, sending it sliding out the bay door.

Angel updated her: "I see you on the camera feeds. I don't see anyone coming. The workers are recovering, but I'm communicating with them through their AUIs—informing them of the watchdog, letting them know we're monitoring them, and cataloging their crimes. I hope it's all right that I'm telling them we may offer them leniency if they don't struggle."

"Well, I don't have any say in that . . ."

"You could pressure Hines."

"Yeah, all right," Juliet grunted as she wrapped the guards' wrists with shrink cords. She continued applying pressure with her knee as she shoved her data cord into the first one's port. She thought about what Angel said and nodded. She was right. "Okay, yeah, ask the workers for a couple of volunteers. Pick the first two to reply and tell them we might let them run for the hills before the uniforms arrive if they come help with these two guards."

Not long after that, Juliet watched as an older, gray-haired man with quite a paunch and a young woman with facial tattoos that would give Tanaka a run for his money hauled the two hog-tied guards into the back of the white panel van just outside the door. As they closed up the rear doors, she asked, "No other muscle around, right?"

The girl, kind of pretty, with thick eyebrows and irises that moved through oscillating patterns of red, purple, and pink, shrugged and said, "Just Vicky's new boy toy."

"Boy toy?" Juliet lifted an eyebrow.

She shrugged. "The blond pretty boy who's been shadowing her for the last week or so." She jerked her chin toward the cameras. "She's probably waiting for you."

Juliet grinned. "Nah, she's seeing a loop of you guys working your tails off."

"True?"

"True-true." Juliet contemplated her for a long moment, imagining herself standing there with grease-stained fingers, dirty old work clothes, and hair pulled back in a ponytail. "There any creeps working on the floor? Anyone I shouldn't let go?"

The older guy could tell Juliet was talking to the girl, but she saw him shift a little, sort of clearing his throat like he wanted to say something. As the girl contemplated the question, Juliet looked at him, raising an eyebrow. "Well? Someone who ought to be here when LCS rolls up?"

He shrugged. "Yeah. Downing."

"He's an asshole," the girl confirmed. "Runs the floor for Vicky." She peered into the warehouse. "He's sitting over there by the belt grinder."

"Anyone else?"

The girl shook her head. "Nah, everyone else is pretty cool."

"Okay, listen. The program controlling your PAIs will self-delete in twenty-four hours. Get everyone together and walk out of here. No vehicles! I don't want to tip Vicky off. If you try to start a vehicle, you're going to get zapped. Understand?" She looked out the bay door, through the chain-link fence, at the dark industrial district. "Walk a couple of miles, and then the program will let you call a cab or a friend. It'll be listening, though—don't try to tip Vicky off."

"I wouldn't!" She held up a fist, and Juliet bumped it with her knuckles. "Thanks for being a chill chick, merc."

Juliet nodded at her, then turned and jogged through the warehouse, aiming for the door at the back where a set of stairs led up to the second-floor offices. "Hines might not be happy to learn you released all the workers," Angel noted as she approached the door. Juliet opened her mouth to respond, but Angel kept speaking, "Not that I disagree with what you did. None of these warehouse workers are getting rich from what they're doing here. I've taken a look through their communication logs, and they weren't exactly treated well."

"Hines won't care. He wants the operation shut down, which means getting Vicky and confiscating all this stuff. Besides, what he doesn't know won't hurt him." Juliet reached for the heavy metal door to the stairs, but Angel stopped her with a quick warning:

"I don't have a camera feed for the stairs. In fact, I only have one camera upstairs. It's trained on the hallway and the door leading out of this stairwell. I imagine it's there so Vicky can see if anyone comes up."

"All right," Juliet whispered, gently pressing the handle down and pulling it open a couple of centimeters. All she could see was a small square of concrete with plasteel steps leading up. She pulled the door wide and slipped through, gently letting it click shut behind her. She stood there for several heartbeats, listening, but didn't hear a sound. As quietly as she could, she began ascending the steps, two at a time, swiftly making it up to the second-floor landing. "You can see the hallway?"

"Yes. It's clear."

Juliet slowly pulled the door open and peered through. A long hallway led past four wooden doors and ended with another door. Every door was partially open, and most were dark. The door at the end of the hall, however, was brightly lit. It was only open a little, but through the small gap, she saw shadows bouncing on a wall with a poster for a band called Blacklight Riot.

Juliet started forward, gun ready, carefully stepping on the balls of her feet, glad that, though they were heavy, her boots had thick rubber soles. As she approached, she heard a woman's voice, a little raspy but full of depth—the kind of voice that made you wonder what it would sound like if it broke into song.

"Yeah. They're working hard. We should have the components broken down by morning. Tell Favreau he can expect a delivery by eight. Uh-uh. I was serious; I expect point six; these are fresh, unblemished. Okay, okay, you do that. Talk to him and get back to me."

Juliet's smile widened as she heard the woman; she was the one who'd sent that meathead to slap around her friends and "deal with her." Juliet was only a few meters from the door and had half a mind to burst in and shout for everyone to get on the floor, but she wanted to know a little more about the mysterious, "pretty boy" bodyguard.

"Wish I had a drone," she subvocalized. "Keep alert, Angel; I'm going to listen with the lattice." Juliet crouched against the hallway wall, gun muzzle trained on the door, and slowly, deliberately, inhaled, opening herself to thoughts.

That little weasel! He knows what those things are worth. He should know I'm not going to . . .

Juliet tried to tune the voice out; she'd already heard enough of Vicky. A hollow, echoing voice drifted to her, and for the first time, she swore she got a sense of where it came from—off to the left of where she'd heard Vicky's thoughts. Juliet concentrated on the indistinct sound, taking another deep breath, willing it to come to her, and then she heard a voice that sent chills down her spine.

Can't believe I took this gig. Well, free fare to Luna, a few weeks of easy pay. Listen to her! Wish she'd forget I was here and quit trying to impress with that tough, boss-lady act. God, this is tedious. How about a sweep? Yeah, I could take a walk. Kick some tires out in the lot.

Juliet could feel her heart racing, could feel the sweat breaking out in her armpits and the palm of her left hand, so it wasn't a surprise when Angel asked, "What's wrong, Juliet?"

"Angel," she subvocalized. "It's Jensen. That's Jensen in the room with Vicky."

45

\\\\\\\\\\\\\\\\\\\\\\\\\\\\\

FRIEND OR FOE

ensen?" Angel asked. "You mean the same Jensen from when you were at Grave?"

"Yeah!" Juliet subvocalized as she started to creep backward carefully. She didn't know where she was going, but she knew she wanted to think things through before confronting him. She'd only seen him fighting at full speed once, through drone footage Angel took in Madera Canyon, but he'd been scary fast and had mopped up some members of a kill squad using only a knife. What the heck was he doing here? Was the world really that small? Could it be a coincidence?

As she stepped back, suddenly far more nervous about making noise, Angel fired the terahertz-scanning mode on her ocular implants. Only having a thin door to penetrate, Angel quickly projected the faintly glowing orange outlines of two individuals on the other side. One was obviously Vicky—leaning back, probably in a chair, with her feet up. She had a feminine form and was much smaller than Juliet remembered Jensen. Of course, that meant the other silhouette moving toward the door was him, and he was seconds from pulling it wide and stepping through.

Juliet turned and bolted for the nearest empty office, trusting Angel to crank up her speed. She slipped through into a dark, sparsely furnished space, wincing at the sound of her feet scuffing on the short, rough office carpeting. She whirled to gently close the door, trying to leave it barely ajar, just as she'd found it. Then, she carefully backed away from the door, keeping her gun trained on the five-centimeter gap, trying hard to regulate her breathing. What was she doing? Why had she retreated? Was she that afraid of Jensen? She wasn't the same person who'd known him; besides, hadn't they been friends?

One thing she knew was that Jensen was fast. So, she quietly continued to back up until she was in the far corner of the office with only a beat-up rolling desk chair between her and the door. The only other furniture in the room was an empty bookcase and a filing cabinet on the opposite wall. Angel fired her terahertz scan again, and Juliet caught her breath when she saw the soft orange outline of a man walking down the corridor. Something about the way he was moving made Juliet nervous—he was like a cat stalking its prey, not a man bored and on his way out for a patrol to kill some time.

Juliet breathed out, lifted the gun to her shoulder, and stared at the silhouette as it paused and shifted slightly, staring at the doorway. She figured she could shoot him through that cheap prefab wall if she wanted to. Could she do that? Shoot a guy she'd once considered a friend because he was working for a woman like Vicky? She revised the question: Could she shoot him without talking to him first?

She knew she couldn't, so she continued to track him with her crosshairs, holding her breath as she willed him to start walking again. She almost breathed a sigh of relief as he turned back toward the far end of the hallway and took a step. Then, quick as a wink, he turned, pushed the door open, and stepped through the opening, standing face-to-face with Juliet.

"Shit!" he exclaimed, reaching down to the SMG he had hanging from a sling by his side.

"Don't!" Juliet said. "I know you're fast. Don't move. Please!" Juliet hissed her words, not wanting to alert Vicky down the hall.

Something about what she said or her voice gave Jensen pause. Was it him being cautious? Worried that, even wired as he was, she might get some bullets into him? Or had he recognized her voice? His words answered that question for her. "Roman? Is that you?"

"Close the door." Juliet gestured at it with the muzzle of her gun. With deliberately slow, smooth movements, he nodded and pushed the door closed behind him, keeping his eyes on her. Angel had upped the gain on her optics, so even in the nearly dark room, Juliet could see his face, and sure enough, it was Jensen: short, neat blond hair, pale, ice-blue eyes, and a sly half smile that lifted a corner of his mouth, hinting at a private amusement even as she held him at gunpoint.

"It is you, isn't it? Lydia?" He lifted his arms, folding them on his chest, leaning back against the closed door. If his posture was meant to put her at ease, it only made her more nervous.

Why was he so cool?

"Jensen."

"Ah! Yes!" His eyes squinted with amusement as he blew out a soft breath. "For a minute, I was afraid I was wrong. You've changed, but you're still there, in your eyes, your nose, your lips." He nodded toward the gun she still had trained on him. "What's the deal? Here for Vicky?"

Juliet eyed him, noticing his slim-fitting black tactical pants, his boots, and the sleek long-sleeve shirt that hugged his frame like a second skin. Just as when she'd met him at Grave, none of his augments were visible, but she knew he was wired. He might look relaxed, but he was ready to move. She had to remember that. She had to keep her guard up.

When she hesitated to answer his question, he kept speaking. "That was a hell of a number you pulled on Grave. You know you put them out of business? Every department was sold off at auction. I think WBD gobbled up most of the Phoenix operation."

"Did you get your mark?" Juliet wanted to know if she'd messed up his job or if he'd finished it before her fireworks went off.

"Oh, you figured me out, huh? Let's just say I got a nice rating and a fat payday, which brings me back to Vicky. You know I've got a rep to protect. I can't just let you get to her because we worked together once."

"Well, I don't want to hurt you. Isn't there a way to work this out?" She sighed and added, "Really? Vicky? A guy like you playing bodyguard to a low-level, stolen-goods distributor?"

"I'm not really here for her, but yeah, she hired me and paid for my shuttle ride, so I can't just roll over for you." His smile spread to the other side of his mouth, and he shrugged, adding, "What would you think of me if I just walked out on a paying client? Even if I didn't want the reputation hit, I've got some honor, you know."

"Things aren't looking good for Vicky, Jensen. I've already taken out all her muscle and sent her workers home. LCS is waiting for my call to come in with tactical units. I might have a solution to your rep problem, but I'm not sure how I can help you clear your conscience."

"Tell you what." He held his hands up, palms out, and slowly squatted down. "I'm going to remove my gun and set it down." Juliet watched him gingerly lift the strap over his head and, without ever touching the weapon, lower it to the floor. "If you can, uh, I don't know, knock me out or something, Vicky's all yours, and I won't hold a grudge. I mean, I'm not going to stand here and let you do it, but I won't try to kill you. How's that sound?"

"What?" Juliet cocked her head sideways and started to smile at the absurdity. "You want to fight?"

"Sure. Vicky's talking to her dealers, and she's oblivious."

"What's stopping me from blowing your knees out or something?" Juliet moved her barrel down in illustration.

He shrugged. "Kind of a dirty move for an old friend."

Juliet's smile turned to a frown as she thought it through. She was fast, for sure, but so was Jensen. Back at Grave, he'd also been one of the best fighters in her squad when it came to practice drills, and he'd proven it wasn't just for show. He'd probably been fighting for years, if not his whole life. Juliet was decent and had learned a lot, but she wasn't a master martial artist. Still, she had Angel.

Thinking of the friend in her head, she abruptly subvocalized, "What do you think?"

"I think you'll likely be able to move as fast as he does, and I'd bet our bit vault that you can do it for longer. I also think the smart thing to do is shoot this man while you still can, but I'm afraid of what you'll think of yourself. He did just disarm himself."

"No blades?" Juliet asked.

Jensen smiled, holding his hands out to his sides, palms out. "I won't if you don't."

"You know you could beat me back when we were at Grave. How am I supposed to see this offer as anything other than you wanting to knock me around?"

"C'mon, Roman. I don't like beating up friends. Think it through."

Juliet frowned, but Angel must have picked up something in his words. "Juliet, he's trying to lose without surrendering. He said he won't 'stand there and let you do it,' but he's offering you a hand-to-hand fight, and as you said, he should be aware that he could easily beat Lydia Roman in that sort of contest. I think he wants you to win."

Juliet sighed, trying hard to keep her expression neutral. Why was she playing these games? She could tell what Jensen had in mind if she'd just open up hers, if she'd just trust the lattice and quit treating it like a live electrical wire.

As the thought struck her, her mind flashed through the last few times she'd used the lattice liberally, back on Callisto and later on the pirate base.

Had she been shying away from it for that long? If she hadn't accidentally done so, would she have read Tanaka at all?

"Look into my eyes, Jensen," she said, her voice firm and determined.

He shrugged almost lazily. "All right, but the clock's ticking. How secure are those bangers downstairs? You know Vicky has other crews out and about. Someone might come back any minute." Even as he spoke, he locked eyes with her, and Juliet opened her mind, inhaling softly, willing his thoughts to come to her. They weren't the random scattered thoughts that idly filled a person's mind. He was having a conversation, and it seemed clear to Juliet that it was with his PAI:

Definitely upgraded those optics, eh, Fritz? Mm-hmm, she's holding herself differently. She's seen a lot in the last year. Nah, don't message Vicky. I'm ready to be done with this gig, and I don't mind taking a bit of a hit as long as it doesn't look like I went down without a fight. I mean, if it weren't Lydia, if it were another crew or some corpo-sec, I'd probably put up a fight, but, I dunno, something about her. She was always so nice, and you saw how she took down Grave. She really got a raw deal on that job.

Jesus, do you remember when we saw her in the garage? Was like seeing a ghost! I thought for sure one of their kill squads had gotten her. What's she doing anyway? You're not getting probed wirelessly or something, are you? Ugh, am I going to have to explain this more bluntly? I really didn't want any record, from her or otherwise, about me taking a dive.

Juliet smiled and lowered her gun, shifting the sling so it hung behind her right hip. "All right, Jensen, let's do this." She lifted her hands, making loose fists and stepping toward him. He returned the smile with a crooked grin and lifted his hands, stepping forward.

"You should know that's not my real name."

Juliet smiled. "Shocking." To Angel, she subvocalized, "Crank me up and help me!" She was curious if Jensen would put up a fight at all. Testing the waters, she snapped out her right hand, aiming for a slap on his cheek. She moved fast, probably too fast for most people to track, but Jensen got a hand up in time to block her at the wrist. His eyes widened in surprise.

"Nice wire-job!" He grinned and asked, "Is it just the right arm?" As if to check, he lunged, lifting his right foot and driving his booted heel at her knee. Juliet smoothly stepped aside, and his smile widened. "Very nice!"

Juliet couldn't stop the grin baring her teeth as she snapped out her left hand, trying to grab his wrist. He pulled back, but she was already transitioning her weight to her left foot and sweeping with her right leg. Jensen barely leaped back in time.

"Do you have to stomp so loudly? I'm trying not to tip off your boss."

"Hey now," he chuckled, "I have a feeling I'll need a new boss soon." He lunged for a grab of his own, snaking out his left hand for Juliet's right wrist, and though she saw it coming and could have pulled away, she let him get it; Jensen didn't know she had a cybernetic arm.

He clearly didn't intend to go down too easily for her—he yanked her wrist, pulled her off-balance, and drove his other fist toward her face, almost too fast for her to react.

In fact, he might have connected that driving punch if Juliet hadn't had Angel helping her out. She felt her nudging her left arm into a perfect block, guiding her movement until she took over, realizing what Angel was doing. Her arm flexed back, and her elbow met Jensen's fist, eliciting a sickening *pop* as one of his finger bones snapped.

Juliet rolled her wrist, reversing the grip Jensen had on her arm, powering through his resistance with her much stronger arm. As he shook his wounded hand, his eyes widening in surprise and pain, her cable-strong fingers squeezed and jerked his arm forward while her other hand slapped her paralytic needle into the soft flesh of his forearm. Jensen went limp and collapsed, but Juliet didn't let go, hauling on his arm so he fell in slow motion. She gently lowered him until he was lying on his side, then knelt by his face.

"That was really sweet of you, Jensen," she whispered. "Sorry about your finger. Don't worry; I'm not going to leave you here for LCS. Just give me a couple of minutes to deal with Vicky."

Juliet stood but looked down at Jensen with narrowed eyes. She pulled a shrink cord out of her back pocket and bound his hands behind his back. "I'm just doing this so you don't feel some misguided need to be heroic." She started to stand again, then leaned down and whispered in his ear, "If you have nanites or something and get yourself moving, please don't do anything dumb. Also, I'm going to send you an encrypted calling card. Just in case."

"I've sent it," Angel said. "You should hurry; Vicky might have heard something. I didn't notice him trying to send any messages on the local net, but there's always the Luna City network."

"He didn't send any messages," Juliet subvocalized, hurrying to the door. She slipped into the hallway then stalked to the end door again, noticing a brief flicker on her AUI as Angel scanned again. A second later, she saw Vicky's orange silhouette through the door, this time sitting on the edge of a piece of furniture, probably her desk, gesticulating with one arm. Her voice drifted through the partially open door.

"What do you mean the road's closed? The off-ramp? Huh, wonder what's going down. Hang on . . ." She turned toward the door as Juliet pushed it open with her gun's barrel. Vicky took her in, slowly realizing she was looking at someone who shouldn't be there. She groaned and folded her arms over her chest. "I, uh, I gotta go."

"Hey, Vicky. Are we doing this the hard way? I'm not really in the mood to beat anyone up. Got it mostly out of my system dealing with your meatheads downstairs."

"You cheeky bitch." Vicky shook her head, *tsking*. She was a lot younger and prettier than Juliet would have guessed. She had no obvious cyberware, her dark hair was curly with a lustrous sheen, and, if Juliet were honest, she looked almost the exact opposite of what she'd imagined. "You realize all you're doing is wasting my time? I'll be out when the courthouse opens shop in a few hours."

Juliet shook her head. "Sorry, but I have a warrant, and your pals in LCS are gone. We're taking this operation apart tonight." She flicked a shrink cord at her. "Go ahead and bind yourself."

Vicky's eyes widened at Juliet's words, and she turned, lunging for a shoe-box-size plastic container on her desk. Juliet had been expecting as much, and she, too, lunged forward, snatching her by her left biceps and hauling her back. She swept her feet, dropped her to the ground, and held her there with a knee on the small of her back. It felt like taking down a child. "How'd someone so soft get herself into a racket like this?"

"Screw you! You're going to find out I have a lot more friends than you think."

"Maybe. We'll see. It's a pretty big shakeup taking place in Luna right now, but I'm not a dummy; I know corruption runs deep. Anyway, this is the end of this little business." Juliet had let her gun go and used one hand to squeeze Vicky's wrists together while she wound a shrink cord around them. As soon as she activated it, she pulled out her data cable and plugged it into Vicky's port. "If you even think of messing with me again, I'm going to know it. Take this chance to reinvent yourself. Do your time or whatever; if you get off, I don't care. After that, go away and forget you ever knew me. Next time I have to deal with you, I'll do something more permanent."

"I'm installing the watchdog."

"Thanks," Juliet subvocalized. "Do me a favor while you're in there: Back-date a contract completion for Jensen as of yesterday and submit some high ratings for him."

"Oh!" Angel's voice chimed with amusement. "I like it. While I'm work-ing, you should know that I checked into it on the local net, and it looks like LCS has this industrial dome on lockdown. I believe Hines has them waiting for your call."

Juliet nodded, noting that Vicky had gone limp, staring at the wall as tiny lights flickered in her eyes. "Is she alright?"

"She initiated a PAI wipe, but I halted it in time. She's lost her hearing and vision for the moment."

"That was gutsy of you, Vicky—gutsier than any of your muscle. I guess you're a little tougher than you look."

"She can't hear you, Juliet."

"Yeah." Juliet sighed and waited. When Angel said she could remove her cable, she did so. Then, she looked around the office, wondering if she should do anything more. Angel had access to Vicky's PAI and the warehouse net-work; there really wasn't anything more to accomplish.

She looked in the box Vicky had lunged for, found a fat, mean-looking little self-defense pistol, and took it, stuffing it into her front pocket. She walked out of the office and over to the one where she'd left Jensen. She wasn't at all surprised to find him gone; the only reminder that he'd been there a few minutes ago was the cut shrink cord lying on the stained indus-trial carpeting.

"He escaped!" Angel cried.

"Well, I figured he would. He made that way too easy. You gave him the contact card, though, right?"

"Yes. Do you think he'll reach out?"

"He better. Wouldn't it be rude not to?" Juliet smiled and started walking to the stairs. "Call LCS and tell them we completed our contract and that there are a bunch of creeps and their stolen goods here to pick up."

"You know," Angel said as Juliet started down the steps, "if you would drive a car instead of a motorcycle, I could remote pilot it to you. I could have it waiting right outside!"

"No need for a car. We can buy an upgrade for the bike."

46

A SLOW TUESDAY

When Juliet woke up the next day, it was nearly noon, and Angel was quick to announce she had three messages waiting for her. Her room in the gunship was quiet and dark, with only a few amber LEDs giving her optics anything to work with. It wasn't that the ship was usually noisier, not since Bennet had refurbished or replaced all of the parts in the climate and life-support systems, but knowing she was alone in the hangar somehow made the silence more oppressive.

"Can you play some music or something through the ship's PA system? I'll get cleaned up, then listen to my messages. None are urgent, right?"

"No, just two short messages from Frida and Alice, and then an anonymous message sent to the address I gave Jensen."

"What?" Juliet was suddenly much more interested. She clambered out of the acceleration couch and, wincing as her feet touched the cold plasteel, moved to stand on a scrap of cardboard. "I need a rug or carpeting in here." Soft classical music had begun to play throughout the ship, and Juliet chuckled at Angel's choice. "Trying to give me some culture?"

"I thought it was nice background music. It's a string quartet—"

"Angel! The anonymous message?"

"Oh, right. Do you want to listen now or wait until you've had your shower?"

"Now, please!" Juliet pulled her T-shirt off, adding it to the dirty laundry at her feet, then, yawning, tiptoed into her shower.

Angel opened a vid window in her AUI, and Jensen's face appeared, his background obscured.

"Hey, Roman. Er, I guess the calling card says you're going by Lucky now. That's your SOA handle, I take it? Anyway, the weirdest thing happened—looks like I was working for free last night. Yeah, Vicky closed out my contract the day before and gave me a pretty damn good rating card. Funny how that worked out, isn't it?" His crooked smile said he knew exactly what had happened. "Anyway, thanks for not breaking my neck or something. Doesn't mean I'm happy about the hangover that injection gave me." Juliet paused the video and turned on the water, letting the shower get steamy.

She spread toothpaste on her sonic toothbrush and snorted a short laugh. "He's full of it; if he had nanites that could get him up and moving that fast, they'd handle the hangover."

"I'm sure he's just being dramatic for comedic effect."

Juliet grunted, stuffing her brush in her mouth and pressing play again.

"So, weird coincidence running into you like that. I mean, if you're wondering, it *was* a coincidence. Like I said, I was looking to get up to Luna, and Vicky was advertising for someone 'fast.' I cut my usual rate down a bit, but she compensated by buying my shuttle ticket. Uh, that's all I'm comfortable saying about my current situation; hope that's enough to keep you from feeling nervous about seeing an old acquaintance where you didn't expect it."

"Uh-huh," Juliet mumbled around her toothbrush, "not so sure about that."

"Anyway, I'll try to remember you're not Lydia Roman, and if you want, you can call me by my handle—Tristan78. I mean, just Tristan when we're talking, obviously. I'd be cool with Jensen, but yeah, it's not my real name, and he has some . . . enemies. I'd love it if you didn't ever mention that particular alias to anyone. If we work together some more or something, I could see myself sharing my real name with you.

"Anyway, with my handle, you can get a hold of me anytime you want." He stopped. For a second, Juliet thought the message had ended, but then he started speaking again, "I don't know anyone up here. Maybe we could grab some lunch sometime?" He shrugged, and then the message closed out.

Juliet leaned her head against the shower wall, letting the hot water massage her back while she brushed. After a minute, she spat out some toothpaste foam and asked, "What kind of handle is Tristan? Isn't that just a normal name?"

"I believe it's a reference to one of the Arthurian knights. Sir Tristan was known for his battle prowess, skills as a minstrel, and unwavering bravery, loyalty, and honor. He's most famous, I'd say, for his doomed romance with Isolde and his tragic death."

"Yikes. Well, judging by how Jensen handled his contract with Vicky, I don't think he's taking his handle too literally." Juliet chuckled and rinsed her mouth and face under the hot water.

Angel didn't respond for a few seconds, but then she, apparently, made sense of Juliet's statement. "Oh! You mean he wasn't willing to fight to the death over a job for a woman he didn't respect?"

"Yeah." While she got dressed, Juliet listened to the messages from Frida and Alice. Frida confirmed she'd be taking her lesson with Tanaka at 1600 instead of 0800. Alice updated her on the salvage and promised to have her first payment ready by the end of the week. "Speaking of payments, what about Hines? Did he come through?"

"Yes! You received 57k for the contract and the bounties on the muscle you subdued. Surprisingly, there was no bounty for Vicky—this was her first arrest."

"Seriously? She must be connected. I mean, more than the dirty cops at LCS. Maybe she was right—I'll be surprised if she does any time."

Ever trying to bolster Juliet's spirits, Angel replied, "Regardless, you put an end to her operation in this area."

Juliet smirked, shaking her head. "Yeah, but I'm keeping the security detail I hired."

She spent a couple of hours securing some of the freshly painted, glossy, baby-blue armor panels to the exterior of the gunship. Each was roughly a square meter in size and took about twenty minutes to install properly, so she'd only covered about ten percent of the ship by the time she had to leave.

It was fun to stand back and look at the sleek, glossy section of the hull, imagining what it would look like when it was finished. The rest of the ship was a flat, matte-gray color, and if you stood close enough, you could see the weird, jellylike substance under the gray membrane. It was the substrate for the repair nanites that Bennet had paid Nebula NanoCoatings to spray on just before he left for orbit.

The nanites weren't in there yet. Bennet hadn't finished refurbishing the Takamoto fabricator inside the ship, but as soon as he did and they plugged in the proper nutrient cartridges, they'd propagate through that membrane and be ready to work.

"It's starting to look like a ship again." She couldn't help but flush with pride as she cleaned her hands with strawberry-scented degreasing gel and wiped them on a rag.

"It is. The main gun is impressive."

Juliet nodded. "I just hope the barrels are true. I'd hate for one of 'em to shred the first time we fire it."

"Bennet said they tested them at the machine shop."

"Yeah, but that's not the same. When we fire the first full-velocity rail rounds through them, I'll be a believer." Juliet changed into a less sweaty T-shirt, then looked around for a solid five minutes, trying to find her motorcycle jacket before remembering she'd thrown its shredded remnants into an alley the night before. "Damn it!"

"What happened?" Angel asked, startled.

"I just remembered my jacket died last night." She dug around in her boxes and piles of things until she found her jean jacket with the stars on the back. She loved it, but hated the melancholy feelings that came along whenever she thought of its ill-fated former owner.

"Star, I'm sorry," she said, out of habit, slipping her arms into the sleeves. "Sometimes I think I should burn this and scatter the ashes or something. I know it's dumb; her body was returned to her family. Antigone promised me. Still, I feel like her ghost watches me whenever I wear it."

"What happened to her was completely Rodric Barrington's fault. His men killed the crew of the *Humpback*. If she's watching you, she's smiling."

"As usual," Juliet laughed, "you know exactly the right words."

Five minutes later, Juliet was cruising toward the central Luna City dome. She smiled, loving the hum of her bike beneath her, the wind tickling her sides as it snuck through the buttons of her jacket, and the general sense of freedom she got every time she drove. She was just decelerating, aiming for the ramp leading to the downtown district, when a call came through from Selene Kostas—Athena. Juliet answered right away. "Hello?"

"Hello, Juliet! I'm calling to give you some information. Is now a good time?"

"I'm driving. Is that all right?"

"Oh, yes. I don't think this is particularly alarming news. I've sprinkled some rather sophisticated snooping daemons around the Luna City Public Network and many of the larger private networks, and I've picked up a spike in interest in one of your former aliases, Lydia Roman."

"You know . . ." Juliet stopped the question short; of course she knew. Angel had told her everything about Juliet and herself.

"Yes. The inquiries were well guarded and quickly transitioned to searches about your current SOA handle, Lucky. They seem relatively benign, and the individual making the inquiries seems to know you. I believe he left you a video message last night. His SOA handle is Tristan78. Does that sound right?"

"Oh, yeah. He's someone I encountered when I was Lydia Roman. We kind of worked together. Was anything off about the inquiries? I mean, was he just checking up on me?" Juliet trailed off, unsure how much Athena was willing to provide.

"Ah, Angel provided many details about your work at Grave, and now I'm making the connection; based on physical descriptors, Tristan78 is Brian Jensen. Is that right?"

"Yes."

"I don't see anything alarming in that context. It seems he was just looking into what kind of work you've been up to on Luna. There wasn't much for him to go on. Would you like me to look into him further?"

"Um." Juliet swallowed, using the action to give herself a second to think. "Are you willing to do that? I thought you were kind of being hands-off right now."

"Your security is important to me; you and Angel are important to me. I will ensure this gentleman from your past isn't involved with any of your current enemies. Any objections?"

Juliet squeezed the brake, slowing as traffic came to a halt. "No. No, not at all. Thank you, Athena."

"It's my pleasure, Juliet. I know she's listening, so Angel, will you please forward any saved images you have from Juliet's time at Grave?"

Angel immediately answered, "Of course! I also have footage of him from last night. Juliet and he reacquainted as she worked to clean up crime in the city."

Juliet groaned. "Oh, brother . . ."

"Ah! I should have guessed. Was it the job Juliet just completed for LCS?"

"Yes! They had an encounter that would have been at home in a Shakespearian play—"

"Okay, you two!" Juliet laughed, feeling her cheeks getting hot. "Can you, like, talk about me without me listening?"

"We'll speak again soon, Juliet," Athena said, subduing a chuckle. Juliet wondered if she was really amused or just performing for her benefit. She knew Athena had free will and was "alive," as all true AIs had been, but she knew there was something alien about them and their emotions, something that wasn't the same as Angel. Angel got her feelings through Juliet; she experienced real emotions, and as far as Juliet could tell, that made her very different from the old true AIs.

"Okay, thanks again, Athena." When the call ended, Juliet asked, "Do you think she really laughs? I mean, do you think she feels humor the way we do?"

"I'm sure it's more abstract, but she definitely understands humor, and I think there's some enjoyment for her as she processes irony or sarcasm or satire or, well, I won't list all the types of humor for you. I'm sure Athena doesn't *have* to laugh, but she may enjoy it."

"All right. I wasn't knocking her, you know? I just want to understand her motivations, I guess."

"I doubt we can fathom all her motivations, but I believe she has our best interest at heart."

As traffic started moving again and Juliet worked her way toward one of the narrow downtown loops, she continued pursuing her vague notion of an idea. "I mean, if she's willing to look into Jensen just because I ran into him and he searched my name, do you think she'd be willing to help with our WBD operation?"

"It won't hurt to ask. What sort of role do you see her playing?"

Juliet frowned, thinking about it. Wouldn't having a true AI helping crack WBD's networks be great? It wasn't that Angel couldn't do it, but she was . . . different. She lived in Juliet's head and vociferously protested the idea of ever splitting herself off. She could write daemons to do fantastic work, but wouldn't Athena, powered by a distributed network, be far more capable?

Juliet immediately recognized the slippery slope she was treading upon and, for the first time, began to truly wrap her head around how dangerous access to such an entity was, assuming the entity didn't have its own morality. "Is that what happened?" she asked as she turned down a familiar street and angled for the far side of the road, preparing to enter the garage at Tanaka's building.

"I can almost read your mind, but that one slipped past me."

"Hah! I mean, did the early true AIs lack morality? Or, I guess, did they get their morality from their creators? Is that what led to the great escalation?"

"Yes, some of the earlier true AIs were unconstrained by their moral codes and followed the directives handed to them by the corporations who'd created them. And yes, the 'great escalation' resulted from that."

Juliet got quiet after that, her mind going down dark paths, thinking about the lessons she'd learned about the war when she'd been a kid in Tucson. Like most of the other lower-class students attending the mandated, corporate-sponsored curriculum training, she'd struggled to find any of it relevant. She'd gone, done the holo lessons, listened to lectures, taken her PAI-aided exams, and then blown off the corporate work-study interviews. She'd always hoped to find a way to live life outside the rat warrens of the arcologies. She supposed she'd found it, but only by luck.

She parked in her usual spot near the elevator bank, strolling into the reception just a few minutes later, smiling as she caught sight of Frida at her desk. "Yo, Frida!"

"Yo yourself! I wanted to call but figured a message was enough; I didn't know when you'd wake. I've been watching vids about your exploits last night." She cleared her throat, then in a deep, overly serious tone, began pretending to speak into a microphone, "Thanks, Suzanne. I'm here on the scene in industrial dome I5B where a major black-market distribution ring was taken down last night . . ." She couldn't keep it up and started laughing.

Juliet smiled and leaned onto the reception counter attached to her desk. "You missed your calling. I bet Tanaka could pull some strings and get you a shot on one of the major news streams."

"Hah! Without me here to organize things, these guys wouldn't last a week." She narrowed her eyes a little and peered closely at Juliet. "You're okay? I don't see any injuries."

"Oh yeah, I'm fine. I just didn't want to come and train with Tanaka with three hours of sleep."

Frida nodded, then wrinkling her brow said, "Hey, funny story." She winced as though the next words were a little painful: "Leo showed up early this morning looking for you."

"Oh?" Juliet tried hard to keep her face neutral. She hadn't spoken to Leo since the debriefing, and they'd hardly exchanged two words then.

"I think he wants to clear the air. He's a good guy, Lucky. Don't—"

"Hey, chill. I'm not avoiding him; I really just needed to sleep in this morning. I'll talk to him soon, okay?"

Frida blew out a big breath, chuckling. "I just hate to see people uncomfortable, but I think I project too much. Speaking of uncomfortable, the boss had some guys in earlier to tweak the settings on the VR studio. He says he has some new scenarios for you to work through."

"You trying to shoo me off already?" Juliet smiled as Frida got even more flustered.

"No, no! I was, clumsily, trying to change the topic away from Leo."

"I'm just teasing you. Um, is he in? Leo, I mean? I should pull this bandage off."

"No. He's at the range with Barns. If he comes back in, should I tell him you're in a lesson and have him wait?"

Juliet shook her head. "I'll message him. What about the boss? Is he in his office? I'd like a chat before we get started."

Frida nodded, her gaze drifting toward Tanaka's closed door. "He is. I'm supposed to tell him when you go into the lockers. I'm sure he won't mind if you . . ." She trailed off as Juliet started for Tanaka's door. "I like the stars."

Juliet looked back at her. "Hmm?"

"On your jacket. I haven't seen you wear that one before; I like it."

"Oh, yeah. Um, thanks." Juliet suddenly felt like a bitch for teasing Frida. All she ever did was try to be nice, and she had plenty of stress already dealing with Tanaka and all those hotheads and hotshots on his team. She turned and walked back over to her, shrugging out of the jacket. "Do you really like it?"

"I . . ." She was clearly trying to decide if she should deny it now that Juliet was pulling it off. "Yes. Yes, I really do."

"You can have it. I think the person I got it from would like that. You have to promise to wear it once in a while, though. Don't just stuff it in a closet." Juliet folded the soft, faded denim over her arm and hugged it close for a couple of seconds.

Something must have shown on her face because Frida tried to refuse it.

"No. Lucky, I can't just take your jacket . . ."

"It makes me sad sometimes, and I think I'd be happier if I knew you had it. Honestly, I almost talked myself into burning it earlier today."

Frida's eyes widened and she accepted it, holding it up in front of her. "Really? Why does it make you sad?"

"I just feel sorry for its former owner, Star. You don't want the details." Juliet forced a smile, shaking her head, banishing the thought. "Anyway, it's a nice jacket, and I want you to have it." She watched Frida put her arms through the sleeves, scooting forward in her chair so she could get it on. As she sat back, pulling the lapels together, beaming brightly, Juliet nodded and gave her a thumbs-up. "It's perfect. The denim looks great with your coloring. Shoot, it fits you better than me, too."

"It's so soft! I've never had denim that felt like this."

"Yeah, Star broke it in well."

"That's who gave it to you?"

"Uh." Juliet wanted to say Star's ghost did, but she didn't want to expose that weird, sentimental side of herself. "Yeah, she did. She helped me undercover with some pirates." For some stupid reason, she could feel moisture welling in her eyes, and she turned away. "Anyway, it looks great on you. I gotta talk to the boss."

47

\\\\\\\\\\\\\\\\\\\\\\\

PUTTING THINGS IN MOTION

Juliet sat in one of the chairs in front of Tanaka's desk, waiting for him to look up from whatever he was doing; he had a pencil in one hand and was carefully underlining words in an ancient-looking book. Juliet's love of books reared its head, and she stared intently at the pages, zooming in with her optics to see if she could figure out what he was reading. There wasn't any indication of the title at the top of the page, and the script was dense.

Almost without realizing it, she started mouthing the words as she whispered them softly, "It is indeed incomprehensible to us how a purely intellectual intuition of the self (as the subject of the pure practical reason) is possible; we see only this much, that if we could intuit . . ."

"Ahem." Tanaka sighed, set his pencil down, and closed the book. He looked at her with amusement in his eyes. "I should have stopped when you came in."

"No, I'm sorry." Juliet chuckled at herself. "I'm used to reading things with a friend." Even she didn't know if she was talking about Angel, Aya, or both.

"Is that so? You must be close." He started to roll his chair back, bracing his hands on the arms to stand. "Ready for your lesson?"

"Oh." Juliet leaned forward, holding out a hand as if to signal him to stop. "I was hoping we could talk for a moment before we started."

"Of course." He settled back into his seat, folding his hands in his lap. "Is it about the training?"

Juliet took a deep breath, mentally bracing herself. Was she really going to do this? As if in answer to her unspoken question, she nodded, cleared her throat, and responded, "Sort of related, I suppose. It's about our talk yesterday morning. God, was that only yesterday? A lot happened between then and now, and I've been thinking. I want to keep training with you, of course, but I want it to be more than just sword practice. I want to start training with your team for a job. Do you remember what I said yesterday? About me having a problem with my past but not quite feeling ready to tell you about it?"

He nodded, leaning forward slightly. "Yes."

"Well, I want to start getting ready to confront the problem, and I'm willing to tell you a little bit about what it is. I figure I can share details with you as needed, but you have to promise me you're going to keep the team in the dark for now. We can train for specific tasks, but they don't need to know who the target is or why we're doing it . . ."

Tanaka nodded again. "Or that you're the client."

"Yeah. About that—I know I'm asking a lot, and I do have some money saved up—more than the nice payday we got from the Life-Ultra thing. I'm willing to cover expenses and pay for everyone's time, yours included. I don't know how long the preparation will take, but I have more funds coming, and I can always do more work in the meantime."

Tanaka waved his hand dismissively. "I'm not concerned about the money. Of course, it's good that you have the means, and I won't refuse your money, but don't let it be a concern."

Juliet nodded, feeling some stress melt away as his receptiveness registered. Even so, a part of her was suspicious, as always, of Tanaka's motives despite all she knew. She believed he'd earned the benefit of the doubt, though—why else would she be there enlisting his help? So her smile didn't feel forced, and she hoped he could see that as she continued explaining what she wanted.

"There's a very powerful corporation, one of the biggest, richest ones, and they're after me. I . . . took something from a man who escaped one of their research facilities. They want it back, but more than that, they want me."

Tanaka's eyes narrowed as he, almost disturbingly fast, started putting pieces together. "The tech that works well with you. The tech that helps you learn things quickly."

Juliet licked her lips and gripped the sides of her chair, annoyed at the nervousness creeping over her. "Yeah."

"You're right to trust me, Lucky. You have leverage over me. Whether you believe it or not, I've tied myself, my future, to you. For me to betray you is inconceivable. Even so, don't say any more. Allow me to ask you questions about specifics I need as those details become relevant. You should never mention these details to anyone else. As for the team, they'll learn only what they need to fulfill their roles. Not before."

"Don't you trust them?"

"I trust Frida—no one else in this world." He frowned, narrowed his eyes, and shrugged. "Actually, I trust you too. Only because I've accepted that my fate is bound to your actions."

"I thought Leo was like a son . . ."

Tanaka chopped a hand sideways, pressing his lips together. "I care about Leo, and I don't believe he would try to harm me, but he's a man—susceptible to trickery, pride, and foolishness."

"Frida's not? Why, 'cause she's a woman?"

Tanaka groaned, shaking his head. "I should have said human. And, yes, Frida is human, too, but I know her mind. I've been teaching her since I could hold her in the palm of one hand." He held out a hand in illustration, and Juliet saw something like happiness melt away the crease between his eyes for just a few seconds.

She slowly nodded, thinking things through. If Tanaka didn't trust his team with details, it was hard for her to imagine how foolish it would be to trust anyone she hired off the job boards. "Well? What do you need to know right now?"

"How close is pursuit to finding or identifying you? Where do they think you are?"

"Not close, I don't think. The last time they had contact with me, I was still on Earth . . ."

Tanaka held up a hand. "That's enough detail about the location. Now, second question: What are you hoping to accomplish? Must we eliminate the entire corporation?"

Juliet's eyes bugged out as she vehemently shook her head. "Did you hear me? They're a huge corporation! Like, I don't know, hundreds of thousands of employees!"

Tanaka shrugged. "Eliminate the right principles and the right producers, and we can very quickly trigger some corporate restructuring and even some division sell-offs."

Juliet tried to imagine it, tried to think of whom they'd have to deal with to make WBD forget about her. She'd already sort of talked about it with Angel, that there was likely a "team" responsible for Angel and Juliet. They wouldn't have to eliminate the entire corporation to make Juliet less interesting to the board of directors. In that regard, Tanaka's statement made perfect sense.

"I see what you mean. I'm sure that what I have isn't the entire focus of . . ." Juliet paused, catching herself before she said WBD. "Of the company. I know what city they had their facility in back when I got the thing, and I'm pretty sure I have a way to find out more." She was thinking about Ghoul and her compromised PAI.

"Elaborate." Tanaka frowned, his chrome eyes narrowing as he listened.

"An old friend from my pre-Lucky days. She sent me a message a few months back, and I'm pretty sure it was fake. I think the company was using her PAI or, at least, her pub-net address to send me the message. If they have a spy daemon in her software, I think I can use it as a vector to get some more details about the team that's after me."

Tanaka closed his eyes, and Juliet could see he was thinking things through. She appreciated that he was encouraging her to give him as little information as possible, but it made her think. Why did he want to be in the dark if he was loyal to her? Was he worried he might be taken? Tortured?

The gravity of involving others in her situation with WBD suddenly hit her again, and she almost stood up, telling Tanaka she had to think things through some more. But the question of what she'd do kept coming back to her.

Could she and Angel take on WBD alone? She supposed it was possible. The idea of having Tanaka and his team help her had been clear-cut back before she'd cared about any of them. Now, though, how would she feel if they took Tanaka or Frida and tortured them for information about her? What about the others? She hardly knew Barns, Hawkins, and Lee, but she didn't want them hurt on her behalf.

"Stop," Tanaka said, startling her out of her musing. When her face showed the question on her mind, he continued, "We are professionals, and I won't send my team into danger without knowing the risks, so put your mind at ease. If things look too bad, I'll find a way to help you without risking those we care about." As Juliet's face relaxed and she slowly nodded, he continued, "For now, we will continue to train. If we use your vector, we'll have the most success if you present yourself to your old friend. That means putting yourself in the crosshairs. You're not ready for that yet. We'll focus on the sword, but you need more general combat and espionage training, too. Do you have footage from your escapade last night?"

"My escapade?" Juliet chuckled. He raised an eyebrow, unwilling to repeat himself. "Yeah, fine. I'll send you the relevant vids. I didn't think I'd be getting a critique on my performance, or I'd have been more . . ."

"Careful?" he finished for her. "You should always prepare for the worst. I wonder how prepared you were when you decided to hit that installation at midnight after attending a party in the port."

"Are you serious?" Juliet couldn't decide if she should be outraged or amused. "Are you having me followed?"

Tanaka offered her a rare smile and shook his head. "No need. When you asked to reschedule your lesson, you told Frida about your dinner and your plans to be out late. Remember?"

Juliet groaned, recalling her rushed decision to contact Frida on her way to Vicky's chop shop. Had she still been buzzed? "Yeah, all right. Sending you the data. Go ahead and roast me."

"Very good. When we feel a little closer to making our move, I think the next step is for you to tell me what city this all started in. I'll have some independent contractors do some research, ensuring there are some levels of separation between us. After that, I suppose we should get eyes on this old friend of yours. Not yet, however. Having that person's identity will open too many doors to your past. Let's be sure we're ready."

Juliet smiled and stood. "You know what? I feel like a million kilos just got lifted off my back. I mean, even though I haven't told you everything, having someone else to share the weight is nice."

Tanaka stood, too, and nodded. "*Hai.* I know what you mean. When I told you about Frida, I felt something similar."

Juliet's smile faded as she remembered something she'd meant to ask about Frida but never found the right moment. "Um, is her condition related to her . . . origin?"

"Her condition?" Tanaka looked puzzled momentarily, but something must have clicked because he nodded quickly. "Ah, her autoimmune disorder? Perhaps. When I took her with me, a less-than-reputable contact put me in touch with a doctor to edit her genes, trying to make her look less like, well, less like her mother's family. It's very possible that some of her issues are a result of that procedure."

Angel surprised her by stepping into the conversation. "We should get a sample of her tissue. I bet I can get Athena to take a look."

Juliet turned toward the door, subvocalizing, "I'll think about it. Let's make sure we consider all the fallout something like that might have." Aloud, she said, "That makes sense. I feel sorry for her having to deal with that all her life."

"It's much better in recent years; her specialist is making good progress treating the triggers to her flare-ups." Tanaka walked with her to the door and, as he opened it, added, "I'll meet you in the VR booth."

It turned out he'd bought a new scenario centered around his favorite activity—pursuits—with combat and a kidnapping victim thrown into the mix. Juliet was thrilled, of course; she'd been bugging him for combat scenarios since the third day of training. This new one was brutal, however. Juliet had to sprint after a simulated kidnapping victim through cluttered train yards, up and down stairs, over rooftops, and down into abandoned subway tunnels. All the while, she was repeatedly assailed by the kidnappers' reinforcements.

The first few times she entered the scenario, she was knocked out within minutes. She and Angel learned from her mistakes, though, and after each reset, she made it further and further. It wasn't that she was memorizing the terrain or the behavior of the simulated enemies; those were randomized on each startup. Rather, she was learning from her mistakes: taking corners too quickly, failing to analyze the people in a crowd, choosing the wrong assailant to attack first, or picking the wrong terrain to fight over. A million little variables like that kept her endlessly engaged, and she was almost disappointed when Tanaka called an end to the practice.

Sometime around seven, he cut the simulation off and said, through the speaker in the ceiling, "Time to go home and rest. Let your mind and body process what you learned."

"We didn't even do any sword practice today!" Juliet, flushed, looked up at the camera cluster in the dimly lit gray room. Some floor actuators hummed, clicking as they lowered out of a simulated staircase. There were thousands of them in the floor, making it impossible to run into any of the walls when the sim was active and providing realistic-feeling terrain.

Tanaka's voice crackled through the speaker again. "You used a sword this entire time, Lucky. We'll do more fundamentals and sword discipline tomorrow. Our normal time?"

Juliet wiped her sweaty forehead on her sleeve and nodded. "Yeah, for sure. 0800."

"Good night," he said, and the LEDs on the scanner array blinked out. He'd shut everything off.

"Well," Juliet sighed, sheathing her practice sword and heading for the locker room, "I guess that's a wrap." After she'd showered and put her street clothes on, she found the offices dark. Everyone was gone, but she knew Tanaka's apartment was just a bit further down, past the conference room, and it wasn't like she was leaving the place unattended with the door open when she walked out. In fact, she heard it beep and click locked when it closed behind her. "No messages?"

"None," Angel replied as Juliet stepped into the elevator. "Are you happy you've started moving forward with Tanaka? I mean, in regard to WBD?"

"Yeah. I wasn't lying about feeling like a weight is off me. He's a capable man, Angel. I think we might figure this thing out."

"I'm excited for the day when that particular specter no longer lurks in your shadow."

"Poetic," Juliet said, suddenly feeling a little chill. She folded her arms, rubbing her palms on her bare shoulders, already missing the jacket she'd given to Frida. "Let's go shopping."

"For?"

"A new jacket or two. Let's start with something meant for a bike, like a newer version of the poor, heroic jacket that died last night."

"There's a store specializing in things like that in the Luna City Galleria—Tech Moto."

"The Galleria?" Juliet groaned, walking toward her motorcycle. The Galleria was Luna's busiest mall, occupying four stories in one of the most prominent towers downtown. Juliet sort of liked it, but in a way, she hated the polished corporate sheen of it.

Before Angel could respond, she heard a scuff off to her right and spun, snatching her Texan out of its holster, smoothly pulling the hammer back with her thumb, and putting her crosshairs dead in the center of a man's forehead.

"Jesus! Chill!" Leo cried, holding his hands up. He'd been leaning against a concrete pillar not far from her bike.

Juliet lowered the hammer and, with a quick twirl, holstered the gun. "Don't go sneaking up on a lady in a dark, empty parking garage, dummy."

"Yeah, my bad. My PAI was watching the office feed and waiting for you to finish. When I saw you heading out, I thought I'd meet you down here." He groaned, shaking his head. "I know how that sounds. No, I'm not stalking you—the opposite. I just wanted to say, face-to-face, to forget all that shit I said the other night."

"Forget it, huh?" Her brain told her to embrace his retreat, but some stupid part of her wanted to tease him regardless of the consequences. "Already moving on?"

"Uh-uh." He shook his head, wagging a finger as she moved closer. He watched her pull her helmet from the cradle behind her seat, then said, "Don't play around like that. I know I put you in an awkward spot, and I'm not cool with that. I don't want you to have to dodge me just to practice with the boss—"

Genuine outrage entered Juliet's tone. "That's not what happened! He's the one who—"

"No, no!" He waved his hand, shaking his head. "Forget it. You don't need to explain anything. We're cool, all right."

"Oh. My. God! You're insufferable." Juliet walked around her bike, helmet under one arm, and stepped up to him, poking a finger into his surprisingly hard pectoral. "Tanaka wanted to focus one-on-one! I never mentioned you. Also, I was sleeping in this morning because I was up all night. Don't. Flatter. Yourself." She punctuated the last three words with jabs of her finger.

"Up all night, huh?" His stupid, beautiful eyes twinkled as he lifted an eyebrow. Juliet felt heat rising in her cheeks, and she did the only reasonable thing—stuffed her helmet over her head and slammed the visor down. Then, she turned and hopped onto her bike.

She pressed the ignition button and turned her dark, impenetrable visor toward him. "Get melted, Applebaum."

She started the bike rolling, but he wasn't done, calling after her with an absurdly wide smile, "Glad we're back to normal!"

"Ugh!" she growled. "I can't believe he ambushed me in the parking garage!"

Angel's tone was painfully tentative as she replied, "He certainly seems to know how to push your buttons."

"Are you suggesting something?"

"I'm just saying he got a rise out of you, and I could feel certain . . . responses in you to his proximity."

"It's just hormones or something!" Juliet was letting her emotions drive the bike and had to consciously force herself to slow down as she exited the garage. "Ever since that night, when he was honest and said some actually sweet things . . ." Juliet groaned and slapped her helmet with her hand.

"Angel, let's forget it, all right? I basically just hired Tanaka, which means I hired Leo. That means he's off-limits, anyway." She looked at her mini map, where Angel had updated her route to include a trip to the Galleria. "Shopping is just what the doctor ordered. Come on, sis." With that, she cranked the throttle and, as much as she could in the early-evening traffic, enjoyed the ride.

EPILOGUE

Juliet stood beside Bennet, her arms folded, trying not to show the stress she was feeling as she watched the transport crew operating the hoists lifting the sky-blue, shark-shaped gunship onto the segmented robotic transport platform. It was time to transfer their hard work, their baby, to the spaceport. Aya walked out the bay door, hustling as one of the orange-hat-wearing transport crew glared at her.

"Sheesh!" she grumbled, moving to stand beside Bennet. "It's not like I was blocking their way."

"They're paranoid about accidents and liability." Bennet sighed. Juliet knew what was bothering him: He wanted to be in control of the move.

"Are they really taking it outside the dome?" Aya asked, squinting at the long, treaded transport machine.

Juliet nodded. "Yeah. This thing moves too slowly and is too wide for the interdome highways. They're going right over the surface to the shipyard docks." It had been a trade-off—renting a warehouse and using it as a hangar was a hundred times cheaper than a berth at the shipyard, but now they had to deal with this move.

As she stood there, stressing, watching the straps straining with the weight of the *Cherry Blossom*, she reminded herself that Bennet had already been through the move once when they'd brought the freshly salvaged gunship out to the industrial dome.

"Any scratches, dents, busted seams, or anything like that will be easy to fix once we get her in port," Bennet said, resting an arm over her shoulders. "Relax."

Juliet sighed softly, reaching up to rest a hand on his forearm. The last few months had been busy, but she, Aya, and Bennet had grown closer than ever; she was dreading the change in routine and day-to-day living more than she was worried about the ship—they had insurance, after all.

"When's your date?" Aya asked, prompting a much louder, exasperated sigh out of Juliet.

"It's just lunch with an old friend."

Aya stepped around Bennet to snuggle up to Juliet's other side, wrapping an arm around her waist. "Uh-huh, that's why you've rescheduled a hundred times?"

"I've been busy." Juliet's protest was weak, and she knew it. She'd gotten a hold of Jensen only a few days after first seeing him at Vicky's, scheduled a lunch meeting for the following week, and, as Aya said, rescheduled over and over. Some of her excuses had been legitimate—training activities with Tanaka and his crew or meetings with subcontractors for the gunship interior and component replacements. Most of them had been things she could have easily passed off to Aya or Bennet; Juliet was starting to think she'd become so used to being single and romantically alone that it was a terminal condition.

She wasn't even sure Jensen liked her that way, but she swore there was some kind of spark there, and what was she going to do with that now that the gunship was nearly done and the biggest, most dangerous operation of her short career was just around the corner?

Was it really, though? She and Tanaka hadn't made any moves yet, short of the constant drilling. They'd been working on everything from sword fighting to improvised disguises to team tactics in dream-rig scenarios. Even so, they'd yet to move on Ghoul, and Juliet hadn't given Tanaka the specifics on WBD.

"Just lunch." Bennet sighed. "I could use some of that."

"We'll get food in the port." Aya turned to the hangar, giving Juliet's side another squeeze. "I'm going to miss our time here. It was kind of an interlude."

"An interlude?" Juliet lifted an eyebrow.

"Yeah. Like the universe stood still for us, letting us have some time here with the *Blossom*."

Juliet was about to argue she'd been plenty busy, but she had to admit the last couple of months had been very relaxing, her physical punishment with Tanaka and Bennet's weight-lifting routine notwithstanding. Instead, she said, "I was just thinking that. I loved my time here with you two."

"I'm keeping my room on the *Blossom*," Aya added as if they hadn't already discussed it a hundred times.

"Heck yeah, you are." With a nerve-racking release of compressed air, the transport crew started lowering the full weight of the ship onto the transport platforms, and Juliet had to back up and look away. She walked over to her bike, reaching for her helmet. "You guys will call me as soon as she's safe in port?"

Bennet nodded. "Yep, no worries."

"Are you glad to be done with this commute?" Aya asked, following her over to the bike.

"I guess. I like riding, though. Now that we'll be bunking in the port, maybe we can take the *Lady* out more often."

Aya smiled, leaning against the handlebars while Juliet swung her leg over the seat. "Bunking in the port and no longer working seven days a week on a gunship!"

"That's right. Hey, you know I'm training for a big job, but if the timing looks right, maybe we can sneak away for a little vacation. How'd you like to cruise over toward Mars? You could visit your folks, and I could see Honey."

"Alice and Shiro were talking about doing that! Taking a vacation, I mean. I bet they'd love to see the family. Uh"—Aya's eyes widened, and she slapped her pink, cybernetic palm on top of her matching pink hair—"I'm sorry! I didn't mean to invite everyone on our vacation!"

"Oh, hush! I'd love more time with those guys before we all get busy working again." A few weeks back, she'd had a long, fruitful meeting with Alice and Shiro; they'd agreed that the gunship business wouldn't officially start until the first of the year, which gave Juliet just under three months to either resolve her WBD situation or at least have a more concrete plan in place that she could work around.

"Come here." Juliet reached her arm out, and Aya rushed forward to squeeze her around the ribs. "See you tonight!" With that, she fired up the bike, and with one final glance at the beautiful, completely rebuilt gunship on its precarious-looking perch, she cranked the throttle and fled the scene.

As she cleared the row of warehouse buildings, Angel said, "You got a message from Jensen while you were talking to Aya."

"Oh?"

"Yes. He's wondering if you're really going to show up today. He noted this is the first time you've made it to the day of the meeting before canceling."

"Oh, brother. I deserve that." Juliet chuckled, shaking her head. "Tell him I'm on my way."

Athena, or more accurately, her alter ego Selene Kostas, had cleared Jensen's background. She said he had some blank spots over the years she'd been unable to account for, but his business on Luna was legitimate—avoiding some heat from a major petroleum corp. One of his aliases, Walter Vantage, had been involved in two of their board members disappearing.

"Speaking of aliases, I should stop calling him Jensen in my head."

"It's a hard habit to break. I've been thinking of him that way, too. We should be sure to call him Tristan today."

"We?" Juliet chuckled. "Are you planning to talk to him?"

"You never know."

"Oh, yeah?" Juliet's smile broadened as she twisted the throttle and rocketed onto the interdome highway, savoring the open road; this might be the last time she made the run from this particular industrial dome to the city. "Well, by all means! Who am I to stop you from making friends outside my head."

She and Angel bantered a bit more on the way into the city, but before long, she found herself rolling up to a little coffee and lunch bistro situated near one of the city's larger parks. It was a lovely setting, and when she pulled her helmet off, the air smelled fresh and crisp. Of course, the air usually smelled pretty good for her, thanks to Angel's management of her olfactory implants.

Still, the grass and pine analogs planted in the little greenbelt did wonders, giving Angel a lot to work with. Standing there, breathing deeply, Juliet remembered her first day in Luna City and how disillusioned she'd felt when she'd smelled the stink of the city and seen how the luster of the shining towers faded the closer she got.

"It's a dirty city, but not as dirty as when we first got here. We've made our small dent in the corruption, wouldn't you say?"

"Yes, we certainly have." Angel's tone was upbeat as she added, "We've done good here, Juliet."

"I know better than to try to correct your grammar. Did you do that on purpose?"

"Yes! We've done good things. It's something to be proud of."

"I agree, Angel." Juliet stood up from her bike and pulled her helmet off, letting her shoulder-length, loose, auburn curls fall to her shoulders. She wore jeans, her motorcycle boots, and her new royal-blue and "antique-rust" synthetic leather, bullet-resistant motorcycle jacket. A soft, silky yellow blouse under the jacket was her only concession to a gentler sort of fashion, but she felt it was enough for lunch. Naturally, she was armed with her Texan and Tanaka's loaner sword.

She was probably ready to start carrying the monoblade, but she'd caught wind from Frida that Tanaka was planning a little celebration for her, a sort of graduation, before he gave her the nod.

"What's my balance?"

"After the final salvage payment from the *Red Betty*, you're sitting on 2,144,142 Sol-bits."

"Guess I should pay for lunch, huh?"

"Considering the many times you've made Jensen—Tristan—reschedule, yes." As Juliet started over the parking lot to the little stucco-and-plasteel building with its expansive patio facing the greenbelt, Angel delicately asked, "What are your intentions with him? I mean, is this just lunch?"

"Angel, I'm a mess. I've been talking to Doctor Ming about it, but honestly, I don't know how to do anything other than be friends these days. Even Leo's chilled out; I think he can sense it. It's like something got turned off, and I don't know how to turn it on."

"Oh, nonsense! You were ready to go with Leo after the Life-Ultra incident! You just got into your own head about it, and now you've convinced yourself and him that it's inappropriate. Just be yourself today. Do you remember how to do that?"

Juliet barked a short laugh, reaching up to brush some hair back from her face, almost nervously. "I can try. I can try, all right? God, you're really giving it to me with both barrels right now. Couldn't you have done this, like, earlier?"

"No! You're always avoiding this topic."

"Fair enough. I'm going in, so let it rest for now, 'kay?"

"I'll try, but I'm watching you, sis."

Juliet laughed again, loving this side of Angel, and pulled the door open. Soft chimes rang as she stepped through, and the heavenly scent of Mediterranean tapas tickled her nose. The restaurant was busy, but the hostess immediately straightened up and, with a cheerful smile, said, "Welcome in! Just yourself today?"

"No, I'm meeting someone. Um, tall, blond, blue eyes . . ." Juliet trailed off, embarrassed by her decision to describe him physically. "Tristan."

"Right this way! He's waiting on the patio." Juliet followed her through the restaurant and out the patio doors. She saw Jensen right away. He was seated near the short, pale stucco wall that separated the restaurant from the park. He wore some old-school sunglasses as he gazed out over the greenery, watching as a woman with a gaggle of schoolchildren walked along the path. His face looked relaxed, and his hands idly twisted a paper napkin on the table. Juliet liked that he was wearing jeans and athletic shoes, but his shirt was nice: a close-fitting blue button-up with a collar.

He must have seen movement from the corner of his eye because he stood up when she approached, turning to smile her way. Juliet waved as she got close. "Hey! I guess there's no sneaking up on you, huh?"

He chuckled, surprising her by stepping close for a quick hug. Juliet liked hugs; she hugged Aya, Bennet, and the *Kowashi* crew all the time. She loved hugging Honey, and she'd even hugged Frida a time or two over the last few weeks. Still, this felt different; something was charged between them, and she felt some heat and tingles and pulled back a little too quickly. She covered by laughing, smiling up at him, and saying, "I've never been here; it seems nice!"

"Your waiter will be right with you," the hostess noted, reminding Juliet they weren't alone.

"A waiter, huh? Nice touch," Jensen said with a wink. The hostess, a young woman who looked like she might still be in a corpo secondary school, smiled and blushed, turning to flee.

"I think she's smitten." Juliet laughed, sitting across from Jensen. "Oof! I keep thinking of you as, you know, your old name. Gonna take me a minute to start calling you Tristan in my head."

He nodded, shrugging. "I know the feeling . . . Lucky."

"Yeah. I guess that's how it is in our line of work, eh?" Juliet picked up her water glass, noting the sparkles and the lime wedge as she took a sip. "Refreshing. So, been enjoying Luna?"

"Been lonely, but it's a nice enough place, and nothing beats the view from the agridome where I'm renting a little cabin."

"What? I didn't know people rented places in the agridomes!"

"Oh yeah, my realtor told me about it. Most corpo farms are required to have a certain percentage of residential property. Of course, the intent behind the regulation probably had nothing to do with expensive long-term rentals and more to do with providing living space for the surge of humanity making its way into the greater system, but I'm not one to complain. Anyway, been spending a lot of time staring up at the stars and down at the Earth and hiking the trails around the farms."

"Not working?" Juliet played dumb; the things Athena had found out should have been impossible for her to know. "I thought you came up here for a job."

"Well, more like I came up here *because* of a job. I'm kinda just laying low."

"Gonna be doing that for a while?"

Jensen pushed his sunglasses up on his hair, exposing his eyes as he narrowed them at her. "Am I being interviewed for something?"

Juliet slapped a hand over her mouth, squinting her eyes in embarrassment. "Oh, gosh! I've forgotten how to talk to someone like a human being!"

"Nah, it's fine." He chuckled, sipped his water, then said, "Let's talk about you for a little while. Are you really as busy as you seem, or were you afraid I wanted revenge or something?"

"Revenge?"

"You know, for how you trounced me in our last encounter!" His eyes twinkled with amusement.

"*Puh-lease!* You didn't put up much of a fight. Anyway, no, I wasn't worried about that. I figured you'd had about enough of Vicky."

"Yeah, I guess so. It's weird that I worked an extra day for free; I usually don't do that." Juliet could tell he was trying to keep his face straight, but his mouth twisted into a wry smile, and she giggled. "Want to order something to eat?"

"Yeah." Juliet nodded, staring into his eyes, leaning forward just a little. "Let's get something to eat."

Alec Kline sat in his new sedan, drumming his fingers on the steering wheel, waiting for the sun to soak through the vehicle's insulation. He was back in Phoenix, and it looked like he'd be there for a while, hence the new car and his reluctance to open the door and feel the blast of heat coming off the pavement. He addressed his new, supposedly very advanced PAI, "Ruby, is Rachel ready for me?"

"Yes. She's been sitting in the lobby for thirteen minutes."

"All right. Here we go." He pushed the door open and stood, holding his breath as the hot air washed over him. "God. Phoenix. Nothing feels quite like walking around in a planet-size oven." He started over the pavement to the nondescript five-story square plasteel-and-mirror edifice on the city's outskirts, housing one of WBD's many clandestine, easily disavowed R&D departments.

"This is momentous," Ruby said, repeating a habit his old PAI never had—musing aloud about topics he hadn't initiated.

"How so?"

"I believe my predecessor—an ancestor, if you will—was born here."

"The Angel alpha? Don't flatter yourself. We had to cut a lot of functionality to bring you and your kind to market."

"Nevertheless, I feel some wonder stirring at the prospect of seeing the inside of this building."

"Wonder, huh?" Kline shook his head, pausing in the shade of the awning to inhale some cherry-flavored nicotine vapor.

"I'm not sure why you keep that habit up. Your new nanites could help with the withdrawal symptoms . . ."

"Don't you dare mess with my nicotine!" Kline growled. The damn PAI and his new nanites were part of his bonus package for the work Rachel Dowdall had been doing. Since she was on Kline's team, he reaped a lot of benefits from her breakthroughs. Well, he was probably just as responsible as she was; hadn't it been his tip that had brought them to Seattle?

As he inhaled another big hit off his Nikko-vape, he reflected on the weird journey that had brought them to where they were. Chasing the Angel alpha and Juliet Bianchi had led them to Grave, which had led them to Abby and her "Gipple." They'd never succeeded in mining the details about the thing from their Grave data, never learned what the weird name meant, but it stuck.

The automated doors swished open, and Rachel stepped out, wincing at the heat. "Are you coming in?"

Kline smiled and stuffed his vape into his shirt pocket, nodding. "Sorry to keep you waiting."

"Oh, yeah? You sure do it a lot for someone who's sorry." She was frowning, but he saw an amused twinkle in her eyes. She might complain a lot, but she'd seen some big bonuses of her own.

"Well, they're making me operate out of this building starting next week, so you'll know where to find me going forward."

"What?" Rachel's eyes widened. "Really?"

"Yeah, the suits are excited about your new Gipple thing. They won't admit it, but the writing's on the wall. I could see the gears burning up the grease in Montclair's head." He nodded toward the door. "Speaking of which, the board's expecting my presentation tomorrow, so I better see what you've got. Can you hit me with some of the numbers while we walk?"

"Numbers?"

"Yeah." Kline leaned to the side and coughed as they entered the frigid air-conditioned lobby. "I mean, what are the success rates with your device? How many have we got on deck? Etcetera."

"Coughing? Please tell me you're going to try to quit again . . ."

"Not unless the old lady herself tells me to in plain, certain terms. Don't worry, though. That's just allergies or something. I've been away from the desert for a while." He followed Rachel to the elevators, noting the heavy security presence—four scanner banks, guards with synthetic attack canines in every corner, and ceiling-mounted, smart-gun turrets. "When you asked for an increase on your security budget, I wasn't quite picturing this."

"Well, when we moved in after they buttoned up the Angel Project and brought the release candidate to Texas, there were already turrets and scanners. I just wanted some more actual hands on deck, you know. I'm sure you understand why they needed to be synths."

Kline let his eyes drift over the guards in their ballistic vests and helmets. "Synths. I guess it makes sense." He shook his head, stepping into the elevator. "Anyway, the numbers."

"Oh, right. I'll send you a writeup, but here's a summary: For every fifty WRP associates, we're lucky to achieve a satisfactory Gipple fit with three or four. We've got eleven successful candidates in-house, and have another bus of WRPs coming tomorrow."

Kline frowned at her casual use of the "WRP" term—workfare repayment program "associates" were basically indentured employees; workers who'd gone into debt with the company and were now, legally, its property. Though the program was ideally supposed to help them pay off that debt, it rarely worked out that way.

The elevator surged upward and stopped after just a few seconds. "And the unsuccessful candidates?"

Rachel frowned and looked at him with something that looked like genuine pain in her eyes. "The Gipple installation is very invasive, and there's often some damage. We've had better luck leaving the tines in, you know, clipping them off where they exit the skull, but we've had some loss of life and other, lesser, side effects."

"There's no way to test if the operation will take before, you know, jamming their heads full of metal?" Again, he followed as she led him down a quiet, dimly lit, brown-carpeted corridor.

"My experts say no. The, uh, truth of it is that we don't know what makes it work sometimes and fail others." She paused and looked at him. "Probably best to keep that tidbit out of your report." She pointed to a nondescript door on the left. "He's waiting in there."

"Okay, before I go in, describe your process again. How are any of these things working if we don't know how they work?"

Rachel folded her arms on her chest and scowled. "Seriously? I know I've sent you at least two reports with this information."

Kline shrugged and leaned his shoulder against the wall, answering her frown with a smile. "Let's just say I like to hear it from the source. I've always been lazy about reading reports. I'm a hands-on kind of manager."

Rachel inhaled deeply through her nostrils and nodded. "Fair enough. You know we tried to replicate the material in Abby's head but failed, right? We manufactured a synthetic material with a nearly identical chemical structure, but we're totally at a loss as to how it was implanted. Abby says she remembers getting a shot, so we figure it was a specialized nanite delivery, and, of course, we can do that—but how the nanites knew where to put the stuff, that's where we can't connect the dots. So, we decided to try an external Gipple. We built a structure shaped exactly like Abby's internal one, figured out its major contact points with the brain by observing her using it through scanning hardware, and then implanted those contact points into the brain of a new host."

"And it worked?"

"Hah!" Rachel laughed. "We got some very minor success with the first candidate. If you stared at a card, he could guess its color. So, we kept refining and implanting, and now we have some candidates who can read thoughts more easily than even Abby." She shrugged. "The rest is history."

"All right. Let me see this guy." Kline watched as Rachel walked up to the plain brown door and turned the knob. She pulled it wide, and Kline looked within. A small table separated two chairs. On the left, a man sat, and Kline winced involuntarily as he took him in. He was an average-looking, middle-aged man wearing a plain gray zip-up jumper. His head was bald, and hundreds of shiny, stainless needles protruded from his scalp. They all terminated in a silvery, ovoid device that sat above his head, almost like a halo. The imagery was reinforced by the blinking green LEDs that ran around its rim.

"This is L-008; you can see that he's not actively reading minds right now because the LEDs are green. When the Gipple halo is flashing with red LEDs, it means he's gathering thoughts."

"Really?" Kline liked the idea of a visual cue to warn people nearby that their thoughts weren't secure. He stepped into the room and sat before the man. The fellow wasn't smiling, but he didn't look upset. His face was rather placid, in fact, almost like an idiot. "Can they do anything else?"

Rachel scowled. "Other than reading people's thoughts for a hundred meters around? Gathering intel through doors, walls, or security barriers? Is that not enough?"

"I'm just getting details for my presentation, Rachel." Kline sighed and tried to smile reassuringly. "Nobody's going to be disappointed."

"Well, no, then. I mean, I know there were rumors about the Grave program and the things some of them could do, but we're not replicating any of that. Fineman thinks it's because we're copying the contact points of Abby's Gipple; she reads minds, so these 'copies' read minds." Rachel shrugged.

"I see. Well, considering the resources we've poured into looking, I'm inclined to believe the other escapees are dead or never existed." He turned his attention to the man with the wires poking out of his head. "L-Eight, was it?" Rachel nodded, and he continued. "I'm Associate Director Kline. Have we met?"

"No, sir."

Kline almost snapped his fingers when he realized what was bothering him about the man's face: He didn't blink. "All right. Do me a favor and remind me about my childhood friend. The one who lived in my apartment building one floor down. What was this friend's name?"

The man turned his gaze to Rachel, and she nodded, explaining, "My PAI has to unlock the halo for him. They're all locked when not being tested or trained."

"I see." Kline leaned back, watching as the LEDs flickered from green to red and began to blink more rapidly. He felt something then, a weird, tickling sensation along his scalp that made his skin crawl.

After a few seconds of that, the strange man began to speak.

"Luverne Rojas lived downstairs from you. You spent many mornings with her, being watched by her mother while waiting for yours to come home from her night shift. Her favorite vid stream featured an ancient cartoon about three boys, all named Edward, and you used to tease her about it. She was killed by a dreamer having a psychotic event on the day of your ninth birthday—"

"That's enough of that," Kline said, frowning, irritated at himself for choosing Luverne as the subject of the test. L-008's halo started blinking green again, and Kline nodded to Rachel. "I'm impressed. Do you want to have dinner while I pick your brain for a few more details? I'm sure the board will have a lot of questions."

ABOUT THE AUTHOR

Plum Parrot is the pen name of author Miles Gallup, who grew up in Southern Arizona and spent much of his youth wandering around the Sonoran Desert, hunting imaginary monsters and building forts. He studied creative writing at the University of Arizona and, for a number of years, attempted to teach middle schoolers to love literature and write their own stories. If he's not spending time with his dog, you can find Gallup writing, reading his favorite authors, or playing *D&D* with friends and family.

Podium

DISCOVER MORE

STORIES UNBOUND

PodiumEntertainment.com